THE PAST HAS INVADED THEIR LIVES...AND NOTHING WILL EVER BE THE SAME

ALEXANDRA
Shattered by the decadence and betrayal of a renowned avant-garde designer, she finds true love only to discover that her own life may have been a deception from the beginning....

ZACHARY
A poor boy from the Louisiana bayous who's made the hard climb to the top. His only mistake has been marrying a woman too devious and depraved to escape....

MIRANDA
She gets what she wants, and what she wants is Lord's. And she'll seduce, scheme and sell herself to keep it all...but will her appetites destroy her before she can succeed...?

ELEANOR
For nearly three decades she's searched for the little girl stolen from her. And now that she's certain she's found her, Eleanor is about to solve the brutal truth of her son's murder...and find the killer who got away.

"EXCITING...STEAMY..."
—Affaire de Coeur

JoAnn Ross

Legacy of Lies

With warmest regards,
JoAnn Ross

MIRA BOOKS

ISBN 1-55166-018-0

LEGACY OF LIES

To Jay,
who gives my life meaning

ACKNOWLEDGMENTS

No one can write a book alone, and I've been wonderfully fortunate to have been on the receiving end of a great deal of help.

To everyone who makes writing for MIRA such a joy: Brian Hickey, Hugh O'Neil and Randall Toye, for their unparalleled corporate support; Candy Lee and Karin Stoecker, who told me to write whatever I want (heady advice for any author); Katherine Orr and Stacy Widdrington, who somehow manage to arrange nearly effortless travel; Krystyna de Duleba, for the dazzling artwork (and for actually welcoming my ideas); Dianne Moggy, Amy Moore and Ilana Glaun, who provide editorial support most writers can only dream of; and, of course, my own incomparable editor and friend, Malle Vallik, who many times understands my stories better than I do.

Also, heartfelt gratitude to Robin Lester and Leslie Burton, for all the years; Shelley Mosley and Julie Havir, for the monthly lunches; and Anna Eberhardt, Jan Flores and Patty Gardner Evans, whose phone calls and faxes keep me reasonably sane.

Last, but certainly not least, I'd like to thank my talented son, for believing in his mother. Here's to tons of sales and mailboxes filled with your own royalty checks, Patrick!

Prologue

Santa Barbara, California
April 1958

It rained the day Eleanor Lord buried her only son. A cold wind, bringing with it memories of a winter just past, blew in from the whitecapped gray sea. Not that the inclement weather kept anyone away; it appeared that the entire town of Santa Barbara had turned out. Rows of black umbrellas arced over the grassy knoll like mushrooms.

Nothing like a scandal to draw a crowd, Eleanor thought. After all, it wasn't every day that the scion of America's largest department store family and his wife were murdered.

If a double homicide wasn't enough to set tongues wagging, the fact that the victims were two of the town's leading citizens added grist to the gossip mill. Then there was Anna....

Eleanor's heart clenched at the thought of her missing two-year-old granddaughter. A sob escaped her tightly set lips.

"Are you all right?" Dr. Averill Brandford asked with concern. He was holding an umbrella over her head; his free arm tightened around her shoulders.

"Of course I'm not all right!" she snapped, displaying a spark of her usual fire. "My son and his wife are about to be put in the ground and my granddaughter has vanished from the face of the earth. How would you feel under similar circumstances?"

"Like hell," he answered gruffly. "Don't forget, Robert was my best friend. And Anna's my goddaughter."

Averill Brandford and Robert Lord had grown up together. Clad in rainwear and shiny black boots and armed with shovels, rakes and buckets, they'd dug for clams in the coastal tidelands. Robert had been the pitcher of the Montecito High School baseball team; Averill had been the catcher. Together they'd led the team to three district championships in four years. Inseparable, they'd gone on to USC, pledged the same fraternity and only parted four years later when Robert went east to Harvard Law School and Averill to medical school, making his father, the Lords' head gardener, extremely proud.

Eventually they were reunited in the Southern California coastal town where they'd grown up. These past horrendous days, Averill had been a pillar of support. He'd arrived at the house within minutes of Eleanor's frantic phone call, rarely leaving her side as she waited for the kidnapper's call.

Tears stung her eyes. Resolutely Eleanor blinked them away, vowing not to permit herself to break down until her granddaughter was home safe and sound.

She thanked the minister for his inspiring eulogy, not admitting she hadn't heard a word. Then she turned and began making her way across the mossy turf.

In the distance the Santa Ynez Mountains towered majestically in emerald shades over the red-roofed city; a few hardy souls were playing golf on the velvet greens of the Montecito Country Club.

Out at sea, draped in a shimmering pewter mist, a tall masted fishing boat chugged its way up the Santa Barbara Channel. Watching the slicker-clad men on the deck, Eleanor felt pained to realize that people continued to go about their daily lives, that the earth had not stopped spinning simply because her own world was crumbling down around her.

As she neared her limousine, Santa Barbara's police chief climbed out of his black-and-white squad car, parked behind it, and approached them. The look on his face was not encouraging.

"Good afternoon, Chief Tyrell." Though there were shadows smudged beneath Eleanor's eyes, her gaze was steady and direct.

The police chief lifted his fingers to his hat. "Afternoon, Mrs. Lord." He doffed the hat and began turning it around and around between his fingers. "The FBI located your granddaughter's nanny in Tijuana, ma'am. Rosa Martinez checked into a hotel under an assumed name."

"Thank God, they've found her," Eleanor breathed. "And Anna? Is she well?"

"I'm afraid we don't know."

"What do you mean, you don't know?"

"She didn't have a child with her when she checked in."

"But surely Rosa will tell you where Anna is. Even if she refuses to cooperate, don't you people have ways of encouraging people to talk?" Thoughts of bright lights and rubber hoses flashed through her mind.

"I'm afraid that's impossible." His voice was heavy with discouragement. "The nanny's dead, Mrs. Lord."

"Dead?"

"She hung herself."

"But Anna..." Eleanor felt Averill's fingers tighten on her arm.

"We don't know," Chief Tyrell admitted. "With the nanny gone, no witnesses and no word from the kidnappers, we've run into a dead end."

"But you'll keep looking," Averill insisted.

"Of course. But I'm obliged to tell you, Mrs. Lord," the police chief said, "that the little girl's nanny left a suicide note asking for God's—and your—forgiveness. The FBI's taking the note as a sign that your granddaughter's, uh—" he paused, looking like a man on his way to the gallows "—dead."

No! For the first time in her life, Eleanor felt faint. She took a deep breath, inhaling the mild aroma of petroleum wafting in from the offshore oil derricks; the light-headed sensation passed.

She heard herself thank the police chief for his continued efforts, but her voice sounded strange to her own ears, as if it were coming from the bottom of the sea.

Back at her Montecito estate, she forced herself to remain calm as she accepted condolences from mourners. Finally, mercifully, everyone was gone, leaving her alone with Averill.

"Are you sure you want to stay here tonight?" His handsome face was stamped with professional and personal concern.

"Where would I go? This is my home."

Needing something to do with her hands, Eleanor absently began rearranging a Waterford vase filled with white lilies. The house was overflowing with flowers; the rich profusion of sweet and spicy scents was giving her a blinding headache.

"Would you like some company?" Averill asked solicitously. "I'd be glad to stay."

"No." She shook her head. "I appreciate your concern, Averill, but if you don't mind, it's been a very long day and I'd like to be alone." When he looked inclined to argue, she said, "I'll be fine. Honestly."

He frowned. "If you can't sleep—"

"I'll take one of those tablets you prescribed," she assured him, having no intention of doing any such thing.

She'd succumbed to his medical prompting that first night, only to discover that the pills made her feel as if her head were wrapped in cotton batting. It was important she be alert when the police called to tell her they'd located Anna.

Although he appeared unconvinced, the young doctor finally left. Eleanor sat alone for a long silent time. After being in the public eye all day, she was grateful for the opportunity to allow herself to droop—face, shoulders, spirits.

Finally, when she thought she could manage the act without collapsing, she got to her feet and climbed the elaborate Caroline staircase to the nursery, where she kept her vigil far into the night.

Chapter One

Paris
December 1981

Oblivious to any danger, Alexandra Lyons ran full tilt across the icy street, deftly weaving her way between two taxis, a gunmetal gray Mercedes and a jet-black Ferrari. Her hooded, red wool cape was like the brilliant flash of a cardinal's wing against the wintry gray Paris sky and the falling white snow.

Her long legs, clad in opaque black tights and pointy-toed red cowboy boots, earned a quick toot of the horn and an admiring second look from the driver of the Ferrari.

It was Christmas in Paris. Glittering semicircles of Christmas trees had replaced Rond Point's formal gardens, and garlands of lights had been strung up in the city's leafless trees, turning the Avenue Montaigne and the Champs-Élysées into great white ways, reminding one and all that Paris was, after all, the City of Light.

But Alex's mind was not on the lights, or the joyful season. Her concerns were more personal. And far more urgent.

She was on her way to the *atelier* of Yves Debord to try again to win a coveted position with the French designer. And though she knew her chances of winning a position at the famed house of couture were on a par with catching moondust in her hand, even worse than failing would be to grow old and never have tried.

Emerging ten years ago as haute couture's *enfant terrible*, the designer had been immediately clutched to the *décolleté* bosom of the *nouveaux riches*. Fashion celebrity oozed from the perfumed corners of his *atelier,* glinted off the windshield of his Lamborghini, glowed from the crystal chandeliers in his many homes.

Hostesses in Los Angeles, Dallas and New York fawned over him. He skied in the Alps with movie stars and was welcome at presidential dinner tables in Rome and Washington and Paris.

During Alex's student days in Los Angeles, the Fashion Institute had shown a documentary about the designer directed by Martin Scorsese entitled *Pure Pow: The World of Debord*. Enthralled, Alex had sat through all three showings.

She now paused outside the showroom to catch her breath. Adrenaline coursed through her veins at the sight of her idol's name written in gleaming silver script on the black glass.

"You can do it," she said, giving herself a brisk little pep talk. "The answer to all your dreams is just on the other side of this door. All you have to do is to reach out and grasp it."

She refused to dwell on the fact that after months of daily visits to the *bureau de change* to cash her dwindling supply of traveler's checks, she was almost out of funds.

Her night job, serving beer and wine at a Montparnasse nightclub, barely paid her rent. The hours, however, allowed her to search for work in the fashion houses during the day, and if sleep had become a rare unknown thing, Alex considered that a small price to pay for a chance to fulfill a dream.

Throwing back her shoulders, Alex lifted herself up to her full height of five feet seven inches and then, with her usual bravado, entered the showroom. Behind her, the door clicked shut with the quiet authority of a Mercedes.

The front room, used to greet customers, was a vast sea of cool gray. Modern furniture wrapped in pewter fabric sat atop silvery gray carpet that melded into the gray silk-covered walls. Marie Hélène, Yves Debord's sister and house of couture directress, was seated behind a jet lacquer table.

She was dressed in black wool jersey, her platinum hair parted in the center and pulled into a severe chignon at the nape of her swanlike neck.

When she recognized Alex, she frowned.

"I know," Alex said, holding up a gloved hand to forestall the director's complaint. She pushed back her hood, releasing a thick riot of red-gold hair.

"You've told me innumerable times in the past six months that there aren't any openings. And even if there were, you don't take Americans. But I thought, if you could only take a look at my work—" she held out her portfolio "—you might consider showing my designs to Monsieur Debord."

Alex's chin jutted out as she steeled herself for yet another cool rejection. *Nothing ventured, nothing gained.*

To Alex's amazement, Marie Hélène didn't immediately turn her away as she had all the other times. "Where did you say you studied?" she inquired in a voice as chilly as her looks.

"The Fashion Institute. In L.A."

"Los Angeles," the directress said with a sniff of disdain, as if Alex had just admitted to being an ax murderer. "You're very young," she observed, making Alex's youth sound like a fatal flaw. "When did you graduate?"

"Actually, I didn't. I felt the curriculum put too much emphasis on merchandising and too little on technique." It was the truth, so far as it went. "Besides, I was impatient, so I quit to go to work in New York."

She felt no need to volunteer that a more urgent reason for leaving school had been her mother's diagnosis of ovarian cancer.

As soon as Irene Lyons had called her with the dark news, Alex had gone to the registrar, dropped out of school and, with a recommendation from one of her professors, landed a job with a Seventh Avenue firm that made dresses for discount stores.

"New York?" Marie Hélène's brow climbed her smooth forehead. "Which designer? Beene? Blass? Surely not Klein?"

"Actually, I worked for a company that made clothing for department stores."

She lifted her chin, as if daring Marie Hélène to say a single derogatory word. While not couture, she'd worked damned hard. And although her suggestions to bring a little pizzazz to the discount clothing were more often than not rejected, she was proud of whatever contribution she'd been allowed to make. After her mother's death, no longer having any reason to remain in New York, she'd followed her lifelong dream, making this pilgrimage to the birthplace—and high altar—of couture.

"But I continued to design on my own," she said, holding out the portfolio again.

When the directress continued to ignore the proffered sketches, Alex steeled herself to be rejected once more.

Instead, Marie Hélène rose from her chair with a lithe grace any runway model would have envied and said, "Come with me."

Unwilling to question what had changed the director's mind, Alex rushed after her through the labyrinth of gray walls and silver carpeting. They entered a small Spartan room that could have doubled as an interrogation room in a police station. Or an operating room.

Though the steel shelves on the walls were filled with bolts of fabric, there was not a speck of lint or dust to be seen. Open-heart surgery could have been done on the gray Formica laminated plastic table in the center of the room.

Beside the table was a faceless mannequin. Marie Hélène took a bolt of white toile from one of the shelves, plucked a sketch from a black binder, lay both on the table along with a pair of shears and said, "Let us see if you can drape."

"Drape? But I came here to—"

"I had to dismiss one of our drapers today," the directress said, cutting Alex off with a curt wave of her hand.

Her fingernails were lacquered a frosty white that echoed her glacial attitude. A diamond sparkled on her right hand, catching the light from the fixture above and splitting it into rainbows on the white walls. Those dancing bits of light, were, along with Alex's crimson cape, the only color in the room.

"I discovered she was sleeping with a press attaché for Saint Laurent." Marie Hélène's mouth tightened. "Which of course we cannot allow."

Uncomfortable with the idea of an employer interfering in the personal life of an employee, Alex nevertheless understood the paranoia that was part and parcel of a business where the new season's skirt lengths were guarded with the same ferocity military commanders employed when planning an invasion.

"With the couture shows next month, we must hire a replacement right away," the directress continued. "If you are able to drape properly, I might consider you for the position."

Draping was definitely a long way from designing. But Alex wasn't exactly in a position to be choosy.

She glanced down at the black-and-white pencil sketch, surprised by its rigid shape. Debord had always favored geometric lines, but this evening gown was more severe than most.

"Is there a problem?" Marie Hélène asked frostily.

"Not at all." Alex flashed her a self-assured smile, took off her cape, tossed it casually onto the table, pulled off her red kid gloves and began to work. Less than five minutes later, she stood back and folded her arms over her plaid tunic.

"Done," she announced as calmly as she could.

Marie Hélène's response was to pull a pair of silver-rimmed glasses from the pocket of her black skirt, put them on and begin going over the draped mannequin inch by inch.

Time slowed. The silence was deafening. Alex could hear the steady tick-tick-tick of the clock on the wall.

"Well?" she asked when she couldn't stand the suspense any longer. "Do I get the job?"

The directress didn't answer. Instead, she turned and submitted Alex to a long judicious study that was even more nerve-racking than her examination of Alex's draping skills.

"Where did you get that *outré* outfit?" Marie Hélène's nose was pinched, as if she'd gotten a whiff of Brie that had turned.

Imbued with a steely self-assurance that was partly inborn and partly a legacy from her mother and twin brother, who'd thought the sun rose and set on her, Alex refused to flinch under the unwavering stare. "I designed it myself."

"I thought that might be the case." The woman's tone was not at all flattering. "My brother prefers his employees to wear black. He finds bright colors distracting to the muse."

"I've read Armani feels the same way about maintaining a sensory-still environment," Alex said cheerfully.

The directress visibly recoiled. "Are you comparing the genius of Debord to that Italian son of a transport manager?"

Realizing that insulting the designer—even unintentionally—was no way to gain employment, Alex quickly backtracked.

"Never," she insisted with fervor. "The genius of Debord has no equal."

Marie Hélène studied her over the silver rim of her glasses for another long silent time. Finally the directress made her decision. "I will expect you here at nine o'clock tomorrow morning. If you do not have appropriate attire, you may purchase one of the dresses we keep for just such an occasion. As for your salary..."

The figure was less than what she'd been making at the nightclub. "That's very generous, madame," she murmured, lying through her teeth.

"You will earn every franc."

Undeterred by the veiled threat, Alex thanked the directress for the opportunity, promised to be on time, picked up her portfolio and wound her way back through the maze of hallways.

As she retraced her steps down the Avenue Montaigne, Alex's cowboy boots barely touched the snowy pavement. Having finally breached the directress's seemingly insurmountable parapets, Alexandra Lyons was walking on air.

"If you can make it here, you can make it anywhere," she sang as she clattered down the steps to the metro station. Her robust contralto drew smiles from passing commuters. "I love Paris in the winter, when it drizzles.... Or snows," she improvised. "Boy, oh boy, do I love Paris!"

She was still smiling thirty minutes later as she climbed the stairs to her apartment.

The first thing she did when she walked in the door was to go over to a table draped in a ruffled, red satin skirt that could have belonged to a cancan dancer at the Folies Bergère, and pick up a photo in an antique silver frame.

"Well, guys," she murmured, running her finger over the smiling features of her mother and brother, whose life had been tragically cut short when his car hit a patch of ice and spun out of control on the New Jersey turnpike six years ago. "I got the job. I hope you're proud."

Alex missed them terribly. She decided she probably always would. They'd both had such unwavering confidence in her talent. Such high hopes. Alex had every intention of living up to those lofty expectations.

When she'd left New York, two days after her mother's funeral, she'd been excited. And nervous. But mostly, she'd been devastated.

As the plane had reached cruising level thirty thousand feet over the Atlantic, she'd collapsed and to the distress of the flight attendants, who'd tried their utmost to uphold the Air France tradition of *esprit de service*—even bringing her a glass of the cognac strictly reserved for first-class passengers—she'd wept like a baby.

For the first time in her life, she'd been truly alone. And though she'd been raised to be independent, deep down inside, Alex had been terrified.

Now, against all odds, she'd achieved the first part of her goal. She'd gotten her boot in Debord's black glass door. Next, all she had to do was prove to the designer she was worthy of the opportunity. Once Debord recognized her talent, she'd be bound to win a promotion.

Could she do it?

Her full lips curved into a wide grin. Her amber eyes, touched with golden facets that radiated outward, lighted with Alex's irrepressible lust for life.

"You bet," she decided with a renewed burst of her characteristic optimism.

Chapter Two

Paris
February 1982

Alex's knees were aching. She'd been kneeling in the close confines of the *cabine* for hours, laboring under the watchful arctic eye of Marie Hélène.

Alex was grateful to still have a job. Last week, at the season's *défilé de mode* held in the gilded splendor of the Salon Impérial of the Hôtel Intercontinental, Debord had experienced the fashion media's ugly habit of chewing up designers and spitting them out.

"Fashion for nuns," American *Vogue* had called his totally black-and-white collection. "A *tour de force* of hideous taste," Suzy Menkes of the *International Herald Tribune* declared, attacking the designer's androgynous black jersey for its dismal, breast-flattening style. "A cross between Grace Jones and Dracula," *Women's Wear Daily* said scornfully. Its sister publication, *W*, gave the collection a grade of *S*—for scary—and said Debord's depressing black shrouds looked as if they came right out of the comic strip *Tales from the Crypt*.

After the disastrous showing, the *femmes du monde*, accustomed to making twice-yearly pilgrimages to this revered salon, deserted the French designer, rushing instead to Milan and Debord's long-detested rival, Gianni Sardella.

Surprisingly, Sophie Friedman, daytime television producer and wife of Hollywood mogul Howard Friedman, paid no heed to the fashion mavens. On the contrary, she amazed even the unflappable Marie Hélène by ordering six evening dresses and twice that number of daytime suits.

Considering that each garment was literally built onto the client, Mrs. Friedman and Alex had spent most of the past week locked in the cramped fitting room together.

"I think it makes me look fat," Sophie said, raising her voice over the classical music played throughout the building.

"It is only the white toile that makes it appear so, Mrs. Friedman," Marie Hélène assured her smoothly. "Once it is worked up in the satin, you will discover that black is very slimming."

"Do you think so?" Sophie ran her beringed hands over her substantial hips, tugging at the material. Alex bit back a curse as the pins she'd just inserted pulled loose. The zaftig woman looked unconvinced. "What do you think?" she asked Alex.

Alex was unaccustomed to being addressed by a customer. A mere draper, she was in the lower echelons of the profession.

But Sophie Friedman had already proved herself to be one of Debord's more eccentric clients. Unwilling to accept the idea that man was meant to fly, Sophie eschewed airline travel. The first day in the fitting room, she'd explained how she'd taken a private Pullman from Los Angeles to Grand Central Station, then the *QEII* to Cherbourg, thence to the Avenue Montaigne by Rolls-Royce.

The woman might be eccentric, Alex thought. But she was no fool. "Madame is correct about black being slimming," she hedged.

"So I won't look fat?"

Alex didn't want to alienate Marie Hélène. Those who dared question the directress were summarily dismissed. Without references.

A tendril of unruly hair escaped the chignon at the back of Alex's neck. Buying time, she unhurriedly tucked it back into place. "You're certainly not fat, Madame Friedman."

Actually, that was the truth. So far as it went. If she was to be totally honest, Alex would suggest that Debord was not the right designer for this middle-aged woman. The designer believed women came in two categories: polo ponies—those who were short and round—and Thoroughbreds—tall and slender. He prided himself on designing for the Thoroughbreds.

Using Debord's criteria, Alex decided he would probably consider the tall, robust Mrs. Friedman to be a Clydesdale.

"I've always had big bones," Sophie agreed. "But I still think this dress makes me look fat."

Alex's innate sense of honesty warred with her common sense. As she'd feared, honesty won out.

"Perhaps," she suggested, ignoring Marie Hélène's sharp look, "if we were to use a softer material than satin, perhaps a matte jersey. And draped it, like this." With a few quick changes she concealed the woman's short waist and broad hips and emphasized her firm, uplifted bustline.

Sophie Friedman's eyes lit with approval. "That's just what it needed." She turned to the directress. "Would Monsieur Debord be willing to make the changes?"

"Of course." Marie Hélène's words were tinged with ice, but her tone remained properly subservient. "It is *Madame's* prerogative to alter anything she wishes."

"Then *Madame* wishes." That settled, Sophie looked down at her diamond-studded watch. "*Madame* is also starving."

"We will take a break," Marie Hélène murmured on cue. "It will be my pleasure to bring you lunch, Madame Friedman."

"No offense, Marie Hélène," Sophie said, "but I could use something more substantial than the rabbit food you serve around this place." She looked down at Alex. "How about you?"

"Me?"

Startled, Alex dropped the box of pins, scattering them over the plush gray carpeting. Marie Hélène immediately knelt and threw three handfuls of pins over her shoulder. Alex had grown accustomed to the superstitions accompanying the business. Baste with green thread and you kill a season. Neglect to toss spilled pins over your shoulder and you've guaranteed a dispute. Lily Dache, legendary hat designer, would show on the thirteenth or not at all. Coco Chanel would wait for Antonia Castillo's numerologist to schedule Mr. Castillo's shows, then schedule her own at the same time. The irate designer was rumored to have used a Coco doll and pins for retaliation. Debord himself was famous for not shaving before a show.

"I could use some company, Alexandra," Sophie announced. "It is Alexandra, isn't it?"

"Yes, Madame Friedman," Alex answered from her place on the floor as she gathered up the scattered pins.

"Well, then," Sophie said with the no-nonsense air of a woman accustomed to getting her way, "since I hate to eat alone and you need to eat, why don't you let me buy you lunch?"

Alex could feel the irritation radiating from Marie Hélène's erect body. "Thank you, Mrs. Friedman, but I'm afraid—"

"If you're worried about your boss, I'm sure Monsieur Debord wouldn't mind." Sophie gave Marie Hélène a significant look. "Considering the dough I've dropped in his coffers this week."

Marie Hélène got the message. Loud and clear. "Alexandra," she suggested, as if the idea had been her own, "Why don't you accompany Madame to *déjeuner*. Monsieur Debord has an account at the Caviar Kaspia, if Russian food meets with Madame's approval," she said to Sophie.

"Caviar Kaspia it is," Sophie agreed robustly.

Ten minutes later Alex found herself sitting in a banquette at the legendary Caviar Kaspia. The Franco-Russian restaurant, located above a caviar shop, had long been a favorite of couture customers with time to kill between fittings.

Across the room, Paloma Picasso, wearing a scarlet suit that matched her lipstick, was engrossed in conversation with Yves Saint Laurent. Nearby, Givenchy's *attaché de presse* was doing his best to charm a buyer from Saks Fifth Avenue. Renowned for her no-nonsense, hard-as-nails approach to the business, the buyer had walked out midway through Debord's showing.

"You're an American, aren't you?" Sophie asked as she piled her warm blini with beluga caviar.

"Yes, ma'am."

"So what the hell are you doing here in Paris, pinning overpriced dresses on women with more money than sense?"

Not knowing how to address the last part of that question, Alex opted to focus on her purpose for coming to Paris. "I've wanted to be a designer for as long as I can remember.

"My mother had her own dressmaking business for a time, but she was a single mother—my father left before my twin brother and I were born—and since taking care of two children took up too much time to allow her to continue designing, she ended up doing alterations for department stores and dry cleaners."

Alex frowned as she fiddled with her cutlery. "I've always felt guilty about that."

"Oh, I'm sure your mother never considered it a sacrifice," Sophie said quickly, waving away Alex's concerns with a plump hand laden down with very good diamonds.

"That's what she always insisted whenever I brought it up," Alex agreed. "Anyway, she taught me everything I know about sewing. When I was little, I designed clothes for my dolls. Eventually I worked my way up to creating clothes for her."

"Lucky lady," Sophie said. "What does she think of you working for Debord?"

"She died before I came to Paris."

"I'm sorry."

"She was ill for a long time. In a way, her death was a blessing. After leaving school, I worked on Seventh Avenue for a few years." Alex continued her story, briefly describing her work at the design firm.

"I'll bet you didn't come clear to France to be a draper," Sophie said as she topped the glistening black caviar with a dollop of sour cream.

Alex shrugged, unwilling to admit to her own impatience. Her mother had always cautioned her that destiny wasn't immediate. But Alex couldn't help being in a hurry.

"All my life I've wanted to work in couture. Paris *is* couture." In Paris, entering a house of couture was taken as seriously as entering a convent; indeed, in French, the expression to enter *une maison* was applied to both cases. "And Debord is the best."

When she was in high school, Alex had pinned pictures of Debord cut out of fashion magazines on her bedroom wall, idolizing him in the way other girls had swooned over rock stars.

Although the photographs had come down years ago, she still harbored a secret crush on the designer.

"He *was* the best," Sophie corrected. "This season his stuff stinks to high heaven. In fact, I'd rather suck mud from the La Brea tar pits than wear one of that man's dresses in public."

Secretly appalled by the direction her idol had taken, Alex found herself unable to defend his current collection. "If you feel that way, why are you buying so many pieces?"

"My soon-to-be ex-husband is buying those clothes," Sophie corrected. "And since your boss is the most expensive designer in the business, he was the obvious choice. Even before last week's disastrous show."

Alex realized that Sophie Friedman had come to Paris to buy "fuck-you clothes." Although haute couture's clientele traditionally consisted of wealthy clients linked together in a solid-gold chain that stretched across continents, mistresses and angry discarded wives made up a remarkable percentage of Debord's customers.

American women were infamous for borrowing couture. The always thrifty French purchased *modèles*—samples. Only the Japanese, along with shadowy South American drug baronesses and Arab brides paid full price.

In fact, a recent Saudi wedding was all that was keeping the house from going bankrupt.

"Of course, I'm giving the stuff to charity as soon as I get back to L.A. It does my heart good to think about that two-timing louse buying couture for some Hollywood bag lady." Sophie grinned with wicked spite. "Although, you know, the changes you made on that evening dress made a helluva difference," she allowed. "I think I'll keep that one."

She chewed thoughtfully. "What would you think of having it made up in red?"

Alex, who adored bright primary colors, grinned. "Red would be marvelous. Coco Chanel always said that red—not blue—was the color for blue eyes."

Sophie nodded, clearly satisfied. "Red it is."

The woman appeared in no hurry to leave the restaurant. Finally, after a third cup of espresso that left her nerves jangling, Alex reminded the client of her afternoon fitting.

"First, I want to see your designs," Sophie declared.

"My designs?"

"You do have some examples of your own work, don't you?"

"Well, yes, but..."

Ambition warred with caution in Alex's head. Part of her knew that Marie Hélène was waiting for them to return. Another part of her was anxious to receive someone's—anyone's—opinion on her work.

She had given Marie Hélène her sketches, hoping they might find their way to Debord. For weeks she'd been waiting for a single word of encouragement from the master. Undaunted, she'd begun a new series of designs.

Giving in to her new friend's request, Alex took Sophie to her apartment. It was located two floors above a bakery in a building that boasted the ubiquitous but charming

Parisian iron grillwork, dormer windows, a mansard roof and red clay chimneys. She'd sublet the apartment from an assistant to an assistant editor of *Les Temps Modernes,* who'd taken a year's sabbatical and gone to Greece to write a novel.

The first time Alex had stood at the bedroom window and stared, enchanted, at the Jardin du Luxembourg across the street, she'd decided that the view more than made up for the building's temperamental old-fashioned cage elevator that more often than not required occupants to rely on the stairs.

Alex could have cursed a blue streak when the unpredictable elevator chose this day not to run. But Sophie proved to be a remarkable sport, though she was huffing and puffing by the time they reached Alex's floor.

"Oh!" she exclaimed, looking around the apartment. "This is absolutely delightful."

"I was lucky to find it." Viewing the apartment through the older woman's eyes, Alex saw not its shabbiness, but its charm.

Near the window overlooking the gardens, a chintz chair was surrounded by scraps of bright fabric samples; atop the table beside it was a box of rainbow-bright Caran D'Ache colored pencils and a portfolio. The Swiss pencils, the very same type Picasso had favored, had been an extravagant birthday gift from her mother. Two days later Irene Lyons had died.

But her memory lived on, just as she'd intended; Alex never sat down to sketch without thinking of her.

Drawn as if by radar, Sophie picked up the portfolio and began leafing through the sketches.

"These are wonderful." The fluid lines were draped to emphasize the waist or hips, the asymmetrical hemlines designed to flatter every woman's legs.

Alex glowed. It had been a long time since anything she'd done received recognition.

Sophie paused at the sketch of a long, slip-style evening gown of ebony silk mousseline with midnight lace and a low, plunging back. "This would be perfect for Angeline."

"Angeline?"

"She's a character on *The Edge of Tomorrow*," Sophie revealed absently, her attention captured by a clinging silver gown reminiscent of films of the thirties and forties. "A former hooker turned movie star turned romance writer."

"Oh, I remember her. I watched that show all the time when I was going to fashion school."

"You must watch a lot of old films, too," Sophie guessed.

"I love old movies."

"I figured that. Your artistic vision definitely has a cinematic scope. So, although television admittedly isn't the big screen, how would you like to come to work for me?"

"For you?"

"I've currently got three soaps in production. Since my shows are famous for their glamour, we keep three costumers shopping overtime to supply outfits for each one-hour drama. The after-six wear and lingerie is the toughest to find, so I've been considering hiring someone to design specifically for us. From what I see here, you'd be perfect."

The idea was tempting. Especially after all the months trying to land a job, then these past weeks laboring away in obscurity. But Alex was not yet prepared to let go of her dream.

"It's not that I'm not flattered," she began slowly, choosing her words with extreme caution. "Because I am...."

"But you're hoping that one of these days, that idiot Debord will open his eyes and realize what a talented designer is toiling right beneath his nose."

Alex felt herself blush. "That's pretty much it."

Sophie shrugged her padded shoulders. "Well, if that scenario doesn't happen, just remember, you've always got a job with me." She opened her bag, pulled out a business card and a pen and scribbled a number on the back.

"Here're the phone numbers for my office at the studio, my car, my home and my pager. Give me a call sometime, even if it's just to talk, okay?"

Alex took the card and stuck it away in a desk drawer. "I'd like that. Thank you."

When Alex cast another significant glance at her watch, Sophie sighed with ill-concealed resignation. "All right, I suppose we'd better get back before Marie Hélène sends the fashion police looking for us."

When Alex and Sophie returned to the salon, they found Debord waiting in the *cabine*. Clad in his smock, his sable hair pulled back into a ponytail to display his Gallic cheekbones to advantage, he looked every inch the temperamental artist.

Dior and Balenciaga had started the tradition of the white smock; Yves Saint Laurent and Givenchy continued it. Debord, always pushing against the boundaries of tradition, had altered it to an anthracite gray. Brightening the breast of the gray smock was the red ribbon of the *Chevalier de la Légion d'honneur*. Although he was not tall, beneath the smock, Debord possessed the broad chest and shoulders of a Picasso etching of a bull.

"Ah, Madame Friedman," he said, greeting her Continental style with an air kiss beside each cheek, "it is a pleasure to meet such a discerning woman."

"I like your stuff," Sophie lied adroitly, "although I have to admit, it was a toss-up between you and Gianni Sardella."

The room went suddenly, deathly still. The only sound was the soft strains of Vivaldi playing in the background. Marie Hélène, normally a paragon of composure, blanched.

Alex's dark eyes widened. Surely Mrs. Friedman knew of the antipathy between the two designers! Stories of their mutual loathing were legion. Not only did Debord not permit his rival's name to be spoken in his presence, last spring he allegedly pushed a client down the grand staircase of the Paris Opera for wearing one of Sardella's beaded evening gowns.

All eyes were on Debord. The back-and-forth motion of his jaw suggested that he was grinding his teeth. His eyes had narrowed to hard, dark stones; a vein pulsed dangerously at his temple. Just when Alex thought he was going to explode, he forced a flat smile.

"I am honored you chose me," he said between clenched teeth.

That, more than anything, displayed to Alex how far her employer had fallen. Before this season's showing, he would have shouted something about philistines and demanded Mrs. Friedman leave these hallowed halls and never darken his doorway again.

Sophie appeared undaunted by the tension surrounding them. Indeed, Alex considered, from the twinkle in her eyes, she appeared to be having the time of her life.

"Your reputation is equaled only by your prices, *monsieur,*" she said. "I hope you realize how lucky you are to have Alexandra working for you."

He looked at Alex, as if seeing her for the first time.

"What I can't understand is why she isn't a designer," Sophie declared. "With her talent, along with her Seventh

Avenue experience, I would have thought you'd have wanted her creative input on this season's collection."

"A designer?" Yves looked at his sister. "You did not tell me that Mademoiselle Lyons was a designer."

Marie Hélène looked as if she could have eaten an entire box of Alex's straight pins and spit out staples. "She designed day wear. Little polyester American dresses," she tacked on dismissively, her tongue as sharp as a seamstress's needle.

"They may have been polyester, but if they were like any of the designs I saw this afternoon, they must have sold like hotcakes," Sophie shot back.

Debord turned to Alex. "You have sketches?"

"Yves . . ." Marie Hélène protested.

The designer ignored his sister. "Do you?" he asked Alex again.

Alex finally understood why her sketches had been rejected without comment. Debord had never seen them. Alex shot a quick, blistering glare Marie Hélène's way. The directress responded with a cool, challenging look of her own.

Knowing that to accuse his sister of treachery would definitely not endear herself to the designer, Alex bit her tongue practically in two. "My portfolio is at my apartment." Anger and anticipation had her heart pounding so fast and so hard she wondered if the others could hear it.

"You will bring your sketches to my office first thing tomorrow morning. I will examine them then."

Ignoring his sister's silent disapproval, Debord turned again to Sophie. "I hope you enjoy your gowns, *madame*. As well as the remainder of your time in Paris."

"If the rest of my trip is half as much fun as today has been," Sophie professed, "I'm going have one helluva time." She winked conspiratorially at Alex.

For the first time in her life, Alex understood exactly how Cinderella had felt when her fairy godmother had shown up with that gilded pumpkin coach.

Her idol was finally going to see her sketches!

And when he did, he was bound to realize she was just what he needed to instill new excitement into his fall collection.

Alex indulged in a brief tantalizing fantasy of Debord and herself working together, side by side, spending their days and nights working feverishly to the sounds of Vivaldi, united in a single, brilliant creative effort.

As she returned Sophie Friedman's smile with a dazzling grin of her own, Alex decided that life didn't get much better than this.

Chapter Three

Alex didn't sleep all night. As she dressed for work, running one pair of black panty hose and pulling a button off the front of her dress in her fumbling nervousness, all she could think about was the upcoming moment of truth. When Debord would view her designs.

When she entered the salon, Alex was met with the cold, unwelcoming stare of Marie Hélène.

"*Bonjour, Madame,*" Alex said with far more aplomb than she was feeling.

Marie Hélène did not return her greeting. "Debord is waiting in his office."

Taking a deep breath that should have calmed her, but didn't, Alex headed up the stairs to the designer's penthouse office.

As she paused before the ebony door, with its *Défense d'Entrer* sign, Alex had a very good idea how Marie Antoinette must have felt on her way to the guillotine. Sternly reminding herself that a faint heart never achieved anything, that this was what she'd always wanted, she knocked.

Silence. Then, Debord's deep voice calling out, *"Entrez!"*

Squaring her shoulders, clad in an uplifting, confidence-building scarlet hunting jacket she'd defiantly worn over her black dress, she entered the designer's sanctum sanctorum.

Debord was talking in English on the phone. After gesturing her toward a chair on the visitor's side of his desk, he spun his high-backed chair around and continued his conversation. From his tight, rigidly controlled tone, Alex sensed that the telephone call was not delivering good news.

She took advantage of the delay to study the office. Like the workrooms, everything was pristine. The desk had such a sheen Debord was reflected in its gleaming jet surface. On the stark white wall behind the desk, Debord appeared in triplicate in Warhol portraits.

"Of course, Madame Lord," Debord was saying. "I understand your reluctance to commit funds just now."

Alex watched his fingers twist the telephone cord and had an idea that the designer would love to put those artistic fingers around Madame Lord's neck.

She'd heard about the possibility of Debord designing a line of ready-to-wear for Lord's, the prestigious department store chain. After last week's debacle, the gossip around the *atelier* was that the designer was desperate for such a deal in order to salvage a disastrous season.

Now, unfortunately, it appeared that Eleanor Lord, like everyone else, had deserted Debord.

"Certainly. I will look forward to seeing you at the fall *défilé* in July. We shall, of course, reserve your usual seat. *Certainement,* in the first row."

That statement revealed how important he considered the American executive. Seating was significant at couture showings; indeed, many fashion editors behaved as if their seat assignments were more important than the clothes being shown.

"*Au revoir*, Madame Lord."

The designer muttered a pungent curse, but when he turned toward Alex, his expression was bland. He did, however, lift an inquiring brow at her jacket. When he failed to offer a word of criticism, Alex let out a breath she'd been unaware of holding.

"Americans," he said dismissively. "They cannot understand that risk-taking is the entire point of couture."

"Mrs. Friedman bought your entire collection."

"True. However, I cannot understand why she chose my designs when they are so obviously inappropriate for her figure."

"She told me she likes your work." Alex was not about to reveal Sophie's actual reasons for buying Debord's collection. "And Lady Smythe seemed pleased with that black cocktail dress."

That particular purchase had been viewed as a positive sign, since Miranda Smythe not only happened to be Eleanor Lord's niece and style consultant for the Lord's London store, but was rumored to be the person who'd brought Debord to the department store executive's attention in the first place.

Unfortunately it appeared that when it came to business Lady Smythe had scant influence with her powerful aunt.

"I would feel a great deal better about the sale if Miranda Smythe had actually paid for the dress," he countered. "I cannot understand Marie Hélène. The discounts she allows that woman are tantamount to giving my work away."

Alex was not about to criticize Debord's formidable sister. "I suppose it doesn't hurt to have the wife of a British peer wearing your designs," she said carefully.

"Such things never hurt. But the British are so damnably tightfisted, they seldom buy couture. The average Englishwoman would rather spend her money on commissioning a bronze of her nasty little dogs, or a new horse trailer. Besides, Lady Miranda is about to get a divorce."

Alex had heard Marie Hélène and Françoise, Miranda Lord Baptista Smythe's personal vendeuse, discussing the socialite's marital record just yesterday.

"Let us keep our fingers crossed," Debord decided. "Perhaps, with luck, this time the fickle lady will wed a Kuwaiti prince. They never ask for discounts."

Alex laughed, as she was supposed to.

At last she couldn't stand the suspense a minute longer. "I know you're very busy, Monsieur. Would you like to see my portfolio now?"

"In a moment. First, I would like to know why such a beautiful woman would choose to labor behind the scenes when she could easily be a successful model."

"I'm not thin enough to be a model. Or tall enough. Besides, I've wanted to be a designer forever."

"Forever?" he asked with a faintly mocking smile.

"Well, ever since I watched Susan Hayward in *Back Street*. That's an old American movie," Alex explained at his questioning glance. "She plays a designer. The first time I saw it I fell head over heels in love."

"With Susan Hayward?" He frowned.

"Oh, no." Alex laughed as she followed his train of thought. "Not the actress. I fell in love with the glamour of the business. It became an all-encompassing passion." Her grin was quick and appealing. "Some of my friends would tell you that designing is all I think about."

"Really?" Debord's eyes, so like his sister's, but much warmer, moved slowly over her face. "I find that difficult to believe. A beautiful young woman such as yourself must have some other interests—parties, dances...men. Perhaps one particular man?"

He was watching her carefully now, the blue of his eyes almost obscured by the ebony pupils. Alex swallowed.

"Let me show you my designs." The portfolio was lying across her knees. She began to untie the brown string with fingers that had turned to stone. "I should probably tell you right off that most of the teachers at the institute didn't really like my style," she admitted. "But since I believe this is my best work, I'd really appreciate a master's opinion." Her words tumbled out, as if she were eager to get them behind her.

"I do not understand why Marie Hélène did not tell me about your talent," Debord said as Alex continued to struggle with the thin brown fastener.

Personally, Alex had her own ideas about that, but knowing how close Debord was to his sister, she kept them to herself.

"She's very busy." *Finally!* Cool relief flooded through Alex when the maddening knot gave way.

Yves Debord took her sketches and placed them face-down on the desk. Before looking at them, he pulled a gold cigarette case from his jacket pocket. After lighting a Gauloises, he turned his attention toward the colorful presentations.

Alex was more anxious than she'd ever been in her life. She kept waiting for him to say something—anything!—but he continued to flip through the sketches, front to back, back to front, over and over again.

Did he like them? Hate them? Were her designs as exciting and modern as she perceived them to be? Or were they, as one of her instructors had scathingly proclaimed, clothes for tarts?

Time slowed to a snail's pace. Perspiration began to slip down her sides.

"You are extraordinarily talented," Debord said finally.

"Do you really like them?"

He stubbed out his cigarette. "They are the most innovative designs I've seen in years."

Alex beamed.

"They are also entirely unmarketable."

The words hit like a blow from behind, striking her momentarily mute. "You have flown in the face of tradition," he said in a brusque no-nonsense tone that didn't spare her feelings. "This is costuming for the theater. Not the real world."

She'd heard that accusation before. But never had it stung so badly. "I was trying to be innovative. Like Chanel in the twenties with her tweed suits. And Dior's postwar New Look. The sixties' revolution, when Yves Saint Laurent introduced the pantsuit. And of course, Courreges's minidress."

She took a deep breath. "You just said that couture was about risk. All the great designers—Norell, Beene, you yourself—have gained fame by insisting on having a spirit of their own."

"You have talent, but you do not understand couture," he countered. "A designer must see women as they *want* to be seen."

"That's true," Alex conceded, even as it crossed her mind that, instead of *telling* women what they want, designers should *ask* them what they want.

Patience, she could hear her mother warning her.

"This design, for example." He held up a sketch that happened to be one of her favorites. An evening gown of tiered gold lace over black chiffon, cut like a Flamenco dancer's dress. "This gown would make a woman look as if she were dressing for an American Halloween party."

That hurt. "I can't see what's wrong with thinking of life as a party." *Patience*. "Besides, I thought it was sexy."

"The first thing you must learn, Alexandra, is that husbands want their women to look like ladies. Especially American husbands, who have a habit of marrying younger and younger brides without really knowing their pedigree."

He ignored Alex's sharp intake of breath. "Since the husbands are the ones paying the bills, a wise couturier designs with them in mind."

"That's incredibly chauvinistic."

"Perhaps. It is also true. The British have a saying," Debord continued. "Mutton dressed as lamb. Never forget, Mademoiselle Lyons, that is precisely what we are paid to do."

"But what about celebrating the female form—" Alex couldn't help argue "—instead of focusing on androgynous, sexless women?" When he physically bristled, Alex realized she'd hit uncomfortably close to home with that one. After all, Debord's disastrous new line had carried androgyny to new extremes.

His stony expression would have encouraged a prudent woman to back away. Unfortunately caution had never been Alex's forte.

"You say we must design for the husbands," she said, leaning forward. "I can't believe any man really wants his woman looking like a malnourished twelve-year-old boy."

"Not all men do," Debord acknowledged, his steady gaze taking in the softly feminine curves her stark black dress and scarlet jacket could not entirely conceal. "But the fact remains, Alexandra, wives should look like ladies. Not sirens."

In Alex's mind, there was absolutely nothing wrong with looking like a lady in the daytime and a siren at night. After all, this was a new age. Having proven they could do men's work, Alex believed it was time women started looking like women again.

"May I ask a question?" she said quietly.

"*Certainement.*"

"How can you consider me talented when you hate everything about my designs?"

"On the contrary, I don't hate everything about them. I love the energy, the verve. I think your use of color, while overdone, is *magnifique.*"

"Well," Alex decided on a rippling little sigh, "I suppose that's something."

"It's important." He stood and smiled down at her. "It is time we found a proper outlet for your talents."

"Do you mean—"

"I'm promoting you to assistant designer," Debord confirmed. "I shall inform Marie Hélène that you will be moving upstairs. Immediately."

Joy bubbled up in Alex. It was all she could do to keep from jumping up and flinging her arms around Debord's neck. She knew the broad grin splitting her face must look horrendously gauche, but couldn't keep herself from smiling.

"I don't know how to thank you, *monsieur.*"

"Just do your best. That is all I expect." Debord walked her to the door.

Feigning indifference to Marie Hélène's cold stare, Alex moved her colored pencils and sketch pads into the design office located above the showroom floor.

She was hard at work at her slanted drawing table later that afternoon when Debord entered the office. He made his way slowly around the room, offering a comment on each designer's work. Some were less than flattering, but all were encouraging. Until he got to Alex.

"A zipper is inappropriate," he declared loud enough for everyone in the room to hear. His finger jabbed at the back of her evening gown design. "This gown lacks spirit."

He plucked the slate pencil from her suddenly damp hand and with a few deft flourishes, sketched in a row of satin-covered buttons. "There. Now we have passion."

The buttons running from neckline to hem were admittedly lovely. They were also highly impractical. Alex wondered how a woman would be able to wear such a dress without a maid to fasten her up. And then there was the little matter of getting out of the gown at the end of the evening.

"It would seem to me," she countered mildly, "that trying to deal with fifty tiny, slippery satin buttons running down the back of a dress would tend to stifle passion."

There was a gasp from neighboring tables as the others in the room realized that this newcomer had dared argue with the master. Debord shot her a warning look.

"The way couture differs from ready-to-wear is in the decorating," he said shortly. "Specialness comes from the shape, the cut, the workmanship.

"Embellishing. Some fringe here." He ran his hand over her shoulder. Down the notched black velvet lapel of her scarlet hunting blazer. "A bit of beading here.

"We all must eat, Alexandra. Yet who among us wouldn't prefer a steak tartare to one of your American hot dogs? A glass of wine to water? A *crème brûlée* to some diet gelatin mold?"

"Are you comparing the designs of Debord to fine French cuisine?" Alex dared ask with a smile.

"*Bien sûr.*" He rewarded her with an approving smile of his own. Alex could have spent the remainder of the day basking in its warmth. "I knew you would be an adept pupil, Alexandra."

As he leaned forward, his arm casually brushed against her breast. "Now, let us review your interpretation of a Debord dinner suit."

Chapter Four

Santa Barbara, California
June 1982

The house, perched dramatically atop a hill, was draped in fog. Inside, candles flickered in Wedgwood holders. A fire blazed in the high, stone library fireplace.

Beside the fireplace, two women sat at opposite sides of a small mahogany table. Eleanor Lord wore an ivory silk blouse and linen slacks from Lord's Galleria department.

Across the table, theatrically clad in a lavender turban and a billowy caftan of rainbow chiffon, Clara Kowalski reached into a flowered tapestry bag and pulled out a small amethyst globe.

"The crystal is radiating amazing amounts of positive energy today," Clara said.

"Do you really believe Jarlath can locate Anna?"

Clara clucked her tongue. "Jarlath is merely a guide, Eleanor. Aiding you to evolve to a higher dimension."

"I'd rather he skip the evolution stuff and find my granddaughter," Eleanor muttered.

Eleanor considered herself a logical woman. She had always scoffed at those tales of farmers being kidnapped by aliens. Nor did she believe in the Bermuda Triangle, Bigfoot or the Loch Ness Monster. From the beginning of her marriage, Eleanor had been an equal partner in The Lord's Group, the department store chain established by her husband. When James Lord had died of a heart attack nearly thirty years ago, she took over the business without missing a step.

Despite her advanced years, despite the fact she now preferred doing business from her Santa Barbara home rather than trek down the coast to the chain's Los Angeles headquarters, Eleanor remained vigorous and continued her quest to keep Lord's the most successful department store in the world.

That same single-mindedness that had made Lord's a leader in fashion merchandising contributed to another, even more unrelenting obsession.

Eleanor had vowed to find her granddaughter, whatever it took. And although twenty-four years had passed, she had not stopped trying.

Each year, on the anniversary of Anna's disappearance, she'd place an advertisement offering a generous reward for information regarding her granddaughter's abduction in numerous metropolitan and small-town newspapers.

Thus far, once again, the advertisement had yielded nothing.

A less stubborn woman would have given up what everyone kept telling her was a futile search. But tenacity ran deep in Eleanor's veins. Besides, some inner sense told her she'd know if her granddaughter had been killed. Anna was alive. Of that, Eleanor had absolutely no doubt.

"As a businesswoman, you utilize your left brain, your logical side," Clara was saying. Eleanor returned her thoughts to the séance. "Jarlath will help you get in touch with your intuitive side. Once that doorway is open, you will have your answer."

Eleanor admitted to herself that the medium sounded uncomfortably like one of those frauds Mike Wallace was always unmasking on "60 Minutes." But, not wanting to leave any stone unturned, she was willing to try anything. Even this dabbling in the occult, which undoubtedly had all her Presbyterian ancestors spinning in their graves.

"Well," she said briskly, "let's get started."

Clara placed an Ouija board between them, took a chunk of quartz from her bag and placed it in the center of the board.

"Rock quartz is allied to the energies of the moon," she said. "I've found it makes a more sensitive channel than the usual pointer. The amethyst shade is exceptionally powerful."

Eleanor nodded and wondered, not for the first time, what had made her agree to this farfetched idea.

"Now," Clara said as she lit a stick of incense, "you must clear your mind. Banish all doubts. All cynicism."

Just get on with it, an impatient voice in Eleanor's cynical mind insisted. She shifted restlessly in her seat.

"I'm sensing negative energy," Clara chided. She began to sway. "Jarlath will not come if he is not welcome. Write your negative thoughts on a mental blackboard. Then erase them."

Immensely grateful that no one she knew was witnessing this outlandish scene, Eleanor took a deep breath and tried again.

"Ahhh." Clara nodded. "That's better. Relax your body, Eleanor. Feel yourself growing serene. Open your mind. Allow your physical and spiritual states to become harmonized and aligned," she intoned. She placed her fingers on the chunk of quartz. "Jarlath. Are you there?"

Eleanor watched as the violet stone slowly slid across the board, stopping on *Yes*.

"Welcome, Jarlath. This is my dear friend, Eleanor Lord. She needs your help, Jarlath. Desperately. She is trying to locate her granddaughter, Anna."

Although she knew it to be impossible, with the fire blazing nearby, Eleanor thought the air in the room suddenly felt cooler.

She leaned forward. "Ask him if he's seen Anna."

"Patience," Clara counseled. "Jarlath reveals in his own time." Nevertheless, her next words were, "Is Anna with you?"

No.

"I knew it!" Eleanor crowed triumphantly. Clara's guide was saying what she'd always known herself. Anna was alive!

There was a long pause. Then the gleaming rock moved to *A*. Then *N*. Then *O*. It moved slowly at first, then faster and faster until it had spelled out, *Another wishes to speak*. The flames of the candles suddenly shifted dramatically to the right, as if a wind had caught them. Caught up in the drama of the moment, Eleanor forgot to disbelieve.

"Who is with you?" Clara questioned. "Who wishes to speak with Eleanor Lord?"

This time the amethyst stone raced across the board. Candlelight reflected off its crystalline surface. *Dead*.

"Dear Lord, perhaps it's James. Or Robbie." Eleanor's voice trembled at the thought of her son. "Or Melanie." Her son's beautiful, tragically unhappy wife. Anna's mother.

No.

Clara frowned across the table as if to remind Eleanor just who was in charge of this séance. "Who, then?"

Silence.

"Place your fingers on the stone with mine," Clara advised. "It will increase the energy flow."

Eleanor did as instructed. Haltingly, the quartz began to move. *R. O.* Heat seemed to emanate from the amethyst. Eleanor's fingertips grew warm. *S.*

"Rosa," Eleanor gasped. Anna's nanny.

Confirming her thoughts, the crystal stopped on *A.* Eleanor felt light-headed. Spots danced in front of her eyes. The fire flared. Though there was no wind outdoors, the glass panes in the windows began to rattle. Then everything went dark.

"You're overreacting," Eleanor insisted an hour later. She was still in the library. And she was a very long way from being in a good mood. "It was merely a little heart flutter. Nothing more."

Dr. Averill Brandford frowned as he took the seventy-one-year-old woman's pulse. "That's your opinion. I hadn't realized you'd gotten your medical degree."

Having been called here from the yacht harbor where he moored his ketch, Averill was casually clad in a blue polo shirt, white duck slacks and navy Top-Siders. His face was tanned and his hair was sunstreaked from sailing excursions off the coast.

"You always did have a smart mouth, Averill," Eleanor returned. "I remember the summer you boys turned seven and you taught Robbie to curse. Although I'll admit to finding the episode moderately amusing, James did not share my feelings. It was a week before Robbie could sit down."

"It was winter. And we were nine." A tape recorder on a nearby table was playing Indian flute music. He turned it off. "And for the record, it was Robbie who taught me." He went over to the desk. "I'm checking you into the hospital for tests."

"That's ridiculous. I'm fine."

"Let's just make certain, shall we?"

"Do they teach all you doctors to be such sons-of-bitches in medical school?"

"The very first semester. Along with how to pad our medicare bills."

"Smart mouth." Eleanor shook her head in disgust.

Her hair, like her attitude, had steadfastly refused to give in to age. It was as richly auburn as it had been when she was a girl, save for a streak of silver at her temple, which had occurred overnight, after the tragic double murder and kidnapping.

"I think you should listen to Averill, Eleanor," the other man in the room, Zachary Deveraux, counseled with quiet authority.

"This isn't fair. You're ganging up on me."

"Whatever it takes," the tall, dark-haired man returned easily, appearing unfazed by her blistering glare.

Zachary was leaning against a leather wall, arms crossed over his chest, his legs crossed at the ankles. Unlike the doctor's recreational attire, Zach was wearing a conservative dark suit, white shirt and navy tie. His shoes, remarkably staid for even this Republican stronghold, were wing tips.

"As president of The Lord's Group, it's my responsibility to do everything I can to keep the company strong. You're more than a vital asset, Eleanor," he said with a slight French-patois accent that hinted at his Louisiana Cajun roots. "You're the lifeblood of the chain. We need you."

His dark eyes, more black than brown, warmed. His harshly cut masculine lips curved in a coaxing smile. "*I* need you."

Although she might be in her eighth decade, Eleanor was a long way from dead. Was there a woman with blood still stirring in her veins who could resist that blatantly seductive smile?

Before she could accuse him of pulling out all the stops to win his way, the library door opened and Clara burst into the room. An overpowering scent of orrisroot and clove emanated from the silver *pomme d'ambre* she wore around her neck.

"Eleanor, dear." Moving with the force of a bulldozer, she practically knocked both men over as she rushed to the side of the sofa. "I've been absolutely frantic ever since your two bodyguards banished me from the room."

She shot a blistering glare first at Averill, then another directly at Zach, who merely stared back. The only sign of his annoyance were his lips, which tightened into a grim line.

Eleanor's slender hand disappeared between the woman's two pink pudgy ones. "I'm fine, Clara. Really," she insisted. "It was merely a flutter. Nothing to be concerned about."

"Of course not," Clara Kowalski agreed heartily. "Don't you worry, dear. I have just the tonic you need in the greenhouse."

She smiled reassuringly. "A little extract of hawthorn, followed by some pipsissewa tea. That will definitely do the trick."

"I believe you've done enough tricks for today, Mrs. Kowalski," Averill said.

Crimson flooded the elderly woman's face, clashing with her lavender turban. "I am not a magician, Doctor. I do not do tricks."

"Oh, no?" Zach countered, scowling at the Ouija board. "Looks like just another fun evening at home with Hecate."

"Zachary," Eleanor murmured her disapproval. "You mustn't talk that way. Clara's my friend. And she's been very helpful. We almost had a breakthrough."

"A breakthrough?" He didn't conceal his scorn concerning Clara Kowalski's alleged psychic powers.

"We nearly made contact with Rosa, Anna's departed nanny." Clara's eyes, nearly hidden by folds of pink fat, dared him to challenge her claim.

"Clara's guide said Rosa was willing to talk to us," Eleanor said.

"Ah, yes, the infamous guide," Zach agreed. "What was the guy's name again? Jaws?"

"Jarlath!" Clara snapped.

"That's right." Zach nodded. "Summer sales could be stronger this season. How about asking old Jarlath to see what he can do about bringing more shoppers into the stores?"

"Jarlath does not control things," Clara replied waspishly. "He is a spiritual guide, not a fortune-teller."

"Sounds a helluva lot like voodoo to me." Zach turned back to Eleanor, his exasperation obvious. "Dammit, Eleanor—"

"Don't you see, Zachary," she interrupted earnestly, "Rosa can tell us what happened to Anna."

The two men exchanged weary, resigned looks. Zach raked his hand through his jet hair and cursed softly in the Acadian French, that during his childhood years, had been the only language spoken in his bayou home.

"Eleanor," Averill said softly. Gently. "It's been twenty-four years since Robbie and Melanie were..." He paused, selecting his words carefully. "Since Anna disappeared," he said, instead. "Don't you think it's time you gave it up?"

"I promised Robbie I'd find Anna. Since I never broke a promise to my son while he was alive, I'll be damned if I start with this one."

"I'm only suggesting a few days in the hospital," Averill said. "For tests. And some well-deserved rest. After all, you need to be in tip-top shape to keep up your search. If that's what you insist on doing."

"It is." But Eleanor's determined expression wavered. Her gaze went to the table, where they'd been so close to contacting the nanny.

"It won't hurt to have a checkup before we leave for the Paris shows next month," Zachary pointed out with the unwavering logic she'd always admired.

In so many ways Zach reminded Eleanor of her dear James. Granted, their backgrounds were vastly different. But even discounting her late husband's family wealth, both James Lord and Zachary Deveraux were quintessential self-made men.

Zachary had been her personal discovery. Eleanor had watched his meteoric progress with a certain secret pride. And although he didn't yet know it, she was grooming him to take over the reins of the Lord's chain when she retired.

Upon her death, this man she'd come to think of as a son would receive enough of the family stock to ensure control of The Lord's Group. But included in her will was a provision for Anna to receive the bulk of Eleanor's personal estate.

"All right. Three days," Eleanor said finally, ignoring Clara's frustrated huff. "Then if you won't release me, I'm checking myself out."

Although Eleanor knew Zach was more than capable of handling business, she insisted on remaining a vital part of Lord's. She'd seen too many of her male colleagues retire, only to drop dead of a heart attack six months later. Eleanor had no intention of joining their ranks.

"Three days," Averill agreed. "That's all I'm asking."

"And I want Clara to have a bed in my room."

"Impossible," Zach ground out before Averill could respond. His rugged face could have been chiseled from granite. "There's no way you're going to get any rest with Sybil the Soothsayer hovering over you like one of Macbeth's damned witches."

Clara's scowl darkened. She crossed her arms over her abundant bosom and glared at him. "Has anyone ever told you that you have a very negative aura, Mr. Deveraux?"

"All the time," he snapped.

"Eleanor—" Averill deftly entered the debate "—Zach's right. You need rest. Time away from all this." He waved his hand, encompassing the accumulation of mystical accoutrements that had taken over the house.

Eleanor held her ground. "Those are my terms, Averill. Take them or leave them."

Professional demeanor was abandoned as he allowed his frustration to show. "There are times when I can't decide whether you are the most obstinate woman I've ever met or simply crazy," he muttered, picking up the receiver to make the arrangements.

If she was insulted, Eleanor didn't reveal it. "That's precisely the reason I'm going to find Anna."

Chapter Five

Two days later, Miranda Lord Baptista Smythe burst into Eleanor's hospital room. She was fashionably thin and sported a sleek blond hairdo that was as much a signature of her British Ascot class as her accent. Although she was in her midforties, her complexion, thanks to a benevolent British climate and the clever hand of her plastic surgeon, was as smooth and unlined as that of a girl in her twenties.

"Dear, dear Aunt Eleanor," she greeted the older woman with a brush of powdered cheek. "I rushed over from London on the Concorde as soon as I heard! Honestly, I don't understand how you could have let that horrid old witch get you so upset!"

"Clara doesn't upset me, Miranda," Eleanor said mildly.

"She gave you a heart attack."

"It was a flutter. And Clara had nothing to do with it."

Miranda took a cigarette from her Gucci bag and was prepared to light it when she caught sight of the No Smoking—Oxygen in Use sign posted beside Eleanor's hospital bed.

"Those things already killed your mother," Eleanor pointed out knowingly.

"Living like some over-the-hill party girl, squandering her inheritance from my father, instead of putting it somewhere safe such as blue-chip stocks or bonds, is what killed my mother," Miranda said. "Why, if it weren't for all the money she threw away on those damned gigolos, I wouldn't be fighting to keep the wolves away from the door."

Lawrence Lord, James's younger brother and business partner, and Miranda's father, had been an avid tennis fan and nationally ranked amateur player. Forty-six years ago, when he'd returned from a trip to Wimbledon with news that he had fallen in love with the genteel daughter of an impoverished viscount, James had established a Lord's in London and made his brother president of the new European branch, where Miranda now worked as a style consultant.

"You're far from destitute, dear," Eleanor reminded Miranda. "Your salary is generous. And you still have your stock."

"That's another thing." Miranda began to pace, the skirt of her emerald silk YSL dress rustling with each long stride. "My barrister assures me the prenuptial agreement will be upheld, but in the meantime, Martin is demanding a share of London Lord's."

Eleanor frowned. She knew Miranda's latest marriage—to a London bond trader—was in the process of ending, as had her marriage to a Brazilian polo player before it, in divorce. But she hadn't been informed of this unfortunate legal development.

"Well, we certainly can't have that," she said.

"I'd shoot Martin through his black heart with one of his antique shotguns before I let him get his greedy, aristocratic hands on the family business," Miranda agreed grimly.

"I believe we can defuse this little problem without resorting to violence," Eleanor murmured. "Why don't I ask Zach to meet with your attorney? Or even with Martin himself? Zachary can be very persuasive." Eleanor knew from personal experience that Lord's president also wasn't above employing street-fighter skills when necessary.

Frown lines etched their way into Miranda's smooth forehead. "If you think it will help. Although I still prefer the idea of shooting the bastard. Or perhaps putting poison in his sherry."

As if aware of how unpleasant she sounded, she said, "But enough about my petty problems. Let me arrange your pillows, Auntie. You need your rest."

Her niece's pretense of concern grated. Before Miranda's dramatic entrance, Eleanor had overheard her talking with Averill outside the room.

Averill had spoken gently, in the reassuring way doctors had. Although with proper care she probably had many years left, if Eleanor's heart did fail, Miranda would be able to glean comfort from the fact that her aunt had had a full life. And though she would be missed, all that Eleanor had done would remain as a memorial.

Averill had reminded Eleanor of a man rehearsing a eulogy. The unctuous testimonial had made her mad enough to want to spit nails.

"The rumors of my impending death have been greatly exaggerated," she paraphrased Mark Twain now.

"Of course, Auntie," Miranda agreed quickly. Too quickly, Eleanor mused. "We all know you're going to live forever."

Well, maybe not forever. But if Averill or Miranda thought she was going to die anytime soon, they had another think coming. Because Eleanor refused to leave this world until Anna was back home again. Where she belonged.

"Miranda, dear, would you do me a favor?"

"Of course."

"Would you please find Clara? I believe she's in the cafeteria."

Miranda's forced smile revealed her distaste for Clara, but she held her tongue. "Of course."

"Oh, and Miranda?"

She turned in the doorway. "Yes?"

"Ask her to bring her tarot cards. I had a dream about Anna when I dozed off earlier. I think a reading is in order."

A nerve twitched at the corner of Miranda's red lips. "Whatever you say, Aunt Eleanor."

Zach sat in a corner of the hospital cafeteria, drinking coffee from a brown-and-white cardboard cup and eating a ham-and-Swiss-cheese sandwich. The coffee tasted like battery acid, the cheese was processed, the dark rye bread stale.

His mind was not on his unsavory meal. It was on what he was going to do about Eleanor. Every morning, when he went to work, he was in charge of millions of dollars and thousands of Lord's employees. He was intelligent, capable and clever. So why the hell couldn't he figure out what to do about Eleanor's unwavering efforts to locate her missing granddaughter? A granddaughter who'd likely been dead for twenty-four years.

Zach polished off the thick, unappetizing coffee and lost in thought, began methodically tearing the cardboard cup to pieces. On some level, he was vaguely aware of a growing commotion nearby. But since this was a hospital and there was always some tragedy occurring, he paid the raised voices no heed.

Last year Eleanor had been convinced she'd discovered Anna. The woman, a blackjack dealer in a Las Vegas casino, had been an obvious impostor. It was also obvious she'd been put up to the charade by her boyfriend, a low-level gangster.

But when Zach had argued that the things the woman professed to remember about the Montecito house and the family could be found in newspaper morgues and style magazines, Eleanor, her steely logic fogged by unrelenting desire, had refused to listen.

Ignoring Zach's protests, Eleanor had moved the woman and her boyfriend into her home, treating them like family. Nothing, absolutely nothing, was too good for her darling "Anna." On one memorable day, Zach had arrived in Santa Barbara with the quarterly reports just as Eleanor and "Anna" returned home laden down with resort clothes, dresses, and elegant evening gowns—suitable for all the parties Anna would be attending, Eleanor had pointed out. Later that same afternoon, a red Corvette from a local Chevrolet dealer had been delivered.

Although Zach detested anything resembling a lie, he had reminded himself that what Eleanor was seeking was family. That being the case, did it really matter all that much if this newly discovered family member was not really tied by blood?

It did.

Six weeks after their arrival at Eleanor's door, the unsavory pair absconded with all the gifts Eleanor had bestowed upon the woman she'd believed to be her granddaughter, along with several thousand dollars from the household expenses checking account, a tea set crafted by Paul Revere that had been in the family for two hundred years, and a stunning diamond-and-pearl necklace set in platinum that James had given Eleanor on the occasion of their son Robert's birth.

Had it not been for the necklace, Eleanor, horribly embarrassed by her uncharacteristic mistake in judgment, undoubtedly would have let the matter go. But the sentimental value of that jewelry overrode any fear of public humiliation.

She'd pressed charges, and two weeks later, the couple was discovered celebrating their good fortune in Cancun. Well aware that what he was doing was bribery, Zach traveled to Mexico with an attaché case filled with American dollars to grease the normally slow-moving machinery of Mexican justice.

He was successful. The fugitives were extradited to California, charged and convicted.

Although still slightly bothered by the way he'd skated along the razor's edge of principle—bribery and veiled threats were not his usual method of doing business—Zach did not for a single moment regret his actions.

The son of an impoverished Louisiana trapper and sugarcane farmer, Zach had come up the hard way and was immensely proud of his white-collar status. He also understood that it was not that great a distance between wearing a starched shirt and suit in his executive suite to his early days laboring in a sweat-stained T-shirt on the loading dock of the New Orleans Lord's.

Eleanor Lord had offered Zach wealth, security and the opportunity to prove himself. There was nothing he wouldn't do for her.

The voices in the cafeteria grew louder, infiltrating their way into his thoughts. When he recognized Clara's voice, he looked over to see what the witch was up to now.

She was engaged in an argument with another woman whom Zach recognized as Eleanor's niece. Eleanor kept a crystal-framed photo of Miranda Lord, smiling up at her first husband, the dashing, unfaithful Brazilian polo player, on her desk.

Deciding he'd better intervene before the two women started pulling hair, Zach cursed and pushed himself to his feet.

Clara's pudgy face was as crimson as today's turban, while equally bright color stained Miranda's cheekbones.

"Excuse me," he murmured, from behind Miranda's shoulder, "but you ladies are drawing a crowd."

Miranda spun around. "Who the bloody hell do you think you are?"

Her green eyes were flashing like emeralds and her complexion reminded him of the Devonshire cream he'd sampled the time Eleanor, intent on teaching him manners, had taken him to afternoon tea at the Biltmore.

"If you do not mind, Mr. Deveraux," Clara said, giving him her usual glare, "we are having a discussion."

"Sounded more like an argument to me."

"Mr. Deveraux?" One perfectly shaped blond brow lifted. The fury faded from her bright eyes, replaced by blatant feminine interest. "*You're* Aunt Eleanor's famous Zachary?"

Miranda Lord was reminiscent of an F. Scott Fitzgerald heroine. One of those bright, shining people, like Daisy from *The Great Gatsby*. Zach felt a burst of masculine pride that she knew of him. "Not all that famous."

"On the contrary." Her lips curved, and he was reminded of a cat regarding a succulent saucer of cream. "You're practically all Auntie talks about. And although I knew you were a change from those old fogies who usually sit on the board, I don't know why she never mentioned how—" she allowed her eyes to sweep slowly over him "—substantial you are."

When her gaze lingered a heartbeat too long on his thighs, Zach knew he was being expertly, seductively summed up.

Her openly predatory gaze returned to his face. "I'm so sorry," she cooed. "All this has been so upsetting that I've completely forgotten my manners." She held out a slim, perfectly manicured hand. "I'm Miranda Lord. Soon to be the former Lady, or Mrs. Martin-the-bastard-Smythe." Her silvery, breathless voice, a voice Judy Holliday had invented and Marilyn Monroe had perfected, carried an unmistakable British upper class tinge.

"I heard about your divorce." Her hand felt soft and smooth. "I'm sorry."

"Oh, you shouldn't be," Miranda insisted. "Personally, I look on divorce as not so much of an ending, as a new beginning."

She gave him a suggestive smile before turning back to Clara. "My aunt wishes to see you. Oh, and she wants you to bring your tarot cards."

"Well, why didn't you say so in the first place?" Clara huffed. Gathering up her immense shoulder bag, she waddled from the bustling cafeteria.

"Do you suppose," Miranda suggested, "that if we threw water on Clara, she might melt?"

Zach threw back his head and laughed. A rich, booming release of sound that eased the tension. "It's definitely worth a try."

"Why don't we discuss the logistics? Over coffee." She glanced disparagingly around the room. "I'm absolutely exhausted from traveling. But I doubt the chef at this bleak establishment knows how to brew a proper pot of tea."

"No problem. I know just the place."

Placing a palm at her elbow, he led her out of the hospital.

Ten minutes later, they were sitting in the Biltmore's La Sala lounge. The lounge, with its wealth of polished stonework, luxuriant greenery and comfortable, overstuffed sofas and armchairs, was the most gracious in the city.

"I really am so horribly worried about Aunt Eleanor," Miranda said over porcelain cups of impeccably brewed Earl Grey tea. Her heady, exotic scent bloomed in the warmth of the room, mingling with the aroma of cedar from the fireplace.

"Join the club," Zach said. "If it's any consolation, there's no sign of senile dementia."

"You actually considered that possibility?"

"Of course. Your aunt's a logical, pragmatic woman—"

"Except when it comes to her darling Anna."

"Except when it comes to Anna," Zach agreed. "But although she's admittedly driven and obsessive when it comes to finding her granddaughter, it's only been these last few months that she's decided to try the spirit world."

"That is so bizarre," Miranda murmured. "I had my barrister retain a private detective when Clara moved into the house with Aunt Eleanor." She frowned. "Did you know she's a widow? Three times over? And that all her husbands have been wealthy?"

"I had her checked out, too." Zach knew Eleanor would hit the roof if she found out about his investigation, but that didn't stop him from wanting to protect her. "One of her neighbors insists Clara poisoned her husbands with her herbs."

"How horrible!"

"It would be if it was true. But the police lieutenant I spoke with said that same neighbor calls up after 'Crime Stoppers' reports on the news to say she's seen the criminal lurking around her neighborhood. He also assured me that there was no evidence of foul play in any of Clara's husbands' deaths."

"Are you telling me you believe she's innocent?"

Zach shrugged. "At the moment, I can only conclude that Clara Kowalski simply seems to have better luck with her plants than with her husbands. But I'm keeping an eye on her."

Miranda leaned forward and placed a hand on his arm. "You've no idea how that relieves my mind, Zachary. To know that someone besides me cares what happens to Aunt Eleanor."

Sitting back again, she spread some frothy cream atop a scone, added a dab of dark red currant jam and took a bite. "Sublime," she said on a soft, pleased sigh. "You have marvelous tastes in restaurants, Mr. Deveraux."

Her lips left a red mark like a crescent moon on the scone; a dab of cream remained at the corner of her mouth. When she licked it away, Zach felt his body harden.

"Thanks." He took a long swallow of tea and wished it was Scotch.

"From your disapproval of Auntie's foray into the spirit realm, I take it you don't believe in things that go bump in the night?"

"No. Although I grew up surrounded by voodoo, I've never bought into the spirit world."

"Voodoo?" Miranda leaned forward, every muscle in her body taut with interest. Once again she reminded Zach of Fitzgerald's Daisy. Her voice suggested moonlight and starshine and champagne; her eyes were dazzling jewels.

"I grew up in Louisiana," Zach revealed. "While it's not nearly as prevalent as it once was, voodoo still lives on in local superstitions and medicines."

"Louisiana," Miranda mused reflectively. Zach watched the wheels turning inside that gorgeous blond head. "But of course," she said, clapping her hands. "That explains the accent I keep hearing. You're a Cajun!"

She was looking at him with the overt fascination one might give to a newly discovered species of animal. "Is it true what they say about your people?"

"What do they say?"

Zach braced himself for the usual stereotypical description of fire-eating swamp dwellers who communicated in an archaic French only they could understand and who had yet to join the nineteenth century, let alone the twentieth.

"That your motto is *Laissez les bons temps rouler?*"

"Let the good times roll?" Zach smiled. "Absolutely." He tried to remember the last time in his own life recently that the *bons temps* had *rouler*ed and came up blank.

"I'm so relieved." Her silky voice caressed, like sensually delicate fingers, making Zach consider suggesting they walk to the lobby check-in and get a room.

"So often the most wonderful things you hear turn out to be an exaggeration. And a crashing disappointment." Miranda's expression revealed that she was finding Zach anything but a disappointment.

"It must be difficult," Miranda mused, "trying to run the business while Aunt Eleanor's locked away in the library with that horrid old witch conducting séances."

"I'm managing," Zach said.

Some inner instinct warned him that Eleanor's niece might have a hidden agenda. The board needed Miranda's vote at this year's annual meeting. Zach wasn't about to give her any hint that the chain's future was not as sound as ever. Which it was. He wouldn't allow it to be otherwise.

"Perhaps things will get better for you," she suggested.

Zach would have had to have been deaf to miss the invitation in her tone. When she smiled at him over the rim of her teacup, he felt another slow pull deep in his groin.

"Perhaps they will," he agreed.

She inclined her head charmingly. Then, recrossing her legs with an erotic swish of silk, she gave him an enticing flash of lacy garter and smooth thigh.

It had begun to rain; a steady drizzle that streamed down the windows and made the line between ocean and sky blur.

"I'm afraid I must confess I don't really keep up on the details of the American end of the business," she admitted. "I have enough to keep me busy with the London store. And, of course, my ongoing effort to increase the chain's couture lines.

"But I do know that Lord's headquarters are in Los Angeles. Before Auntie's unfortunate attack, had you come here to Santa Barbara on business? Or pleasure?"

This morning he would have answered business. But since there was no mistaking her signals, Zach answered, "A bit of both."

"I've always admired a man who knows how to play as hard as he works." She took another sip of tea and eyed him expectantly from under the silken fringe of her expertly dyed lashes. Leaning forward, she placed her hand on his knee and looked him directly in the eye. "Now that you've done your duty and provided me with much needed sustenance, I suppose we should return to the hospital. Heaven knows what that horrid woman has done to Aunt Eleanor's blood pressure."

Her demeanor, as they left the lounge and waited for the valet to bring Zach's Mercedes, revealed that returning to the hospital was definitely not her first choice.

"I have some business to discuss with Eleanor. And then you'll probably want to visit with her again," Zach said ten minutes later as he pulled into the hospital parking area.

"Aunt Eleanor and I have a great deal of catching up to do," Miranda agreed.

"I thought you might. After your visit, I'll take you back to the house."

"I'd appreciate that. If you're certain I won't be intruding on your busy schedule."

She was. But Zach didn't care. *Laissez les bons temps rouler.* His mind was practically writhing with erotic images. "I'll shuffle things around while you're with Eleanor." He cut the engine and pocketed the key.

"That's very kind of you."

"And then, after you get settled in at the house, we'll go out to dinner."

"It sounds positively delightful," Miranda said.

Unable to resist the creamy lure of her skin another minute, Zach ran the back of his hand down her cheek.

"And then, after dinner, you'll spend the night with me," he declared in a firm, deep voice that brooked not a single argument. "All night. In my room. In my bed."

Miranda's lips curved in a slow, seductive smile that burned as hot as an Olympic flame. "Yes."

Chapter Six

Paris

Alex's days, weeks and months flowed into each other like long ocean swells as she labored under Debord's watchful, unrelenting eye.

The designer continued to closely monitor her work, brutally subtracting a flounce here, dispensing with what she considered marvelously sexy feathered trim there, all the while treating her to a dizzying array of seemingly casual touches and intimate smiles that left her weak in the knees.

His personal attention to his new protégée did not go unnoticed by the other assistant designers. Jealousy, that ugly emotion rampant in the fashion business, reared its green head on an almost daily basis.

More than once Alex arrived at work only to find that the "cleaning woman" had mistakenly tossed out yesterday's sketches. Or a colleague "accidentally" spilled coffee over designs she'd labored past midnight to finish. Even her beloved pencils disappeared, fortuitously discovered buried beneath some discarded towels in the change room.

Although the others steadfastly refused to accept her, nothing could banish the joy Alex felt every time she entered the studio.

Four months after her promotion, Debord invited Alex out to dinner. Refusing to play coy, she immediately accepted.

They dined at the Café le Flore, a place that remained unchanged from the days when Picasso had made it his unofficial salon and Jean-Paul Sartre and Simone de Beauvoir had sat out the German occupation at a table in the back.

But Alex's mind was not on the past but the future. The immediate future, to be exact. She wore one of her own creations, which had been designed to capture and hold a man's attention. Created of tissue lamé, the strapless dress dipped to her waist in the back. The sparkling gold fabric duplicated the lightest strands in her multihued hair; layers of black net petticoat peeked enticingly from beneath the billowy skirt.

Glittery gold stockings, ridiculously impractical backless high heels and gold chandelier earrings that dusted her shoulders completed the festive look.

"Did I tell you that I plan to include two of your designs in the fall line?" Debord asked.

"No!" Pleasure surged through her. "Which ones?"

"The silk dinner suit with the sarong-style skirt, for one. It should work up nicely in smoke."

Her tawny eyebrows crashed down toward her nose. "Gray?"

"Purple is inappropriate."

Momentarily putting aside her excitement that the master had chosen her work, Alex crossed her legs with a quick, irritated rustle of ebony petticoats. "It's not purple. It's amethyst. Jewel toned." Alex had intended to press to have it also offered in ruby, emerald and sapphire.

"More women can wear gray than purple. The suit will be offered in smoke. And, of course, black."

Of course, Alex thought. Although she knew she should be thrilled, she felt like a mother who'd just handed over her only child to the Gypsies.

"What other design did you like?"

Although asking Alex to hold her tongue was a little like asking her to stop breathing, she was clever enough to know that getting into an argument with Debord over the line that would ultimately bear his name would prove a fatal mistake.

Patience, she reminded herself for the umpteenth time in months.

"The velvet evening dress with the gold braid."

"Oh, that's one of my favorites." After the brutal change he was making to her dinner suit, Alex could hardly believe he'd actually selected her most flamboyant and sexy design. "I'm surprised you like it," she admitted.

He lifted an amused brow. "Because it is cut to showcase a woman's curves?"

"Well, yes, actually. I know you usually prefer to design for a thinner female shape."

Debord's gaze moved over her, taking in the softly feminine curves displayed by her gilt dress.

"Although I will not take back what I said about men preferring their wives to dress like ladies, I will admit that you are definitely correct about one thing, *chérie.*"

His voice lowered, becoming deep and intimate. His gaze caressed her breasts, causing her nipples to harden into little points that pressed painfully against the gold tissue lamé.

Alex swallowed. "What's that?"

"A man tires of fashionably bone-thin women."

His unwavering gaze was rife with sexual promise. A woman could drown in those eyes, Alex mused. And this man wouldn't lift a finger to save her. Such thoughts, which should have frightened her away, strangely only made her want this passionate, talented man all the more.

Conversation lulled as they sat close enough for their thighs to touch on the red banquette, exchanging glances that grew longer and more heated as the evening progressed.

When she suggested they have their after-dinner drinks at her apartment, Alex was only following her heart, bringing things to their natural conclusion.

Their lovemaking, she told herself as they stood side by side in the slow, creaky elevator, had always been inevitable. With the single-mindedness that had allowed her to achieve, at the relatively young age of twenty-six, so much of her dream, she couldn't put aside her belief that she and Debord were destined to be together. In every way. The elevator finally reached her floor. The ornate brass door opened. Alex walked with Debord down the hall, her full skirt swaying.

When she went to open her apartment door, the key stubbornly stuck in the lock. She twisted it viciously. Nothing.

"Allow me." Alex could have wept with relief when Debord took over. The door opened, as if by magic.

"Would you like something to drink?" Suddenly horrendously nervous, Alex found her arsenal of feminine allure had mysteriously deserted her. "Some wine? Cognac? Coffee?"

"Cognac will be fine."

"Cognac it is." Although it cost far more than she could comfortably afford, Alex had purchased the expensive Rémy Martin that afternoon. Just in case.

She poured the dark brandy into two balloon glasses, handing one to Debord. His fingers, as they curved around the glass, were long and tapered. The thought of those fingers stroking her body sent a jolt of desire surging through her.

As they sipped their drinks, a pregnant silence settled over them. Debord was the first to break it. He put down his glass on the table in front of him, took hers from her nerveless fingers and placed it beside his. Then he turned toward her.

"You are beautiful, Alexandra Lyons." He trailed his fingers up her throat. "And so very talented."

They were precisely the words she'd been hoping—longing—to hear. "Do you really, honestly think so?" she whispered.

His hands were warm and strong and gentle as they cradled her head. His smile warmed her to the core. *"Bien sûr."*

Desire clouded her mind even as his words thrilled her. Warmth seemed to leave his fingertips and enter her bloodstream, flowing through her, down her legs, through her arms to her fingertips, waves of shimmering, silvery light.

His lips captured hers in a devastatingly long, deliriously deep kiss that left her drugged. She felt hot. Feverish. She wanted to melt into him, she wanted to feel his naked body next to hers, she wanted to immerse herself in the scent of his flesh. Never had Alex known such need! She pressed herself against him. She felt his hardness and wanted him deep inside her.

He stood up and looked down at her for a heartstoppingly long time, his expression unfathomable. When he finally extended his hand, she took it, allowing him to pull her to her feet.

Very slowly, he unzipped her dress. It fell to the floor in a gilt-and-jet puddle at her feet. Alex stepped out of it.

She was wearing a lace-trimmed, strapless, gold satin teddy, and a pair of thigh-high gold stockings. As he carried her into the adjoining bedroom, Alex clung to him mindlessly, eager to go wherever he took her.

She didn't question how her underclothes were whisked from her. She only knew that they disappeared, as if by magic.

And then Debord's clothes were gone as well. He stood beside the bed, blatantly aroused. The ancient bedsprings creaked as he lay down beside her. "You are so voluptuous, *ma cocotte*." His fingers closed over her full, aching breasts. "So hot." His tongue laved her burning flesh.

He touched her, kissed her, licked her all over—her neck, her breasts, the backs of her knees, her stomach, on the insides of her thighs, in the furrow between her buttocks, even her toes.

He lay bare all her feminine secrets, all the while murmuring seductive suggestions in French that thrilled her.

It was torment. Torment mingled with escalating pleasure. The exciting, feverish floating feelings built even higher. Her body flushed strawberry pink.

"Please." Alex wanted him wildly. Madly. She begged him to take her. "I don't think...I need..." She could stand this no longer.

But he taunted her with his control, stripping away her defenses layer by layer, leaving her raw and vulnerable.

And then finally he took her. As the passion rose, furiously like a wind before a thunderstorm, Alex clung to Debord, surrendering to the rhythm. To him.

The designer arched his back for a long, charged moment, every gleaming muscle in his body cast into sharp relief. Heat flooded through Alex's body, echoing his pri-

mal cry. It was as if the flame of their passion had ignited
into a blinding fireball, searing them together for all time.

Forever, she thought as she lay in the strong protective
circle of his arms, her lips curved in a secret womanly smile.
The final phase of her life's plan had blessedly come true.
Just as she'd always dreamed. She and Debord were now
inexorably linked—creative minds, spirits and bodies.
Forever.

London

Located in the heart of modern London, The City, as it
was known, was considered by many to be the wealthiest
square mile on earth. It was also synonymous with power.
Roman legions had once camped on land now taken over
by towering high-rise office buildings, medieval guilds had
plied their trades here, and swashbuckling capitalists—men
who financed wars and countries—had transacted million-
pound deals on the strength of a gentleman's handshake.

These days, Americans and Japanese were rushing into
The City in droves, clutching stuffed briefcases and folded
editions of the *Financial Times*. The deals now made in The
City tended to be about French films, Arab oil imports and
shopping centers.

"You've come a long way from the bayou, boy," Zach
murmured as he watched a flock of pigeons circling the
dome of St. Paul's Cathedral.

"You talking to me?" the taxi driver asked, looking at
his fare in the rearview mirror.

"No. Just thinking out loud."

The driver shrugged and concentrated on making his way
through the crush of traffic.

The business day was coming to a close. Workers poured
forth from the buildings, headed toward the Underground
which would take them back to their homes in Knights-

bridge and Mayfair. Buses forged their way through the crowded streets.

Tomorrow morning the same people would all rush back, talking fast, working hard, coming up with innovative new ways to make dizzying amounts of money. Because one thing that never changed was that money remained the lifeblood of The City.

Just as money was the reason for Zach's being in London. He'd come here on Lord's business. Or at least that was what he'd been trying to tell himself.

But the minute Miranda's butler opened the door, Zach knew that the overriding reason he'd flown across a continent and an ocean was to be with the woman he'd not been able to get out of his mind for the past three weeks.

He knew he was behaving uncharacteristically. He couldn't remember a time, even during his horny teenage years, when he'd been so obsessed with sex. Of course, he'd never met a woman like Miranda Lord before, either, Zach mused as he followed the dark-suited butler into the drawing room.

"It's done," he greeted her without preamble.

"Done?" She stubbed out her cigarette in a Lalique ashtray and crossed the room on a swish of crimson silk. "Do you mean..."

Feeling like a knight returning after a successful Crusade, he set his briefcase on a priceless Louis Quinze table and extracted a single piece of paper.

"Lord Smythe deeply regrets having caused you emotional distress. As proof of his willingness to accept full blame in the breakup of your marriage, not only has he dropped all claims against your assets, but he insists on paying all legal fees having to do not only with his attempt to acquire your Lord's stock, but the divorce, as well."

"Surely you jest!" She grasped the piece of paper from his hand, her avid eyes eating up the lines of text. "You darling, wonderful man." Her voice was a low, satisfied purr. She pressed her hand against his chest, moving it lower. Then lower still. "How ever can I thank you?"

There was nothing subtle about her stroking fingers or the invitation gleaming in her eyes. Zach had come to the conclusion that directness was one of Miranda's greatest charms.

"I'm sure you'll think of something," he said amiably.

Much, much later, Zach telephoned Eleanor from Miranda's antique bed and amazed his employer by announcing that he was taking five rare days off.

Since they couldn't make love twenty-four hours a day, Zach and Miranda managed to leave the bed from time to time. Miranda proved an enthusiastic tour guide as she took Zach to all the attractions. Hyde Park, the Tower of London, Kensington Gardens.

She also took him to the London Lord's. For a man in charge of a chain of department stores, Zach was an anomaly in that he'd always hated shopping. But unable to resist Miranda's polished charms, he spent an afternoon following her through the big store, and while he couldn't get excited about the aisles of china and linen, he had to admit that the cashmere sweater she selected for him was quite comfortable.

One evening they attended a concert at Albert Hall, immortalized by the Beatles in their *Sergeant Pepper* album. "Did you know," Miranda offered, as they climbed into the back seat of the Daimler limousine that was waiting to take them back to her townhouse after the concert, "when Tom Jones played here, women actually threw their underwear onto the stage?"

Zach arched a brow. "Surely not proper English women," he said with feigned shock.

Miranda nodded. "So I've been told."

Her eyes glittered like the diamonds she wore at her ears and throat. Her gown was little more than a slip, which clung to every curve of her body, outlining the pert up-thrust of her breasts and rounded buttocks in a shimmer of silver satin. It was obvious she was wearing nothing underneath it.

"Sounds like I'm in the wrong business," Zach said. It had begun to rain; the steady drizzle diffused the street-lights and made the streets glisten like black glass.

Miranda's sultry laugh promised myriad sensual plea-sures. "You have absolutely nothing to worry about in the bedroom department." She pushed the button that caused the thick, tinted glass to rise between the front and back seats.

Kneeling in front of Zach, she unzipped his slacks, then bent her head, draping his groin in a curtain of blond silk as she lowered her glossy lips over him. With every pull of her mouth, Zach came closer to exploding. When he didn't think he could hold back another moment, he yanked her back up onto the seat, arranging her so that she was lying across his lap.

She sprawled wantonly across him, her silver kid shoes on the seat, her skirt riding high on thighs, which, illumi-nated by the glow of the streetlights, gleamed like porce-lain.

He trailed his fingers up her thighs in a seductive pat-tern that left her trembling. When he caressed her mound and played with the pale blond hair covering it, Miranda squirmed and arched her back, pressing against his hand.

Threading his fingers through the soft pubic curls, he began stroking her moist vaginal lips. "Tell me what you want," he ordered, crazed to hear it. He'd never had an acquisitive streak. But from the first minute he'd seen her, he'd wanted Miranda. During these past five days, he'd discovered he was a greedy man. The more he had, the more he wanted.

"You, dammit," she complained on a low moan that had nothing to do with surrender. "I want you."

Zach kissed her deeply, tasting himself on her lips. Then he turned her in his arms, his hands spanning her waist and with one swift, strong movement, lowered her onto him.

Naked flesh seared naked flesh as Miranda met his challenge; her pelvis ground into his, her white teeth nipped at his neck.

The ripe scent of passion filled the car; their bodies were hot and slick with it. Zach's fingers dug into her skin, he suckled greedily on her breasts, and she felt a corresponding tightening deep within her.

She rode him relentlessly, up and down, harder and faster, demanding more and more until they crossed the finish line together. Exhausted, she collapsed against him.

They stayed together for a long time, neither having the inclination nor the energy to move. The only sound was their heavy, ragged breathing and the soft patter of rain on the roof of the limousine.

"I believe I've made a decision," Miranda murmured against his chest.

"What's that?"

She tilted her head back and smiled up at him. "After the Paris shows, I believe I'll take a holiday in America."

"How long a holiday?"

"I was thinking a fortnight. That would also give me an opportunity to examine all the new things you and Aunt Eleanor have been doing with the American stores. I'm always on the lookout for new ideas for the London Lord's."

Zach had already discovered that underneath Miranda's patina of steamy sexual appeal lay a quicksilver brain. She'd been a driving force behind Lord's couture boutiques, and although the deal with Debord had fallen through, she'd been lobbying Eleanor nonstop to give the *avant-garde* designer yet another chance.

"New ideas are the lifeblood of retailing," he agreed mildly.

"And then, of course, there's Auntie's unfortunate friendship with Mrs. Kowalski. Someone has to help you keep an eye on her."

Seeing through Miranda's flimsy excuses, Zach enjoyed the idea that this unbelievably sexy creature was willing to cross an ocean for him—a former bayou brat who hadn't worn shoes until he'd gone to school.

"I think," he said, as he felt himself growing hard again, "that's an excellent idea."

Chapter Seven

Paris

Debord's fall show took place late on a cold, rainy evening in July. Instead of the traditional runway, a huge wooden platform had been constructed over the Olympic-size pool at the Ritz Hotel. Seated around the pool, looking like so many judges at a diving competition, the world's fashion herd had gathered to see if they would be writing the former wunderkind's obituary. Like locusts, the rich and famous, along with thousands of buyers and thousands of fashion reporters, had winged their way to Paris. By the time the last model had twirled her way down the platform, these arbiters of society chic would either praise or bury the king of fashion.

They were, as always, prepared to do either.

No attempt had been made to protect celebrities from the omnipresent paparazzi. Seated in the front rows as many were, they were obvious targets, forced to put up with the hordes of photographers who ambushed them at point-blank range, camera shutters sounding like rain on a tin roof.

"Over here, Bianca," they called out to the former Mrs. Jagger, hidden behind a pair of wraparound sunglasses. "Look this way! ... Hey, Ivana, how about giving us one of those million-dollar smiles!" This too, was part of the ambience. The razzle-dazzle game of couture.

Also on hand were a trio of Saudi Arabian wives, properly draped in black for the occasion and accompanied by a phalanx of turbaned, grim-faced bodyguards who'd caused a stir when they'd refused to give up their daggers. From time to time the men's hands would slip inside their dark jackets, ensuring that their automatic pistols were still nestled in their shoulder holsters.

In the pit around the platform the photographers stood on their camera cases for a better view. One enterprising photographer from the *Baltimore Sun* had brought along her own folding stepladder. When the trophy wife of a Wall Street trader continued to loudly complain that a photographer from a big Texas daily was blocking her view, he merely flashed her a snappy salute with his stubby middle finger and kept snapping away.

In the midst of all this sat Miranda and Eleanor Lord. Although one of the prized gilt chairs had also been reserved for Zach, he preferred to watch the show from the back of the crowd.

Backstage, chaos reigned supreme.

Trying to do ten things at once, Alex thought the hectic scene resembled the worst of Lewis Carroll's Wonderland. The surrealistic Mad Hatter's Tea Party, perhaps. Models in various stages of undress raced about like tardy white rabbits, hotly pursued by hairdressers who teased and spritzed, and dressers who tortured them into clothing no normal body could wear even as makeup artists wielded false eyelashes and stubby red pencils and complained that absolutely no one, dear heart, was holding still long enough to draw in a decent lipline!

Debord paced, barked orders and chain-smoked.

"Dammit, Alexandra," he snapped, "you have put the wrong earrings on Monique! She is to wear the crystal teardrops with that gown. Not the tourmalines!"

He viciously yanked the offensive jewelry from the model's earlobes, making both Alex and the model glad they were clip-ons. "*Merde*. Foolish girl! What am I paying you for?"

"Sorry," she murmured, changing the earrings without pointing out that indeed, Debord himself had specified the green tourmalines. Three times.

On the other side of the curtain, their performances timed with stopwatch precision, sleek, sloe-eyed models glided across the platform beneath the unforgiving glare of arc lights.

"*Numéro cinq,* number five...Place des Vosges," a voice announced as a trio of towering mannequins, clad in trousers and smoking jackets, done up in Debord's signature black and gray, marched past the onlookers.

"*Numéro treize,* number thirteen...Jardins du Luxembourg." This season Debord had chosen to name his collection after familiar Paris landmarks.

"*Numéro vingt,* number twenty...Palais-Royal...."

It was soon apparent to all assembled that this collection was more eclectic than usual. One of the smoking jackets boasted wide gold lapels, and a pair of jet trousers were shown with an eye-catching, beaded tuxedo jacket.

No one knew, of course, that the glittery additions had been Alex's contribution. Since a couture line bore the name of the designer, assistants' efforts routinely went unrewarded.

Alex had finally talked Debord into trying her silk dinner suit in some other hue besides black and gray. Although he'd steadfastly refused to make it up in her beloved amethyst, the burst of applause the suit received when shown in the rich ruby made her heart swell with pride.

"Turn for me, baby," the male photographers called out, whistling flirtatiously as the model spun and twirled.

The familiar ponchos from last season returned,. along with huge shawls flung over the shoulder and allowed to hang on the ground. Several of the shawls were fringed; many were offered in graduated colors, from misty mauve through dark heather to the deep, rich, royal purple Alex had been denied in the suit.

The applause grew more enthusiastic with each number. Indeed, editors from *Vogue* and *Bazaar* stood up to salute Alex's other effort—a voluptuous velvet evening gown shown in a stunning, pimento red that added a flare of fire to the collection. From her viewing spot behind the curtain, Alex was certain she saw Grace Mirabella wipe away a tear with the knuckle of an index finger.

By the time the show ended with the traditional wedding gown, this one white satin and studded with seed pearls, the verdict was clear. Surrounded by television lights, Debord joined a dozen models on the stage as the crowd bravoed wildly.

Within moments his unshaven jaw was smeared with the lipstick of his admirers. He had successfully reclaimed his place at the uppermost tier of the fashion pack; he was, everyone agreed, a genius!

"Well," Eleanor said, raising her voice to be heard over the enthusiastic applause, "that was quite inspiring. I do believe it's time to invite Debord into our corporate family."

"The show certainly seems to be a success," Zach said. He'd left the back of the room and joined the two women.

"I told you the man was worth his weight in gold to Lord's," Miranda said. Her face had the kind of beatific expression Zach usually associated with religious paintings.

Neither Zach nor Eleanor brought up Debord's earlier disaster. After today's triumph, there was no need.

"No point in trying to talk business with the guy now," Zach decided, eyeing the crowd of women surrounding the designer.

"Tomorrow will be soon enough," Eleanor agreed.

She was suddenly more tired than she cared to admit. But the way Zachary had been hovering over her like an overprotective guard dog ever since that silly heart flutter she'd experienced during the séance, she knew that if she confessed the slightest fatigue, he'd rush her immediately to the Hôpital Américain.

Zach turned to Miranda. "Ready for dinner?"

"If you don't mind, darling, I think I'll stay and schedule my fittings with Marie Hélène."

"Now?" Zach's expression revealed that he damn well did mind. He'd been looking forward to ravishing her in the suite's hedonistic marble tub.

"You know what they say." Miranda's smile reminded Zach of a sleek, pampered cat. "Never put off until tomorrow what you can do today."

She linked her arms around his neck and brought his mouth down to hers, apparently oblivious to their audience and the whirring sound of camera motor drives freezing the heated kiss on film.

"I won't be long," she murmured caressingly. Her pelvis pressed against his groin in a blatantly sexual promise. "I promise. After all, we can't miss Debord's party."

As her wet tongue insinuated itself between his firmly set lips, Zach relented, as he'd known all along he would.

The private party celebrating Debord's triumph was held in a converted Catholic Church in the first *arrondisse-*

ment. The gilded altar and carved oak pews had been replaced by three balconies, five bars, a giant video screen
and three dance floors.

The guests were a mix of high society, artists, models,
and the occasional Grand Prix driver and soccer star; the
music was just as eclectic, ranging from the tango and bossa
nova to fifties' and sixties' rock and roll.

Alex was standing on the edge of the crowd beneath a
towering white Gothic pillar—one of many holding up an
arched, gilded ceiling emblazoned with chubby cherubs—
sipping champagne and watching the frenzied activity when
Debord materialized beside her.

"Are you ready to leave *mon petit chou?*"

She looked up at him, surprised. "So soon? Don't you
want to celebrate?"

"That's precisely what I had in mind." He plucked her
glass from her hand and placed it on the tray of a passing
waiter.

He put his arm around her, ushering her through the
throng of merrymakers, pausing now and again to accept
glittering accolades.

Anticipation shimmered in the close interior of his
Lamborghini. He reached over and slid his hand beneath
the hem of her dress. Few women possessing such bright
hair would dare wear the scintillating pink hue; confident
in her unerring sense of style, Alex resembled a brilliant
candle.

"It was a good day, *non?*"

His caressing touch on her leg was making her melt. "A
wonderful day," she breathed.

"And it will be an even better night." His fingers tightened, squeezing her thigh so that she knew he would leave
a bruise. It would not be the first mark of passion he'd in-
flicted during these past weeks together, and if his husky

tone was a promise of things to come, it would not be the last.

He returned his hand to the steering wheel and continued driving. "I received good news tonight," he told her. "From Lady Smythe."

Alex had seen him talking to the British heiress She hadn't recognized Miranda's escort, a tall, handsome man who'd literally stood head and shoulders above the other guests.

"She bought your entire collection," Alex guessed.

"Better. Eleanor Lord has finally seen the light."

Alex remembered the call she'd interrupted the day months ago when she'd shown Debord her sketches. The call canceling Lord's proposed collaboration with the designer. "Do you mean—"

"There will soon be an Yves Debord collection in every Lord's store in America," he revealed with not a little satisfaction. "And, of course, London."

"That's wonderful! I'm so happy for you!" She waited for him to mention her own small contribution to his successful line.

"It is about time that old woman recognized my genius," he said, instead.

Reminding herself that without his oversize ego, Debord would not be the man she'd fallen in love with, Alex tried not to be hurt by his dismissal of her efforts. She realized he could not acknowledge her publicly. But it would have been nice if at least privately, he'd given her a smidgen of credit.

Trying to look on the bright side, that some of the richest women in the world would soon be wearing her designs, Alex reminded herself how lucky she was.

Here she was in Paris, the most romantic city in the world, about to make love to the man who'd played a starring role in her romantic fantasies for years. She would not ruin the moment by wishing for more than Debord was prepared to give.

As they passed the magnificent Église du Dome, Napoléon's final resting place, Alex realized that Debord was taking her to his home. It was the first time he had. Her heart soaring, Alex took the gesture as an important shift in their relationship.

"Welcome to my little *maisonette*," he said as they entered his *hôtel particulier*.

Unlike the stark modernism of his *atelier*, where she knew she could work for a hundred years and never feel comfortable, Alex found Debord's Paris residence charming.

He'd decorated it in the colors of eighteenth-century France—sunny golds, flame reds, rich browns. The walls were expertly lacquered and trimmed with marblized bases and moldings. Small, skirted tables were adorned with candid photographs of the designer with Nancy Reagan, Placido Domingo, Princess Grace, all testaments to Debord's high-gloss life.

As Debord led Alex up the stairway to his bedroom, she caught a fleeting glimpse of the art lining the walls, and although she was no expert, she did recognize a Dali giraffe woman, a Monet Gypsy and a Picasso sketch.

They entered the bedroom. Outside the window, a white, unbelievably large full moon looked as if it had been pasted onto the midnight black sky.

She held her arms out toward this man she loved, anticipating his kiss. But he turned away to light the fire some unseen servant had laid. "Take off your clothes," he commanded brusquely.

Although it was not the romantic approach she would have wished for on this special night, Alex obliged. But by the time she'd dispensed with the final scrap of silk and lace, the heat that his dark gaze could always instill in her had begun to cool.

His expression remained inscrutable, his eyes devoid of warmth. She stood there, hands by her sides, firelight gleaming over her nude body, growing more and more uneasy.

His dark eyes continued to hold her wary gaze with the sheer strength of his not inconsiderable will as took off his own clothing. When he put his arm around her and led her to the bed, Alex's heart leapt. Now would come the tenderness, the love, she'd been yearning for.

But instead of kissing her, as she'd expected, after drawing her down onto the smooth Egyptian-cotton sheets, Debord's teeth closed sharply on her earlobe.

"What are you doing?" Shocked, she touched her stinging lobe, startled to see the drop of crimson on her fingertip.

Once more, his eyes locked on hers as he took her finger between his lips and licked the faint drop of blood from it. There was a menace in his gaze that frightened her.

"Making love to you, Alexandra, of course. What did you think?"

"I don't want this." A dark shadow moved across the ghostly moon. Another moved over her heart. Her earlobe throbbed; the warmth between her thighs went cold.

Alex tried to turn her head away, but his fingers grasped her chin and forced her face back to his.

"Of course you do," he said. "You want me to penetrate you, to possess you."

"Yves, please. Let me go."

"You know that's not what you want."

When she tried to pull away, he tightened his hold. His eyes glittered dangerously, and for a moment Alex thought he was going to hit her. Afraid, but unwilling to show it, she held her ground, refusing to flinch.

He obviously mistook her silence for consent. His lips curved in a cruel, unfamiliar smile. "I promise to make this a night you will remember always."

Before Alex could determine whether to take his words as a promise or a threat, Debord pinned her wrists above her head and thrust into her dryness, smothering her startled cry with his mouth.

At first she fought him, but she was no match for his superior strength. A vicious, backhanded blow cracked across her face like a gunshot.

He took her with a savage, relentless, animal ferocity. Finally, when she didn't think she could stand the searing pain another moment, he collapsed on top of her, his passion spent.

The moon reemerged from behind the cloud. Alex lay bathed in its cold white light, feeling cruelly violated and sadder than she'd ever felt in her life. He shifted onto his side, his elbow resting on the rumpled sheet, his head propped on his hand, and looked down at her. Unwilling to meet his gaze, Alex covered her eyes with her forearm. She heard the bedroom door open. Surprised, since she could feel Debord still lying beside her, watching her with his unwavering intensity, she removed her arm and looked up.

The newcomer was Marie Hélène. The woman was standing over them, clad only in a crotch-length strand of pearls. For the first time since Alex had known her, she was smiling.

"Ah, *ma chère*." As if nothing unusual had happened, as if it were commonplace for his sister to arrive unannounced and undressed in his bedroom, Debord rose and drew the nude woman into his arms, showing her the tenderness he'd denied Alex.

"Your timing is perfect," he murmured when their long, openmouthed kiss finally ended. He looked down at Alex. "Isn't it, *chérie?*"

As they smiled down on her with benevolent, expectant lust in their eyes, Alex realized that this was not the first time the brother and sister had engaged in such activities.

Self-awareness came crashing down on her like a bomb. She'd thought she was oh, so sophisticated, with her darling little Paris apartment and her fancy couture career and her French lover!

Now she realized that deep down inside, where it really counted, she was just a country bumpkin who'd come to the big city and lost her heart. The trick was to escape before she also lost her soul.

Although every muscle in her body was screaming, she managed to push herself to her feet. Her nose was running. Wiping it, she saw the bright blood on her hand.

"Speaking of timing, I think it's past time that I went home." She managed, with effort, to push the words past the sob that was lodged in her throat.

She looked frantically around the room, searching for her wispy panties and stockings. When she couldn't spot them, she reminded herself that the important thing was to escape this nightmare.

"Surely you do not intend to leave now?" Debord questioned with an arched, mocking brow. "Not when the celebration is just getting started?"

Vomit rose in Alex's throat. She swallowed it back down again. "If you think I'm going to—" her voice was muffled by the dress she was pulling over her head "—play musical beds with you and Morticia here, you're sadly mistaken."

"Alexandra." Debord caught her arm and shook his head in mock chagrin. "I have spent these past weeks patiently introducing you to a world of erotic pleasures. I've taught you passion. I've taught you to set free your darkest, most innermost emotions."

That much was true. Some of the things he'd asked Alex to do in the name of love had made her grateful that her bedroom was usually so dark he couldn't see her blush. Many of them she hadn't enjoyed. But he obviously had. And at the time, to her, making Debord happy had been the important thing.

"A *ménage à trois* with Marie Hélène is simply the next step in your education."

Her blood was like ice in her veins; it pounded behind her eyes like a jackhammer. "You're both disgusting." What the hell had happened to her shoes?

"I warned you about Americans," Marie Hélène sniffed, slanting a knowing glance at her brother.

"I thought you were turning into a sophisticate," Debord told Alex. His fingers tightened painfully on her upper arm. "But *non*, my sister was right about you. You are merely a silly schoolgirl with dreams of Prince Charming on a white charger."

Something that felt horribly like hysteria began to bubble up inside Alex. She struggled for dignity, vowing she would not let them see her cry.

"You're certainly entitled to your opinion."

Shaking free of his possessive touch, she marched barefoot toward the door with an amazing amount of contemptuous disdain for a woman whose lifelong dream had just been shattered.

She paused in the bedroom doorway, raked her gaze over the unholy coven of two and said, "Oh, and by the way. I quit."

Debord revealed not a scintilla of surprise. He nodded his head even as he wrapped his arm around Marie Hélène's nude waist, drawing his sister tightly to his side.

"That is your choice. Just remember, Alexandra, any designs you created while employed by the House of Debord belong to me. If you attempt to take them elsewhere, I will make certain that you never work again."

After what he'd done tonight to her body, not to mention her pride and self-esteem, this threat seemed nothing. Less than nothing. Indeed, rather than frighten her, his words turned her into a towering pillar of wrath.

"You're fucking welcome to them," Alex shouted with renewed bravado. "Since they're the only decent thing in your new line."

She slammed the door behind her, feeling a faint satisfaction when she heard a painting fall from the wall. Running back down the stairs, as if the devil himself were on her heels, she left the house.

The street was dark and empty. Numb as she was, the only way she knew she was still walking was that the stone sidewalk felt cold and wet and rough against her bare feet.

Finally, blessedly, a taxi appeared. She flagged it down, grateful when the bulky, mustachioed man displayed no interest in the fact that she was alone on the street at this time of night without any shoes.

Her head was splitting by the time she reached her apartment, but her nose, for the time being, had stopped bleeding. The elevator, naturally, had chosen this night to stop working, forcing her to climb the stairs. Each step proved an effort.

In a delayed reaction to the events of the past hour, as soon as she entered the safety of her apartment, Alex began to shake. She barely made it to the small cubbyhole masquerading as a bathroom before throwing up all the champagne and caviar she'd had at the party celebrating Debord's brilliant showing. She flushed the toilet, longed to wash her face, but was too tired to stand up again. So she remained there on the tile floor, her back against the wall, knees drawn up to her chest, arms wrapped around her legs.

Resting her sore cheek against her knees, Alex finally allowed herself to cry.

A long time later, after she'd run out of tears, she brushed her teeth, then took a shower, scrubbing herself viciously in a futile attempt to wash tonight out of her mind, to rid her body of Debord's touch. His scent. His seed.

The hot water turned tepid. Then cold. Alex rubbed her reddened skin dry, pulled on the most sexless, oversize pair of sweats she owned, then dragged herself back out into the hall to the pay phone.

With trembling fingers, she managed to place a collect call to the States.

The following morning, she piled suitcases filled with her clothing, sketch pads and her pencils into the back of a taxi.

Turning her back on the city that had for so long represented her most heartfelt dream, Alex was on her way to California, determined to begin a new life.

In the luxurious first-class section of the Air France jet winging its way over the Atlantic, Eleanor, Miranda and Zach sipped champagne and orange juice cocktails, and toasted Miranda's newest discovery.

Twenty-six rows back, Alex was shoved between a woman with a crying baby and a portly businessman who'd made two passes before the plane had even taxied down the runway.

How had she been so stupid to allow herself to fall under the spell of such a horrible, self-indulgent man as Debord?

The answer came to her as the jet chased the waning moon across the night-black sky. The truth, as unpalatable as it might be, was that she'd closed her eyes to any faults her idol might possess. She'd seen in the designer only what she'd wanted to see. Flattering images born in a teenage girl's romantic fantasies.

And now, because of her foolishness, the dream that had sustained her for years, the dream that had fed her soul during those long periods of personal struggle, had disintegrated like a puff of smoke from a Left Bank chimney.

Chapter Eight

Los Angeles

Wallowing in self-pity had never been Alex's style. By the time her flight landed at LAX, she'd roused herself out of the abyss and managed to regain most of her usual bravado. Her experience with Debord, as exhilarating, fulfilling and ultimately horrendous as it had been, was over.

And now, Alex vowed, as the flight attendant bid her *adieu* with a professional smile, there would be no looking back.

Sophie Friedman was waiting for Alex at the door of the jetway. Her admiring gaze swept over Alex, clad in a scoopnecked cotton peasant dress. Embroidered pink flowers bloomed on the billowy mint green skirt, appearing like Queen Anne's lace on an Alpine meadow. Impractical for traveling, the outfit was one of Alex's favorites. She'd worn it hoping it would raise her spirits. It hadn't.

"Lord, child, you remind me of a half-wild Tyrolean shepherdess. Hell, if I had any sense, I'd turn in my producer's card, become an agent, drive you straight to the nearest studio, negotiate a multipicture, multimillion-dollar deal, then sit by my swimming pool and wait for the bucks to roll in." Before Alex could insist she had no theatrical ambitions, Sophie was filling her in on the latest episode in her divorce, which she dubbed "The Hundred Years' War."

Sophie didn't stop talking the entire time it took to collect Alex's luggage. Although she interrupted herself constantly, from what Alex could discern, this latest skirmish had begun over custody of Prince Andrew, more familiarly known as Randy Andy, a champion Yorkshire terrier who'd been declared Stud of the Year by the American Kennel Club. Or perhaps it was Sophie's estranged producer husband who was the stud. Alex wasn't quite sure. Alex's depression momentarily lifted when she saw the white car purring beside the curb outside the terminal. "A limo?"

"Just the usual star treatment."

"I'm hardly a star," Alex murmured as the dark-suited driver swept open the passenger door.

"Not yet. But stick with me, kid, and you will be."

The seats were wide and white and smelled of leather balm. After they settled in, Sophie leaned forward and gave Alex a very intense look. "Is that an example of Debord's handiwork?"

Alex's hand went instinctively to her cheek, covering the bruise she thought she'd successfully hidden with concealer and makeup. "I don't want to talk about it." She was still too embarrassed to admit to such a horrid lapse in judgment.

"I was thinking about getting Prince Andrew neutered. To keep my rat of a husband from getting any stud fees," Sophie revealed. "But I've got a better idea. Why don't we take the nut cutters and do a snip job on a certain French designer?"

Alex smiled in spite of herself. "He's not worth the jail time. But thanks, anyway."

"Men," Sophie muttered. "Just because God gave them a set of balls, they think they rule the fucking world.

"Do you believe in fate?" Sophie changed the subject suddenly as the limousine eased into the bumper-to-bumper, circling and suicidal lane changing that was standard driving procedure at the nation's third-busiest airport.

Alex cringed as a white Jaguar abruptly cut off a blue BMW, earning a blast of a horn and an expansive hand gesture from the BMW's driver. "Not really."

"Neither did I." Sophie took a bottle of Dom Pérignon from a bucket filled with ice and poured the sparkling wine into two glasses. "Having come up the hard way, I always figured if you wanted to get ahead, you needed to make your own luck."

Murmuring her thanks, Alex accepted the proffered flute. "That's pretty much what I've always thought."

She certainly hadn't waited for fate to secure her a job with Debord. Alex frowned as she thought about the treacherous, amoral designer.

Sophie observed Alex's scowl without comment. "But," she revealed, "since meeting you, I've changed my mind."

"Oh?" Alex took a sip of the champagne, enjoying the way the tiny bubbles exploded on her tongue.

"I was getting ready to call you when you telephoned."

"About designing for your daytime soaps?"

"Not exactly."

"Oh?" Surely Sophie wouldn't have invited her to Hollywood and met her at the airport with a stretch limousine to tell her she'd changed her mind, would she?

Alex didn't believe Sophie capable of such behavior, but she'd recently discovered that when everything seemed to be coming up roses, it was prudent to watch out for thorns.

"Last month I got an invitation to lunch from this network honcho. Seems they did a market study with some focus groups, and my soaps blew away all the competition."

"I'm not surprised. They're wonderfully written."

"Bless the girl!" Sophie lifted her expressive eyes heavenward. "She didn't even tack on the usual 'for soaps.'

"Anyway," she continued, "although it hasn't been announced yet, I just signed to create a weekly nighttime television drama with a continuing storyline. A prime-time soap, so to speak."

"Like 'Dallas'?" Alex had seen the show in Paris. Although it seemed strange watching Larry Hagman and Victoria Principal speaking French, soon she, like the rest of the world, was addicted to the story revolving around the wealthy Texas oil family.

"Like 'Dallas,'" Sophie confirmed. "But the network guys want more glitz and glamour than the Ewing family. More sex and sin."

She refilled their glasses. "Which naturally made me think of you. Well, your designs, anyway. Whatever sex and sin you have in your private life is your own business."

Alex's expression remained outwardly calm even as Sophie's reference to sex made her hands turn to ice. "I'm flattered."

"Don't be. I told you I thought your creative vision was cinematic. Which was why I couldn't understand why you'd want to hide all that creative light beneath Yves Debord's barrel."

Alex didn't want to talk about Debord. "Tell me about the story line."

"Well, it's still in the planning stages, but the plot revolves around a fiftyish New Orleans oil baron and the three women in his life—his conniving ex-wife, who has maintained a chunk of the business and is always trying to finagle more, his saintly current wife who does her best to make his mansion a home, and his young, ambitious mistress, a dancer working on Bourbon Street. I want to set a hot, steamy atmosphere. Sort of a cross between Tennessee Williams and Harold Robbins.''

Such disparate personalities would offer myriad design opportunities, Alex mused. ''That sounds like a challenge.''

''Don't worry. We've got plenty of time. The network wants an extravagant look to 'Blue Bayou' and I didn't want to be rushed into putting a sloppy show on the air, so I worked a deal allowing us to spend the entire upcoming season creating story lines, getting actors under contract, designing sets and wardrobes. Then the show's going to premiere as a miniseries over three consecutive nights during Sweeps week. We've got a twenty-six-week guarantee, which is double the norm for new show contracts.''

''Twenty-six weeks. That's a lot of wardrobe.''

''I plan to use enough beadwork to keep an entire village in India working overtime.''

''That won't be inexpensive,'' Alex felt obliged to warn.

''Not to worry. The network brass is behind us all the way. We're going to do a lot of shooting on location, and as for wardrobe, the sky's the limit.''

The woman's enthusiasm was contagious. Alex felt a slow smile spread across her own face. ''It sounds wonderful.''

''Doesn't it?'' Sophie lifted her glass in a salute. ''To 'Blue Bayou.' And the lady who's going to make it shine.''

''To 'Blue Bayou,''' Alex agreed absently.

She was relieved to discover that although he may have stripped her of a dream, Debord hadn't killed her optimism. Rich colors and fabrics were already spinning around in her mind, changing and tilting like the facets of a kaleidoscope.

Professing a desire to clinch the deal over lunch, Sophie whisked Alex off to the famed Bullocks Wilshire Tearoom, high atop the landmark 1929 Art Deco store. The restaurant, a longtime Los Angeles tradition, boasted a high-domed ceiling and, Sophie claimed, the best Caesar salad in town.

As she leaned back in the comfortable chair and watched the lanky models from the department store sashay around the room, Alex found herself sharing Sophie's belief that perhaps there was something to be said for fate, after all.

While Alex and Sophie celebrated their new artistic collaboration, Miranda was entering an office building on Sunset Boulevard, not far from Frederick's famed purple lingerie palace.

The sign on the glass door said Galbraith and Bailey. Though Jonathon Bailey had been dead for more than a quarter century, Theodore Galbraith had not removed his former law partner's name from the door. He was a man comfortable with tradition. A man of principle. Principles Miranda had every intent of testing.

She'd dressed carefully for this meeting, in a black silk Geoffrey Beene dress that set off her pale skin and displayed an intriguing bit of décolletage. She'd pulled her blond hair back into a society-girl style at the nape of her neck, held with a black satin bow. Her Italian pumps boasted four-inch heels that made her silk-clad legs look as if they went all the way up to her neck.

"Dear, dear Teddy," she greeted the attorney with a warm smile that suggested secrets to share. "It's been too long! How kind of you to make time for me in your busy schedule."

Theodore Galbraith rose quickly and went around his partner's desk to greet her. "When a beautiful woman invites an old fogie like me to lunch, I not only make time, my dear," he responded with a twinkle, "I clear my calendar for the day."

Galbraith was a balding, rumpled man in his late sixties. A contemporary of James and Eleanor Lord, he'd been their lawyer since the beginning, when James had opened his first store. Unlike the new wave of trendy L.A. attorneys, who favored silk Bijan blazers, linen trousers and sockless loafers, Galbraith was not overly concerned with outward appearances.

But Miranda knew the man's aging Saville Row suit, the frayed cuffs on his monogrammed white shirt, the half glasses purchased from a rack at the Walgreens drugstore down the street, all belied a brilliant legal mind.

"Shame on you for talking that way," she scolded lightly. "Why, you're not at all old, Teddy." She took hold of both his hands, allowing her slender white ones to rest in his blue-veined ones slightly longer than necessary. Arthritis had swollen his knuckles, but his grip remained firm and sure. "On the contrary, you are just reaching your prime."

A pleased flush rose from his white collar. "That's a vast exaggeration, Miranda," he said, "but since, like most men, I plead guilty to being highly susceptible to feminine flattery, I won't argue with you."

"It isn't flattery at all. It's true," she lied deftly. "And I know it's very naughty of me to call you on such late notice, but I must be returning to London soon, and I'm so very concerned about Aunt Eleanor."

He frowned. "I do hope she hasn't had another occurrence of that heart problem."

"Oh, no, nothing like that, thank goodness," Miranda hastened to assure him. "But she has been behaving quite strangely lately. I felt it prudent to obtain advice."

His fuzzy white eyebrows lifted above the rim of his reading glasses. "Legal advice?"

"Not really." She lowered her eyes to the faded carpet, as if trying to frame her answer. "Actually," she murmured as she met his waiting gaze again, "I came to you, Teddy, because you're her dearest friend. And I'm terribly afraid Aunt Eleanor is going to need all the friends she can get."

"Oh, my. This does sound ominous."

"Wait until you hear the entire story."

They lunched at the Polo Lounge, where it was apparent that the attorney enjoyed being seen in the company of a much younger, attractive woman. Miranda knew he'd been widowed for nearly as long as he'd been running the office without a partner. Her spies had also told her that for the past decade, he'd been living a scholarly, celibate existence more suited to a Trappist monk than a rich attorney in Lotus Land.

Well, that would soon change. Teddy Galbraith didn't know it, she thought with an inward smile as she refilled their glasses from a second bottle of Tattinger champagne, but he was about to get lucky.

They were both slightly tipsy when her driver finally returned them to his office. Teddy more than her. But she'd been careful that he hadn't gotten too drunk. She definitely hadn't wanted to render the elderly attorney impotent.

"I can't believe Eleanor's involved in the mumbo jumbo spirit world," he said for the umpteenth time. He'd been upset by Miranda's description of the séances, not to mention the suspicious circumstances surrounding the deaths of Clara Kowalski's former husbands. "She's always been such a sensible woman."

"I know. That's what makes her behavior all the more bizarre," Miranda agreed earnestly.

It was late afternoon. His secretary had gone for the day, leaving them alone in the office. Miranda sat down on the leather sofa and crossed her legs.

For a moment he seemed tempted to join her on the couch. She smiled to herself as he overcame the temptation and chose the high-backed chair behind his desk, instead. If he thought that wide expanse of oak was going to protect him, she mused wickedly, the old dear was sadly mistaken.

"I do wish there was something, anything, we could do," she murmured.

He ran a hand over his head, ruffling his wispy white hair, torn between dual loyalties. "I agree this is worrisome, Miranda." Unaccustomed to drinking in the middle of the day, his tongue felt thick and awkward, forcing him to speak slowly.

"But as I've already explained, what you've told me this afternoon, as upsetting as it admittedly is, is simply not enough for a judge to rule in your favor."

She leaned forward, giving him an unrestricted view of her cleavage. "But what if that horrid Mrs. Kowalski has convinced Aunt Eleanor to change her will? What if Eleanor's going to give the old witch control of Lord's? What if Clara is plotting to kill my aunt?"

Sexual feelings he'd successfully locked away in cold storage long ago stirred. With obvious effort, he dragged his gaze from those perfect white globes.

"Miranda, I'm sorry." His voice was strained. Even with the extra effort, he knew he was slurring his words. "You know I can't discuss your aunt's will."

"I understand all about attorney/client privilege." She rose and crossed the room with a smooth, pantherlike stride. "But you have to understand how very, very important this is to me, Teddy."

She knelt beside his chair, wrapping him in a cloak of obsession as she gazed up into his round, red-cheeked face, her green eyes gleaming with implied sex.

"If I could only have a teensy little peek." She ran a seashell pink fingernail up his leg. "To reassure myself."

"Miranda, dear." His voice was rough, choked. "I'd like to help you, but I truly can't."

"I'd be ever so grateful." Her stroking touch grazed the fly of his very un-Californian chalk-striped trousers, kindling embers he'd thought long dead. Her eyes locked on his as she deliberately unfastened his belt. "You've no idea how extremely grateful I can be." Her tongue slid wetly over her glossy lips.

She slowly lowered the zipper. When her palm brushed against the front of his baggy, old-fashioned boxer shorts, he jumped as if she'd touched a hot wire to his flesh.

"I can't," he tried again, clearly torn between dual needs. "It would be a breach of ethics."

"I promise no one will ever know." When she began stroking the flaccid flesh beneath the white cotton fly, he leaned his head against the back of his chair and closed his eyes.

"Miranda..." He wanted her to stop. He wanted her never to stop. His head spun, his body burned.

With a deft, practiced touch, she freed his semierect penis. "Just a glimpse, Teddy." She bent her blond head and kissed it lightly, making him groan. "That's all I want." Her tongue darted catlike across the tip.

"Oh, God." It had been years since he'd known a woman's touch, and Theodore Galbraith was loath to stop the glorious feeling flowing through his veins, like a hot, wet summer storm after a long season of drought.

His arthritic hands curled around the wooden arms of his executive chair. He thought he'd burst into tears when she suddenly stopped her sweet torment.

"I'll make you a deal, Teddy."

"What kind of deal?" he croaked.

His head spun, his body throbbed, and at that moment he would have done anything she asked. He would have crawled naked to Bel Air and back over broken glass. He would have betrayed every client he still had. He would have committed murder for such rapturous ecstasy.

"I'll be nice to you." She licked her glossy lips. "And you be nice to me in return. It will be our little secret."

"Our little secret," he echoed, watching her pink tongue with fascination.

It was an astonishing performance. Theodore Galbraith hadn't always been a celibate sixty-eight-year-old man. Indeed, in his salad days he'd sampled some of the best sex Hollywood had to offer.

But never had he experienced anything that equaled Miranda Lord. He'd heard rumors over the years that she was a woman of uninhibited sexual appetites. Those rumors, he was discovering to his delight, were absolutely true.

"I won't whisper a word to anyone." She bent her head and touched her lips to his dry ones, kissing him with little licks and nips that promised so much more. At the same time, she pressed her palm against his throbbing shaft.

Yes, a truly remarkable performance, he thought. And ultimately irresistible. "You'll have to read it here."

His surrender was rewarded with a satisfied, feline smile that told the attorney she'd never expected any other outcome.

"Whatever you say, Teddy, dear."

She kissed him then. A deep, wet, soul kiss that took his breath away. Although he was trembling with hunger, with need, Theodore grew frustrated when his penis remained only semierect.

That wasn't about to deter Miranda. "Don't worry," she crooned silkily. "I'll take care of everything." She ran her fingers through his thin hair and treated him to a warm, intimate smile. "You just relax, Teddy, dear. And enjoy."

With those confidence-building words ringing in his ears, she went to work, alternating gentle bites and long licks, covering his shaft with saliva, sucking the tip, while massaging his testicles with cleverly wicked fingers.

His blood began pounding in his veins, his ears, his now straining cock. It crossed his mind that although his penis had risen to the challenge, his galloping heart was still that of an old man.

It didn't matter, he decided as she finally placed her wet mouth fully over him, taking him in deeper than any woman ever had. As he bucked furiously, thrusting himself into that glorious, moist cavern, he decided that if this turned out to be his time to die, he couldn't think of a better way to go.

Coherent thought disintegrated, and with one final mighty spasm he exploded.

When he could think again the room was redolent with the raunchy scent of sex and he felt reborn.

Miranda left him sprawled limply in the chair and walked over to the bank of filing cabinets.

She bent down to open the drawer marked *L-M*, giving him a provocative view of shapely buttocks that would have made him hard again if he'd been ten years younger. As it was, he was content to enjoy the view.

She murmured the client names to herself as she flipped through the manila files.

"Aha!" She retrieved one thick file, then turned, flashing him a brilliant smile over her shoulder. "Eureka."

As he watched her green eyes avidly skim through the pages of legalese, Theodore Galbraith's head began to clear.

The mists gradually parted. His body cooled.

Too late he thought of his longtime friend and client, Eleanor Lord. And what he had done.

Chapter Nine

It was healing work, which kept Alex from regretting the loss of her dream of a life in Paris couture. It was exhausting work, which allowed her to fall into a deep and dreamless sleep each night. And it was exciting work, which encouraged her to greet each new morning with optimism.

As for men, the debacle with Debord had made her take a long hard look at her past relationships.

It was her sophomore year at Phoenix's Thunderbird High School that she'd finally—at last!—gotten her period, and her body, as if anxious to make up for lost time, had sprinted into womanhood. Adolescent boys began falling all over themselves, trying to lure this dazzling wonder of femininity into the back seats of their Dodge Chargers and Ford Mustangs.

Alex had found their juvenile, unsubtle seduction attempts admittedly flattering. She liked them buzzing so intently around her, like a hive of drones around their queen bee.

However, wise beyond her years, she realized they only saw her attractive packaging. Those boys had absolutely no interest in who she was inside, in her hopes and dreams and goals. That being the case, while she might permit a bit of heavy breathing and some harmless groping in the back row of the movie theater, she steadfastly refused to ''go all the way.''

It was during her first year at the Fashion Institute that she willingly surrendered her virginity to a fashion photographer twenty-five years her senior who'd come to L.A. to shoot a spread for *Vogue* and had agreed as a favor for a friend—an instructor at the institute—to give a lecture while in town.

Alex had not been surprised when he asked her to dinner that night. Nor was she surprised when dinner melded into breakfast. She was ready to make love; she'd only been waiting for the right man.

Max Jones had been funny and kind and sexy, and when he returned to Manhattan, as she'd known all along he must, Alex had not harbored a single regret.

A pattern she hadn't even realized she'd been setting continued. Indeed, if Alex possessed a fatal flaw, it was her unfortunate habit of getting involved with domineering older men.

Her last lover before leaving for Paris had been a Seventh Avenue district sales representative nearly twice her age. But unlike the man to whom she'd joyfully given her virginity, Herb Stein was overbearing and possessive.

Which was why, when he began employing every emotional trick in the book to keep her from going to Paris, she'd broken off the affair and concentrated on making her mother's last days as comfortable as possible.

Irene Lyons, outspoken to the end, had always argued against Alex's romantic choices. ''Of course, you don't need to be Freud,'' she'd say, whenever Alex returned from dinner with one of these cookie-cutter characters, ''to realize that you're looking for a father figure, Alexandra, dear.''

And although she'd steadfastly denied her mother's claim, Alex's experience with Debord had stripped the blinders from her eyes, forcing her to face a bitter truth about herself.

Her mother had been right. All her lovers had been cut from the same cloth. Such an unpalatable revelation made her realize it was time for a drastic change.

Other women may have vowed simply to modify the self-destructive pattern by turning toward men their own age. Not Alex. Never one to do anything in half measures, with a determination a Carmelite nun might have envied, she vowed not to even think about sex.

With the same tenacity she'd used to gain employment in Paris, Alex set about changing her image, too. Although it was not easy, she purposefully dimmed the glowing aura of vibrant energy in which she usually moved. She narrowed her normally animated gestures and muted her voice. She even went so far as to eschew her usual flamboyant colors, opting instead for more somber hues.

"We waited for you," Sophie complained late one November afternoon, "until the turkey turned as dry as shoe leather."

Sophie had invited her to Thanksgiving dinner with a group of friends. "I'm sorry. I really intended to come...."

"But you got sidetracked. Again."

Alex's answering smile was sheepishly apologetic. "I thought of a new idea for Tiffany's wedding gown."

A newly devised plot twist now had the stripper marrying the oil tycoon's son while continuing her affair with her groom's father. A perfectionist by nature, Alex had discarded three gown ideas Sophie had found delightful.

"By the time I was satisfied with the sketch, it was too late to call."

"Peter was disappointed."

Peter Collins was an Australian actor who'd come to the States and gotten his start in Sophie's daytime drama, "The Edge of Tomorrow." Since the stunningly profitable release of his first major adventure film three months ago, he'd shot like a comet to the top of the A-list of every hostess in town.

"I'm sure he'll survive," Alex murmured dryly. She had no interest in meeting any man. Even one who was being touted as an Australian Harrison Ford.

"Besides," she argued, "didn't I see his picture on the cover of *People* with Debra Winger? The caption said they were about to become engaged."

"That was a publicity date for their new picture. Peter doesn't date actresses. He believes they're too self-involved."

The older woman frowned with well-meaning concern. "You know, darling, as much as I appreciate your devotion to 'Blue Bayou,' you're in danger of becoming an workaholic."

"This from a woman who's been known to sleep in her office to save the commute time," Alex said. "Besides, you don't have to worry about me. I'm happier than I've ever been in my life."

Despite Alex's profession of happiness, it had not escaped Sophie's notice that the light that had shone so brightly in her eyes in Paris had been snuffed out like a candle in an icy wind. Sophie had remained quiet the past five months, waiting for Alex to come to her for a heart-to-heart talk. She realized, with her unerring ability to get beneath the surface of a character, that Alex's metamorphosis had been purposefully planned and executed.

But what Alex didn't realize, Sophie mused now, was that her subterfuge wasn't working. Because all she had to do was walk into a room and it was instantly illuminated by her talent, her independence, and her natural beauty of face and spirit.

Although she was willing to grant Alex her secrets, Sophie had not reached such high echelons in a male-dominated business without being persistent. "You say you're happy. Even so, how do you know Peter wouldn't be the icing on the cake?"

Unwilling to discuss her love life, or lack of it, even with this woman who'd become her best friend, Alex decided it was time to change the subject. "Don't you want to see what I was working on?"

She handed Sophie the sketches. The diversion proved successful. As the producer oohed and aahed over the billowy white vision of crystal-studded tulle and lace, ideas of matchmaking were immediately forgotten.

After convincing Eleanor she should be given the job of organizing the Yves Debord boutiques in all the Lord's stores—after all, who knew the designer's genius better than she?—Miranda threw herself into the task, traveling all over the United States. Although her work was time-consuming, she was careful to fit in regular trips to California.

She and Zach spent Thanksgiving in Santa Barbara with Eleanor. Although Miranda was far from pleased that Clara was still in residence, after reading her aunt's will, she did not feel as threatened by the witch's presence. Especially after paying another visit to Theodore Galbraith, ensuring his promise to notify her if Eleanor decided to revise her will.

The day after Thanksgiving, they returned to Zach's Los Angeles apartment. And to his bed, where they proceeded to ravish one another with a hunger that had not lessened since that first electrifying meeting. Two days later, they were still there.

"Have I ever told you how magnificent you are?" Miranda purred with satisfaction. Her head rested on his damp chest, her fingers playing in the pelt of hair, and her long legs were entwined with his.

"I believe you've mentioned it," Zach murmured drowsily. After two days of ravenous and near-continuous sex, he was finally satiated. "Occasionally." On this late November day, it was still warm enough for air-conditioning. When the cool breeze blew over their sweat-moistened flesh, he pulled the sheet up to cover them. "But it's always nice to hear."

Miranda smiled at him. "I've never met a man like you."

Zach returned the smile with a lazy, satisfied one of his own. "Nor I a woman like you." It was the truth. From the first moment he'd seen Miranda, he'd wanted her. And the need, rather than abating, grew stronger each time they were together this way.

Although he hated to admit to any weakness, Zach realized that somehow, when he hadn't been looking, he'd crossed the line between merely wanting Miranda and needing her. As other men were addicted to the bottle, or gambling, Zach had been lured into obsession with the sultry siren call of sex.

Their work for Lord's kept them apart for days, even weeks, at a time. But whenever the need grew unmanageable, which it always did, one of them would pick up the phone and call the other, and within hours they'd be in bed, driving one another mad.

Miranda was, quite simply, Zach's weakness. The only thing that kept him from denying it was that his need was not one-sided. In fact, although he hadn't really been keeping score, it had not escaped Zach's notice that Miranda had been the one to initiate the majority of these stolen interludes.

"Deborah Langley asked me again when we were going to make an announcement," Miranda said. The society matron had been Averill's companion at Eleanor's holiday dinner party.

"An announcement?" His body soothed, Zach's mind had wandered to a vexsome zoning problem regarding a planned underground parking garage at the new Atlanta Lord's.

"It's embarrassing, this going steady like a pair of teenagers."

He glanced at her, surprised. He'd never received any sign that Miranda gave a damn what anyone thought.

"I'd hardly call it going steady," he said, "since we're hardly ever seen in public."

And then only at the glitzy functions Miranda insisted were *de rigueur* for making and keeping business-society contacts. Although Zach hated any event that forced him into a dinner jacket, he had to admit that couture and jewelry sales inevitably rose after such an appearance.

"It is difficult," Miranda agreed on a sigh. "Our schedules keep us apart so much that when we do get together I don't want to share you with anyone."

Zach knew that feeling all too well.

"But that doesn't mean people don't know we're what the society columnists call an *item*," she tacked on.

Screw the columnists, Zach wanted to say. "Does our affair really embarrass you?" he asked, instead.

"Do you want the truth?"

Having always been honest with Miranda, it had never occurred to Zach that she might not have been equally forthright with him. "Of course."

She gazed up at him through smoky lashes. "Yes, it does embarrass me when I hear people whispering that you don't care enough about me to make our relationship official."

"By official, I assume you're talking about marriage."

"Yes."

On the rare occasion Zach thought about life beyond work, he imagined that if and when he did marry, the union would be based on respect and trust and shared dreams. Having witnessed the wealth of love his parents had shown one another, he'd expected to share that same closeness of mind and spirit with his wife.

All he and Miranda seemed to share were their bodies. And, of course, Lord's.

As if reading his mind, Miranda framed his frowning face with her palms and gave him a slow, reassuring smile.

"Darling Zachary," she murmured on a voice that was half smoke, half honey, "there's no reason to look so grim. I'm not some silly young girl looking for a mythical Grand Love."

Her lips plucked at his enticingly. "What we have together is quite enough." Her fingers trailed down his chest. "More than enough."

Zach had always prided himself on his rational, decision-making abilities. He inevitably weighed every bit of evidence, analyzed all data, lined up facts and figures on a mental ledger. That was exactly what he did now.

On the plus side of the ledger, Miranda was a charming companion. She was a willing, enthusiastic, demanding and amazingly inventive lover. Even after all these months together, knowing that she found him sexually irresistible continued to be a potent aphrodisiac.

On the negative side, she had the irritating habit of showing him off to her jet-setting friends in a way that made Zach feel like an Angus bull on display at a stock show.

Once, when he'd complained about her behavior, she'd broken into hysterical tears, asserting between choking sobs that she was sorry if she'd made him angry. It was just that she was so marvelously proud of him and adored him so that it was hard to hide her happiness. By the time he'd managed to calm her down, Zach had felt like an unappreciative ass.

Miranda was more than a little emotional, not to mention maddeningly complicated, but she was also stunningly beautiful and highly intelligent. And when it came to Lord's, she'd surprised him by being every bit as driven as he.

There was also the inescapable fact that she was a highly sexed animal. If she couldn't satisfy her innate lust with him, her need would drive her into the arms—and the beds—of others. Just the thought of another man tasting that fragrant warm flesh made a red mist billow in front of Zach's eyes.

But marriage?

There were various ways of dealing with a Gordian knot. You could try to untie it, dooming yourself to failure. If you were Alexander the Great, you could simply say to hell with ancient prophesies and cut it.

Or, Zach considered thoughtfully, as he gazed down into Miranda's intense, glittering eyes, you could just accept it the way it was, enjoying the intricacy of its workmanship.

Pushing lingering misgivings into the farthest corner of his mind, with one deft, strong move, he lifted her onto his newly aroused body, claiming possession.

"I think," he said, as Miranda fitted him tightly inside her and began to ride, "it's time I made an honest woman of you."

Chapter Ten

Zach and Miranda's wedding, held three days before Christmas, was the highlight of the Santa Barbara social season.

The bride was beautiful in a Geoffrey Beene cocktail suit of ivory peau de soie, with which she wore a cream, wide-brimmed hat and the pearls Zach had given her for an engagement present.

The groom was handsome in a dark suit, but to the amusement of all gathered, appeared uncharacteristically nervous. The flowers were from Eleanor's greenhouse, the champagne was from France, and the wedding gifts came in blue Tiffany boxes.

After the ceremony, the happy couple flew to Brazil for their holiday honeymoon. Rio de Janeiro had a beat and a beauty all its own. The Cariocas' renowned zest for living was so evident that first-time visitors could be excused for half expecting pedestrians walking along the pink-tiled sidewalks to break into a samba.

Miranda couldn't remember when she'd felt so grand. Even the light afternoon rain couldn't dampen her spirits.

Here she was, in the sexiest, most uninhibited city in the world, lying in bed next to a handsome husband whose lust equaled her own.

Last night, she'd talked Zach into visiting a club in Copacabana, where for a small cover charge, they were given an eye-opening glimpse of Rio in the raw. The motto of the underground nightclub seemed to be Anything Goes. Men danced with men, women with women, in pairs, sometimes threesomes, and if there was a lot more than dancing going on in the dark corners, the management turned a blind eye.

Although Zach had professed distaste for the more blatantly outrageous displays, after returning to their hotel at dawn, he'd taken her with a savage passion that definitely belied his earlier condemnation.

But it was more than great sex that had Miranda floating on air. By becoming Mrs. Zachary Deveraux, she'd pulled off the coup of a lifetime.

At first she'd been furious to discover that Eleanor was leaving control of Lord's to Zach. There was, unsurprisingly, the obligatory bequest to Anna, whom everyone knew was dead. Any good attorney could break that clause.

It wasn't that Miranda had been disinherited. On the contrary, Eleanor had bequeathed her a lump sum of two million dollars and several exquisite pieces of jewelry, including an incomparable jaguar pin once worn by the Duchess of Windsor.

Along with the jewelry, Miranda was to receive the oversize Caravaggio of St. Matthew the tax collector that hung in a gold frame on the library wall, the Cézanne still life from the dining room and a valuable scale model of the London Lord's, complete with Gothic ornaments and flying buttresses.

But the one thing Miranda wasn't going to gain by her aunt's death was the one thing she most wanted: power.

Undaunted, after an initial outburst of rage that had required her to apologize profusely to Teddy Galbraith and to replace the shattered Waterford globe he'd used for thirty years as paperweight, Miranda had devised a new plan.

If she couldn't inherit control of Lord's, she'd earn it the old-fashioned way: by marriage.

Miranda glanced at her sleeping husband. Deciding she deserved a reward for devising such a brilliant solution, she slipped out of bed, dressed and took a taxi to Mesbla, Rio's answer to Macy's.

The department store was bustling. Miranda strolled idly past the fragrant cosmetics counters, past innumerable alligator belts and leather purses, and through the shoe department. She took the escalator to all eleven floors, perusing everything from lingerie to linens to pots and pans. But she could find nothing that shouted, *Choose Me!*

Finally she returned to the main floor and stood by the displays of costume jewelry. Across the aisle, behind the locked glass-topped counter displaying fine jewelry, a salesclerk with coffee-dark eyes and thick hair that fell to her waist was busily trying to convince a covey of young Japanese tourists that they couldn't leave Brazil without a pair of pink tourmaline earrings.

Nearby, a teenage girl, squeezed seductively into a flowered dress a samba dancer would have lusted after, tried on necklace after necklace, looking for the perfect accessory to her beauty.

Miranda plucked a pair of gold hoops from the costume-jewelery display and held them up to her earlobes, examining herself in the round mirror on the counter. They were regretfully common.

She returned them to the rack, choosing instead a pair of pearls surrounded by Austrian crystals. The cultured pearls definitely lacked luster. The faux rubies were too muddy, the sapphires too blue.

And then she saw them. A pair of glittering green stones set in gold. She clipped them on and smiled at her reflection.

Perfect. She looked over at the salesclerk, who had moved on to pushing aquamarines. Satisfied with her choice, Miranda took off the earrings and, with one last casual glance around, slipped them into her crocodile Hermès bag.

Excitement surged through her. She was heady with it. Her blood pounding, she walked quickly back the way she had come.

She'd just made it to the heavy glass doors, when an overweight, middle-aged man, wearing the dark blue uniform of authority the world over, stepped in front of her.

"Excuse me, Madame," he said in heavily accented English. He put a beefy hand on the sleeve of her black silk dress. "If you would please come with me?"

Displaying her usual flair for extravagance, Sophie arranged to transport the entire cast and crew of her three daytime soaps to Colorado for a week on the slopes during that unproductive time between Christmas and New Year's. Also along for the celebration were several actors and actresses she'd pegged to star in "Blue Bayou," and the new writers, many of whom she'd hired away from other daytime productions.

In the beginning, Alex had tried to beg off.

"There's still so much to do," she complained, frustrated by Sophie's tendency to continually tinker with the script, expunging story lines, adding others, creating havoc with Alex's costuming plans.

"Don't you worry about a thing," Sophie said blithely. She smiled, thinking about the surprise she had waiting for this workaholic young woman who had come to mean so much to her. "Things will all work out fine. They always do."

"I have a feeling you won't be so sanguine when Tiffany doesn't have a thing to wear for the opening scene when the show debuts."

"Tiffany has a body that won't quit. Just having her play her part in the buff would probably send ratings through the roof."

Alex laughed and caved in.

While Alex was growing up, her mother, seemingly possessed with wanderlust, had constantly moved their small family from town to town, state to state. Although they'd spent nearly a year in Durango, Alex had never visited Aspen. The former mining town did not disappoint.

From her first glimpse, the snow-clad valley reminded Alex of a Currier and Ives print. She found the Victorian architecture and quaint shops charming, the scenery inspiring, and the people friendlier than she'd imagined.

Of course, Alex allowed, part of her instant acceptance into Aspen's lofty social stratum was undoubtedly because her hostess was a driving force in the alpine community.

Sophie's ski chalet, which she had wrested from her husband during the bitter divorce negotiations, was nestled at the base of Buttermilk Mountain, two miles from the village center. The enormous house had walls made up almost entirely of triple-paned glass, offering an extraordinary panorama of blue sky, craggy mountains and deep drifts of blindingly white powder snow. In nearly every room of the house, fires blazed merrily away in stone fireplaces.

In the living room, a fifteen-foot Christmas tree, decorated with Western and Native American ornaments, towered above the assembled guests, reaching for the lofty, cantilevered ceiling. Outside the sliding glass doors, steam rose high in the crisp, dry mountain air from a huge hot tub.

On the third night of her visit, Alex was sitting at the pine desk in her room, her bright head bent over her sketchbook.

"Knock, knock" came a voice from the open door.

She glanced up. It was Stone Michaels, signed to play Tiffany's former high school sweetheart, a jazz saxophonist. When she'd first seen the attractive couple together, Alex had thought they looked like Ken and Barbie.

"I've been searching the entire house for you."

With an inward sigh, she put down the royal blue pencil. Stone was Sophie's latest attempt at matchmaking. After discovering the aspiring actor/musician pumping gas at the Arco station on Sunset, the producer had set her sights on casting him as the man in Alex's life.

"I'm sorry," she said. "I was taking a shower and this thought occurred to me, and—"

"And you just couldn't rest until you got it down on paper," Stone finished. He entered the room on a long, loose-hipped stride reminiscent of James Dean. He was carrying a glass of white wine in each hand. He held one out to Alex.

She accepted the glass. "Guilty."

"I'm the same way when I'm working on a character sketch."

Alex smiled up at him as she took a sip of the wine. "This is great. Thanks."

"My pleasure." He glanced down, trying to catch a glimpse of her newest design.

Alex turned the pad over. A perfectionist by nature, she didn't like anyone seeing her work until she'd completed it to her satisfaction.

Tilting his sun-streaked head, he sipped his wine and studied her. "I thought you were going to soak your aching bones in the hot tub."

At Sophie's urging, she'd spent the day taking ski lessons from a gorgeous hunk who talked like Arnold Schwarzenegger, looked like Robert Redford and skied like Phil Mahre. After several humbling hours struggling to learn the logistics of schussing, herringbone and snowplows, after tumbling again and again into drifts of thick white powder, every muscle in her body was screaming in protest.

Which was why, when she'd returned to the house, Alex had allowed Stone to talk her into joining the gregarious group in the spa. At the time, the idea of all those jets of hot water massaging her aching body sounded like Nirvana.

But then, as so often happened, while she was standing beneath the pelting shower, a new design for a velvet-and-lace cocktail suit popped into her mind, and she'd rushed to get the thought onto paper.

"You know," Stone said when she didn't immediately answer, "if I didn't have the obligatory Hollywood stud superego, I'd think you were ignoring me." His friendly smile took the whine from his accusation.

"That's not true." Alex sipped a little more of her drink. "I seem to remember going into town with you just last night."

"With five other people acting as chaperons," he reminded her. "And you only stayed long enough to dance a couple of numbers. Hell, Alex, you were back here by nine."

Stone was nice. But pushy. She wished he'd hit on someone else. Like Brenda, a writer who hadn't tried to hide her crush on him.

"I'm sorry." Alex brushed his hand away when he began toying with her earring. "But I was exhausted. My body hasn't adjusted to this altitude."

He gave her a chiding look over the rim of his glass. "You're making this awfully hard, Alex."

"This?"

"You." He took her hand. "Me." Brushed his lips over her knuckles. "Us."

Tired and sore, she was not up to playing games. He'd been tossing these sexual innuendos her way since they'd boarded the private train in L.A. Not wanting to get into an argument, she'd tried to ignore them.

Which had been, Alex decided, a mistake. "There isn't going to be any us," she insisted firmly, tugging her hand free.

"Are you so sure about that?"

"Positive." Alex could feel her temper beginning to fray. "I'm sorry, Stone. I think you're a nice guy. And I like you."

"I like you, too." Encouraged, he tugged on the ends of her hair.

Once again, she brushed his intimate touch away. "I like you as a friend. A 'Blue Bayou' colleague. But right now my work is so demanding I don't have time for a relationship."

"That's okay by me." This time his grin was blatantly suggestive. "I'd settle for a holiday fling."

Why was it, Alex wondered, that the gorgeous ones were inevitably so damn dense? Reminding herself they'd be working on the same program and it wouldn't do to antagonize him, she put her glass down on the desk, stood up, placed both her hands on his broad shoulders and looked him straight in the eye.

"Stone, listen to me. I am not in the market for an affair or a holiday fling. I came up here to relax. Which is very hard to do when you keep trying to get me horizontal."

He stared at her for a long time like someone who couldn't quite comprehend the language. "You really mean that, don't you?" he asked finally with obvious surprise.

"I really, really mean it."

When he raked his long fingers through his gilt hair, looking strangely hurt and definitely confused, Alex's heart softened. "I really should get back to work. Why don't you take Brenda a glass of wine?"

"Brenda?"

"The new writer Sophie stole away from 'The Guiding Light.' You know, the redhead."

"The tall, skinny one?"

Alex's frustrated sigh ruffled her bangs. "Willowy, Stone. The term is willowy. And in case you didn't notice, she's got dynamite legs."

"I was too busy chasing you to notice anyone else." His Paul Newman blue eyes turned thoughtful. "It probably wouldn't be a bad idea to get to know her," he mused aloud. "If she's a writer, she might like my input on my character."

She might also be inclined to pad the part, Alex tacked on silently what he hadn't bothered to say. Stone Michaels might be dense. But he wasn't stupid.

"I think that's an excellent idea." She flashed him a bright, encouraging grin. "Good luck."

"Thanks, Alex. You're a peach." He bent his head, gave her a brief unthreatening kiss, then headed toward the door, stopping momentarily in front of the mirror. After finger combing his wavy, collar-length hair to his satisfaction, he left the room whistling.

Alex laughed, grateful she'd withdrawn from the romance sweepstakes. Then, shaking her head, she turned the sketch pad over again and began reworking the suit's lace-trimmed lapels.

* * *

Although Rio was a bustling metropolis by day, by night it truly came alive. The streets filled with stunningly attractive people and clubs were packed with dancing and singing bodies. Zach and Miranda's luxurious hotel suite boasted a breathtaking view of Guanabara Bay, but at the moment, Zach's attention was not on the lights surrounding the gumdrop shape of Sugarloaf Mountain.

Instead, he was pacing the floor, frustration pounding through every pore.

"I don't understand," he repeated for the umpteenth time. "You have a purse filled with credit cards. Not to mention the five thousand dollars in traveler's checks."

"A little more than that, actually," Miranda said with a calm smile that made him want to shake her.

"So why the hell did you feel the need to lift those earrings?"

When he'd first received the telephone call from the manager of Mesbla, awakening him from a much needed nap, Zach had been certain it must be a mistake. When he arrived at the store's security offices, he'd learned it was all too true. His bride of three days had been caught redhanded stealing a pair of fifty-dollar earrings.

"They weren't even real emeralds, goddammit," he said.

"But they were lovely, nevertheless. For costume jewelry."

"So why didn't you just pay for them? Like everyone else?"

"What fun would that be?"

She sighed prettily as she went over to the bar and retrieved a bottle of champagne. Ignoring his smoldering fury, she expertly opened it. A wisp of vapor followed the cork. She poured the champagne into two flutes.

"Please, darling," she murmured, coaxing him to calm with her expressive eyes, her lush lips, "this is our honeymoon. Let's not spend it fighting."

Resisting an overwhelming urge to punch a hole in the wall, Zach thrust his hands through his hair. "Goddammit, Miranda—"

"Take a sip." She held the glass out to him. Zach grimly decided that Eve must have looked a great deal like Miranda did at this moment when she presented Adam with that shiny red apple to take his mind off that serpent hovering overhead. "It's a very special vintage. The concierge spent a great deal of time locating it. Just for you."

Shaking his head with mute frustration, Zach took a drink. Although the champagne was excellent, for a fleeting moment, he had a sudden urge for a cold beer. A Jax in a long-necked bottle.

You're the one who was so all-fired eager to leave the bayou, he reminded himself. You're the one who wanted to be a big shot. He might have grown up without the right name or address. He might have grown up without ever hearing of Chippendale or Baccarat or Royal Doulton.

And his working-class family had not possessed any money at all, let alone the kind of old money—respectable, fuck-you money—that was stashed away in Eleanor Lord's vault.

Unable to count on social contacts, Zachary had gotten where he was on brain and guts and hard work, along with a willingness to take risks.

And it had all paid off. In spades.

He was now the very wealthy president of an international company. He was a registered Republican, despite the fact he usually voted Democratic; he worshiped in the Episcopalian church, though there were times when his mind automatically responded in the Latin of his altar-boy days. He belonged to all the right clubs, even while secretly considering golf excruciatingly boring.

And last, but definitely not least, he was now married to an unbelievably sexy, stunningly beautiful woman from the gilded, fairy-tale world of the Social Register. So dammit, why did he feel as if something was missing?

Perhaps because he'd just found out that his society bride was also a common, garden-variety shoplifter.

"We have to settle this, Miranda."

"Would it help if I told you that I'm terribly sorry?" Her voice was low and throaty. Her bedroom voice. "And that it will never, ever, happen again?"

She put her hand on his cheek. "It was just one of those crazy urges." Her eyes were wide and guileless. "And you know how impossible it is for me to resist my urges. Please don't be mad at me.

"I'll do anything to make this afternoon up to you, darling," she said breathlessly. When the tip of her tongue touched the top of her glossy red lip, Zach flashed back to this morning. The memory of the incredible things she had done with that tongue was all it took to make him hard. "Absolutely anything."

She was manipulating him, using sex to get what she wanted. But even knowing that didn't make him want her any less.

Reading the reluctant acceptance in her husband's eyes, Miranda put her glass down on a nearby table. And then she began to languidly undress, displaying seductive skills that a striptease artist headlining at the Folies Bergère would have envied.

Her eyes were dark with sex and sin as she unbuttoned her silk dress and allowed it to slide down her body, where it drifted into ebony petals on the plush blue carpet.

Her wispy bra was next. She shrugged out of it, revealing breasts as full as ripe melons. Her nipples were already hard. She stood there, smiling at him, wearing nothing but a sinfully sexy garter belt, black lace-topped stockings and skyscraper-high heels, a statuesque marvel of female perfection.

By the time she'd dispensed with the last bit of satin and lace, Zach's body was throbbing.

Their lovemaking, although quick and frenzied, was as torrid as ever. But unlike all those other times, tonight Zach's explosive orgasm left him feeling strangely unfulfilled.

Chapter Eleven

Nineteen months after Alex's return to the States the shooting for "Blue Bayou" began with a bang on location—New Orleans during Mardi Gras. Excited about seeing her designs in action, Alex had accompanied the crew to the city.

Even the knowledge that Debord and his sister would be in town for the opening of the new Lord's department store could not burst her bubble of pleasure.

"I cannot believe you," Mary Beth Olson, the actress who was playing Tiffany, complained on their last afternoon in the city.

Alex glanced up from the skirt she'd been repinning, correcting minuscule flaws in the costuming that had shown up during taping. Although the location shooting had been completed, the costume would be worn again when the inside shots were taped back in California.

"What do you mean?"

"She means," Olivia Drew, who played the oil tycoon's wife, said, "that you are turning out to be a stick-in-the-mud."

"It's the next-to-last night of Mardi Gras and you still haven't seen a single parade," Mary Beth complained.

"I've been working."

"That's all you do. Honestly, girl, you're more industrious than one of Santa's little elves."

"All the taping's been done," Olivia coaxed. Even Sophie had not been fearless enough to attempt to get decent footage on the final two nights of carnival. Fortunately there had been large crowds and several parades during their five days in the city. The New Orleans footage would be mixed with that shot on the sound stage at the Century City studio. "Come out and play."

The idea was appealing. Alex had admittedly been a little envious, watching the cast enjoying themselves while she'd remained behind in the hotel making last-minute changes to the extensive wardrobe.

She'd been working nonstop since her return to the States. And although her intense schedule had been self-imposed, perhaps it was time she had a little fun. As a hard, driving beat filtered up from the crowded French Quarter street below, Alex could feel herself weakening.

"I suppose it wouldn't hurt. For just a little while."

That was all it took. An hour or so later, Alex was standing in front of the mirror, staring at the unfamiliar reflection. The off-the-shoulder dress, in Mardi Gras shades of purple, green and gold, and so diaphanous it skated the very fringes of decency, was one Alex had designed for Tiffany. Her arms were covered in gold bracelets; gold hoops swung from her ears to her bare, polished shoulders.

She looked good. Better than good, Alex decided. What was really surprising was that she felt as alluring as she looked. After having worked so hard to subdue her image these past months since escaping Debord, Alex felt a stirring of the female sexuality she'd locked away deep inside.

"Lord, you look like a very wealthy, very sexy Gypsy," Olivia drawled, putting in her two cents' worth.

For a woman whose role required her to wear Chanel knockoffs as she arranged flowers in Ming vases around the mansion, tonight Olivia had gone for broke with a jet leather mini and halter top, complete with a spiked necklace, over-the-thigh ebony boots and a vicious-looking black riding crop. She looked, Mary Beth had exclaimed, like a biker's wet dream.

No slouch in the costume department herself, after a visit to a shop on Chartres Street, Mary Beth had returned to the hotel dressed like a very sexy Pocahontas, complete with suede bikini and towering feathered headdress.

On this night before Fat Tuesday, Bourbon Street was, unsurprisingly, packed with boisterous merrymakers carrying paper cups filled with Hurricanes, the city's famed and lethal blend of rum and passion-fruit punch.

"I think I'm going to go back to the hotel!" Alex shouted to be heard over the din of a Dixieland jazz band two hours later.

"So soon?" Olivia swayed on her high heels and was helpfully steadied by a well-muscled man dressed like the cowboy from the Village People. She was obviously drunk, but so were most of the people in the bar and on the street.

It seemed to Alex as if all restrictions of gender, manners, morals and social status had been dispensed with. Old and young, male and female, rich and poor, seemed to have been mixed together and blended like one of the frothy red Hurricanes.

"I'm getting a headache." She wasn't, though she would be if she stayed out much longer.

"I've got some aspirin," Mary Beth offered, digging through her shoulder bag.

"That's all right. Really."

"Just a minute. I know they're here somewhere." She dumped the entire bag onto the bar, sending coins scattering to the floor along with a crumpled pack of cigarettes and a small pink plastic case. "Oh my God," she cried drunkenly, "I dropped my diaphragm!"

As three men, one dressed as Marie Antoinette, immediately bent down to retrieve it, the actress dissolved into giggles. She was still laughing when Alex left the bar.

Returning to the hotel was easier said than done. A parade float passed, preceded by musicians dressed as creatures from the sea: pink coral, sea horses, exotic fish and shells, moving with sinuous twists and turns as they played, as if buffeted by undersea currents. Following was the float itself, depicting Odysseus tied to the mast, resisting the Sirens, who stopped their seduction efforts every so often to throw plastic doubloons and strings of beads to the enthusiastic, masked and costumed spectators.

Jazz poured out of every open doorway. Battling her way through the raucous, jostling crowd, Alex had reached the corner of Bourbon and St. Peter's Streets when she suddenly found the sidewalk blocked by three very young and very drunken sailors.

"Well," one of them drawled, eyeing her with lust in his glazed eyes, "if it isn't a little Gypsy fortune-teller."

Alex stepped into the street to move around them. Unfortunately the trio moved, as well. "How about reading my palm, sweetheart?" another sailor suggested.

He held his hand out to her. Alex ignored it, glancing instead over his shoulder, looking for the mounted patrolman she'd seen on this corner earlier.

"If you'll excuse me . . ." She moved the other way, her unease building as they moved with her.

"Don't be in such a hurry, sugar," the first man said. He took hold of her arm and leaned close enough for her to smell the whiskey on his breath. Anger churned with a growing fear inside her, but when she tried to pull away, his fingers tightened, digging into her flesh.

If these three weren't enough, another man appeared behind her.

"There you are, sweetheart," Zach said to Alex with feigned cheer. "I thought I'd lost you in Ryan's." He'd been returning to his hotel from the new store when he'd spotted the woman in obvious trouble.

Didn't she realize, Zach wondered, that for a woman to appear alone on what was, during this week at least, the most hedonistic street in America, dressed in a ridiculously sexy outfit like that was like waving a red flag in front of a bunch of crazed bulls?

When his arm looped possessively around her shoulder, Alex stiffened.

"Where the hell did you go?" An edge of irritation crept into Zach's tone. "I came back from the john and you were gone."

Alex was nothing if not quick. Although she had no idea who her rescuer was, she read the reassuring message in his eyes and picked up on the conversation.

"It was so crowded I went out for a breath of fresh air and got swept away with the crowd."

"I was worried." He brushed her gilt bangs from her forehead with a tender, concerned gesture, then turned to the trio who'd begun muttering among themselves.

"Thanks for watching out for the little woman for me," Zach said, acknowledging the trio for the first time. He reached into his pocket and pulled out some folded bills. "Let me buy you a beer for your assistance."

The others, weaving on their feet, eyed the steely determination in Zach's eyes and mumbled their agreement. The one who'd been manhandling Alex was not so malleable.

"We were about to have ourselves a little party."

"Good night for it," Zach agreed. He flashed a smile that failed to reach his eyes. "Have fun." He turned, taking Alex with him and began to walk away, only to have the sailor step belligerently in front of him.

"We were planning to have a party with the little Gypsy."

When Zach felt Alex begin to tremble, he tightened his arm around her shoulder. "I'm afraid there's been a small misunderstanding." His voice was amiable enough, but his dark eyes had turned as hard as obsidian. "This lady's taken. So why don't you boys go find yourself some more-willing companionship. Unless you'd rather talk with the Shore Patrol." Along with the deepened bayou patois, a dangerous edge had crept into his voice.

There was a long, silent moment as both men held their ground. Finally the sailor shrugged. "Hey man, she's all yours," he muttered. With that he turned and staggered away, his companions following drunkenly behind.

Alex released a long, pent-up breath and was prepared to thank him when he turned on her. "Are you always this reckless, lady? Or are you merely stupid?"

He was standing in front of her in a spread-leg, feet-planted stance that made her think that, instead of that dark suit, he should be wearing a pirate costume. All he was lacking, she thought, was an eye patch and a cutlass.

Alex had already had enough trouble with men tonight; she didn't need any lectures from this one, no matter how well intentioned.

"Are you always this rude?" she countered.

"If you're so concerned about manners, you're definitely in the wrong town at the wrong time. You're just damn lucky I came along when I did. Where are you staying? We'd better get you back to your hotel before some other drunk decides to play king of the Gypsies."

Her palms were still damp from fear. "I'm more than capable of getting back to the hotel on my own."

"Dressed like that, you probably won't make it to the next corner. This isn't exactly a Boy Scout convention going on in town. And you, lady, are a rape just waiting to happen."

"This dress isn't any more seductive than any other costume on the street. And it's a lot less sexy than most." Her eyes, as gold as a buccaneer's doubloons, flashed sparks.

"True enough. But most of the women out here aren't you."

Alex supposed his words could have been taken as a compliment, but there was nothing complimentary about his tone.

"Are you always this charming?" she asked sweetly. "Or does rescuing strange women just bring out the best in you?"

They stood there, toe-to-toe, face-to-face.

And that's when it happened. Zach smiled. An unexpected smile that changed his features, humanizing the man and making him horrendously, dangerously sexy.

"Hell, I'm sorry," he said with absolute honesty. "I don't suppose it's any excuse that I've had a lousy day and I took out my frustrations on you."

Alex shrugged. "You were probably right about a woman alone in this crowd," she admitted reluctantly. "Although I didn't start out alone."

"Lose your husband somewhere along the way?"

"I'm not married."

"So you were with a date?" he probed with a casualness he was suddenly a long way from feeling.

"Actually, I was with friends. But I wanted to go back to the hotel and they wanted to stay out and party."

"If I apologize for being such a jerk, how about letting me walk you back to your hotel? I'm not quite ready to call it a night," he said, conveniently forgetting that only minutes before he couldn't wait to get back to his suite on the top floor of the Royal Orleans.

Something was happening between them. Something more charged than mere sexual tension. All around Zach and Alex, the Mardi Gras festivities flowed, but the pair remained in the center of the celebratory throng of people, an isolated, private island.

"I'd like that," she said in a perfectly rational voice although her eyes displayed her own suddenly turbulent emotions.

"Terrific." He held out his hand. "By the way, I'm Zachary Deveraux."

"Alexandra Lyons." As she took his outstretched hand, the vibrations the seemingly casual handshake set off hummed inside her like a tuning fork.

The Jean Lafitte Hotel, named for the legendary New Orleans pirate and smuggler, was a restored eighteenth-century town house, a romantic place of courtyards filled with tropical plants and private, wrought-iron balconies, in the heart of the Vieux Carré. The walk to the Jean Lafitte from Bourbon Street normally took no more than five minutes. Tonight, with the crowds, it took almost half an hour.

"Would you like to come in for a drink?" Alex asked. She was unwilling to let him get away so soon.

Zach reminded himself that he was a married man. That these feelings he was experiencing for Alexandra Lyons were not only wrong, but dangerous.

Although his marriage was turning out to be a horrendous mistake, Zach never played around. Not that there weren't always available women, both married and unmarried, who let it be known they would not be adverse to spending a stolen afternoon indulging in illicit pleasures.

But Zach had always considered himself a man of his word, and marriage vows were exactly that. Vows. *For better or for worse.*

"I'd like a drink," he said, ignoring the nagging voice of caution in the back of his mind.

Not surprisingly the Jean Lafitte's All That Jazz bar, along with the l'Escale dining room and the Gazebo Salon were packed.

In for a penny, in for a pound. Telling herself she had no other choice, Alex said, "I suppose we could go upstairs and call room service." As she waited for his answer, Alex realized she'd forgotten how to breathe.

Zach knew it was wrong. He realized he would be treading on very thin ice. But at this moment, on this freewheeling, carnival night, with the sound of Louis Armstrong floating on the breeze, Zach felt his usually dependable self-control slipping away like grains of sand—or strands of her magnificent red-gold hair—between his fingers.

"Sounds great," he heard himself saying before he could come to his senses and change his mind.

While Zach struggled with his conscience, Miranda and a companion strolled arm in arm into a bar near the Mississippi River levee. Tucked away in Miranda's quilted Chanel bag was a lovely pair of suede gloves she'd lifted that afternoon from the Canal Street Maison Blanche.

Although from the outside, the dimly lighted cocktail lounge looked like any other in the historic Vieux Carré, the management catered to a unique clientele. After ordering Sazeracs, Miranda and her escort managed to squeeze, just barely, into a spot on the crowded, postage-stamp-size dance floor.

As she felt Marie Hélène's long slender fingers settle on her waist, Zach's wife smiled with anticipation.

Chapter Twelve

Alex's hotel room was actually a minisuite, with an alcove containing a couch and easy chair adjoining the bedroom, which allowed them to keep their visit on a proper plane even as unspoken feelings swirled around them.

Alex had never met a man who was more easy to talk with. She found herself telling him more about herself than she'd ever told anyone—about growing up with her mother and twin brother, about the way they never stayed in one town or even one state for more than a year, about the pain and loneliness she suffered at first David's, then her mother's death.

It was as if, once she started talking, she couldn't stop. She told him all about her dreams of becoming a designer. And about her time working in New York and more recently in Paris. She told him what she could about "Blue Bayou" without divulging the plotline, which Sophie guarded as ferociously as a mother bear protecting her cubs.

Alex did not mention her affair with Debord. It wasn't that she was ashamed of it. On the contrary, she was rather proud of the way she'd picked herself up, dusted herself off and started over.

She didn't mention it because looking back, it seemed as if the affair and its dreadful conclusion had all happened to some other woman. A far more foolish, more naive woman.

"Gracious," she said, when she finally ran down. "I've been doing all the talking."

Zach refilled their glasses from the bottle of wine they'd ordered from room service. "I like hearing you talk." Her enthusiasm for life was contagious. And although she worked in Tinseltown, it was obvious she hadn't gone Hollywood. She was, he considered, the most natural woman he'd ever met.

The simple compliment shouldn't give her so much pleasure. But it did. "But I don't know anything about you," she protested. "Other than you should be wearing a coat of shining armor instead of that Brooks Brothers suit."

"I didn't own a suit until I graduated from college," he surprised himself by saying. Although he was not ashamed of his humble roots, he was not in the habit of sharing his past. Let alone with someone he'd just met.

"Ah." She curled up in the corner of the couch, tucking her legs beneath her flowing skirt. "A self-made man."

"With a little help from some friends."

Zach told her briefly about his life growing up in Lafourche Parish, of the early years fishing and trapping with his father.

"My father died when I was ten," he said when she asked about his parents. Alex murmured a sound of sympathy. She knew firsthand the pain of losing a parent as an adult. She couldn't imagine how she'd have survived if her mother had died while she and David were still children.

"Was yours a large family?" she asked.

"I was the oldest in a family of eight kids. One boy and seven girls."

"Gracious. You were definitely outnumbered."

"I didn't mind."

Imbued with a deep sense of duty and an even deeper sense of family, Zach had immediately stepped into the role of second parent. When his mother, desperate for additional funds to feed her family, went to work as a domestic in town, Zach took over the household chores, which made him not only an excellent cook, but the only ten-year-old boy in the bayou who could weave a French braid.

"When I was sixteen, I got a summer job working on the loading dock at the New Orleans Lord's," he continued his story. "The old one. A new one just opened today on Canal Street."

Alex nodded. "So I heard." She'd fretted some about running into Debord. When she arrived in town and saw how many thousands of people came to New Orleans during festival, she realized she'd been foolish to worry. The odds against seeing the horrid man again were astronomical. "I've always liked Lord's. Their buyers have a tremendous sense of style."

"Thanks. I'll pass the word along."

"It's a long way from the loading dock to the executive offices," she prompted, growing more curious about this unique man by the moment. "Are you manager of the new store?"

"Actually, I'm president of the company."

She wasn't all that surprised. Zachary Deveraux radiated power. "I'm impressed."

"I was lucky. I got some breaks along the way."

Alex liked the fact that he didn't have an enormous ego. Actually, she had a feeling this was a man who would succeed at whatever he chose. With or without any breaks along the way.

When she told him what she was thinking, he shrugged. "To tell the truth, my senior year of high school, the loading-dock manager offered me a full-time job after graduation. I wanted to take it."

"But?"

"My mother hit the roof. She wanted me to go to college."

"I think that's every mother's dream for her children. My mother scrimped for years so I could attend the Fashion Institute." She'd also vehemently protested when Alex had dropped out to take care of her.

"It wasn't a common goal in the bayou," Zach revealed. "In my father's day, any young Acadian who considered college was considered lazy. But my folks realized times were changing. They knew my future lay working out among the Americaines."

"Americaines?"

"That's how Cajuns refer to non-Acadian Louisianans."

"Oh." Alex considered that for a moment. "It must have been difficult," she murmured. "When I first arrived in France, I might as well have landed on the moon, things seemed so different from what I was used to."

So she was insightful, as well as beautiful. That made her, Zach considered, even more dangerous.

"I got used to it," he said, purposefully understating what had indeed been a major cultural adjustment.

She took a sip of wine and eyed him with bright interest. "Where did you go to college?"

"I got a football scholarship at Tulane, right here in the city." Which had allowed him to continue to work part-time at Lord's, where he'd been promoted to the sales floor. The money he'd earned he'd sent home to his mother.

She envisioned him wearing shoulder pads and those tight white pants and decided he must have looked magnificent. "Were you any good?"

Zach shrugged. "My sack statistics weren't bad." Actually, they'd been so impressive he'd garnered the pros' attention. "But my junior year I injured my knee in the final game of the season, which quashed my dreams of NFL stardom."

"You must have been terribly disappointed." Alex knew all too well the power of youthful dreams.

"For a while. But if there was one thing life had taught me, it was how to punt."

Another thing they had in common, Alex mused. If she was keeping score. Which she wasn't.

Hell. Of course she was.

"So, to make a long story short, I graduated with degrees in business and marketing—" he didn't mention those degrees had been cum laude "—and moved into management. In a few months, I went back to business school for my MBA."

That had been Eleanor's doing. Six months after he'd begun work full-time, he'd suggested a new inventory system that had garnered her attention. Recognizing potential when she saw it, Eleanor offered to pay his tuition to Harvard Business School.

Although he'd refused her charity, Zach did accept the money as a loan, payable on installment when he graduated.

"Then I returned to work at Lord's L.A. headquarters." He spread his hands. "End of story," he said, leaving out his meteoric rise to vice president and finally president.

Alex suspected there was a great deal more to the story than he was telling.

"Your wife must be very proud of you," she murmured, wishing she could ignore the gold band on his left hand.

"I suppose so." His lack of enthusiasm was in direct contrast to his earlier tone.

"Is she in town with you?"

"Since Miranda's in charge of setting up the Debord boutiques, she came for the opening." He'd been neither surprised nor disappointed when his wife had opted to spend the evening with the designer and his iceberg of a sister, rather than with her husband.

Since returning from their honeymoon thirteen months ago, Zach doubted if he and Miranda had spent more than five consecutive days together. Their work was demanding. And it required a great deal of travel. But, he'd asked himself time and time again, if they truly loved one another, wouldn't they make the time to be together?

Unfortunately whenever his wife did deign to join him at the French Normandy-style manor she'd convinced him to buy in Brentwood, it was as if a dangerous wind had swept into the house, disturbing the calm, predictable routine of his existence.

Alex watched the scowl darken his features. "Your wife is Miranda Smythe?" Try as she might, she could not envision this man married to the mercurial Lady Smythe. She knew the old adage about opposites attracting, but Zachary Deveraux and Miranda Lord Baptista Smythe had to be the mismatch of the millennium.

"That *was* her name," Zach allowed. "Do you know her?"

"I've seen her picture in the magazines." To reveal any more would bring up her time with Debord, and Alex refused to allow that bastard to ruin a wonderful night. As if to remind himself that he was married, Zach spent the next half hour telling Alex what he could about his wife.

He told her about the success of the Debord boutiques. He did not mention Miranda's recreational shoplifting. Hardly a week went by that Zach didn't receive a discreet bill in the mail for some item his wife had not been able to resist taking.

Fortunately, after that experience in Rio, Miranda had stuck to stores where they had an account. Apparently she wasn't willing to risk incarceration over a Hermès scarf or a bottle of Obsession, both of which she could easily afford.

He lauded Miranda's inspired remodeling job at the London Lord's. He did not mention the glacier that had begun creeping inexorably over their marriage bed after their return from Rio.

Nor did he admit the truth that sex had been the coinage of his and Miranda's odd-couple relationship from the beginning. And now, having just recently celebrated their first anniversary on separate continents, that relationship was already approaching bankruptcy.

He expressed, with honest admiration, his wife's unerring sense of style and her ability to draw British society to the store's special events, thus increasing customer loyalty.

He left unsaid that these days her conversation skills, when she did trouble to speak to him, seemed limited to clothes and parties and race horses, and gossip about face-lifts and tummy tucks and what wife had run off with her karate instructor and what yacht club member of the Newport-Palm Beach crowd was committing adultery with what married princess of some European pocket principality he'd never even heard of.

He also didn't relate his belief that Miranda was so busy going places, seeing and being seen with the right people with the most money, she had precious little time for normal, everyday activities.

Despite his discretion, Alex had no difficulty reading between the lines. From what Zach didn't say about his marriage, she realized that all was not well in the Deveraux household.

Which was, she told herself firmly, none of her business. As attracted to Zach as she was, she had no desire to get involved with a married man. Feeling the pall settle over the room, Zach returned the conversation to Alex's reason for being in New Orleans in the first place. For nearly nineteen months, she'd lived, eaten, slept and dreamed "Blue Bayou." It was, quite literally, the most important thing in her life.

And on this long Mardi Gras night, it didn't take much encouragement for her to talk about the show and, more specifically, her costuming.

Pink fingers of dawn began creeping above the wrought-iron railing when Alex finally ran out of steam.

"I can't believe we've been talking all night," she said.

"Time has a way of flying during Mardi Gras." Zach knew he should get up from his chair, thank her for a lovely evening and return to the Royal Orleans, where just perhaps, his errant wife may have returned by now.

They fell silent, Zach sprawled in the chair, Alex curled up in the corner of the flowered sofa, watching as the rising sun streaked the sky over the courtyard in a dazzling display of gold and ruby rays.

During their hours together, he'd come to realize that Alexandra Lyons was a warm and caring, talented and special woman. Zach found himself unwilling to say goodbye just yet.

The effect she was having on his body was considerable—and not entirely unexpected. After all, he'd been celibate for months, and Alexandra Lyons was a ravishing woman. As a normal, heterosexual male, Zach was not immune to attractive women. What was coming as a distinct surprise was what Alexandra was doing to his mind. He wanted her, he realized. And for a helluva lot more than an adulterous roll in the hay.

Quicksand, Zach warned himself. Take one more step and you're in deep, deep trouble.

"My mother's getting married today," he revealed. "I don't suppose you've ever been to a Cajun wedding."

She briefly thought of a time when she'd been foolish enough to think she'd be planning her own Paris wedding. "No. But from what you've said about Cajun parties, I'll bet they're special."

"They are. How would you like to experience one first-hand?"

Yes, yes, her unruly heart called in reply. "With you?" she asked cautiously.

"I'd like your company." Although his tone remained matter-of-fact, his eyes were unnervingly intimate, setting off warning bells.

"What about your wife?" she had to ask.

"Miranda's not going. She's not exactly wild about my humble rural roots."

Before their marriage, Miranda had displayed a burning fascination with everything about Zach: his Louisiana childhood, his family, his hardscrabble, pull-himself-up-by-the-bootstraps success story, his work at Lord's.

These days, she found everything about their life together boring. Santa Barbara was boring. Los Angeles was boring. California. Constant sunshine. All were so, so boring. Even Zach, she'd accused on more than one stormy occasion, screeching at him in a voice high enough to risk shattering her precious collection of crystal, had become bloody, bloody boring! In Miranda's eyes, her husband had committed the cardinal sin.

It hadn't taken Zach long, after they were married, to discover that he'd never really known Miranda at all. His wife reinvented herself every day in the mirror. Everything Miranda did, everything she said, was another brush stroke in that carefully drawn self-portrait.

If he was disillusioned with his marriage, which he most definitely was, Zach knew that he had no one to blame but himself. He'd understood from the beginning that Miranda led life in the fast lane.

The only problem was that during this past year Zach had begun to feel more and more as if he were standing all alone in the roadway, facing the fatal rush of oncoming traffic.

"If you're worried about not getting any sleep," Zach said, unreasonably unnerved by her hesitation, "the ceremony's not until this evening. I thought I'd return to my hotel, then meet you back here around two or three."

Before putting her feelings on such a restrictive rein, Alex had not been a woman to guide her emotions. More often, she allowed them to guide her. And although such behavior might be considered foolhardy, especially when it led her into the type of trouble she experienced with Debord, in the balance, her life had been rewarding.

She was, quite honestly, weary of trying to live a lie, of pretending to be someone she was not. She was tired of her dark and proper clothing, her subdued behavior. It was as if by donning this bright Gypsy outfit last night, she'd let the genie of her own daring, slightly reckless personality out of the bottle, and Alex didn't know if she'd want to put it back even if she could. And she suspected she couldn't.

Knowing that she was already too attracted to this very married man and telling herself she should refuse, Alex took a deep breath, threw caution to the winds and said, "I'd love to attend your mother's wedding with you, Zachary."

Chapter Thirteen

Alex felt the change in Zach as they drove away from the city. Soon after they'd crossed the iron bridge spanning the Mississippi River, he tuned the car radio to a station playing an infectious, toe-tapping medley he told her was called zydeco. As "The Lake Arthur Stomp" gave way to "Jolie Blonde," Zach visibly relaxed.

They sped along a highway that spread like a long gray ribbon over swampland, past stretches of sugarcane fields and rice paddies. Blue herons glided soundlessly among magnificent cypress trees, bearded in Spanish moss, which the sun backlit in ghostly gold; nutria and muskrats paddled along, furry shadows in the dark waters.

A silence descended that could be described as companionable, if only the participants hadn't been so studiously avoiding feelings too risky to acknowledge out loud.

"This is so beautiful," Alex said quietly after a while.

"We call it the trembling prairie. Roots sink deep here."

She knew he was not talking about the knobby cypress roots, which rose out of the water. "You must miss it a great deal."

"It's good to get back home," he agreed. "Once the bayou gets into your blood, I don't think you can ever get it out. Even if you want to."

"Which you don't."

"No."

His familiarity with the seemingly unfathomable maze of dirt roads and waterways reminded Alex of what she'd once read about a nomad's ability to find his way home over miles of shifting desert sands. From the fact that he'd risen so quickly in the Lord's organization, it was obvious he possessed an enormous talent for business. But she suspected that it was here, in this misty, mystical land, that Zachary felt truly comfortable.

The wedding, held in Zach's former waterfront home, was a vibrant celebration of family and community. Eve Deveraux, who was marrying a nearby rancher, gave Alex a warm greeting.

"Thank you for celebrating our happiness with us today," she said. Although her smile was sincere, Alex thought she detected a fleeting concern in the dark eyes that so resembled her son's.

A beautiful woman in her fifties, Eve had chosen a royal blue dress, cut on the bias and falling to just below the knee. Alex decided it definitely suited her.

Zach's paternal grandmother was more outspoken than her daughter-in-law. After giving Zach a huge hug, she stepped back, gave his companion a long, probing once-over with eyes that reminded Alex of a curious bird and said without preamble, "You have known heartache."

Although startled, Alex kept her smile from slipping. "What woman hasn't?"

The elderly woman didn't respond to Alex's flippant remark. "There will be more to come," she pronounced. "But in the long run, you will find the love you deserve."

"Maman," Eve murmured. "Please…" She slanted Alex an apologetic look.

Zach's grandmother ignored the quiet warning. "As for you, boy," she said, tilting her white head back to look a long, long way up into Zach's face, *"Lâchez pas la patate."*

Zach's answering grin was meant to charm his grandmother, but Alex found herself mesmerized by its warmth. "Why don't you tell me what you really think?" he suggested blandly.

The maternal concern Alex had witnessed earlier in Zach's mother's gaze was back as Eve skillfully led them away to introduce Alex to the rest of the huge Deveraux clan.

The wedding feast was a culinary extravaganza—spicy gumbo, jambalaya, crayfish and filet of alligator topped with Tabasco sauce hot enough to clear Alex's sinuses. The mood was as joyful as the food was lavish; dust from the dancers' feet and smoke from the barbecue grills rose into the cooling air.

More than once Alex was pulled, laughing, into a conga line led by guests dressed in Mardi Gras costumes, and by the time the sun had set over the water, she decided that she must have danced with at least twenty of Zach's cousins.

"I envy you," she murmured when she found herself in Zach's arms for the first time since their arrival hours earlier. As the marsh gas flickered a phosphorous green, the band started interspersing a few ballads in with the livelier dance tunes.

"Why?" Zach asked, his attention distracted by her eyes, which were shining like antique gold in the light of the campfires that had been set.

"You have so many people who care about you. And love you."

"I suppose, where life is hard, family becomes even more important," he said thoughtfully. "I have a photo of Dad and Mom and my sisters and me all picking Grand-mère's sugarcane. Last year, when I became president of Lord's, I had an artist copy it.

"Whenever I start getting cocky, I look at that painting on my office wall and remember where I came from. And what's important."

She was not surprised by the story. Watching Zach with his family and friends had revealed a side of the man she suspected few people were permitted to see. Did his wife know the real Zachary Deveraux? Or had Lady Miranda set her sights only on the high-powered executive?

The fact that Zach had brought her to his mother's wedding, rather than Miranda, provided the answer to that question, she decided.

"Your grandmother's an interesting woman," she murmured.

Zach laughed. A deep rumbling sound Alex found herself liking too much for safety. "That's one way to describe her. She's stubborn, like all us Deveraux. And she claims to have second sight. Like her own *grand-mère.*"

"Do you believe her?"

Zach shrugged. "When I was a kid, I didn't. But one fall when I was thirteen, I couldn't find a deer all season. We really needed the venison to get us through the winter. That's when she told me exactly where to go.

"Deciding I didn't have anything to lose, I took her advice and found an enormous buck standing beside a cypress as if he'd been waiting for me to come and shoot him. After that, I started listening to her more often."

"What about tonight? What did she tell you?"

"Oh, that." Zach knew his grandmother didn't approve of his wife. He also knew she approved of divorce even less.

"It's an old Cajun expression—'Don't drop the potato.' Loosely translated, it means 'Hang in there.'"

"Oh." When she felt his body tense, Alex opted against questioning him further.

He danced her away from the others to a hidden place of shadows beneath a grove of trees. They swayed to the sultry romantic ballad, his chin atop her hair, her fingers linked around his neck.

And even when the music stopped, they stood there for a long, immeasurable time, still clasped together, looking into each other's eyes, silently exchanging seductive messages too dangerous to put into words.

"Alexandra." There was a husky poignancy in his voice.

Looking up at him, Alex saw a man who'd just come to the stark realization that his life has, in the space of a single day, been changed forever. She could recognize the tumultuous emotions because she was feeling the same way.

Alex knew she was playing with fire. She also knew one of them was likely to get burned, and more than likely it would be her. But at this absolutely perfect moment in time, she didn't care.

Zach had spent the entire day valiantly trying to keep his hands off her, but it had been like fighting an undertow. Dammit, he'd never claimed to be bucking for sainthood.

He brushed his fingers down her cheek, following the slow, seductive movement with his eyes. "You are, without a doubt, the most beautiful woman here today."

The soft touch of his fingers made Alex's blood hum. "The bride's the most beautiful woman at her wedding," she argued on a shaky little whisper.

"Maman's always been beautiful." His hand trailed down her throat as he took in the sight of her, clad in a moss green dress and forest green suede boots that reminded him of a wood nymph.

Last night, in theatrical makeup, Alexa peared lush and sultry and vampish. Earlier to face flushed from a heady mixture of sun and e pleasure, she'd possessed a bright, breezy type of conformist beauty that had reminded him of Audrey Hepburn's Holly Golightly.

Tonight in the moonlight, with a dusting of freckles scattered across the bridge of her nose, Alexandra Lyons seemed delicate and vulnerable.

"But you," he alleged gravely, "are absolutely exquisite."

Slowly, giving her time to read his intention and back away, he framed her face between his large, reassuring hands and with the utmost deliberation and gravity, lowered his mouth to hers.

With a patience he'd never known he possessed, Zach took his time to kiss her tingling lips from one corner to the other, loving her for a long, delicious time with only his mouth. As his lips tempted, cajoled, caressed, Alex's world was reinvented.

Beguiled, she closed her eyes, twined her arms around his neck and allowed her mind to empty. She melted into his exquisite kiss because at this suspended moment in time, to do otherwise would have been to deny her own feelings. And to deny her emotions would have been contrary to her honest nature.

Caught up in the wonder of Alex, Zach savored her every sigh, each soft moan. As her warm breath shuddered out of her, he forgot all the reasons why this was wrong; as he heard his name murmured against his mouth he could only think how perfectly Alexandra Lyons fit in his arms.

His lips skimmed over her face, drinking in the tantalizing taste of her skin before returning to her mouth.

The kiss could have lasted a minute. An hour. An eternity. When it finally ended, Zach was as disoriented as if ʌomeone had just informed him that the laws of physics had been suspended, and down was now up, up down, and gravity no longer existed.

Not quite knowing how to tell her what he was feeling, he said her name again—"Alexandra"—savoring the pure sweetness of it. The pleasure. The absolute joy. He wound a strand of gleaming hair around his finger into a ringlet; he released it and it immediately sprang back into the mass of riotous waves. Although he knew it was masochistic, Zach imagined what that silky hair would feel like against his naked chest. His thighs.

"This is…" His voice trailed off, and all he could do was shake his head in wonder and frustration.

"Unexpected," Alex filled in for him. "Exciting. Frightening."

"Terrifying," Zach concurred.

The one description neither of them was prepared to resort to was *mistake*.

"I want to be honest with you, Alexandra. I *need* to be honest with you. The problem is, I have the feeling that whatever I say is going to come out wrong."

"This can't go anywhere." Alex's voice was soft and resigned.

He wished she'd argue. Shout. Anything but this quiet acceptance. "Not now. Although you'll probably never believe this, I'm not the type of man who plays around on his wife."

"I believe it. Because I'm not the kind of woman who has affairs with married men."

"I don't want to hurt you."

But he would hurt her, Alex knew. Oh, he wouldn't mean to. But she could see the heartbreak coming, like the headlight of a runaway freight train approaching in a tunnel.

"I was going to ask if you'd let me show you the real Louisiana tomorrow."

Alex could hear the regret in his tone. "But?" she asked softly.

"I received a phone call a while ago," he said, telling her nothing she didn't know. She'd watched him go into his mother's house, wondered if it was his wife calling and noticed his grim expression when he'd emerged several minutes later.

"There was a fire at a Lord's store under construction in Santa Monica. They think it was started by a welder's torch."

"I hope no one was hurt."

"Fortunately, no. But the city fire inspector's going to be on the site first thing in the morning. Since I should be there, I had to change my flight. There's a plane leaving at 4:30 in the morning, which will get me back to L.A. in time."

"Four-thirty." *So soon.*

He heard the soft shimmer of regret in her tone. "I'm sorry."

Alex managed a wobbly smile. "We still have the rest of tonight." The smile moved to her eyes. "I'm going to change my flight so we can return to California together, Zachary. And then I want to dance with you at your mother's wedding."

"And then?" Zach had a feeling he wasn't going to like her answer.

He didn't. "And then," she continued quietly, firmly, "once we land at LAX, you'll return to your life. And I'll go back to mine."

Part of him knew she was right. But then his gaze moved to her mouth—Jesus, her sweet, soft, delectable mouth!—and he found himself wishing she'd suggest they run away together. To some faraway, romantic South Sea island where no one would ever find them and they could spend the rest of their days making love and feeding each other tropical fruit. Passion fruit.

"You can really walk away from whatever's happening between us here? Just like that?" His voice, his eyes, testified to his disbelief.

Unable to speak past the sudden lump in her throat, Alex merely nodded.

Even as she tried to tell herself that these few golden hours together would be enough, as they danced and kissed and whispered and sighed, she felt horribly like Cinderella facing the countdown of that treacherous palace clock. Later, as they drove in heavy silence back along the darkened highway toward New Orleans, Alex half expected Zach's rental car to turn into a pumpkin.

The stolen hours passed all too quickly. Hidden beneath the blue blanket in the first-class section they had all to themselves at this unpalatable hour of the morning, they kissed like lovesick teenagers, their bodies aching with feverish yearning.

Finally the long day caught up with Alex and she fell asleep, her head on Zach's shoulder, her legs curled up beneath her on the seat.

While the plane sped closer and closer to Los Angeles, Zach remained awake. Indulging himself in the pure pleasure of watching Alex undetected, he wished for the impossible. As the plane made its inevitable approach into LAX, the change in engine speed roused Alex from her light slumber. She escaped to the lavatory, dragged a brush through her tangled hair, splashed cold water on her face, took several deep breaths and reminded herself that as wonderful as her romantic interlude with Zach had been, it was time to return to the real world.

Reality was Los Angeles, with its smog and soaring property prices, traffic jams and escalating crime. Reality was Zach returning to his Century City offices. Reality was her continuing her work for Sophie.

Reality was Zach's marriage.

And his wife.

They stood face-to-face, close enough to touch, but not daring to as the bustling early-morning crowd in the terminal surged around them.

Although Zach didn't want to let Alex get away, he couldn't escape the unpalatable fact that he was married. And while he suspected Alex might be willing to meet him for the occasional rendezvous, he could not play with her emotions that way.

Divorce was, of course, an option. But the last time he'd suggested it to Miranda, she'd lost her temper, become hysterical and taken an overdose of Valium. She hadn't taken enough to kill herself, the doctor had assured Zach.

But she had achieved her objective. She'd scared the hell out of her husband.

Looking back on that fateful day when he'd first met Miranda Lord Baptista Smythe, Zach knew he'd been foolishly led with his hormones and not his heart. Or his brain.

And now, the price for the unbridled lust he'd once felt for the woman who was now his wife, for better or for worse, would be to live with the bad bargain he'd made.

"You know, this is a small town, really," he said. "Perhaps we'll run into one another."

"Perhaps." The sheen of moisture in Alex's eyes belied her falsely bright tone.

They both knew it would not happen. They could not allow it to happen. Because the chemistry between them was too potent to allow them to remain merely friends.

Alex was putting on such a goddamn good show of being cheerful and brave. Zach thought this would all be a helluva lot easier if she'd break down and cry. Or shout.

Forsaking all others. The vow he'd willingly taken felt as heavy and burdensome as Jacob Marley's chains.

Unable to resist, he touched her cheek. "Goodbye, Alexandra."

The tender touch threatened to be her undoing. "Goodbye, Zach."

As her eyes filled with hot, frustrated tears, Alex turned and walked away, the heels of her suede boots clicking a rapid staccato on the tile floor.

Zach stood there, his fists shoved deep into the pockets of his slacks, his heart aching. He desperately wanted to call her back, but knew it would only hurt her more if he did.

Chapter Fourteen

Deciding she was a disaster just waiting to happen when it came to romance, Alex threw herself back into the one thing she could control in her life—safe, soothing work.

When she wasn't hard at work, she ran along the packed sand, mile after mile, until her physical pain equaled her emotional pain. And then she ran farther still, until the ocean breeze dried her salty tears and she was too exhausted to dwell on what might have been if she'd only met Zach during that brief window of time when they'd both been in Paris. Before he'd married Miranda.

The first episode of "Blue Bayou" proved a blockbuster hit, outscoring even "The Cosby Show" in the overnight ratings.

The media, unsurprisingly, panned the glitzy soap opera. One particularly harsh critic declared that Americans possessed a limitless desire to identify with the upper classes. That being the case, he'd gone on sarcastically, it was no wonder they'd all tuned in to watch a show where the characters, who changed clothes between the appetizer and soup course, appeared to be the classiest people on television.

Undeterred by the strident criticism, Sophie laughed all the way to the bank.

"Blue Bayou" quickly became not only America's number-one television show, but was also watched by citizens of seventy other countries, including Iceland, Japan and Bangladesh.

And, as Sophie had predicted, Alex's designs made her a rising star in Tinseltown. Even critics who hated the program couldn't resist a positive mention of the dazzling wardrobe.

Her imaginative costuming expressed the basic conflict around which the steamy nighttime drama revolved. Typically the wicked ex-wife would strike a blow with a black crepe cocktail dress trimmed with rhinestones along a plunging neckline, while the saintly current wife would counter with a pink peplum jacket accented by thin silver piping.

Across town the exotic dancer/mistress would go shopping in a sequined blue baseball jacket over a ribbed red silk tank top and tight white shorts.

And every week, without fail, the studio mail room was flooded with letters from fans wanting to know where they could buy those ultraglamorous Hollywood fashions for themselves.

To Sophie's delight and Alex's surprise, Alex was nominated for a coveted Emmy for television costuming. As she dressed for the awards program, Alex said a silent prayer of thanks to whatever fickle fates or gods had led Sophie to Debord's salon that long-ago day.

Television might not be couture. But from the cold dead ashes of that lost dream, like a legendary phoenix, another had risen. One Alex had already determined was a lot more fun.

* * *

While Alex sat with her nerves in a tangle amid so many of Tinseltown's glitterati—albeit in the back of the auditorium with the rest of the technical nominees—Eleanor Lord was in the den of her Santa Barbara home, watching the live television broadcast with Clara Kowalski.

Although Clara had yet to contact the nanny, or anyone else on the other side for that matter, Eleanor enjoyed her company and refused to give up hope that someday they would learn the truth about her granddaughter's disappearance.

But tonight Eleanor's mind was not focused on Anna. It was centered, as was so often the case, on business. She never missed an Emmy or Oscar presentation; inevitably, knockoffs of the actresses' evening dresses would begin appearing in the stores almost as soon as the broadcast was over. And Eleanor knew from past experience that customers from Seattle to Miami would expect to find them in their local Lord's.

"Damn," she muttered as Jane Curtin received the Emmy for lead actress in a comedy.

"I like 'Kate and Allie,' " Clara offered.

"It's a nice enough program. And the woman's a fine actress," Eleanor agreed. "But she isn't exactly a fashion celebrity. This isn't going to help sales at all."

Her irritation increased as the awards show progressed. This was definitely turning out not to be a year for glamour, she thought dejectedly, when Tyne Daly won an award for her role as detective in the popular "Cagney and Lacey."

It was during the costume category that Eleanor perked up. On a personal level, she and Clara never missed an episode of "Blue Bayou"; as a retailing executive, she was hoping the dazzling costuming worn on the show would encourage designers to instill more glamour into their distressingly predictable ready-to-wear lines. Anything to bring more women into the stores.

"Clara!" Eleanor pressed her hand against her heart, which had trebled its beat as she watched the young woman going up on stage to accept her award. "Look!"

"Isn't that the most gorgeous dress you've ever seen!" Clara agreed enthusiastically, taking in the gown that was even more special and exciting than the evening's festivities. The fire-engine red silk mousseline, adorned with several trompe l'oeil necklaces of glittering Austrian crystal beads, fell in a long fluid column to the floor.

"Not the dress!" Eleanor snapped, earning a surprised and injured look from her friend. "The girl, dammit! Look at that girl!"

"She's lovely. And slender enough to get away with such a figure-revealing dress. I wonder if she's wearing anything underneath it," Clara mused. "I can't see any panty lines."

"The hell with panty lines," Eleanor said impatiently. "It's her, Clara. It's my Anna!"

"It can't be!"

"Look at the portrait," Eleanor insisted. "Alexandra Lyons could be me at her age." Clara's gaze went from Eleanor to the television, to the portrait above the fireplace of Eleanor, painted as a young bride, then back to Eleanor. "Perhaps there's a resemblance," she conceded. "But—"

"It's Anna! I know it is." Eleanor picked up the desk phone and dialed the familiar Los Angeles number.

"Do you have the television on?" she demanded, dispensing with any polite greeting when the male voice answered.

"Not at the moment," Zach said. "Miranda's in town, and she's throwing a dinner party for a bunch of Los Angeles anglophiles and expatriated British nobility who claim to be 'languishing away' in lotusland. Why?"

"Because I've seen Anna."

He sighed. "On TV?" Zach half expected to hear Eleanor claim that her missing granddaughter had just popped up as a guest star on "St. Elsewhere."

"On the Emmy broadcast. She just won an award. She's going by the name Alexandra Lyons."

The name rang an instantaneous and painful bell. Hardly a day went by that Zach didn't find himself thinking about Alex with regret. "You're kidding."

"You know I would never kid about a thing like this." Anna's image had faded from the screen, replaced by a car commercial. "It's her, Zachary!"

"Eleanor," Zach said patiently, "that's impossible. I met Alexandra Lyons in New Orleans."

"You never told me that."

"There was nothing to tell." That wasn't true, but his feelings for Alex were no one's business but his own.

"It's her, Zachary," Eleanor repeated stubbornly.

"I'll tell you what," he suggested, "if you promise to calm down, I'll look into it first thing in the morning."

"I want you to check it out now."

"Short of going downtown and crashing the awards ceremony, which will be over by the time I arrive, there isn't a helluva lot I can do tonight," he pointed out reasonably. "But I promise to call the studio as soon as the switchboard opens in the morning. All right?"

"No, it's not all right. But I suppose it'll have to do," Eleanor grumbled.

After reassuring her yet again, Zach hung up, wondering as he did so if Eleanor's obsession would ever fade. After placing a call to Averill and asking the doctor to run by the house and check on the elderly woman, Zach returned to the gilt-trimmed and mirrored dining room, wishing for a party featuring a steaming pot of spicy crayfish, some equally spicy zydeco music and a sweet-smelling, sexy strawberry blonde to hold in his arms.

All night long.

Two weeks later, Zach was in Santa Barbara, sipping a Scotch as Eleanor read the portfolio the private detective had compiled.

"Alex Lyons was born in Raleigh, North Carolina," he revealed. "Her mother's name was Irene Lyons. Her father was listed as 'unknown' on her birth certificate. It was, by the way, a double birth. She had a fraternal twin brother. David Lyons died in his teens. A drunk driver hit his car late one night."

"How tragic."

"Isn't it?" Zach remembered the pain on Alex's face when she'd told him about her twin's death. "The brother is the key. Even if Irene Lyons was in on Anna's kidnapping, she couldn't have pulled a boy child the same age out of the air."

Eleanor waved his words away. "Perhaps she already had a son of her own. Perhaps she always wanted a daughter, so she took my Anna."

Zach bit back his frustration and struggled for patience. "The birth certificates for both children list them as twins."

"Birth certificates can be forged."

Zach's jaw tightened as he recalled the debacle with the blackjack dealer. It was happening all over again. "True. But there's no reason to believe these were. Or that she's Anna."

"There's one way to find out for sure."

"You're not going to tell her what you suspect?"

"No. Believe it or not, Zachary, even this old dog can learn a few new tricks. I'm not going to tip my hand. At least not yet."

Zach's relief was short-lived.

"You know," Eleanor mused aloud, "it's been a long time since I had a party."

"I suppose Alexandra Lyons's name is at the top of the invitation list."

Eleanor smiled for the first time since Zach had arrived with the dossier. "Of course."

As he left the estate, though he knew it was wrong, Zach found himself looking forward to seeing Alexandra Lyons again. Oh, there was no way he believed she would ultimately prove to be Anna Lord. But perhaps, he told himself during the drive back to L.A., now that fate was about to throw them together again, he'd discover that his usually faultless memory had merely exaggerated Alexandra's charms.

Perhaps she was nothing more than a romantic, moonlit bayou fantasy.

The hell she was.

"I don't understand you," Sophie complained. "Eleanor Lord is one of the most influential people in the state. Hell, probably the entire country. To be invited to one of her soirees is a coup."

"I know that," Alex mumbled, running her fingernail along the gilt edge of the invitation.

"And it's for a good cause."

"I know that, too." But couldn't she just skip the fundraising party and write out a generous check to the Save the Beaches Foundation?

"So what's the problem?"

Even as Alex continued to vacillate over the next two days, she knew that the real reason for her indecision could be spelled out in two words: Zachary Deveraux. She wanted to see him again, if for no other reason than to prove to herself that the chemistry she remembered was nothing more than the product of a dazzling, crazy Mardi Gras night and a steamy, mystical bayou day.

But another part of her was afraid of what would happen if she did attend the party and discovered that the emotional bond they shared during those long hours together turned out to be real.

It had taken her a long time to expunge Zach from her mind; sometimes entire days went by when she managed not to think of him, yet all she'd have to do was drive past a Lord's store and all those bittersweet memories would come flooding back.

As for the long, lonely nighttime hours, although she'd throw herself off the top of the "Blue Bayou" billboard towering over Sunset Strip before admitting it, the truth was that Zachary Deveraux continued to play a starring role in far too many of her erotic dreams.

Reminding herself that her mother had brought her up to take risks, after several sleepless nights and anxiety-filled days, during which Sophie nagged incessantly, Alex finally decided to accept Eleanor Lord's invitation.

Uncharacteristically, she dithered over her dress for days, trying on and discarding everything in her closet before moving on to the show's wardrobe department. Claiming it heightened the program's visibility, Sophie enouraged the "Blue Bayou" cast to borrow clothing for personal appearances. She'd made the same offer to Alex, who'd never seriously considered doing so until now.

But even these glamorous gowns weren't quite right. Because Alex wanted something new. Something that was all hers. Something that would knock Zachary Deveraux's socks off.

She stayed up for three nights, draping and stitching, ripping and restitching. The night of the party, as she ran her bath, she tossed in colorful crystals and scented oil from

Victoria's Secret into the hot water with the careless aban-
donment of a teenager preparing for the senior prom.

Which was exactly how she felt, Alex admitted, as she
soaked in the perfumed water, sipping a glass of preparty
champagne to soothe her tangled nerves.

Chapter Fifteen

Rather than make her guests drive up the coast to her Santa Barbara estate, Eleanor had booked the swank Rex Il Ristorante for the evening. The building, which had once housed the city's most elegant haberdasher, clothier to the Duke of Windsor and the Shah of Iran, among others, had been turned into a lushly romantic place—a tribute to Hollywood in its heyday.

Swathed in soft hues of peach, plum and mauve, the main dining room resembled the grand salon of a luxury liner. Art Deco chairs and cozy love seats were not merely furniture, but curvaceous, sensual pink shells and calla lilies; glass tables appeared to float on crystal bases.

Despite the lingering nervousness she felt from the moment she walked through the etched Lalique doors, Alex was absolutely enchanted.

She'd no sooner entered the room when she was greeted by her hostess. "My dear," Eleanor Lord said, taking both Alex's hands in her beringed ones, "don't you look absolutely stunning!" Her gaze swept approvingly over the short scarlet sarong. Alex had spent hours sewing glittering gold beads onto the strapless bodice. "I assume this marvelous gown is your own design."

"It is," Alex said with a smile.

"With such talent, it's no wonder you won an Emmy. You've no idea how pleased I am you could make our little party."

Although the elderly woman's smile was warm and inviting, there was something about the way Eleanor was looking at her—deep and hard—that made Alex vaguely uneasy.

"I'm honored to be invited."

"It's we who should be honored," Eleanor corrected absently. Her gaze was riveted on Alex's face. "It's not often we're in the company of artistic genius."

Alex laughed at that and managed to relax. Just a little. "That's definitely an exaggeration, but I was taught at a very early age that a proper guest never argues with her hostess."

"That's absolutely right," Eleanor agreed. Something indiscernible flashed in her eyes, something that came and went so quickly Alex nearly missed it. "It sounds as if your mother paid more attention to Emily Post than Dr. Spock." Her voice went up a little on the end, turning the observation into a question, but before Alex could respond, a tall, distinguished, silver-haired man in black tie approached.

"Eleanor, don't tell me you're going to keep this lovely creature to yourself all evening," he complained. "Not when everyone's dying to meet Hollywood's newest celebrity."

The moment for private conversation had passed. Alex was introduced to a dizzying number of people, most of whom she'd watched on television and movie screens for years.

All the time she remained devastatingly aware of Zach, looking resplendent and too handsome for comfort in black tie. Having practiced her polite, casual greeting all afternoon, she waited for him to approach. An hour later, she was still waiting.

Finally, feeling a need for solitude, Alex climbed the stairway to the circular mezzanine promenade, where intimately arranged conversation areas allowed for private *tête-à-têtes*.

Settling into a comfortable, mauve-and-pink suede seashell, she watched the dancers glide across the black marble floor and found herself picturing a billowy, white tulle dance dress, shimmering with crystal beadwork, the type of dress Ginger Rogers might have worn. The type of dress that would be perfect for the oil man's wife to wear in the season's end cliff-hanger charity ball scene.

"Makes you wish you'd been around for the days of the Coconut Grove and the Copacabana, doesn't it?" an all too familiar voice murmured. Lost in her creative muse, Alex hadn't heard Zach come up beside her.

The deep sound strummed a hundred, a thousand, hidden chords in Alex. Feeling the color rise in her cheeks, she looked up into the ruggedly handsome face she'd tried so hard to forget.

She had to force herself to remember how to breathe. *Inhale.* "I half expect to see Rita Hayworth dancing cheek to cheek with the Ali Khan," she admitted. *Exhale.*

Oh, God. It was happening all over again. What made her think she could ever forget this man? And the dizzy, terrifying, wonderful way he could make her feel.

"While he whispers sweet nothings in her shell pink ear," Zach said, reminding them both of a time when he'd held her in his arms and told her again and again how beautiful she was. How sweet. How exquisitely unique. He casually flicked a finger at her dangling gold earring. "Hello."

"Hi." *Stop that!* Alex instructed her lips, which had curved into a foolish, adoring teenager's smile. *Inhale.*

"Congratulations on your Emmy."

"Thank you." *Exhale.*

"I'm no expert on women's fashions, but according to my mother, who never misses an episode of 'Blue Bayou,' you were a shoo-in to win."

At the mention of Eve, Alex's smile turned warm and genuine. "How is she?"

"Wonderful." He sat down across from her, close enough that their knees were almost touching. "I visited last month, and she's still glowing like a new bride. I think it must be love."

Alex's soft answering laugh made Zach realize exactly how long it had been since he'd heard that rich, vibrating sound. And how much he'd mourned its absence. "That's sweet," she said.

"I think so, too. She's wild about that dress you made for her, by the way. It was a very nice thing to do."

"I had such a marvelous time at her wedding, I wanted to find some way to repay her." Alex couldn't believe she'd actually brought up that magic, romantic night. *Stupid, stupid, stupid!*

Zach had spent the past hour nursing a single drink while he made polite small talk. Sipping and smiling and chatting, all the time watching Alex. And now, as she crossed her legs, clad in shimmering stockings that reminded him of stardust, he had an urge to whisk her out of there and take her for a midnight stroll on the beach. Just the two of them. Alone, with only the full, benevolent moon and sparkling stars to keep them company.

"It was a good time, wasn't it?"

Not wanting to lie, but unwilling to admit it had been the best time of her life, Alex lowered her gaze so he wouldn't see the dangerous yearnings that had leapt into her heart.

She was wearing her hair the same way she'd worn it for the Emmy broadcast, piled high atop her head in wild, sexy disarray and looking as if it might tumble down over her bare shoulders with the slightest provocation. She'd precariously secured the bright concoction with a trio of jeweled combs. Zach had a perverse urge to pluck those combs loose so he could watch the gilt waves cascade free.

He reached out and brushed away an errant curl that had escaped to tumble down her cheek. At the feathery feel of his fingertip against her skin, Alex's mind emptied.

"I'm glad you came," Zach said.

"I almost didn't."

Another silence settled. They exchanged a long look rife with sensual temptations. Alex felt as if she were standing on a precipice and it would take only the slightest nudge to send her toppling over the edge.

Dragging her gaze from his, Alex glanced around with a casualness she was a long way from feeling. "Where's your wife?"

The question spoke volumes. Zach wondered if Alex actually thought he was coming on to her because Miranda was out of the country.

That wasn't the case, even though he admittedly wasn't as upstanding a husband as he'd been when he'd first met Alex. A few months after Mardi Gras, in a futile attempt to convince himself that what he'd felt for Alexandra Lyons could be felt for any intelligent, beautiful woman, he'd entered into a discreet, noncompromising, brief and emotionless affair with a local and very married television anchorwoman, which had left him feeling guilty and even lonelier than before.

"We need to talk."

"I don't think that's a very good idea." Remembering where they were, and who they were, she glanced around to make certain no one was standing within hearing distance. "I'm sorry, Zach. But I'm not into sneaking around."

"Dammit, I'm not asking you to—"

"I know." She put her hand on his arm and felt the muscle tense. "You want to talk. But we both know it wouldn't stop at that, and eventually, although we wouldn't mean to, we'd end up hurting everyone."

Did she think he wasn't hurting now? Hell, just being close to her without being able to touch her, to kiss her, was ripping his heart to ribbons. He was surprised that the mauve carpeting wasn't soaked red with his blood.

"Do you have any idea," he said roughly, "how much I've missed you?" The hell with protecting his male ego.

"Yes. Because not a day has gone by since New Orleans that I haven't wondered if I did the right thing walking away from you."

On the table in front of them a crystal Art Deco vase held a single pink rose. Unreasonably nervous, Alex began plucking unconsciously at the velvety petals. "But I know that I did. Because it's obvious that your relationship with Miranda—" there, she'd said her rival's name without choking "—is important enough to keep you in your marriage."

"Dammit, Alexandra, you don't understand."

"That's where you're wrong, Zach," she said softly. "I understand only too well."

The fact, as much as she wished otherwise, was that Zach was married. That was all she needed to know. End of story.

At least it should have been. But although she'd tried her best to avoid thinking about Zach, tried to convince herself that he'd been nothing more than a Mardi Gras fling, she now realized that their time together in New Orleans had left behind some smoldering embers that only needed the slightest breath of air, the most fleeting touch of a match, to ignite.

* * *

Miranda arrived late at the gala party. The first thing she did when she entered the room was grab a flute of Mumm champagne from a passing tray. Sipping the bubbly liquid, she began idly looking around the room, trying to locate her aunt's newest folly.

She spotted the interloper talking to, of all people, Zachary. And from the look on his face, Miranda realized that Eleanor wasn't the only one intrigued with Alexandra Lyons.

She tossed down the champagne, following it with two more in rapid succession. Then, fortified for battle, she crossed the room with long, purposeful strides.

"Darling!" she gushed, ignoring Alex completely as she captured Zach's face between her palms and gave him a long, inappropriately intimate, openmouthed kiss.

"I would have been here sooner," she said when they finally came up for air. "But my plane was stacked up for hours over LAX. I barely had time to throw on a decent dress and redo my face."

"You look lovely as always," Zach said on cue, wiping the scarlet lipstick from his mouth with his handkerchief.

He recognized the long, sinuous, skintight black gown as being from Yves Debord's latest collection. Even with her generous discount, the evening dress had been outrageously expensive. Although she'd assured him that the design was the very height of fashion, Zach thought the dress, with its layers of jet sequins, made Miranda resemble a snake. Or an eel.

"And you always say the right thing. I suppose that's only one of the reasons I adore you so." She gave him another wet kiss that stained his cheek and made Zach wonder what the hell his wife was up to now. He couldn't remember the last time Miranda had shown him even a scintilla of affection.

As if noticing Zach's companion for the first time, Miranda cast wide, expectant, green eyes Alex's way. "Zachary, darling," she cooed, "you're forgetting your manners. Aren't you going to introduce me to your friend?"

Of course, Zach realized. Miranda was staking her claim, on the Lord's empire, as well as on her husband. He could practically feel No Trespassing being stamped on his chest.

"Miranda, Alexandra Lyons. Alexandra, this is Miranda." There was a brief, all too noticeable pause. "My wife."

"Not *the* Alexandra Lyons!" Miranda looked at Alex as if admiring a newly cut precious stone. "The Emmy-winning costume designer the entire city is abuzz about?"

Miranda's photographs, which had graced the glossy pages of last month's *Town and Country,* had not begun to do her justice. Her blond hair swung in sleek, polished wings; there was an innate superiority in the way she dressed, the way she moved, the absolute perfection of face and figure. Zach's wife was a dazzling blend of glacial beauty and smoldering sexuality.

Alex hated her on sight.

"I'm not sure the entire city is abuzz," she said mildly, steadfastly ignoring the apologetic look Zach was trying to send her way. "But yes, I did just win an Emmy."

"I knew it!" Miranda clapped her hands. A diamond the size of the Taj Mahal glittered coldly on the ring finger of her left hand. "Of course I'm much too busy to watch the telly, but my dear Aunt Eleanor would never miss an episode of your little show. I do believe she's hooked," Miranda confided in a conspiratorial tone.

"Along with much of the television-viewing world," Zach broke in, determined to somehow spare Alex his wife's whip of a tongue. Although their marriage bed had become as arid as the Sahara, for some reason he could not understand, Miranda was an insanely jealous woman.

Woe to the female who was caught talking to him alone, double woe to the woman who dared to smile at him, even in passing. And woe, woe, triple woe to the poor unsuspecting female who might display even the faintest interest in Miranda Lord Baptista Smythe Deveraux's latest husband.

As she returned Miranda's predator smile with a bland, polite one of her own, Alex found herself grateful for the woman's interruption.

She could not—would not!—let herself fall in love with Zach. No way. Absolutely not. Only fools fell in love with married men, Alex reminded herself. Fools or women with strong suicidal streaks.

"Well, it's certainly been wonderful meeting both of you," she said. All right, so it was a lie. But only a little white one. Besides, from the dangerous, possessive glint in Miranda's gem-bright eyes, Alex knew better than to admit she and Zach had met before. "But I'm afraid I must be going."

"Oh?" Miranda's glossy lips formed into a perfect, pouty O of regret. "So soon? We've barely had time to get acquainted."

"I'm sorry. But we're taping early tomorrow morning."

"I'll walk you out," Zach said. As he'd feared, his casual remark drew a dark, fatal glance from his wife.

Lord, if looks could kill, Alex thought, Zachary Deveraux would be six feet under. "Thank you," she said, declining his offer firmly, "but that really isn't necessary."

Alex prided herself on getting through the obligatory parting conversation with Eleanor Lord, making her way back downstairs and remembering to tip the liveried parking valet.

It was only when she was all alone in the privacy of the new red Porsche that Friedman Television Productions had leased for her as a reward for winning the Emmy, driving through the darkened Los Angeles streets back to Venice, that Alex finally allowed herself to weep.

Chapter Sixteen

Lord's executive offices were located in Century City, built on land that had once been 20th Century Fox's back lot and had housed Sunnybrook Farm, Peyton Place and Boot Hill. Before that, the valuable Los Angeles real estate had been cowboy star Tom Mix's ranch.

The day after the party, Zach sat in his office in one of the two towers, which had so altered the Los Angeles skyline, going over the monthly sales figures with Eleanor.

He found it difficult to keep his mind on the report. Because he knew that just across the way, in the vast network entertainment center on the other side of the sculpture garden, "Blue Bayou" was taping.

The memory of those stolen, magical hours with Alex in Louisiana flickered seductively through his mind, teasing him with sensual memories and erotic wishes.

"What about the Texas Fashion House acquisition?" Eleanor asked, leafing through the thick sheaf of papers.

Since opportunities for new stores nationwide were limited, expansion-minded chains like Lord's were forced to seek market share by acquiring existing stores in other cities. Zach was currently negotiating to purchase a small chain of boutiques in San Antonio, Houston and Dallas.

Known throughout the retail industry for sales growth, Lord's was adding floor space at a faster rate than any other chain in the country. Expansion under Zach's leadership had fueled a thirty-three percent sales gain during the past five-year period.

Still, unlike so many of his contemporaries, who were leveraged up to their eyebrows, Zach was a conservative businessman. He slept easily each night knowing that under his leadership, The Lord's Group would survive—indeed, thrive—when the inevitable down cycle did occur.

"They've turned out to be more heavily leveraged than we first thought," he revealed. "However, since our debt-to-capital ratio is down considerably since last quarter, that shouldn't prove a problem."

"Good. Neiman-Marcus is opening a new store in Dallas. I don't want to lose market share there."

"I'll see that we don't." What was Alex doing right now?

Eleanor knew that on a lesser man, such innate confidence would have sounded like arrogance. On Zach it was an understatement. "I have every faith in you, Zachary."

She put the Texas figures aside. "By the way, did you receive my memo about the boutique lighting?"

"About dividing the various departments with neon signs?"

"That's the one. Clara and I went shopping yesterday in the Rodeo Drive store and were met with a distressing phalanx of dress racks."

"Well, it is a dress store," Zach said. Was Alex standing at a window in that twin tower, perhaps, looking out across the complex, thinking of him and wondering if he was thinking of her?

"True. But the store seemed boring."

"I believe the term you and the decorator agreed on last year during all those months of planning the remodeling was 'sophisticated and timeless,'" Zach reminded her.

"I liked the plans on paper," Eleanor conceded grumpily. "But in reality, there's just no *pow*. We need to liven things up."

"Don't tell me you want to hire perfume terrorists like they have at some stores."

During his last trip to Manhattan, on the way to a first-floor escalator in a major department store, he'd gotten attacked by a frighteningly aggressive young woman who'd leapt out from behind a counter and sprayed Polo cologne on him. Zach had spent the rest of the afternoon yearning for a shower.

"Nothing that drastic," she assured him. "But these are exciting, fast-moving times, Zach. And our stores should reflect that. The minute a customer enters Lord's, she should experience a sensual overload that gives her an immediate sense of something going on. A happening."

"I think happenings went out with the sixties."

"Don't be difficult. You know what I mean. Neon is bright and lively, and I think we ought to implement it in the Rodeo Drive store. If it works the way I think it will, we can take it nationwide."

"I'll get work started on the designs." He'd learned not to argue with Eleanor's innate sense of marketing.

"Good. While you're at it, have the design staff add some spotlights to brighten up our more special merchandise, as if they were on stage. Center stage."

"Spotlights," he murmured, jotting it down, along with a note to have the construction department ensure there would be enough capacity for the increased electrical demand. One thing they didn't need was another fire.

They were momentarily interrupted by his secretary, who arrived with the latest sales figures. Last quarter Zach had installed a much envied management information and control system that provided hourly updates on sales and inventory in every department of every store in the country.

Such a state-of-the-art computer system allowed Lord's buyers to recognize both the dogs and the hot sellers quickly. It also revealed regional trends; what sold well in Dallas or Los Angeles didn't necessarily work in Peoria or Buffalo.

He gave a copy of the report to Eleanor, keeping one for himself. "Debord's sales are still slipping," he pointed out unnecessarily.

"I know." Eleanor's lips drew down in a frown. It was not often she made a judgment in error. But when she did she characteristically made a quick correction. "Do you happen to know what it would cost us to buy out the last year of his contract?"

Zach had anticipated that question.

"You're always one step ahead of me," she complained when he answered quickly off the top of his head. In truth, she wanted it no other way. "I don't understand what happened," she mused. "The line we saw in Paris, when we signed him to that contract, was wonderfully energetic. I thought it would leap out of the stores."

"Which it did. First-quarter sales were unprecedented."

"And have been going downhill ever since. Just like his fashions. Oh, well." She shook her bright head. "We'll just pay the man off and be done with it."

"You know," Zach said, "although I'll agree with you that his designs lack something, it isn't completely Debord's fault. All the designer lines, as well as the store brand names in other chains, have experienced slippage this past year."

"I know. I've been giving that some thought and have decided that clothing has become so ubiquitous that we department stores are living our own version of every chic woman's private nightmare. Every store in every mall in every city has the exact same clothes....

"We need something new. A look that says, Only Available Here."

Zach's attention had wandered again, across the sculpture garden, over the landscaped plaza, to Alex. "I suppose you have something in mind," he murmured absently.

"You know me so well." Eleanor sat back in her chair, crossed her legs and said, "Here's my plan."

Her next words, spoken in that brook-no-argument tone he'd learned to respect, brought Zach back to reality with a resounding crash.

Alex was sitting on the porch of her rented home in Venice, watching the waves roll relentlessly onto the packed sand. The sun had sliced its way through the smog, splintering the sky with shafts of pure gold. The clarity of the light intensified the landscape, making the water sparkle like crystal beneath the gleaming sapphire sky.

Like so many residents of the City of Angels, Alex knew she was guilty of taking the benevolent weather for granted. It took mornings like this to make one stop and bask in the pure glory of California sunshine.

Unfortunately she was not to be given that luxury today. Because in a few short hours she was scheduled to have lunch with Eleanor Lord. And Zachary Deveraux.

Six days had passed since she'd encountered Zach at Eleanor's fund-raising party. Six long days and six equally long and restless nights. In trying to keep up with Sophie's demands that "Blue Bayou" remain the glitziest, most dazzling show on television, along with struggling to live up to her own design reputation, which seemed to be ballooning into the stratosphere since the Emmy, Alex's work required her undivided attention.

So why the hell couldn't she stop thinking about Zach?

Although she'd fought it, he'd infiltrated her thoughts. Which she must not allow! A lifetime of experience had taught her that everything was transitory—here today, gone tomorrow. Homes, schools, work, relationships.

Nothing was forever.

Especially relationships.

With a sigh, she went back into the house. She stood under the shower, head back, allowing the water to sluice over her, willing it to dampen her desire for a man she had no business thinking about.

He was married, for God's sake, she reminded herself firmly as she rubbed herself dry with enough vigor to practically scrape away a layer of skin. And she'd seen enough women badly burned by unhappy experiences with married men to vow that she'd never make that mistake herself. Even if the man in question caused her pulse to jump with a single glance, or her heart to turn somersaults with a mere touch.

The company dining room in the Lord's Century City office complex was, as Alex would have expected, exquisitely decorated. Dove gray silk walls blended quietly with the soft blue sky outside the tall windows, which wrapped the room in nonstop views.

Rosewood gleamed, glazed pale pewter tile glimmered underfoot. Oriental vases claimed space in arched wall niches, while special-effects lighting illuminated priceless Impressionist paintings.

Although she'd been nervous about this meeting, Alex tried to relax as Eleanor greeted her warmly and congratulated her again on her Emmy, then complimented her work, the dress she'd worn to the party, the outfit she'd chosen to wear today.

Other than greeting her politely, Zach remained silent. But as she exchanged preluncheon small talk with the department store owner, Alex was all too aware of him leaning back in his chair, his nonchalant pose doing nothing to soften his innate power.

The lunch, a fresh Alaska king crab and shrimp salad topped with raspberry vinaigrette and served by a blue-suited butler, was a superb example of California cuisine. The polite conversation continued over lunch as they discussed the weather, the Lakers and, of course, "Blue Bayou," the plot line of which Alex knew, but could not reveal.

And still Alex had no idea why she'd been invited here today.

The plates were cleared. Finally, after a dessert of pears poached in California champagne, Eleanor said, "I have a proposition for you, Alexandra."

"A proposition?"

"I'd like you to adapt your glamorous television designs for Lord's ready-to-wear market."

The Limoges cup filled with coffee was halfway to her lips. Alex slowly lowered it back to the table. "Like your Lady Lord's line?"

"Not at all," Eleanor corrected quickly. "Actually, I always had my personal doubts about Lady Lord's. The only reason we initiated the line was it seemed like a good idea at the time. After all, everyone else was establishing private-label clothes. But there was a problem we didn't foresee."

"The latest focus-group study revealed customers view private labels as knockoffs," Zach said, entering the conversation. "Which was Eleanor's concern all along," he added, giving credence to his employer's instincts.

"Actually, the report said customers perceive private labels as the kind of frumpy, cheap stuff you'd see on the first floor," Eleanor revealed. "Store brands are, unfortunately, viewed as the bottom of the line. Which is definitely not where we would position your designs.

"We'd insist on exclusivity, of course. But we are willing to pay for that privilege." The figure she suggested was higher than the deal Debord had reportedly cut with the chain. "And, naturally, we would work out a generous commission schedule," Eleanor tacked on matter-of-factly.

Alex was, quite literally, stunned. The idea was intriguing, the money being offered staggering. But the deal also came with a definite downside. And that was that if she agreed, she would undoubtedly be forced into frequent contact with the very man she'd vowed to stay away from.

That brought up another even more unpalatable thought. What if this had been all Zach's idea? What if he was willing to spend Lord's money to force her into an intimate relationship?

Eleanor misunderstood Alex's hesitation. "I realize that couture gets all the headlines. But perhaps you've heard of something Prince Matchabelli once said: 'When customers come to you in Rolls-Royces, you go home on the subway—'"

"When customers come to you on the subway, you go home in a Rolls-Royce," Alex filled in the rest of the quote. She shot Zach a sharp look, earning only a bland one in return.

"Exactly." Eleanor smiled her approval. "Besides," she said, "you wouldn't be designing clothing for K Mart, Alexandra. Lord's is decidedly upscale. And as I was telling Zach just the other day, with all the department store chains now carrying the same designers, fashion has grown boring.

"It will give Lord's extra clout to have its own line. You've a remarkable gift, Alexandra, dear. Together we could bring that gift to women all across America."

"How would it be displayed?" Alex asked, intrigued in spite of herself.

"Oh, I'm so glad you asked that question."

Eleanor reached into the leather-bound portfolio on the chair beside her and pulled out a series of sketches, which she handed across the table to Alex. "I took the liberty of commissioning these specifically for this meeting."

Alex stared in wonder at the dazzling artist's renderings of an in-store boutique featuring the Alexandra Lyons Blue Bayou collection. Exclusively at Lord's.

The drawings were incredibly detailed, making Alex wonder if Eleanor always worked at such warp speed. She glanced at Zach, who merely shrugged, revealing his own surprise with the artwork.

"I've always wanted to have my name up in lights," Alex murmured, half in truth, half in jest.

"Blue neon," Eleanor agreed robustly. "And now I think it's time to relinquish the floor to Lord's brilliant president."

Zach pushed himself to his feet, trying, as he had been for the past hour, to keep focused on the conversation at hand. Ever since Alex had arrived, bright and brazen in a red blazer and sinfully short, pleated white skirt that made her look like a nubile cheerleader he'd been fighting a losing battle to keep his mind on work.

"'Blue Bayou' is the number-one show in the world," he said, telling Alex nothing she didn't already know. "Our research shows that an extraordinary number of women want an opportunity to wear your glamorous Hollywood fashions. And men want to buy the intimate apparel for their wives or lovers."

"The studio does receive a lot of mail from fans," Alex agreed. She wondered if Zach's research had also revealed the transvestites and professional female impersonators who'd professed a desire to own the sexy fashions.

He pulled out a stack of colorful computer-generated charts depicting wholesale and retail costs of producing the line, the estimated potential sales, profit, loss, her share, until her head was whirling with numbers, which made it even more difficult to keep her mind on business.

Because try as she might, and as irritated as she was at him, as Alex watched Zach pointing out the various statistics, she kept focusing on his strong dark hands rather than the numbers depicted, remembering with vivid, painful detail how they had been capable of creating such warmth. Such pleasure. Such deep and aching need.

"I'm overwhelmed," she said quietly.

Eleanor would've had to be deaf to miss the hesitation in Alex's tone. "But?" she coaxed.

"I'm not certain my contract allows me to enter into outside agreements."

"Your contract with Friedman Television Production Company gives you sole ownership of your designs," Zach assured her. "There's no conflict."

Alex was not surprised that Zach would know the details of her two-page contract with Sophie. He would not have invited her to this business meeting *without* knowing.

"I'm sure your producer would enjoy the additional promotion for her program," Eleanor said.

Alex knew she was being offered a once-in-a-lifetime opportunity. She wanted the chance so badly she could taste it. But she was worried about her unruly feelings for Zachary, and angry that he'd manipulated her into this uncomfortable situation in the first place.

"I'd like to give you a decision, but my horoscope said I shouldn't enter into any business agreements until Jupiter aligns with Mars."

"When will that be?" Impatience surrounded Eleanor like a shimmering life force.

"I don't know," Alex said, regretting the flippant answer the moment it left her lips. "I'm sorry, I was just kidding. I never read my horoscope." Actually she did. But she only chose to believe the positive messages. "But I would like a few days to think it over."

"How many days?" Eleanor's earlier restraint began to slip.

Zach put a calming hand on the older woman's arm. "Take all the time you need," he told Alex.

After promising Eleanor that she would make her decision within the next few days, Alex left the suite of offices, relieved when Zach allowed her to walk away without a word.

She was in the parking garage, congratulating herself on escaping without incident, when he caught up with her.

"Go away." Alex marched toward her Porsche, her heels clattering on the concrete floor.

"You're angry at me," he diagnosed.

She spun around, her color rising. "You're damn right I am!"

Zach wasn't all that bothered by her flare of temper. An angry woman was not an indifferent one. Although he would have preferred some other response—such as her throwing herself into his arms—at this point he was willing to take whatever he could get.

"I hadn't realized you'd consider the chance to have your name become a household word an insult."

"It's not the offer. It's the way you manipulated things just to throw us together again that I'm furious about."

He rocked back on his heels and regarded her, his eyes shuttered. "I'm not in the habit of manipulating women into my bed. Nor have I ever paid for a woman's favors. The offer is only for your work, Alex. Not your body."

"Are you saying this wasn't your idea?"

"Actually, I argued against it."

That statement, calmly spoken and so obviously the truth, took some of the wind out of her sails. "Don't you like my work?"

"Why do I get the feeling I'm in a no-win conversation?" Alex could hear the dry humor in his voice.

"Beats me," she retorted, refusing to let him see he'd hurt her feelings. When she turned to walk away, he caught hold of her hand.

"Alex." It was just her name. But uttered with such depth of emotion it had the power to stop her in her tracks.

She shook her head. "I have to go."

"I know." He stroked the back of her hand, leaving an unsettling trail of heat in its path.

Their gazes met and held. And Alex felt a strange little jolt in her heart.

"I'm sorry you thought I was trying to manipulate you."

She shrugged and tried to look away. But she couldn't. "I shouldn't have jumped to conclusions."

"Would it make you feel any better if I told you I'm very impressed with your talent? And that if you were any other designer, any other woman, I would have been beating your door down trying to get your signature on the dotted line?"

They were standing a discreet distance apart, linked by eyes and hands. "It should," she admitted quietly.

"But it doesn't." They were courting disaster. Even knowing that, Zach could not let go of her hand.

"I really ought to leave."

"Not yet." He drew her closer.

"We can't do this," she insisted shakily. It was only a whisper, but easily heard in the cavernous stillness of subterranean garage.

"You know that." He lifted her hand to his lips. "And I know that."

He observed her solemnly, almost sadly, over the top of their linked hands. "So do you want to tell me why the idea feels so right?"

There were reasons. Alex knew there had to be reasons—hundreds of them, thousands, millions of logical, sensible reasons. But heaven help her, with his lips burning her hand and his eyes looking so deeply into hers, as if he could see all the way to her soul, she couldn't think of a single one. "Zach—"

"I love the way you say my name." The thumb of his free hand brushed against her lips, his touch as light as goose down. "Say it again."

"I can't." She pulled her hand away and was appalled to realize she was trembling. Her mind was turning cartwheels; it was a struggle to think straight.

"I have a picture of you. Of us."

"You do?" She had her own pictures, of course. Hundreds of them. Wonderful, romantic, sexy portraits, all in her mind, popping up at the most inopportune times to torment her.

"It's a snapshot taken by one of my brothers-in-law at the wedding. I keep it in my wallet." When she backed away, running up against the driver's door of the red Porsche, Zach moved toward her, closing the distance once more between them.

"We're dancing." He stroked her hair. "There's not a day that goes by that I don't take it out and look at it and think of how right you look, how right you felt, in my arms."

Alex longed for Zach's touch. His kiss. She ached for him. What she craved was wrong, forbidden, and a mortal sin in probably every major religion of the world.

She knew that. But she couldn't help herself.

The need to touch him was overpowering. Just an innocent touch. What could it hurt?

She lifted her hand to his cheek. "I think about you, too. Far too often," she admitted softly. To herself she admitted there was nothing innocent about what was happening here.

"Ah, Alex." He closed his eyes, as if the touch of her fingertips was just the balm he needed. "Do you have any idea—"

"Yes." She pressed her fingertips against his lips, cutting off the words. It was as if once he said the words out loud, once he told her how much he wanted to make love with her, she would be helpless to prevent it. "I do."

She bit her lip and wished her mother had not brought her up to feel responsible for the consequences of her own behavior. "But we can't."

"I know." Zach cursed softly. "And that's what makes this all so damn hard." He took in a deep, shuddering breath. "But I promise not to let my personal feelings stand in the way of your future.

"Eleanor's right. You're extremely talented, and the Blue Bayou collection would be a boon for our bottom line. We need you, Alex. And I think at this point in your career, you could use us, too."

"Of course I could." The opportunity would establish her as a top name in design. Like Cher's sexy television costuming did for Bob Mackie in the seventies. "But do you really think you could keep things on a business level?" she asked doubtfully. If her own feelings were anything to go by, they were sunk.

"I'll do my damnedest."

It was, she allowed, all she could ask for. If she was absolutely honest, she would have to admit it wasn't really what she wanted.

What she wanted, she realized with little surprise, was for Zach to take matters into his own hands. She wanted him to free her of all responsibility. She wanted him to drag her to the floor—all right, perhaps the back seat of the nearest car—and wildly ravish her until neither one of them could move.

But she knew that wasn't going to happen. When and if she decided to make love with Zachary Deveraux, Alex knew, she'd have to be willing to accept the consequences.

"Tell Eleanor I'll seriously consider her offer."

He studied Alex for one final, painful minute. "I will."

He stepped back, giving her room to open the car door. He stood there, silent and watchful as she fastened her seat belt and put the key in the ignition.

And then he watched her drive away.

Alex lectured herself all the way back to the "Blue Bayou" offices. He's married, she reminded herself.

Unhappily married, an argumentative little voice piped up.

That doesn't matter. Unhappily married is still married.

Everyone knows his wife fools around. Since meeting Zach, Alex had developed an almost unhealthy obsession with jet-set gossip. Especially that concerning Miranda Deveraux.

So, if everyone jumped off the roof, she remembered her mother saying, that wouldn't give you permission to jump off, too.

Lord, when had she become so willing to justify bad behavior?

When she'd fallen in love with a married man.

The bottom line was that Zachary Deveraux was married. And that made him off-limits.

Sophie was, unsurprisingly, ecstatic. "This is absolutely fantastic! The high-profile visibility Eleanor Lord is offering will definitely translate into big bucks at syndication time." Watching Sophie's smile, Alex could practically see the dollar signs dancing in her head.

"Not to mention your designs being sold in every major city in the country. My God, girl, do you know what this means?"

"Of course," Alex murmured. Her sketch pad was covered with lopsided stars, proof of her inability to concentrate these days.

Sophie's hands were splayed on her silk-draped hips. "As long as I've known you, I've never seen you as indecisive as you've been these past couple of weeks. First you didn't want to go to Eleanor Lord's party, and now you're hesitating about working with her. What do you have against the woman?"

"Nothing at all," Alex answered honestly, switching to rectangles.

"It's a very good opportunity, Alex."

"It's a terrific opportunity," Alex agreed.

"So what the hell is the problem?"

"I don't know." Not wanting to discuss anything so personal as her feelings for Zach, even with this woman who was both friend and benefactress, Alex laughed off her indecision.

One week later, still worried she was stepping into quicksand, she picked up the telephone.

"I've made a decision."

Her answer shouldn't mean so damn much, Zach told himself. It shouldn't. But it did.

"I'm glad to hear that," he replied mildly.

How was it that even his voice, coming across the wires, could create that now familiar, enervating flood of desire? What was she doing?

She should hang up. Now! Before she found herself in very hot water. Over her head.

She took a deep breath.

"You can draw up the papers."

Chapter Seventeen

The Irish pub, located in, of all places, Pasadena, would definitely not have been Miranda's first choice for an intimate rendezvous. The single thing the out-of-the-way watering hole had going for it, she decided, was that she did not have to worry about running into anyone she knew.

Or more importantly, anyone who knew Zach.

She was on her second martini when the man she'd been waiting for finally showed up.

"You're late."

Mickey O'Rourke shrugged uncaringly as he waved to a pair of uniformed cops seated nearby. From what she'd already determined during her irritating wait, the Hibernian watering hole was a favorite with the police. "Something came up."

She frowned at him over the rim of the iced glass. When he sat down across the table, she caught the unmistakable scent of cheap drugstore cologne. "If you must meet me reeking of other women, I would prefer you find a bedmate with better taste in perfume."

He grinned unrepentantly. "Don't tell me you're jealous."

"Hardly."

The grin widened, a cocky flash of white in his freckled face. He tilted the wooden chair on its back legs and laced his fingers behind his head. The gesture, which she had no doubt was meant to impress, caused his biceps to swell against the sleeves of his navy blue polo shirt.

"You sure about that?" Lines crinkled outward from his boyish blue eyes.

"Absolutely. I was merely pointing out that I am not paying you two hundred dollars a day—"

"Two hundred dollars a day, plus expenses," he reminded her helpfully.

"Plus expenses," she agreed, "to waste time screwing."

"Could have fooled me." He lowered the chair to all four legs again and leaned across the small wooden table toward Miranda. "My balls still ache from our marathon fuckarama in Bungalow Five of the Beverly Hills Hotel last week."

"Must you be so crude?"

"Don't get up on your high horse with me, sweetheart." He ran his hand up her leg beneath the table. His thick square fingers slipped beneath her emerald silk skirt, exploring the soft skin above her stocking top. "I remember you liking it crude." His fingers tightened. "And hard.

"In fact, how about you and I moving this meeting somewhere else. Somewhere more private."

Mickey O'Rourke was everything Miranda despised. He was uneducated, horridly common and, thanks to an unfortunate habit of playing the ponies at Santa Anita racetrack, he was also, despite his hefty fees, always skating on the brink of poverty.

She had no doubt that while her civilized ancestors had been drinking tea and playing polo, his people had amused themselves by painting their naked bodies blue and leaping out of trees.

He showed her no respect. Not in their business meetings or in bed. But, she allowed, the man was hung like a Brahma bull and could keep it up all night. He also had access to something she wanted. Something that made her willing to hang around places like this waiting for him to show up.

"What have you discovered?"

"I'll give you the rundown in a minute. Soon as I get a drink." He signaled the bartender, calling out an order for something called a Black Marble.

"Okay. The information your husband's private cop came up with checks out," he revealed, proving finally that he could, when required, get down to business. "Alex Lyons was born in Raleigh. She had a twin brother who was killed when he was still a kid. There's no record of any father."

"I already know that," Miranda said on a frustrated huff of breath.

"Yeah, but did you know that the mother seemed to have an incurable case of wanderlust?"

Damn. Miranda wondered if O'Rourke was going to turn out to be a waste of money, after all. "The papers I found in my husband's home safe reveal that the family moved a great deal."

"Every year, like clockwork," he agreed. The waitress delivered his drink to the table. He took a taste and nodded his satisfaction.

"You know, Wambaugh invented this drink," he informed Miranda. "Stolichnaya on the rocks with an orange peel and a black olive."

"It sounds absolutely delightful." Her acid tone said otherwise. "Who is Wambaugh?"

"Joseph Wambaugh. The writer," he elaborated at her blank look. "He used to be a cop. Now he writes books about cops."

"Ah. A kindred spirit." Her voice was tinged with sarcasm, letting him know she was fully aware that he'd been dismissed from the LAPD for various infractions, among them allegations of illegal gambling and citizen complaints of police brutality.

His open Irish face closed up. Storm clouds gathered in his blue eyes, reminding Miranda that despite his seeming Celtic charm, O'Rourke could be a very dangerous man. "Christ, you can be a bitch."

"True enough." She took another sip of her martini. Her green eyes turned as frosty as the Beefeater gin. "But let us not forget that I happen to be a very wealthy bitch. Who has thus far paid you a great deal of money for nothing."

"Not exactly for nothing. What would you say if I told you that the Lyons family happened to move hearth and home each spring?"

"Spring?"

"April to be exact." He leaned back in the chair, took another drink and waited.

It did not take long for comprehension to click in. "That's the anniversary of the murders and kidnapping. It's also the same month Eleanor runs her annual newspaper advertisements seeking information concerning Anna."

"Bingo. Interesting coincidence, isn't it?"

"But not proof."

"True enough. But it's a start."

"Yes." She sipped thoughtfully.

"You know, if this Lyons chick does turn out to be Anna Lord, it wouldn't be that difficult to arrange an accident."

"An accident?" The idea, which she honestly hadn't considered, proved surprisingly appealing. "Surely that would be extremely dangerous."

He shrugged again. His shoulders, thickly muscled from daily workouts at Gold's Gym, strained the shirt seams. "Not really." He lifted his glass in a pantomimed farewell to the cops as they left the pub to return to their black-and-white cruiser parked outside.

"Don't forget," rogue cop Mickey O'Rourke reminded Miranda, "I've got a lot of friends in high places."

Miranda toyed with the green plastic toothpick from her drink as she thought about Eleanor Lord's will leaving the bulk of her vast empire to Anna. She thought about the irritating design deal Eleanor had offered Alexandra Lyons.

Then she thought about the way Zachary had been looking at Alex the night of Eleanor's party. From his intense expression, she'd suspected the pair had not been discussing business.

Whether or not Alex Lyons was, indeed, Anna Lord, Miranda realized that the woman still represented a very real threat.

"Let's cross that unsavory little bridge when we come to it," she advised. "In the meantime, I've something else I want you to do."

Reaching into her handbag, she pulled out a photograph. The candid snapshot of Zach had been taken on Ipanema Beach during their honeymoon. Before that unfortunate little episode in the Mesbla store. He was wearing the brief black European swimsuit she'd had to coax him into. His hair was ruffled by the ocean breezes and he was smiling into the camera lens. That was, Miranda considered, the last time she could recall Zach smiling at her.

"This is a photograph of my husband."

O'Rourke nodded in recognition. "Zachary Deveraux. The department-store honcho."

"Yes. I wish to know every time he and Alexandra Lyons are together."

"You got it." He took the snapshot and slipped it into his shirt pocket. "How much coverage do you want? We can do bugs in both their offices and the broad's home, photo stakeouts, around-the-clock surveillance—"

"I want, as you investigator types put it, the works."

"Gonna be expensive."

"I've always believed one gets what one pays for."

"A lady after my own heart." He tossed back his drink, popped the fat black olive into his mouth and slipped his clever hand beneath the table again. "Is this meeting over?"

A familiar warmth that had nothing to do with the two martinis she'd drunk began to flow through Miranda's bloodstream. "I believe so."

"Good." He snapped her garter. "What would you say to a little afternoon delight?"

She'd been planning a brief trip to Saks. A few days ago, while comparison checking their couture lines, she'd seen a silk Chanel scarf she'd found particularly appealing. Miranda weighed the equally attractive choices; both shoplifting and sex always gave her a rush. Then, remembering that long, lust-filled afternoon at the Beverly Hills Hotel last week, she made her decision.

"It will have to be off the clock." She absolutely refused to pay for what was so readily available for free. "You're good, Mr. O'Rourke. But not that good."

"Why don't you withhold judgment on that?" The rogue grin was back. "Until you've seen what I can do with my handcuffs."

That idea, Miranda admitted privately as they left the pub, had definite possibilities.

Chapter Eighteen

With "Blue Bayou" on hiatus and Eleanor's optimistic and energetic plan to launch the retail line in a mere six months, Alex turned all her attention to creating her retail designs.

She was not working in a vacuum. In order to work with Alex on the design concept—and to observe her closely—Eleanor began to spend more and more time in Los Angeles, staying at her bungalow at the Beverly Hills Hotel. Worried that perhaps she'd bitten off a bit more than she could comfortably chew, Alex found the canny retailer's assistance invaluable.

As the first television product licensing venture ever aimed at upper-middle-class adults, the Alexandra Lyons Blue Bayou collection was staking out new retailing territory. The trick was adapting Alex's ultraglamorous costumes into equally alluring, reasonably affordable clothing.

Remembering what Debord had said about knowing exactly who you were designing for before she put pencil to sketch pad, Alex spent hours staking out Lord's stores to get a true fix on her clientele. The quintessential Lord's woman, she determined, was a woman with charm and sophistication and beauty. She was intelligent and successful and as a rule preferred sensual, rather than overtly sexy, clothing.

It was decided from the start that Alex's clothes would not bear any outer labels linking them with the popular television program. After all, Eleanor pointed out succinctly, a Lord's customer was independent and self-confident. She would never purchase anything that might label her as a fashion victim.

"As you can see, I modified certain outfits," Alex explained during a meeting with Eleanor in Zach's vast corner office. She'd been relieved to learn Zach wouldn't be sitting in on the design portion of the meeting. "What works on television doesn't always translate into real life."

Eleanor nodded thoughtfully, comparing the actual still photographs of the actresses wearing the various dresses and suits during taping and the colorful sketches depicting Alex's adaptations.

"That's true," she agreed with a regretful little sigh that suggested her retail marketing sense was warring with her feminine side. "Most women aren't going to put on big, veiled hats to go to the market or the office. More's the pity," she murmured as her gaze lingered a long time on an ultraglamorous, but oh, so huge red hat draped in black flowered lace.

"Oh, I like this." She held up a sketch of a pastel pink gingham dress with a full, gathered skirt. The model in the drawing was holding a prim little handbag and sporting a beribboned straw boater. "It reminds me of Leslie Caron in *Gigi*, with a touch of Brigitte Bardot in *Babette Goes to War*."

"That's the idea," Alex admitted with a quick, only slightly sheepish grin. "Those films were on late-night cable back-to-back the night I was trying to come up with a design for Tiffany to wear back home to the bayou for her sister's wedding.''

Sophie had devised that plot twist after Alex, needing to talk about Zach with someone, had told her about that long ago day.

"The day she got pregnant with her old high-school sweetheart's baby," Eleanor remembered. "Gracious, that was a hot scene! The night Clara and I watched that episode, I half expected their lovemaking to set off the smoke detector."

She grinned and fanned herself dramatically with the sketch; for not the first time since they'd begun working together, Alex found it difficult to believe that Eleanor was actually in her seventies. Her appearance, along with her unwavering zest for life, made her seem decades younger.

"The contrast between that sexy scene and that sweet fifties-style dress was brilliant," Eleanor said, unstinting as always with her praise.

Alex returned the warm smile. "Thanks."

At the time, Sophie had worried that the dress wasn't as blatantly obvious as the rest of Tiffany's wardrobe. But Alex had argued that the exaggeratedly innocent gingham would work. And it had, better than she could have hoped.

"The Tiffany wardrobe is certainly different from what we usually feature at Lord's," Eleanor mused, flipping through the sketches for the umpteenth time.

Eleanor's careful study of the sketches reminded Alex of the time Debord had first examined her portfolio. Back then, she'd felt certain she would die from anxiety. Now she had more confidence, and while she admittedly worried that the older woman might reject her suggested designs, she knew such a rejection was not the end of the world.

"It is a slightly younger look," Alex said carefully.

She'd been worried about that ever since Zach's demographics had revealed the average Lord's charge-card customer was nearly a decade older than the Bourbon Street stripper character. But conversely, letters from younger viewers made up a large proportion of "Blue Bayou's" fan mail.

And although she'd never claim to be a retailer, from a purely practical viewpoint, Alex thought it foolish to ignore such sales potential.

"Definitely younger," Eleanor agreed. Her gaze lingered on a blue-and-green plaid pleated skirt and white blouse reminiscent of a Catholic school uniform. The only difference was that the skirt was scandalously short and shot with gleaming gold threads, and the blouse was created from diaphanous silk organza. *Schoolgirl sex.*

"What you've done is wonderful, Alex. It's about time Lord's had an infusion of new blood."

As she dug into her portfolio for the lingerie collection, Alex released a breath she'd been unaware of holding.

"I realize that marketing really isn't my field," Alex said, distracted momentarily by Zach's arrival. Knowing he kept a very close eye—and an equally tight fist—on the Lord's bankbook, Alex had been expecting him.

Today they were going to discuss factories, and she had a very good idea that she and Zachary Deveraux were about to have their first serious disagreement.

"But," she continued, returning her attention to Eleanor, "an idea occurred to me I want to share with you."

"What idea is that?"

"I thought you might want to consider having actual customers appear in some of the print advertising."

"Like those mink ads?"

"Exactly. Except they always use famous faces. I thought it might be fun to show that any woman can be a star wearing clothing from the Blue Bayou collection."

A curtain of silence settled over the room. Alex could practically see the wheels turning inside Eleanor's head.

"I love it." She clapped her hands together and gave Alex a look that reminded her of the gold stars teachers used to put on her papers. "You definitely have a flair for retailing."

A genetic flare, Eleanor decided, exchanging a brief, I-told-you-so look with Zach.

Alex grinned, enjoying the praise and the moment. She'd been admittedly nervous about working with Eleanor. And not only because the job would entail seeing Zach on a regular basis. Stories regarding the elderly retailer's impatient, often curt tongue and short temper were legion; independently minded herself, Alex had worried that she and Eleanor Lord might clash on a regular basis.

But instead, they worked flawlessly together. For two women of different generations, raised in such disparate life-styles, she and Eleanor were, Alex had discovered to her surprise, remarkably alike.

As much as Alex enjoyed her work for Lord's, she quickly discovered she'd been right to worry about working so closely with Zach. The truth, as much as she tried to deny it to Sophie, as much as she wished it otherwise, was that she possessed a burning passion for a man she was forced to work with, a man she could only see in public, a man she didn't dare permit herself to be alone with anywhere but in his office.

And even there they tended to keep the door open by mutual unspoken agreement, making Marge, his secretary, or better yet, Eleanor, their chaperone. And on the rare occasion they did find themselves alone, they maintained an inviolate border between personal and business conversations.

"The important thing is to find a factory that will give us low labor costs and efficient delivery," Zach began without preamble when Eleanor turned the meeting over to him.

"And right now, from a cost-per-unit criteria, we can get the biggest bang for our bucks in Korea."

Alex had been expecting this. She was also ready for it. "I won't allow the Alexandra Lyons collection to be manufactured by miserably underpaid women in some horrid Seoul workshop."

"*You* won't allow?" He reined in a burst of irritation that was threatening to ignite a temper he thought he'd put away when he'd donned his expensive Brooks Brothers suits.

"That's right."

Alex folded her arms and turned her gaze to the oil painting on the wall depicting Zach with his parents, sisters and grandmother working the family sugarcane farm. She remembered him telling her how it reminded him of his roots.

"And quite honestly, knowing your background," she added, "I'm amazed that you'd consider exploiting the less fortunate."

Eleanor, watching the exchange with interest, made a slight sound that could have been a cough. Or a smothered laugh.

"I fail to see where giving impoverished citizens honest employment is exploiting the less fortunate."

"Did you actually visit any of those so-called factories?"

Zach had the grace to flush. Alex watched the color rise from his white shirt collar and felt a flicker of hope.

"They're not that bad," he argued. But his voice lacked conviction.

"Not that bad?" She raised her voice, realizing immediately she'd taken the wrong tack when his ebony brows came crashing down toward those midnight dark eyes. "Zach." She lowered her voice. *Patience*. "They're horrible."

"I suppose you've been there?" His normally mild tone was edged with a sarcasm she was unaccustomed to hearing from this man.

"Actually, I have. When I was working on Seventh Avenue, one of the foreign reps had a heart attack, so I was sent in his place."

A cloud moved across her face at the memory of those vile, dark workrooms redolent with the stench of sweat and *kimchi,* where half-naked laborers toiled eighty or more hours a week for a miserly wage.

"The first one I saw had some unpronounceable name, but like all the others I visited, it should have been called Pandemonium."

The capital of Hell in *Paradise Lost.* It was, Zach admitted reluctantly, a deadly accurate description. He'd found the shops as unpalatable as Alex had. But despite his moral misgivings, his first loyalty was, as always, to Lord's.

"Look, Alex, I'll agree that in a perfect world, everyone would live in nice little houses with picket fences surrounding lush green lawns and spreading elm trees. But we're talking about the real world. Where life isn't always fair."

Her exquisite face, which haunted too many of both his sleeping and waking hours, had closed up. Realizing that she wasn't buying this argument, Zach decided to try another tack.

"I don't know if you're aware that The Lord's Group gives a very generous amount of its corporate profits to charity each year," he began slowly, shifting into the same lecturing mode he used when delivering the annual report to the stockholders.

"Which in turn generates a very healthy tax write-off," she countered.

"That's beside the point, dammit! Would you just let me finish?"

"Go right ahead."

"Fine." He gave her a warning look. "My point is, Lord's contributions assist a great many needy people. What moral victory would be achieved if the company went bankrupt and that money stopped flowing into charitable coffers?"

"Lord, talk about false justification," Alex muttered. "If you truly believe that, Zachary, I'm amazed you get any sleep at night. But since you seem to only understand the bottom line, Mr. President, let me spell things out for you in black and white. In case you've forgotten, my contract with Lord's gives me manufacturing approval."

"I recall that clause." All too well. He'd argued against it, but Eleanor, damn her, had been immovable.

"Fine. Then I'm only going to say this once. Any clothing line with my name on it will not be manufactured in South Korea. Or Taiwan, or Indonesia or Mexico. The clothing will be made here, in the United States, by American workers."

"You sound like a campaign speech," he muttered.

"And you sound like an apologist for Big Business. That's my bottom line, Zach. Take it or leave it. But let me warn you, if you don't agree, I'll take my designs and go home."

"Oh, we wouldn't want you to do that," Eleanor insisted quickly, finally entering into the argument. "Surely we can come up with some compromise."

"There's a garment factory in Brooklyn," Alex said, reaching into her portfolio and taking out a business card, which she held out to Zach. "I've done business with them before. They're efficient, relatively inexpensive, and they don't treat their workers like indentured servants."

There was no point in arguing any longer, Zach decided. He'd investigate Alex's damn factory, and if it wasn't competitive, he was just going to have to make her see the light.

After all, she wasn't designing clothes for her dolls any longer. Or her mother. This was business. Pure and simple.

He plucked the card from her fingers. "I'll check it out."

She gave him a sweet smile that was only slightly tinged with sarcasm. "Thank you. I'd appreciate that."

"So, have you decided where you're going to debut the collection?" Zach asked Eleanor.

Eleanor frowned. She'd been worrying about that exact question for weeks. "I suppose the Rodeo Drive store would be the most obvious."

"But you've never been one to settle for the obvious," Zach said with a slow, intimate smile that, although focused on Eleanor, managed to warm Alex, who was seated across the small round table from him, to the core.

She dug her nails into her palms, denying the need to reach across that space and touch her hand to his cheek.

"That's what keeps Lord's on top," Eleanor agreed. "There's always Manhattan. We'd ensure a great deal of fashion press that way." Her lack of enthusiasm showed in her flat tone.

"May I make a suggestion?" Zach asked.

"Of course."

"How about Chicago?"

"Chicago?"

"We're opening a new store there next quarter," he reminded her unnecessarily. "It wouldn't be a bad place to showcase the Alexandra Lyons collection."

"Like we did with Debord in New Orleans."

"Like New Orleans," Zach echoed, his words directed toward Eleanor, but his dark eyes on Alex.

Eleanor, caught up in the logistics of Zach's suggestion, failed to notice that her two favorite people had become snared in the silvery strands of an emotionally sticky web.

Zach watched the shared memories shimmer in Alex's remarkable amber eyes. He saw her full lips part ever so slightly, as if she were remembering that night of desperate kisses.

"That's an excellent idea, Zachary." Eleanor's voice shattered the thick tension strung between Zach and Alex. "Women in Los Angeles and Manhattan have grown horribly blasé. What we need is the excitement a wildly enthusiastic Chicago audience can bring to Alex's marvelous clothing."

Alex shook off her lingering desire, as well as the guilt she always experienced when she found herself wishing for a life with Zach, and allowed herself to be swept up by Eleanor's enthusiasm.

"I have another idea," she suggested, as if the thought had just occurred to her. "Along with the professional models, what would you say to having the actual actresses from 'Blue Bayou' take part in the show?"

Eleanor's eyes lighted up like a child getting her first glimpse of a Christmas tree. "That would certainly add Hollywood pizzazz to an already glamorous collection. But do you think Sophie Friedman would agree?"

"In a minute." Alex laughed, thinking of how Sophie's calculator brain had begun clicking away the dollars of free publicity when she'd suggested the idea to the producer over Cobb salads at the Bistro Garden yesterday.

Alex's clear laughter reminded Zach of summer sunshine on an Alpine lake. Desire stirred in him, as unwelcome as distant rumbles signaling a thunderstorm and just as impossible to fend off.

Chapter Nineteen

Moonlight streamed into the room. Candlelight glowed, creating flickering shadows on the wall. A bed, draped in a canopy of gauze netting, dominated the room. A couple lay atop satin sheets, arms and legs entangled. The woman was clad in a clinging white slip. The man was wearing a pair of jeans. His muscled chest was bare.

"You are so beautiful." There was reverent awe in his tone as his hand moved up her thigh, slipping beneath the hem of the slip. "I've been going crazy thinking about you. About us."

The woman smiled, pleased with her feminine power. "Ah've been thinkin' about you, too, sugah." She rolled over on top of him, fitting her lush curves to his hard male angles.

His hands cupped her buttocks, holding her hard against him. "Even while you're making love to you husband?"

"*Especially* while Ah'm makin' love to my husband," she promised on a silvery laugh.

"Cut!" The director's voice shattered the sensual moment. "Dammit, Mary Beth, I'm still seeing panty lines."

"I am not taking off my underwear," the actress countered. "That's the kind of stuff that gets into the *Enquirer.*"

"I doubt Tiffany would even wear panties," Stone Michaels suggested helpfully.

Mary Beth Olson turned on him. "You're just trying to figure out a way to get me naked."

"Not me!" The handsome actor held up his hands and glanced toward the control booth, where his bride of six weeks sat following the action on the script she'd fine-tuned just the night before. Since beginning his relationship with Brenda, the show's head writer, Stone's part had, as Alex had predicted, grown considerably.

But he hadn't needed to marry to ensure fame. Not when the show's female audience found him the ultimate hunk. *People* magazine had recently voted him the sexiest man alive, and Helen Gurley Brown was talking to his agent about a *Cosmopolitan* centerfold.

"Why don't we put Mary Beth in a teddy?" Alex, who was standing on the sidelines, suggested.

"It has to be white," the director warned. "White works best with moonlight and candles."

"How about ivory?"

He rubbed his chin. "I suppose that'll do."

"I've got just the thing. I'll be right back."

"Okay, boys and girls! Lunch!" the director shouted.

"Lunch," the assistant director echoed.

Alex turned to leave the soundstage when she suddenly came face-to-face with Zach's wife. "Mrs. Deveraux?"

Miranda nodded. "Ms. Lyons."

"This is a surprise."

Miranda's sharp gaze didn't miss Alex's discomfort. "Not a pleasant one, I take it."

Alex straightened. "I'm sorry if I sounded rude. It's just that this isn't one of my better days." Although the writers stayed the same, directors changed on a regular, sometimes weekly basis.

The one they had now seemed determined to make things difficult. He'd changed the clothing cues innumerable times, keeping her running a marathon back and forth between the soundstage and the costuming department. She wasn't the only one being worn to a frazzle. Alex had heard the hairdresser threaten to do something painful and probably anatomically impossible with her curling iron after he'd had her restyle Olivia's hair three times.

"I can see you're busy," Miranda said agreeably. "So, I'll be brief and to the point." She leaned forward, placing a manicured hand on Alex's arm. Her diamond wedding band glittered. "It's about my husband."

"What about him?"

"I want you to stay away from him."

She was now so close her breath fanned Alex's cheek. Her green eyes had turned flat and cold. Alex felt a chill race up her spine. "Your husband and I work together, Mrs. Deveraux. That's all."

"Don't try to lie to me, because I know what you're up to." Animosity etched vertical furrows next to Miranda's perfectly drawn lips. "First you insinuate yourself into Eleanor's life just like all the others—"

"All the others? What—"

Miranda cut her off with a furious wave of the hand. "You've wormed your way into my aunt's life. And now you're after my husband."

Her voice was low and controlled, but Alex would have been no more shaken if Miranda had suddenly begun to rant and rave. The fury she saw on Zach's wife's face and in her eyes was more frightening than any display of temper.

Miranda's fingers tightened on Alex's arm. Her nails dug deep into Alex's flesh. "You must understand, I can make things very difficult for you. And for Zach."

Alex knew, without a shadow of a doubt, that Miranda was telling the absolute truth. "I'm not having an affair with your husband, Mrs. Deveraux," she insisted.

"See that you don't." Miranda's deadly smile reminded Alex of a shark. "Unless you wish to suffer the consequences. And believe me, dear," she said with silky menace, "the consequences of crossing me are not at all pretty."

Outraged that Miranda dared to show up at her workplace and threaten her, and concerned that the woman just might resort to physical violence, Alex was turned momentarily speechless.

Tension hummed between them, a living, breathing, thing.

"Alex? Is anything wrong?"

Alex could have kissed Sophie for interrupting.

"Nothing at all," she managed through lips that had gone as dry as dust. "Mrs. Deveraux is just leaving."

"That's right," Miranda agreed with the trademark public smile that had graced the glossy pages of *Town and Country* and *Tattler* on numerous occasions. "I'm already late for a luncheon date with my husband. And you know, Ms. Lyons, how Zachary hates to be kept waiting."

She loosened her death grip on Alex's arm. "I enjoyed our little chat, dear. We must do it again sometime soon."

"What the hell was that all about?" Sophie demanded, hands on her hips, as they watched Miranda Deveraux walk away.

Alex fought a shiver and wiped the dampness from her hands onto her poppy suede skirt. "She thinks I'm sleeping with her husband."

Sophie lifted a brow. "Did she actually threaten you?"

Alex shrugged and tried to tell herself she'd only imagined the fatal threat in Miranda's green eyes. That's what came from hanging around a soap opera all day, she decided. Life started looking like some stormy television drama.

"Not in so many words."

"Then why are you as white as new snow?" Sophie's expression was one of concern. "Perhaps you ought to talk to Zach about setting her straight."

"No." Alex released a deep breath. "I haven't done anything for her to be jealous about. And since I have no intention of having an affair with Zach everything will be okay."

But as she headed off again to retrieve the ivory satin teddy, Alex couldn't quite shake a lingering feeling of unease.

Six hours later, the taping finally completed to the satisfaction of the unrelenting, obsessive-compulsive director, Alex left the nearly deserted studio.

When she reached the Porsche, parked in her reserved spot—the spot with her name clearly stenciled on the concrete curb in bright white lettering—she found all four tires flat.

Alex was admittedly relieved when, as the weeks passed, there were no further incidents.

Immersed in the Blue Bayou collection, along with designing for the show, she worked even harder. After a run on the beach every morning, she'd settle down with a pot of coffee and her sketch pad. Lunch, when she remembered to stop and eat, was more coffee and a sandwich. Dinner often went ignored completely.

She slept little and ate less. Pounds drifted away unnoticed.

"What the hell are you doing to yourself?" Zach asked one rainy afternoon when she arrived at his office for a budget meeting.

He'd been away on a lengthy inspection tour of potential new building sites. She'd been both relieved and disappointed when nearly three weeks passed without seeing him. But now that they were finally alone Alex realized she needn't have worried about Zach trying to seduce her.

On the contrary, he was looking at her with something uncomfortably akin to horror.

"I have no idea what you're talking about." Exhaustion made her tone sharper than usual. A lingering cold she'd not been able to shake made her cough.

"When was the last time you looked in a mirror? You look like shit." Her peaches-and-cream complexion had the unhealthy pallor of paste, her unpainted lips were chalky pale, and her usually remarkable eyes were red-rimmed. Her cashmere cardigan sweater hung on her too-thin frame.

"Gee," she said in a saccharine tone, "thanks a lot. Anyone ever tell you that you're wonderful for a woman's ego?"

She ran a trembling hand over her red wool slacks. She'd worn the trousers with a matching sweater, hoping the vivid color would not only brighten the dreary day but add some color to her cheeks, as well. From Zach's disapproving words and harshly critical look, she guessed her ploy had failed.

"Didn't anyone ever tell you that the pale, consumptive look went out with Camille?"

"Wow, you *are* complimentary," she muttered. "Where's Eleanor?"

"In Santa Barbara. This lousy weather has her arthritis acting up. Averill thought she ought to stay in."

"Oh. So it's just going to be the two of us?"

"Got a problem with that?" he challenged softly.

"None at all," she lied. She thought about suggesting that his wife might, but didn't. "Let's get down to business."

As she struggled to keep her attention focused on the multitude of figures Zach kept flashing at her, Alex considered that there were times when her mind seemed every bit as foggy as the slate gray day outside the bank of floor-to-ceiling windows.

On more than one occasion lately, she'd walk into a room and forget why she was there. Or she'd dial the phone to ask Zach a question or share with him her latest idea, only to have the thought erased from her mind when his rich, deep, voice came on the line.

They'd be discussing the pricing of the Blue Bayou clothing, when her gaze would suddenly be captured by the sight of his fingers holding the sheet of lettuce-green ledger paper and all the figures would flee her mind, like dry leaves blown away by gale-force autumn winds.

But the past. Ah, Alex considered, as she found herself drowning in the glittering black depths of Zach's gaze, the past was an entirely different story! The past, most specifically her time in Louisiana with Zach, was crystal clear, sparkling with the brilliance of an alpine mountain stream.

She'd hoped time would have dulled her memories. She'd prayed she would forget how his touch made her knees weak, how his arms wrapped around her waist had felt so very right.

But despite her hopes, her prayers, her best intentions, everything about that distant, all too brief and frustratingly unconsummated romance remained etched on her rebellious mind in the same perfect detail as the facets on the Waterford crystal in the Lord's corporate dining room.

Alex's mind was spinning treacherously out of control. As she did too often these days, she found herself thinking terrible, uncharitable thoughts. She hoped for irreconcilable differences in their marriage; she wished that Miranda would run away with one of her many rumored lovers.

Sometimes, late at night, lying in her lonely bed, staring up at the ceiling, though she knew it was unforgivable, she imagined turning on the television news to hear that the Concorde had crashed over the Alps, and although the crew had survived, the sole passenger—socialite and department store heiress Miranda Lord Baptista Smythe Deveraux—had tragically died.

She pictured herself rushing to Zach's side, offering her heartfelt solace. It was then that he'd tell her what she'd longed to hear—that he'd never loved Miranda, that the only woman he'd ever loved, would ever love, was her. And then finally, blissfully, he'd draw her into his arms.

Sometimes she'd picture them making love on the beach beneath a full white moon, or in a deep marble tub filled to overflowing with frothy white bubbles. Other times she'd imagine him undressing her slowly, reverently, beside a white-draped canopy bed strewn with snowy rose petals.

Yet another fantasy had them making love in a warm Polynesian lagoon behind a thundering waterfall, while the tropical setting sun turned the water a dazzling, blinding gold. The location changed, but the words and the exhilarating feelings were always the same. Alex knew her fantasies were horribly wrong. Even sinful. But she couldn't help herself.

"Alex? Are you all right?"

Zach's deep, concerned voice made her realize that her mind had been drifting again. "I'm fine. Can we just forget about me and get back to work?"

He frowned, but having already discovered that Alex's tenacity rivaled even Eleanor's, he decided there was no point in wasting either time or her obviously depleted energy by arguing.

"I've decided to use the Brooklyn factory for production."

Such news should have made her ecstatic. All she could manage was a nod, which she regretted when the movement sent rocks tumbling around inside her head. "I'm glad," she said quietly. Too quietly, Zach thought.

"That's about all I have for today," he lied. Actually, he'd wanted to question her about going over budget again on trim for the lingerie line, but looking at her pale face, he decided any discussions about whether or not she'd really needed all those ostrich feathers could wait.

"Well, that didn't take long."

Alex didn't bother to hide her relief; she'd half expected to receive a reprimand about the gorgeous feathers she'd bought for Tiffany's negligee set. Eager to escape the office before he mentioned her little extravagance, she stood up too fast.

Her head swam; the room began to spin; little dots danced in front of her eyes.

Then the floor tilted and rushed up at her.

Chapter Twenty

Zach was at Alex's side before she reached the plush carpeting. His hands caught her upper arms and he lowered her to the chair.

"Why the hell didn't you tell my secretary you were sick when she scheduled this meeting?" he growled.

As angry as he was at Alex for her blatant disregard for her health, he was even angrier at himself for not having noticed how ill she was. "We could have postponed it until you were feeling better."

"I didn't want to postpone, because we're running out of time as it is. Besides, it's just a cold."

"Colds don't make you faint. And scheduling isn't your problem."

"I thought—"

"You think too damn much." Squatting, he placed the back of his hand against her forehead. "You've got a fever."

Her flesh was raging hot and clammy at the same time. Something alien ripped through Zach, something that felt a great deal like fear. "I'm taking you to the hospital emergency room."

"You're overreacting." Why didn't he just leave her alone? Alex tried to stand and was immediately pushed back down. "It's just a cold," she repeated. "And perhaps a bit too much work."

"How about a lot too much work? When was the last time you had a decent meal?"

"I had spaghetti last night." The noodles and tomato sauce had tasted like the cardboard box they'd come in. She'd thrown away most of the microwave meal. "And I don't want to go to any hospital."

"Tough."

"Dammit, Zach—" Her planned protest was cut off by a deep, wracking cough that went on and on.

He swore at her richly. "That's it." With a speed that caused her head to start spinning again, his fingers curved around her shoulders and he hauled her to her feet.

"Don't touch me."

"I've been trying like hell not to touch you for weeks," he retorted. "But thanks to your lack of concern for your own health, we're both just going to have to put up with it." Ignoring her hurt intake of breath, he said, "Do you think you can walk?"

"Of course." She hoped.

"Then come on." He half-carried, half-dragged her out the office door. "Call Dan Matheson at Presbyterian General," he barked uncharacteristically at his secretary. "Tell him I'm bringing in a patient."

"You don't have to call anyone," Alex countermanded, "because I'm not going to any hospital."

Zach's hold on her tightened. "Shut up." His tone was brusque and unsympathetic. To his secretary he said, "Tell Matheson we'll be there in ten minutes. Fifteen tops."

With that, Zach hauled Alex into the private elevator from his office suite.

"You can't treat me this way," she complained as he jabbed the button. "I don't work for you. In case you've forgotten, Zachary Deveraux, I'm a privately licensed contractor. That contract I signed with Lord's doesn't give you the right to interfere in my personal life."

He jerked her close against him, literally holding her on her feet. "If you don't quit wasting valuable energy talking, I'm going to have to resort to a left hook to shut you up."

"You wouldn't dare!"

Of course he wouldn't. He'd never in his entire life struck a woman. Not even Miranda, who'd certainly tempted him on enough occasions.

"I wouldn't put it to the test if I were you," he said.

They reached the underground garage. As they exited the elevator, Alex's knees sagged. Zach caught her when she stumbled and scooped her up in his arms.

"I said I could walk," she complained.

"Yeah, you were doing a real great job." He wanted to hold her close against his chest and never let go. He wanted to take care of her. And not just today, but all the days of their lives.

"I don't know what you're so mad about," she grumbled. Succumbing to the irresistible lure of his strong shoulder, she rested her head against the gray wool.

"Stupidity always makes me angry. You should be old enough to take care of yourself without a keeper."

"I've had a lot of work to do."

He managed to unlock the door of his car and deposit her in the passenger seat and buckle her seat belt. "Ever heard of delegating?"

"My name's going to be on the label." When the garage began spinning, she leaned her head against the leather seat back and closed her eyes. "If I want the clothes to be perfect, which I do, I have to take full responsibility."

"Just what the world needs. Another dead over-achiever."

"I wish you'd just leave me alone."

"That makes two of us," he snapped. "But in case you haven't been paying attention during all those meetings, The Lord's Group is investing one helluva lot of money in you, Alexandra Lyons. I'm not about to let anything happen to that investment."

"That's what all this is about? Money?"

"What the hell do you think?"

His husky growl sent a warmth flowing through her that Alex feared had nothing to do with her fever. She opened her eyes and found herself looking directly into his. "Dammit, Alex," he said, softening his demeanor and his tone, "don't argue. Not now."

He brushed her cheek with his knuckles in a slow, tender sweep she knew was meant to soothe rather than arouse, but nevertheless created a violent rush of feeling deep inside her.

Dragging her gaze from his, she glanced around the lushly appointed interior, which smelled of leather and wood. "Nice car."

"Thanks. I like it."

As a kid, he'd pored over the pages of his uncle's *Motor Trend* magazines, practically drooling over the dazzling, unaffordable cars. If anyone had ever told him he'd actually own a Jaguar like this one, he'd have wondered just what kind of cigarettes they'd been smoking.

"Looks like you'd need a pilot's license to drive it," she murmured, taking in the multitude of dials on the dash. When those dials began to dance, she leaned her head back again, closed her eyes and allowed her mind to drift as Zach drove through the wet streets.

At her insistence, he allowed her to walk into the hospital, but kept one strong arm around her for support. She was relieved when he didn't declare his intention of accompanying her into the examining room. She wasn't up to another confrontation.

"I don't believe it," she murmured an hour later when they were back in the Jag.

"Neither do I." His expression was as grim as she'd ever seen it; his stony jaw could have been chiseled from granite. "Christ, how the hell could you not notice you had pneumonia?"

"I really wish you'd quit yelling at me," she complained weakly.

"Sorry," he muttered, sounding as if he meant it.

"I thought it was just a cold." Then, in a frail voice so unlike her own usual robust one, she said, "Thank you."

He slanted her a look. "You're welcome."

Alex would have given anything to know what he was thinking, but his gaze was expertly and frustratingly shuttered. Groggy from her fever and light-headed from the injection the doctor had given her, Alex didn't question how Zach knew where she lived.

Nor did she protest when he lifted her from the passenger seat and carried her into the funky pink-and-yellow bungalow on Venice Beach, one of a handful that had managed to evade falling prey to greedy land developers' bulldozers.

Warning bells began to peal when he headed unerringly toward her bedroom, but her mind was too fogged to offer up a single word of complaint.

He sat her down on the edge of the bed. The bits and pieces of fabric and papers scattered over the puffy comforter emblazoned with wildflowers were mute testimony to the fact that she'd been working when she should have been sleeping.

"This is ridiculous," he muttered, gathering up the colorful swatches.

"Wrong. It's Italian silk."

"Cute, Alex. Real cute." He tossed the fabric and sketches onto a nearby wicker table.

"Need any help getting undressed?" he asked with more casualness than he was feeling.

Christ, it was getting harder and harder to be around this woman without wanting her! Even dressed as she was, engulfed in that oversize scarlet sweater, too-baggy slacks and black boots, even with her Rudolph-red nose and her too-pale cheeks, even knowing how sick she was, Zach still had a burning desire to touch her.

He longed to slip his hand beneath the hem of her sweater and caress the flesh he knew would be even softer than the crimson cashmere. These long and frustrating months of working so closely with her, at the same time forcing himself to keep his distance, had taken their emotional toll on him.

"I think I can manage it."

Relief and regret washed over him. It was, Zach reminded himself, for the best. "I'll wait in the other room. Shout if you need anything."

Although it wasn't easy, he forced himself to cool his heels in her living room, taking the opportunity to study the room that bore her own personal stamp in the same way as her unique designs.

Casual wicker furniture with bright blue-and-yellow sailcloth cushions sat on a bleached oak floor. In the center of the room, colorful hot-air balloons took flight on a sky blue rug. Green plants flourished in brightly flowered ceramic cache pots. Art posters hung on the snow-white walls.

A pair of red shoes with ridiculously high heels rested haphazardly on the rug in front of the wicker sofa, surrounded by more scraps of vivid silks and glowing satins. A small plastic globe rested on a nearby table, the scene inside depicting the New York skyline. Other similar globes displayed the St. Louis arch, the Golden Gate Bridge, the Seattle space needle and the Alamo, making Zach remember her telling him about her youthful Gypsy existence.

One plastic globe in particular captured his attention; he picked it up and turned it over, causing snow to fall on St. Louis Cathedral across the street from New Orleans's Jackson Square.

Zach experienced a pang of bittersweet remembrance and wondered if there were times when Alex held this same toy world in her palms and thought of him.

Sighing, he returned the globe to its place and continued his study of the room, searching for clues about Alex's life. He took special note of the framed photo of a middle-aged gray-haired woman and a smiling, dark-haired boy atop a table painted to resemble a bright yellow sunflower.

Her mother and brother, Zach decided, looking for a resemblance to Alex and finding none.

Perhaps Eleanor was right.

You're letting anxiety about the lady warp your mind, pal. Zach reminded himself that of the eight kids in his family, he and his sister Maggie resembled his mother, Paula and Lorraine resembled their dad, and the other four girls didn't really look like either parent. Or each other.

That being the case, there really wasn't any reason for Alex to look like her mother. And her twin, he reminded himself, was not identical, but fraternal.

He went into the pocket-size, old-fashioned kitchen which, while painted a sunny yellow with a bright blue ceiling and smelling of Christmas due to the pyramid of clove-studded oranges on the creamy ceramic tile, didn't look as if it had changed since the house was built, probably in the thirties. He filled a red enamel kettle with water for tea, then stood at the window, hands jammed into the pockets of his slacks gazing out at the sea, which was draped by the misty rain in a silvery blanket of fog, while his mind was filled, as it was too often these days, with thoughts of Alex.

He'd come to realize that Alexandra Lyons was smart and sweet and dazzlingly talented. Her stunning beauty was only illuminated by the blaze of her fiercely independent ambition, an ambition he clearly recognized, possessing a fair share of that character trait himself.

She was, without a doubt, the most fascinating and intriguing—and ill, he reminded himself firmly—woman he'd ever met.

His thoughts were shattered by the shrill whistle of the kettle. As he poured the water over a Constant Comment tea bag he'd found in a flowered canister on the open shelf, he glanced up at the whimsical black-and-white cat clock and realized she'd been in the bedroom a very long time. What the hell was she doing? Taking the tea with him, he went back to the bedroom and tapped lightly on the door. Once. Twice, then a third time. When she didn't answer, he decided to risk her ire and go in.

She was sprawled atop the comforter, appearing dead to the world. Zach experienced a momentary panic that was eased when he viewed the slow rise and fall of her chest. Her breathing was shallow and strained, but it was steady.

Bending down, working gently so as not to disturb her, Zach unzipped her knee-length boots and slipped them off. Her red socks, then her slacks followed.

"Oh, hell." Zach groaned when he discovered the scrap of crimson lace cut high on her delicately rounded hips. Trust this woman not to wear nice, safe, white cotton underpants. Although, he considered, his gaze lingering on that soft shadow of femininity between her long legs, Alex could probably make even a nun's drawers look sexy.

Frowning, he set to work on the sweater, unbuttoning it with fingers that were not nearly as steady as they should have been. As he'd feared, her bra matched those ridiculous panties. It was as scarlet as sin.

Standing beside the bed, staring down at the provocative sight, Zach felt like a starving man, his nose pressed against the glass of a bakery, denied even the smallest morsel.

During these past months, Zach had come to the unwilling conclusion that Alex had been designed by the Fates to taunt him, to torment his sleep and drive him crazy with dreams of what he could not—dared not—have. She was a bewitching nymph created solely to teach him that the self-control he'd always prided himself on was nothing more than a well-constructed sham. She was also a bright, intelligent woman who made every other woman he'd ever known pale in comparison.

Exhaling a long sigh, he managed to tuck her beneath the sheets. He bent and touched his lips to hers.

Then, leaving her to sleep, he went into the living room, picked up the receiver of her Mickey Mouse phone and placed a call to Eleanor.

When Alex awoke several hours later, she found herself in the capable hands of the private nurse Zach and Eleanor had hired. When she tried to assure the blond Amazon that she could take care of herself, Inga Nusland simply folded her muscular arms over her ample chest and refused to budge.

By the third day of sinfully hedonistic pampering, during which time the phlegmatic Inga proved herself to be not only a capable nurse but a marvelous cook and baker, Alex decided that perhaps there was something to be said for relaxation, after all.

Chapter Twenty-One

"When are you going to admit she's Anna?" Eleanor demanded.

Zach had come to Santa Barbara to fill the older woman in on Alexandra's recuperation. Although he hadn't returned to that cheerful little bungalow, Inga gave him daily updates, and he'd spoken with her doctor.

"There's still no proof," Zach pointed out as he did every time they had this conversation.

Sometimes, and this was one of them, he almost wished he'd never met Alexandra Lyons, hadn't played Sir Galahad in that long-ago Mardi Gras. But dammit, he had, and now, thanks to him, they were both suffering.

Once, when he was a boy, he'd come across a wild owl struggling impotently to fly with a broken wing. He'd wrapped the crippled bird in his shirt, taken it home, then spent the next two weeks feeding it field mice and nightcrawlers, only to have the ungrateful owl nearly bite off the end of his finger.

No good deed ever goes unpunished, his *grand-mère* had proclaimed. At the time, Zach hadn't known how prophetic her words would prove to be.

"Surely you can see the resemblance?" Eleanor pressed.

"I'll agree she looks a lot like you as a young woman. But that doesn't mean she's your granddaughter. After all, Miranda's your niece, and there's no Lord family resemblance there."

Eleanor scowled at the memory of her niece's call the night before, when she'd asked for a little loan to cover her losses in Monte Carlo. She'd also requested Eleanor not mention the call to Zach, which was bothersome because Eleanor had tried to stay out of the disaster that was Zach and Miranda's marriage.

They were both adults, she'd told herself innumerable times. What they did, or with whom, was their own business. So long as it didn't impact adversely on Lord's.

"Miranda inherited her looks from her mother's gene pool."

Along with, Eleanor worried, her behavior. After marrying Lawrence Lord, Sylvie, the viscount's tennis-playing daughter had proved to be not so genteel, after all. The sad truth was that Sylvie had been a gin-guzzling nymphomaniac.

Zach wished he hadn't brought Miranda up. He didn't want to talk about his wife. He also didn't want to admit that during these months working closely with Alex, he'd noticed things about her that defied any rational explanation.

She possessed certain gestures that he'd witnessed innumerable times in Eleanor herself, along with a stubborn intelligence he couldn't help but admire, even as it frustrated him whenever they found themselves on opposite sides of an issue. Like that damn factory ultimatum.

"Are you planning to share your suspicions with Alex?"

Eleanor sighed. "No. Not yet." From the deep furrows on her brow, Zach suspected she was recalling another time she'd felt so sure she'd found Anna. "Not until after we launch the Blue Bayou collection. But what would be wrong with seeing if we could strike a chord in her memory?"

"Eleanor—"

Eleanor ignored his planned protest. "The poor girl's been working so hard she made herself sick. Even after the doctor pronounces her recovered, she'll still need her rest."

"You're suggesting she recuperate here. In Santa Barbara." It was not a question.

Eleanor's forehead smoothed. "Here," she confirmed. "In the home where she and her father and grandfather were all born."

There was so much to prepare; Eleanor wanted things absolutely perfect when Anna finally returned home.

After ten days of antibiotics, supplemented by biscuits slathered with butter and marmalade, apple strudel, and steaming stews and chicken pies topped with fat, fluffy dumplings, Alex proclaimed herself ready to go back to work.

Her doctor confirmed her self-diagnosis, with the caveat that she begin with a few hours each day, taking time to work herself back to full throttle.

"You're still too pale," Eleanor complained during a visit to Venice. Although she'd gained back several much needed pounds, Alex's complexion continued to lack its normal healthy hue.

"I'll be fine."

"Of course you will. But we need you well rested, Alexandra. The Chicago debut of the Alexandra Lyons collection is only a month away," she reminded her. "And there's no better place to finish your recuperation than my house."

"You want me to come to Santa Barbara? To stay with you?"

"I'd love to have you as a houseguest."

"But I can't leave town. Zach and I still haven't worked out the problem with the music." She was insisting on live musicians while he argued for a less expensive audio tape, which she in turn countered would sound like elevator music.

"That can wait." Eleanor brushed off Alex's worries. "Zach will solve your little impasse. Believe me, dear, he always accomplishes everything he sets out to achieve. Besides, you couldn't have your meeting now, anyway. He's out of town."

"Oh?" Alex said with careful casualness. Against all common sense, she'd been hoping Zach might visit her. He hadn't.

"He's in Toronto. We're entering into negotiations to open our first Lord's in Canada. But right now things are hush-hush."

"I won't tell a soul," Alex promised, vaguely surprised Eleanor had shared confidential business information with her.

"Why, I never thought you would, dear," Eleanor answered mildly. "Now, let me help you pack."

One thing she'd learned during their months together was that like so many other rich, powerful women, Eleanor Lord was more than a little accustomed to getting her way. Rather than stand up to the silken bulldozer currently plucking clothes from her closet, Alex decided to simply relax and go with the flow.

Miranda was furious. And when Miranda was furious, she paced. Zach stood in front of the upstairs bedroom window, looking out over Eleanor's Santa Barbara estate and tried to ignore the furious energy radiating from his wife's every pore.

"I cannot believe she's invited that bloody little impostor into this house!" She was clenching and unclenching her fists, twisting her rings on her long aristocratic fingers, an outward sign of her tumultuous thoughts.

Miranda was not about to be cut out of her inheritance by any calculating con artist. How dare Alexandra Lyons endanger her happiness, her comfort, her entire livelihood this way! The threat she represented hovered over Miranda like a thick, suffocating cloud of noxious smog.

"Your aunt doesn't believe she's an impostor."

He shouldn't be here, Zach told himself. He should be at his office in L.A. Someone had begun quietly buying up outstanding shares of Lord's stock, and as hard as he'd tried, he had not been able to work his way through the maze of holding companies designed to keep the buyer's identity a secret.

But Eleanor had insisted he be on hand for Alex's arrival, and as much as he hated to admit it, he was curious to see how she'd react to the house.

Miranda continued to wear a path across the needle-point cabbage-rose rug. Her furious, restless strides reminded Zach of a tigress that hadn't been fed for a week.

"You realize, of course, that the old woman's gone absolutely batty." She stopped long enough to light a cigarette. Puffs of blue smoke rose to the beamed ceiling as if from a smoldering volcano.

"You're exaggerating again."

"The hell I am. Any qualified psychiatrist would declare her incompetent."

He spun around. "I'm warning you, Miranda, if you try it, I'll block you at every turn."

Miranda took in his glittering dark eyes, his threatening stance, the tautly reigned-in violence simmering just beneath the surface. There was a looming menace about him that was palpable. And extremely exciting.

It had been a long time since she'd managed to garner a reaction other than his usual cold disdain. A rush of sexual anticipation rushed through her loins, making her momentarily forget her fury concerning Eleanor's newest protégée.

"Do you know, darling," she said slowly, switching gears with a blink of her gleaming emerald eyes, "that you are frightfully sexy when you're angry?" Deliberately, with regained control, she approached on a slow, hip-swiveling feline glide he'd once found incredible appealing. Now he just found her obvious seduction attempt depressing.

"It isn't going to work."

She placed her hand against his chest. "Are you so sure about that?" She began toying with the buttons of his shirt. "Do you realize how long it's been since we made love?"

"Made love?" He plucked her hand away. "Is that what you call it?"

"Of course." Refusing to give up, she twined her arms around his neck. "We used to be so good together, Zachary. Remember?" Taking the fact that he hadn't moved away as a sign of encouragement, she pressed her body against his taut, unresisting one.

"Remember that lovely evening in the limousine in London? Remember how we spent the remainder of the night, steeped in sex and sin?" Her voice was a velvety purr; her teeth nipped at his earlobe. "Remember how you told me you'd never met a woman who made you feel the way I did?" She paused and assumed a tragic look. "When did everything go so wrong?"

"How about when you stole those earrings on our honeymoon?"

She sighed prettily. "You never will let me live that down, will you?" Moisture shone in her green eyes. "Perhaps, if we tried again. Perhaps, if I could believe that you truly loved me, no matter what my faults, I could be strong enough to get help for my sickness." On cue, tears began to stream down her face.

She was a remarkable actress, Zach mused distantly. He'd give her that. If he didn't know her so well, he'd actually believe that she regretted the chasm that had grown between them. A gulf as deep and wide as the Grand Canyon.

She went up on her toes and brushed her parted lips against his. "Please, Zachary. Can't we try to put the pieces together again? So we can have a wonderful, heavenly life together?"

She was definitely pulling out all the stops. Her fingers were caressing the back of his neck, her voice was a soft breeze against his mouth and her pelvis was moving seductively against his groin.

She was also out of luck. He didn't need to look down to know that his body was steadfastly refusing to respond.

"And I suppose all I have to do to achieve such Nirvana is help you gain Eleanor's power of attorney and lock her away in some home for addled old ladies."

"Well, you can't deny that she is old," Miranda said. "And even you must admit this latest idea about that little slut of a Hollywood dress designer being her long-lost Anna is proof that she's not completely in her right mind."

"Alexandra Lyons is not a slut." Fed up, he shoved Miranda away with an unexpected force that had her tottling on her high heels. "She just happens to be an extremely talented woman who's overcome a lot of hard knocks by integrity and tenacity and working damn hard."

"So." Miranda's seductive expression turned hard and cold, making her look every bit her age, which just happened to be ten years older than that printed on her California driver's license. "I was right about her all along."

"I don't know what you're talking about." Furious at himself for rising to her bait, Zach turned his back to her, jammed his hands into his pockets and resumed staring out the window.

She thought about the photographs Mickey O'Rourke had given her. Incriminating photos of Zach carrying Alexandra into her house. Photos that, from the intense, concerned expression the camera lens had frozen on her husband's face, suggested their relationship was much more than a mere business alliance.

Miranda hadn't confronted her husband with the damning evidence. Not yet. Although patience had never been her long suit, she was willing, when necessary, to bide her time. But if the conniving little tart thought she could steal both Miranda's husband and her inheritance, she was going to be in for a very rude awakening!

"I've wondered why you've been so indulgent with Auntie's delusion this time." She was practically biting the words off, one at a time and spitting them at him like stones. "Tell me, Zachary, is she any good in bed?"

"I wouldn't know."

A breath hissed from between Miranda's glossy lips. "Liar," she taunted. "I'll bet you know very well. I'll bet the little chit's been spreading her legs for you for months. All the better to convince you to go along with her little scheme to inherit the Lord millions."

His hands curled into fists. "I'm warning you, Miranda—"

"No, darling," she said, her voice a silken threat, "I'm warning you. If you so much as look at that girl again, let alone fuck her, I'll sell my shares of Lord's stock to Nelson Montague so fast yours and Auntie's heads will spin."

"Nelson Montague?"

"Didn't I mention that I'd run into him in Monte Carlo last month?" She examined her polished nails, dragging the moment out for as long as possible. "He was playing baccarat—winning wonderfully, by the way—and I was doing miserably at roulette."

Her eyes gleamed coldly, like green neon. "Well, generous man that he was, he gave me part of his winnings so I wouldn't have to go over my credit limit." She smiled. "We had a wonderful time."

"I'm so happy for you both," Zach said dryly. "And I suppose sometime during this fun-filled evening he offered to buy your shares."

"No."

"No?" She was enjoying herself immensely, Zach realized grimly, tempted to wring her neck for the way she was dragging this out.

"Actually, it was the next morning, after breakfast, that he brought up the stock." That her eyes gleamed with memories of whatever orgy she and Montague had indulged in didn't faze him. She had long ago lost the power to make him jealous.

But the idea of Nelson Montague getting his grubby Australian raider's hands on any Lord's stock bothered the hell out of him.

A former miner who'd made his first millions when he'd struck a mother lode of gem-quality diamonds on Australia's Kimberly plateau, Montague was a ruthless, take-no-prisoners type of businessman who viewed things like laws and ethics as nothing more than petty annoyances to be overcome.

"You're not going to sell." It was not a suggestion. Nor a request. It was an order, pure and simple.

"Not right now," she agreed. "However, Nelson assures me that before long, if I were to sell, he'd have controlling interest in the company you and Auntie care so much about."

Zach damned her dissolute father for having sold his family stock in the first place. If Lawrence Lord hadn't been such a poor excuse for a man, if he hadn't succumbed to gambling fever, if his luck hadn't always been so bad, the company his brother founded would not be in jeopardy now.

"Actually, to tell the truth, I don't really like the man," Miranda confided. "He's coarse and crude."

"He's also the fifth wealthiest man in the world."

"That does make up for a great many faults," she agreed pragmatically. "And I can't deny that I found much of what he was offering quite attractive. Did I tell you he proposed?"

"I don't believe you mentioned it. Tell me, did you accept?"

That would certainly solve one of his problems, Zach considered. Unfortunately it would also mean that Eleanor would end up losing control of Lord's. Something he would not allow to happen.

Although he was more than capable of starting over, Zach knew exactly how much Lord's meant to Eleanor. The company was, quite simply, her life, second only to her quest for Anna. He didn't think her aging heart could take such a loss.

"Of course not, silly boy. How could I? Since I'm already married to you."

"There's also the little matter of that Aussie thug probably killing any wife who dared even think about playing around."

Rumors of the corporate raider beating a former unfaithful mistress to death had been circulating in the international business community for years. The official report was the depressed young woman had jumped from Montague's penthouse terrace.

"Well, there is that," Miranda agreed. "So," she said with a remarkable amount of cheer, considering the mutual antipathy surrounding the discussion, "we're agreed? You keep your hands off that conniving little fortune hunter and help me get Auntie the help she needs, and in return for your husbandly fidelity, I'll not sell my stock."

"I won't let you do anything to Eleanor. You make one move against your aunt and I'll refuse to cover up for your shoplifting ever again."

Frown lines furrowed her porcelain brow. "Honestly, Zachary, you can be so distressingly unbending." She bit her lip and considered her options. Jail was not one of the prettier ones. "All right. I suppose we've reached a stalemate. So long as you're at the helm of Lord's protecting my investment, I'll allow Auntie her little eccentricities.

"But," she continued, her tone growing hard, "I want that girl gone."

"That isn't my decision to make."

Miranda's eyes turned as flinty as her tone. "Then you'd better figure out something, darling. Because if you won't get rid of Alexandra Lyons, I will."

It was not, Zach feared, an idle threat.

Chapter Twenty-Two

Refusing to allow Alex to make the drive up the coast in her weakened condition, Eleanor sent a limo to fetch her. As the white limousine approached the estate, winding its way through avocado orchards and eucalyptus groves, Alex felt as if she were entering another, more privileged world.

She rode through pastures, where Arabian horses galloped across wildflower-dotted fields, their manes flowing in the breeze. The driver paused momentarily at the palacelike wrought-iron security gate hung with bright pink bougainvillea, where an elderly guard welcomed Alexandra to Casa Contenta. His proprietorial air made Alex suspect he'd worked for Eleanor Lord for a very long time.

Majestic, graceful California oaks flanked the long, curving brick driveway which led through even more acres of brilliantly colored formal gardens in full bloom, accented with cascading fountains. Finally they arrived at the sprawling, Spanish-revival mansion.

The house, if such a magnificent display of architecture could be deemed a mere house, perched atop a gentle rise of luxuriant bluegrass, offered panoramic views of pastures, mountains and sea.

The limo had no sooner glided to a stop beneath the wide red-tiled *porte cochère,* when the towering oak doors opened and Eleanor emerged.

"Welcome, Alexandra dear. I've been waiting for you." As she hugged her guest, kissing her on both cheeks, Eleanor wondered what Alexandra would say if she knew exactly how long.

If she'd thought the drive through the Lord estate was like entering another world, Alex was struck momentarily speechless by the baronial splendor of the home's interior.

Sunlight streamed through a bank of skylights, casting a warm yellow glow over the deep red Spanish tile of a reception galleria that was more spacious than many of the apartments Alex and her mother and brother had lived in during their Gypsy years. The hand-carved wooden posts lining the plaster walls and the massive beams adorning the dizzyingly high ceiling overhead recalled California's earlier era of Spanish *dons* and *doñas.*

"Well, Toto, I don't think we're in Kansas anymore," she murmured.

Eleanor laughed. "I realize it seems a little grand at first sight, but we live quite casually." She patted Alex's arm comfortingly. "Let me introduce you to the others."

One grand room followed the other as she led Alex into what she called the library and what, if the rugs had been taken up from the floor and one didn't worry about all those undoubtedly priceless knickknacks perched atop marble pedestals, was large enough to double as a gymnasium. As in the galleria, wood was abundant—in the heavy Mexican furniture, in the built-in bookcases lining the paneled walls, on the high, elaborately honeycombed wood ceiling. They could have held the NBA finals in this room, Alex mused. And still have room down by the massive see-through stone fireplace at the far end for the concession stand.

A portrait of Eleanor as a young woman hung in a gilt frame above the fireplace. Alex stopped in her tracks, stunned. Except for the fact that the portrait's subject had glossy auburn hair and was wearing a wedding gown, she could have been looking in the mirror.

"That was painted a month after my marriage to James," Eleanor said. "I see you've noticed the resemblance."

"It would be hard not to." Alex wondered why Eleanor had never mentioned this before. "They say everyone has a double, but this is incredible."

"Isn't coincidence a remarkable thing?" an all too familiar, distinctly British voice offered from the other side of the vast room. Alex slowly turned.

They were waiting for her. Zach was wearing the same smooth mask of composure he always donned when forced to rein in his emotions, while Miranda looked as if she'd like to pull Alex's hair out, strand by strand. Before she had time to dwell on Miranda's obvious antipathy, Alex was being introduced to a heavyset woman outrageously clad in a rainbow-striped chiffon caftan and matching turban, and a tall, handsome man in his fifties.

Although he appeared momentarily startled by Alex's appearance, Averill quickly recovered.

"Welcome to Santa Barbara, Alexandra," he greeted her warmly. The laugh lines framing his friendly eyes crinkled attractively. "I've been looking forward to meeting Eleanor's brilliant designer. You know," he said, dropping his tone confidentially, "you're all she talks about these days."

"I'm pleased to meet you, Dr. Brandford."

"Please . . . call me Averill." His gaze turned momentarily professional as it swept over her face. "Eleanor says you've had pneumonia. How are you feeling?"

"I'm fine. Well, mostly fine," she amended, when she saw the physician's eyes narrow.

"This is an excellent place for R & R," he assured her. "And perhaps, before you leave, you'll let me take you out on my ketch. You do sail, don't you?" he asked with the air of a man who couldn't imagine otherwise.

"Actually, I've never been sailing."

"Then you must. You'll love it, Alexandra." He rubbed his hands together with anticipation. "There's nothing more invigorating than the tang of the salt spray and the sea breeze in your hair."

"It sounds wonderful," Alex agreed, returning his smile.

There was a momentary lull in the conversation. The way they were all suddenly staring at her made Alex feel like a laboratory specimen.

The suspended moment was broken by the arrival of a housemaid with a trolley of steaming tea and fresh-baked pastries. Over the brief repast, Averill entertained Alex with amusing anecdotes of past sailing adventures.

Zach did not enter the conversation. Nor did Miranda, who seemed content to sip her Scotch and glower at Alex. Eleanor, too, remained oddly quiet, watching Alex with a deep, unwavering gaze that reminded Alex of the first time they'd met.

After a time, fatigue from the trip abetted by the strained atmosphere, began to take its toll.

"You've had a long drive," Eleanor said, noticing Alex's slight, stifled yawn. "Why don't we get you settled into your room?"

"Thank you. I am a little tired," Alex admitted.

She followed Eleanor out of the library, up a gracefully curving staircase and down a hall adorned with framed, formally posed portraits of elegantly clad individuals she assumed were Lord ancestors. For some reason she could not explain, she paused momentarily before a closed door.

Watching Alex stop in front of Anna's nursery, Eleanor experienced a burst of pure victorious pleasure. Of course Anna would remember which door it was!

"Your room is right next door, dear," Eleanor said in a mild tone she was a very long way from feeling.

Shaking her head to rid it of a sudden strange, slightly disorienting sensation, Alex entered a room that was both luxurious and cozy at the same time. The bed, ornately carved from the same dark wood that graced the honeycomb ceiling in the library, was draped with a crocheted comforter.

More crocheted and needlepoint pillows had been scattered at the head of the mattress. There was a fireplace in this room, as well, topped by a hand-carved mantel; needlepoint tapestry rugs were scattered over the polished oak flooring.

Ceiling-high windows looked out over the vast green grounds; from this vantage point, Alex could view a Palladian teahouse, leafy dark green hedges and a red clay tennis court that had been built beside a serene, crystal blue swimming pool.

"It's absolutely lovely," she murmured. "Exquisite, actually."

"I want you to feel at home here, Alex."

She laughed at that. "Never in my wildest dreams could I imagine living in a home like this," she said with her characteristic frankness. "But I know I'll be comfortable," she tacked on quickly in a belated attempt to avoid hurting Eleanor's feelings.

"I do so hope so," Eleanor said fervently. "The bathroom's right through that door. It's stocked with soaps and shampoos and various other items, including a hair dryer, but if you need anything, anything at all, just pick up the phone and dial zero for the housekeeper. She'll be able to get you anything you wish."

"I'll be fine."

"Then I guess I'll leave you to your rest," Eleanor murmured, appearing oddly reluctant to leave.

Something occurred to Alex as the older woman reached the door. "Oh, I could use my suitcase from the limo."

"It's already been brought upstairs," Eleanor assured her. "Maria has already put your things away."

"Maria?"

"Juanita and Jesus' daughter. Juanita is the housekeeper," she explained. "Jesus is our main gardener. He took over after Averill's father, who had the job for years, died. Maria's the upstairs maid."

With that she was gone, leaving Alex to sink onto the bed and stare around at her luxurious surroundings.

"The upstairs maid," she murmured. "Of course." She began to giggle. "Boy, Mom," she said, flinging herself backward onto the mattress and staring up at the restful garden mural painted on the ceiling. "I sure hope you can see me now."

Although Alex was tired, she found she could not relax. After thirty minutes or so, inexplicably drawn to the room next door, she crept back down the hallway, feeling like a cat burglar.

The room was a lovely flowered bower. Dainty pink rose blossoms bloomed on the cream wallpaper, stuffed animals and exquisitely dressed dolls with porcelain faces and hands lay atop a quilt hand-appliquéd with pink and pastel yellow tulips. Peeking out from beneath the quilt was an eyelet dust ruffle accented with pink grosgrain ribbon; more white eyelet draped a round bedside table and framed the windows. A pine rocking horse painted glossy white and boasting a white yarn mane stood in one corner of the room, while a Victorian dollhouse claimed another corner. Entranced, Alex was examining a beautiful wicker carriage, fit for a princess—or her dolls—when Eleanor, who'd come upstairs to fetch her for dinner, entered the room on silent cat feet.

"This was Anna's room."

The quiet voice behind Alex made her jump. "Anna?" A pink-cheeked, cupid-mouthed doll lay in the wicker carriage; Alex reached down and carefully adjusted the battenberg lace christening gown.

"My granddaughter."

"I didn't know you had a granddaughter." Now that she thought about it, Eleanor had never mentioned any family other than her late husband, James. Alex had assumed the couple had been childless.

"Oh, yes." A shadow moved across the older woman's face. "She was the most beautiful child. With a personality like summer sunshine. Even as a baby, she brightened the room with her sweet smile. Her mother, my son Robbie's wife, always accused me of spoiling her, but I never believed it possible to spoil a child with too much love."

"That's what my mother always said," Alex murmured. Although she may not have possessed Anna Lord's wealth of toys and treasures, Alex had always known that she was much loved. "You said *was*," she said, as the thought suddenly occurred to her. "Anna isn't—"

"Dead?" Eleanor broke in, saving Alex from having to say the unthinkable. "No." She shook her auburn head. "No, my Anna isn't dead. Unfortunately her parents are. They were murdered," she revealed. "Downstairs, in the library, twenty-eight years ago. When Anna was only two."

"How tragic!"

"It was horrific," Eleanor said. "But quite honestly, it took a long time for Robbie's and Melanie's—that was my daughter-in-law—deaths to sink in because Anna was kidnapped at the same time."

"Kidnapped?" Alex's startled gaze moved slowly around the room.

"She was taken from her bed the night of the murder." Eleanor was watching Alex carefully. "Naturally, I've left the room exactly as it was that night. The only change I've made was to replace the crib with a child's bed, and now this full-sized Shaker.

"Although the police never found my granddaughter, I've always known Anna will return. I want her room to be waiting for her."

"It's a beautiful room," Alex murmured. "When I was little, I used to dream of a room like this."

"Of course you did." When Alex gave her a quick, puzzled glance, Eleanor hastily added, "Doesn't every little girl?"

"I think so."

Alex walked over to a glossy white bookshelf and ran her hands over the leather-bound classics—*Tom Sawyer, Huckleberry Finn, Robin Hood, Black Beauty, Treasure Island*—which were far too advanced for the two-year-old child Anna Lord had been when she disappeared.

"*Black Beauty* was one of my favorite stories." Alex wondered if Anna's mother had read this book to her at bedtime, as her own mother had done.

"Anna loved horses." Eleanor's eyes misted at the memory. "I wanted to get her a pony for her third birthday, but Melanie thought she was too young. Of course, Papa put me on a horse before I could walk."

The brief flash of temper in Eleanor's eyes suggested that she was recalling the long-ago argument with her daughter-in-law. "My earliest memory is sitting in front of Papa on Moonglow—his favorite Thoroughbred from the family stables—feeling on top of the world."

Once again Alex noticed Eleanor's casual regard toward such vast family wealth. She'd tossed off the comment about the family stables with the same offhand attitude she'd mentioned the upstairs maid. When she'd been younger, during those years when her mother had struggled to keep a roof over their heads and the wolf away from the door, there had been innumerable times when Alex had thought that if only they were rich, all their problems would be solved.

After watching some of Debord's customers, not to mention the chronically dissatisfied Miranda Deveraux, along with having a front-row seat for Sophie's bitterly fought divorce and, now, hearing of the tragedy in Eleanor Lord's privileged life, Alex considered that wealth was not all it was cracked up to be.

Oh, it could certainly buy a great many lovely things, such as this house and its exquisite furnishings. And it could ease a great many financial concerns of day-to-day living. But the one thing money couldn't buy was happiness.

Or, she considered, thinking of Zach and Miranda, love.

"Gracious," Eleanor said, breaking into Alex's thoughts with a soft, self-conscious laugh. "I certainly didn't mean to cast a pall over your first night here." She reached out, rubbing away the lines that thoughts of Zach and his wife had etched into Alex's forehead. The maternal gesture seemed perfectly normal.

"We'd better get downstairs," Eleanor suggested, "before Beatrice starts yelling at me for ruining her dinner."

"Beatrice is the cook," Alex guessed, beginning to get a handle on how things worked around this vast estate.

"That's right. And unfortunately, when God was passing out short fuses, Beatrice must have been first in line, then turned around and gone back for seconds.

"She has a temper that could blow us all off the face of the earth," Eleanor said conspiratorially as they descended the stairs. "But one taste of her heavenly *crème brûlée* and you'll understand why I've let her bully me all these years."

Chapter Twenty-Three

Although the food was as delicious as Eleanor had promised, Alex found dinner to be a decidedly strained affair. Averill's queries about her life, her family, her career, were couched politely enough, but she couldn't quite shake the feeling she was being cross-examined.

As for Zach, Alex doubted if he uttered two words during the entire meal. Miranda also remained silent, although it would have been impossible to miss the cold fury directed Zach's way. That they had quarreled recently was more than a little obvious.

Eleanor, on the other hand, was as charming as usual, entertaining Alex with stories of her colorful family.

Her father's family, Alex learned over a rich salmon bisque, had been the Philadelphia Longworths, business people, leading players in the world cotton market and patrons of the arts. One of Eleanor's Longworth ancestors had established the Longworth Philadelphia Trust Bank, a leading financier of the American Revolution. Another had been on the board of directors of the Pennsylvania Railroad, which, in the City of Brotherly Love, established one as an undisputed member of the city's aristocracy.

Over hearts-of-palm salad, Eleanor told Alex that her mother's family were New Yorkers, whose roots, like the Longworths, predated the revolution and whose forebears included a signer of the Declaration of Independence.

Eleanor had grown up in splendid luxury on a cotton plantation outside Atlanta, Georgia, where her father raised and brokered cotton. Clothes for the ladies of the house came from Christian Dior, Chanel and Madame Grés in Paris.

She attended Foxcroft, that very proper Virginia private school, where she achieved the polish required of a young lady of her station. Like so many of her equally privileged classmates, she summered in Europe with her grandparents. She made a stunning debut at her grandparents' home on Long Island, then was sent to Paris to be "finished."

She'd wed when she was twenty, wearing a wedding gown of beaded, handmade alençon lace—the same gown she was wearing in the painting that had so startled Alex—and carrying a white Bible that had been in the Longworth family since the 1600s.

"James's parents tragically went down on the *Lusitania* when he was a boy," Eleanor divulged over the main course, grilled pheasant with lingonberry sauce. "I've always thought that being orphaned helped my husband develop the independent streak that served him so well when he began the Lord's chain."

"Those must have been exciting times," Alex said.

"They were wonderful." Eleanor smiled reminiscently. "Why, when he decided to move to the Deep South shortly after our marriage, the *Wall Street Journal* declared the region hadn't seen such a sweeping campaign since Sherman marched through Georgia."

"And of course there's always the London Lord's," Miranda reminded her aunt. A bit testily, Alex thought.

"Of course," Eleanor said agreeably. She did not add that she'd always found Miranda's father lacking. Although James had defended his younger brother on numerous occasions, it had been obvious to Eleanor from the start that Lawrence did not possess the intelligence, vitality, or work ethic of his brother. Given the choice between reading a sales report from a regional manager or playing a set of tennis, Lawrence could always be found on the court.

After the dessert cups had been cleared—Eleanor hadn't exaggerated about the hot-tempered Beatrice's *crème brûlée*—the group moved into the library for brandy and coffee.

It was then that Miranda addressed Alex directly for the first time since she'd come downstairs with Eleanor. "From what Zach and Aunt Eleanor tell me, you're the quintessential workaholic, Alex."

Alex looked for the trap, but couldn't find it. "I like to keep busy."

"So I hear. Imagine working so hard that you'd give yourself pneumonia." She refilled her brandy snifter from a Waterford decanter. "How fortunate that Zachary was with you when you collapsed."

The insinuation hovered over the room, just waiting for Alex to pick up on it. "I was grateful for your husband's assistance."

"I'm sure you were." Miranda smiled first at Alex, then Zach, her eyes glittering with anticipation of impending violence, like a spectator at a prize fight. "My husband can be very helpful when he puts his mind to it."

Those dangerous eyes narrowed, giving Alex the feeling she'd just landed in the center of a very deadly bull's-eye.

"Tell me, dear," Miranda said in a silken voice that belied the malice in her gaze, "how do you make time for men in such a busy, allegedly fulfilling life?"

"I manage."

Actually she didn't. Not that there was a shortage of candidates. Actors, agents, heirs to old California fortunes, even a rising young culinary star, whose trendy new Beverly Hills restaurant had Hollywood insiders actually willing to stand in line for a table, had all repeatedly asked Alex out. But she wasn't interested in any of these contenders for her heart.

Because she'd given it to Zach on that magical star-kissed bayou night. And her feelings hadn't changed. She still found Zach fascinating; she still wanted him. He was still married.

"I have the most scintillating idea!" Clara, clad tonight in royal purple, clapped her pudgy hands. "Let's have a séance!"

"No!" Zach and Averill shouted in unison.

"I was speaking to Eleanor." Alex found Clara's waspish tone a direct contrast to her soft, pink features.

All eyes turned to their hostess, who, Alex thought, suddenly looked every day of her seventy-plus years.

"I think," Eleanor said slowly, "that perhaps Alexandra should be given time to settle in before we expose her to the supernatural, Clara, dear."

Out of the corner of her eye, Alex saw Zach and Averill visibly relax. "A séance sounds fascinating," she told Clara not quite truthfully. Although she didn't believe in ghosts, Alex was not all that eager to go dabbling in the afterlife. "Perhaps some other time."

Slightly mollified, Clara spent the next half hour regaling Alex with tales of supernatural manifestations, and although Alex had no desire to insult Eleanor's elderly friend, she was relieved when the dinner party finally broke up.

After extracting a promise from Alex to go sailing soon, Averill left. Zach was next, accompanied upstairs by Miranda who, after several glasses of brandy appeared none too steady on her feet.

Alex rose to go upstairs as well, pausing briefly to wish the two elderly women good-night and to give Eleanor a quick peck on the cheek. Although she realized such behavior was unprofessional, for some reason, in this house at this time, it seemed right.

As she entered the comfortable guest room, Alex realized she was exhausted. Her head ached and she felt both cold and hot at the same time, just as she had in Zach's office. Worried that she might be in danger of a relapse, she poured a glass of water from the crystal carafe that had appeared as if by magic on her bedside table, took two aspirins, then, on second thought, swallowed a third.

"All you need is a good night's sleep," she told herself as she slipped beneath the perfumed sheets.

Unfortunately sleep proved a frustratingly elusive target. Alex tossed and turned, twisting the Egyptian cotton sheets into a restless tangle. The house was dark and silent, with only the occasional creaks as it settled for the night, as old homes seem to do.

It was after two in the morning before she finally drifted off.

Sometime later, awareness filtered slowly into Alex's subconscious mind. Something feathered against her cheek. She groggily brushed it away.

"Go home," a low, deep voice intoned.

Murmuring a protest, Alex rolled over.

"You should not have come."

Alex was emerging from the depths of what she thought to be a dream. The room had gone cold. Alex had curled up in a tight ball in an attempt to keep warm. She felt rather than saw the movement above her. She blinked slowly, trying to focus in the darkness. A strangely familiar, musty scent teased her nostrils.

A gauzy figure was standing over her. As she watched, momentarily transfixed, it began to lower a fluffy down pillow over her face.

She came to full alertness as if a bucket of ice water had been thrown on her. Arms flailing, she struck out wildly at the white-draped figure. Her bloodcurdling screams awakened the entire household.

They all rushed in—Eleanor, Clara, Zach and Miranda—and found her standing beside the bed, shaking like a leaf.

"Alex?" Although her own eyes were wide with lingering fright from being roused so abruptly, Eleanor placed a calming hand on Alex's shoulder. Alex flinched. "What's wrong?"

"Someone was in here." One of them had turned on the light upon entering. She blinked against the brightness.

"Who, dear?"

"Three guesses," Miranda drawled. She shot a blistering glare Zach's way. "And the first two don't count."

Alex was still shaking. She was as white as the pillow lying on the floor by the window. Seeing her in such obvious distress made Zach want to take her in his arms, to hold her until the color returned to her cheeks, to stroke her hair until her fright was vanquished.

"Shut up, Miranda," he said equably. He picked up an afghan from the foot of the bed and draped it over Alex's trembling shoulders. Her turquoise nightshirt ended high on her thighs. Drenched with sweat as it was, it clung to her body. "Are you all right?"

"I—I—I think so." Alex's confused gaze circled the room, taking in the quartet of faces watching her with varying levels of intensity. "I thought I saw someone.

Standing over my bed. And then . . ." She was hit with violent tremors.

Knowing he'd pay for this later, Zach dared Miranda's wrath and put his arm around her. She was as taut as a wire. He could practically feel her nerves crackling.

"And then?" he prompted with a gentleness that had Miranda grinding her teeth and Eleanor looking at him with sharp interest.

She felt so safe in his embrace. So protected. Alex knew she should move away. But she didn't. "I thought he was going to suffocate me. With that pillow."

"The one by the window?"

Alex followed his gaze to the floor below the open window, where the pillow had landed when she'd wildly knocked it out of the intruder's grasp.

"I think so." The entire experience was taking on the surrealistic sensation of a nightmare.

"Ghosts," Clara declared knowingly. She'd wrapped her ample body into a silk kimono embroidered with a fire-breathing dragon. The purple and red rollers in her hair made her look as if she were trying to pick up satellite signals from space. "Perhaps Rosa has finally made contact. Your aura, Alexandra, dear," she confided, "is very strong."

"I rather doubt that Alexandra's midnight visitor was a ghost," Eleanor murmured. She'd long ago given up on Clara's psychic abilities. Especially since her own explanation was so much simpler. It was not lost souls who'd plagued Alex in the lonely dark night, Eleanor surmised. But memories. Memories, perhaps, of a child's last night in this house. The night her mother and father had been murdered.

"Well, the answer is obvious," Miranda said scathingly. Her black silk robe billowed out behind her as she marched across the room and shut the window. "The wind made the white lace curtains billow," she said. "Which to Alex's overactive imagination must have looked like a ghost. That's all there is to it. So, now that the gothic mystery is solved, can we all go back to bed?"

"I'm sorry to have bothered you all," Alex said. She glanced at the window. She could have sworn she'd closed it earlier. "Miranda's right. The curtain makes the most sense. Or a nightmare."

"It was a ghost," Clara repeated with surprising cheer considering the circumstances.

"Good night, Mrs. Kowalski," Zach said firmly.

"But—"

"Come along, Clara." Eleanor seconded Zach's order. "Let's let Alexandra get back to sleep." She kissed Alex on the cheek, gave her a fond look and practically dragged the robust woman from the bedroom.

Miranda folded her arms. "Coming, Zach?"

He knew he should go. But he couldn't. "Go on to bed, Miranda," he instructed, knowing he was further risking her ire, but feeling an even stronger pull to ensure himself that Alex was truly all right. "I'll be along in a minute."

Miranda surprised both Zach and Alex. "Whatever you say," she said sweetly. "Good night, Alex. Sweet dreams."

Her friendly smile matched her pleasant tone. So why, Alex wondered, did she hear a threat behind those sugar-coated words?

"How are you, really?" Zach asked when they were alone.

"Fine." Her voice was frail. "I'm fine," she repeated more firmly this time. "Actually, I'm more embarrassed than frightened."

His hands were stroking her arms, soothing her lingering distress and creating another even more vital. "Do you think it was a dream?"

"What else could it have been?"

"I don't know."

Surely Miranda wouldn't have... No! Zach assured himself. His wife was admittedly a pathologically jealous woman. But even Miranda was not capable of murder.

"It was a dream," she said.

Unable to think of any other plausible solution, Zach murmured an agreement. He drew her against him and ran his hands up and down her back, soothing and stimulating her at the same time.

"You should go."

He brushed his lips against her hair, inhaling its fresh, sunshine scent. "In a minute."

She closed her eyes and rested her cheek against his chest. Alex knew she should send him back to his wife, back to the bed they shared. But she couldn't. Not yet.

"A minute," she breathed. She wrapped her arms around his waist and clung. He was wearing the jeans he'd hurriedly tugged on when awakened by Alex's screams. His chest was bare. And so, so enticing. In a warm haze of need, Alex brushed her lips over his shoulder. His chest.

"Alexandra," he moaned. Her mouth was searing his skin with every breathy kiss.

"Shh." She smiled against his warm flesh. "Just a little more."

Half-blind with need, Zach grasped a handful of fragrant hair and tilted her head back, lifting her gaze to his. "More." His lips hovered inches above hers. His voice was rough and husky.

And then he closed the distance.

A soft, yielding sigh slipped from between her lips to his. She went up on her toes, twining her arms around his neck, clinging tightly. The afghan slipped unnoticed to the floor.

Her body strained against his. Her hot, avid mouth was as urgent and impatient as his. He stroked her through the nightshirt, delighting in the sensuous movements of her body beneath the silk. Beneath his hands. He slipped his hands under the hem and discovered that her flesh, so icy just minutes ago, had warmed.

Fear disintegrated. Her earlier shock dissolved. At this suspended moment in time there was only now. Only Zach.

Through her dazed senses, she could hear him whispering to her, intimate soft words, crazy, wonderful promises.

Zach knew it was foolhardy, allowing the reins on his tautly held hunger to slip here, and now, with the house filled with people and his wife just next door.

He knew it was dangerous. Knew it was wrong. But, God help him, he was only human and she was so soft and so sweet and he'd been so terrified when he'd heard her scream, so relieved when he'd discovered she was all right, that all he could do, dammit, was feel.

Oh, yes! This was what she'd been wanting. Alex had been longing for the taste of his firm lips, dying to feel those strong bold hands against her flesh. She wanted him with a need that bordered on insanity, which is why she didn't back away, even as she knew that what she and Zach were doing was madness.

He pushed the turquoise silk up, giving his lips access to her breasts. As he breathed on the hot flesh, kissed it, licked it, a direct line of fire shot from her taut, tingling nipples to the center of her legs.

She moaned deep in her throat. Her fingers dug into his hips. If this was, indeed, madness, Alex welcomed it with open arms.

With trembling fingers she unsnapped his jeans. But when she reached for him, desperate to drive him as crazy as he was driving her, he caught her wrists.

"Alex, sweetheart." He steadied himself by drawing in deep drafts of air. "We have to stop."

She shook her head, sending her hair out in a shimmering arc. "Not yet."

His body was throbbing, reaching for the touch she was trying to bestow. Zach's head was swimming, and although he wanted nothing more than to drag her to the bed, strip off that scrap of turquoise silk and bury himself deep inside her welcoming heat, he knew that the risk would be too great.

Besides, a nagging little voice of conscience reminded him, only moments ago she'd been terrified. What if her response had been born only out of the need to be comforted? If he went to bed with her now, wouldn't that be taking advantage of her atypical fragility?

And, first and foremost, his agonized, convoluted thought process returned as it always did to the simple fact that he couldn't offer her anything beyond the moment. And to Zach's mind, that was offering her nothing at all.

Alex was looking up at him, her heart shining in her wide, luminous eyes. Then she took a deep shuddering breath, glanced around and belatedly remembered where she was, where they were.

"Thank you."

"For what?" His voice was rough.

"For having the good sense to stop." She combed her fingers through her hair. "If your wife had walked in..."

There was no need to finish the sentence. They both knew the scene that Miranda was capable of creating would not be pretty.

As their gazes met and clung, Alex shivered.

"You're cold." Zach reached for the afghan again.

Alex wrapped her arms around herself in an unconscious gesture of self-protection. "No, not cold. Scared."

He glanced over at the window. "It's closed now. And locked."

She shook her head. "That's not what I'm afraid of. I'm afraid of you."

"Me?" She couldn't have said anything that hurt more.

"Of the way you make me feel."

Zach closed his eyes and dragged his hand down over his face. "Don't feel like the Lone Ranger."

He smiled a crooked, self-deprecating smile as he trailed his fingertips down the side of her somber face, tracing the full shape of her lips before continuing along her jaw and down her throat. Then, heaving a deep sigh of regret, he dropped his hand.

"Do you think you can sleep now?"

"Yes." It was the only lie she'd ever told him. How did he think she could sleep when every pore in her body ached for his touch? Just when she thought she was going to burst into frustrated tears of unfulfillment, humor rose to rescue her. "After a cold shower."

He chuckled at that, as she'd meant him to. "At least Eleanor won't have to worry about running out of hot water with the two of us stuck together under the same roof."

He ran a hand down her hair, gave her a long look overbrimming with emotion. "Good night."

Her smile wobbled, her eyes misted. "Night."

And then he was gone.

Dammit, women slept with married men every day, Alex told herself. And husbands fooled around. Afternoon talk shows routinely discussed the advantages of open marriages, and movies and novels depicting infidelity were becoming so common it seemed that recreational adultery between consenting adults was becoming almost chic.

As she climbed back into bed and pulled the sheets over her head, Alex found herself wishing that her mother had imbued her children with less scruples.

Or that Eve Deveraux had raised a less honorable son.

Chapter Twenty-Four

"Good morning!" Clara greeted Alex the next morning.

"Morning." Alex had come downstairs in desperate need of a cup of coffee. "Good morning, Eleanor."

"Good morning, dear. How are you feeling?"

"Fine." Actually, a maniac was pounding away with a hammer inside her head, but Alex decided a polite white lie was in order. She went over to the antique sideboard and poured a cup of coffee from a silver samovar.

"I was concerned you might have another nightmare," Eleanor said.

Alex stirred in a teaspoon of sugar. "I slept like a baby." Another lie. Beside the samovar were silver bowls of fresh berries and a damask-lined basket of fresh breads and pastries. Alex plucked a blueberry muffin from the basket, put it on a plate and sat down at the table.

"Beatrice will be happy to make whatever else you'd like," Eleanor said. "Some hotcakes, perhaps? French toast? An omelet?"

"This is fine. I'm not much of a breakfast eater."

"You need to get your strength back," Eleanor reminded her.

"I also need to fit into the dress I'm making for the Chicago debut. Thanks to Inga, I've gained at least ten pounds."

"Thank goodness," Eleanor countered. "You were looking far too thin before your collapse."

Alex shrugged. "You know what they say. A woman can never be too rich or too thin."

"I knew the Duchess of Windsor," Eleanor revealed. A wicked light danced in her eyes. "And she might be right about the money, dear. But believe me, the woman looked like a corpse."

"I've always found men prefer curvaceous women," Clara declared robustly. "At least my three husbands did." Her dimpled arms reached out of today's billowy green sleeves and plucked a buttery *croissant* from the basket. Two bran muffins and a cinnamon roll joined the *croissant* on her plate.

"You know, Alex," Clara said around a mouthful of muffin, "I've been thinking about your visitor last night."

"It was a nightmare," Alex demurred. "Or a trick of moonlight."

"That's your logical mind speaking," Clara insisted. "Last night you were operating in your intuitive realm. Tell me, have you ever heard of Resurrection Mary?"

"No, but—"

"She was a beautiful young girl, captivating, with blue eyes and the palest, prettiest flaxen hair. And Lord, she loved to dance! One night she died in an automobile accident going home from a ballroom. That was nearly fifty years ago, yet there are still tales of her rising from her grave in Resurrection Cemetery to go dancing with handsome single men at that same ballroom."

"Really, Clara," Eleanor complained, "I have difficulty believing any single young man would care to dance with a fifty-year-old corpse."

"But she looks just the way she did the night she died," Clara explained. "Of course, the men do report that she seems aloof. Cold."

"I would think she'd be cold," Eleanor snorted.

Clara frowned, obviously piqued that she wasn't being taken seriously. "My point is that there have been so many reportings of Mary, a song was written about her. And there's the young maid who hanged herself in Chicago in 1915 and still haunts the Victorian house where she worked, and the young bride in St. Paul, Minnesota, and—"

"I believe you were making a point?" Eleanor interrupted.

"Well, yes." Clara nodded emphatically, starting her several chins jiggling. "I think there's a very good possibility that this house is being haunted. Perhaps by Melanie."

"Dammit, Clara—" Eleanor began.

"But you've told me she was wearing a white evening dress the night she was killed. And Alexandra's apparition was wearing white. Isn't that so?" she demanded of a bemused Alex.

"It was only a nightmare," Alex repeated weakly, wishing the entire humiliating event had never happened.

Clara folded her arms over her ample bosom. "Well, I believe an exorcism is in order."

"Alex is here to rest," Eleanor said briskly. "There will be no exorcism." She rose and placed her folded napkin on the table. "I have to go over the reports Zach brought up from L.A. yesterday. There are papers that need to be signed."

Her expression softened as she turned to Alex. "I hope you don't mind my abandoning you your first day here."

"Don't worry about me," Alex assured her. "I'll just explore the grounds."

"What a grand idea," Clara agreed robustly after Eleanor had left the dining room. "I'll give you a tour. And of course, you won't want to miss the greenhouse. In fact, you're in luck. I was planning to feed my *Dionaea muscipula* this afternoon. My Venus's-flytrap," she elaborated at Alex's blank look. "I've a nice fat cricket I've been saving just for this occasion."

The idea of watching a plant devour a helpless insect was not Alex's idea of a fun afternoon. "That sounds quite interesting," she lied yet again, "but I just remembered I promised Sophie Friedman some new sketches."

"It's quite fascinating to watch," Clara coaxed.

"Perhaps next time." Alex stood up, flashed the woman an apologetic smile, then escaped the room.

As the afternoon progressed, Alex experienced strange, periodic feelings of *déjà vu*. It was almost as if she'd been here, in Santa Barbara, in this very house before.

But, of course, she assured herself, that was impossible. As impossible as Clara's insistence about restless spirits.

These unsettling emotions, last night's bad dream, along with her continued feeling of being drawn to Anna's nursery, were nothing more than the product of her imagination. The power of suggestion, Alex reminded herself, could be very strong.

On her third day at the house, Clara confronted Alex in the rose garden.

"There you are, Alexandra. I've been searching the entire house for you," she complained, her pink face even rosier than usual. She was out of breath; her ample chest was heaving as if she'd just run a marathon. Today's caftan was the vivid yellow, orange and crimson hue of the Joseph's Coat blossoms Alex had just been admiring.

It crossed Alex's mind that if Clara were truly clairvoyant, she would have known where she was. "Well, you found me."

"I had a vision."

"Another one?" If the elderly woman was to be believed, psychic revelations were a remarkably common occurrence.

"I was in the library, playing canasta with Eleanor, when I just happened to glance over at the fireplace. That's when I saw it."

"It?"

She leaned toward Alex, lowering her voice to a dramatic stage whisper. "There was a lighthouse in the flames."

Almost against her will, Alex was momentarily intrigued. "You can see things in fires?"

"Of course. Didn't I tell you that I am one-eighth Rom?"

"Rom?"

"Romany—Gypsy. My great-grandmother was a *shuvani*," Clara said haughtily. "A wise woman. When I was a girl, she taught me how to divine fortunes from the flames of the *atchen'tan*—the campfire."

"That's very interesting," Alex murmured politely even as she considered, not for the first time, that Clara's talents were definitely being wasted. With her vivid imagination and penchant for storytelling, she could probably clean up writing horror scripts in Hollywood.

"I haven't done it for ages. This time it was totally unconscious...." She shook her head, as if clearing her mind. "A lighthouse means danger. It was at the top of the fire in the position representing the present. But that wasn't all. At the front of the fire, into the future, I saw a monk."

"A monk?"

"Any Gypsy worth her salt knows that a monk is the symbol of deception and subterfuge."

"I see," Alex said, not really seeing anything at all.

"The monk is a warning of some unpleasant incident connected with a man of power and influence. And that's not all."

It never was with Clara. "Oh?"

Clara placed a pudgy pink hand on Alex's arm. "The warning wasn't for me, Alexandra." Her fingers tightened. "It was for you. You must leave Santa Barbara. Now."

Alex gently shrugged off the older woman's touch. "It's not that I don't appreciate the warning, Clara," she said politely, "because I do. But I think I'll take my chances."

Clara bristled. "Well," she huffed, with an angry shake of her turbaned head, "don't say I didn't warn you." With that, she turned and stomped away, her silk caftan billowing around her ample frame like a bright sail against a gale-force wind.

The nightmare came before dawn, slinking into Alex's subconscious mind like a black cat on All Hallows' Eve. She was walking through the fog; cold gray mists curled around her bare legs, brushed over her arms, settled damply in her hair. In the distance she could barely make out a huge, forbidding house.

The dark, damp earth beneath her bare feet had a pungent, yeasty smell. She had no idea whether it was day or night; the world had become a skyless realm where the only colors were black and green. The immense quiet of the shadowy forest closed in on her; the black, gesticulating trees curtaining the narrow path seemed to be reaching for her.

A gust of wind from the nearby storm-tossed sea ruffled her hair; a sudden flash of sulfurous lightning illuminated the land in a stuttering white light.

And then she saw it. The blood. It was everywhere—flowing wetly over the ground like a dark red river, splattering over the rocks, staining her flowing white dress, soaking into her wild, unkempt hair.

Locked in the escalating terror, Alex tossed and turned on her sweat-drenched sheets.

She was no longer alone. A cowled monk was coming toward her, the evil glint of a dagger in his hand. Although she couldn't make out his features in the overwhelming darkness, his eyes gleamed like red-hot coals.

He slowly raised the dagger high above his head and brought it down viciously, directly at her heart.

Alex woke with a jolt just in time, rescuing herself from the monk's murderous intent.

As she paced the floor in the predawn darkness, waiting anxiously for morning, Alex tried to tell herself that the nightmare was nothing more than a figment of her imagination, brought on by the strain of preparing for her upcoming design debut, Miranda's ongoing antipathy, the lingering effects of her illness and her strange conversation in the garden with Clara.

But even as she assured herself that her nightmare was nothing more than the product of her creative mind, Alex couldn't quite make herself believe it.

Not when her skin was still chilled from the icy gray mists. Not when the image of that cowled monk lurked threateningly in her mind's eye. And certainly not when the acrid, suffocating odor of blood lingered in her nostrils.

Despite the good deal of common sense Alex possessed, she couldn't quite shake the feeling that the nightmare that had disturbed her sleep for the past ten nights had been all too real.

The nightmare continued, night after restless night. Disjointed, frightening fragments, scenes hidden in a misty fog. Scenes that asked more questions than they revealed.

Each night before retiring, Eleanor brought Alex a cup of lemon verbena tea, touted by Clara as a near-miraculous sedative. When the tea proved ineffectual, Clara followed up with valerian, an unpleasant brew that smelled like dirty sweat socks and did nothing to help Alex sleep.

Hearing of Alex's insomnia, Averill offered to prescribe something to help her sleep. But wary of prescription drugs, Alex declined.

Seeking other means of relaxing, which had been the point of this trip all along, Alex began taking long walks on the cliff behind the estate, where she'd stare out at the vast Pacific Ocean and try to sort through her unsettled emotions.

Part of her discomfort, she knew, was due to Miranda. Although Zach had returned to L.A., Miranda had remained in Santa Barbara, living in the family wing. Jealousy surrounded the woman like a particularly noxious cloud; she seemed determined to make Alex's life miserable with her sly innuendos. The unrelenting hostile behavior made Alex face the unpalatable truth of Miranda's very real existence in Zach's life.

The fact of his wife existed as solidly as one of the boulders forming the cliff upon which she walked. And unfortunately, though it was more than obvious that Zach and Miranda's marriage was less than idyllic, the beautiful, spiteful Mrs. Deveraux had made it all too clear that she was every bit as immovable as those enormous granite rocks.

Deciding that perhaps she ought to return to the city, where she wouldn't be forced to endure Miranda's presence, Alex returned to the house to find Averill waiting for her on the terrace. He was dressed in chinos, a navy polo shirt and white deck shoes. A white billed cap with gold braid was perched jauntily atop his sun-streaked hair.

"I came by to kidnap you," he said to her cheerfully.

Alex went ice cold. Her hands, her mind, her heart.

"Alexandra?" Eleanor, who'd been sitting on a blue-and-white striped lounge, rose quickly to her feet. "What's wrong?"

"Wrong?" Alex answered through lips that seemed to have turned to stone. What the hell was happening to her these days? She was turning into a hysterical ninny.

"Nothing." She shook her head to clear away the mists, then turned back toward the doctor with a smile. "I must have misunderstood you."

"No." He took off his cap and combed his long, aristocratic fingers through his hair, ruffling a fifty-dollar haircut. "It was my fault. I simply dropped by to invite you sailing. But I should have chosen my words more carefully. Especially since Eleanor has told me that you know about Anna's disappearance."

They were both looking at her as if they expected her either to faint or go screaming off across the manicured lawn at any second. Feeling ridiculously foolish, Alex ignored her lingering disquiet.

"I'd love to go sailing with you, Dr. Brandford."

"Averill," he reminded her with a friendly wink.

He was a very nice, uncomplicated person. And the way he hovered over Eleanor like a dutiful son proved he had a warm and caring nature.

Though she'd vowed never again to get involved with an older man, Alex wondered idly if the good doctor was married. If so, his wife, she decided, was a very lucky woman.

"Averill," she agreed with a smile.

As she ran upstairs to change into a pair of rubber-soled shoes, for the first time since her arrival in Santa Barbara, Alex was feeling almost lighthearted.

Before they left port, Averill gave Alex a brief lesson on the fundamentals of sailing, and while she tried to keep track of the terms, he might as well have been speaking in Sanskrit.

He laughed when she'd admitted her confusion. "I'd be equally lost if you began talking about dress design," he assured her. "I figured out buttons and bra hooks when I was a teenager. Other than that, everything else to do with female clothing remains a mystery."

She knew he was attempting to make her feel less foolish. He succeeded. Alex watched him cast off, maneuvering deftly and confidently around the ropes she knew would have tripped her and sent her flying over the gleaming brass railing.

The sail snapped in the breeze, then billowed, appearing starkly white against the cloudless cerulean sky as he guided the sleek ketch through the channel, out into the sea.

The boat skimmed across the water as Averill followed the jagged shoreline. Up till now, Alexandra's sole boating experience had been a futile attempt to row a cumbersome wooden craft across a Minnesota lake at Girl Scout camp the summer she turned twelve. Back then, all she'd gotten for her laborious efforts were blisters and a lobster red sunburn.

But this was different. This, she mused, as she leaned back and tilted her face up to the California sun, was like flying.

Averill proved to be a wonderful companion, entertaining her with tales of his sailing experiences, including more than one close call when he'd found himself caught in a sudden squall.

"You don't have to worry," he assured her when he viewed her worried frown after one such story. "Today's going to be clear sailing. All the way."

Like Zachary, he managed to appear supremely self-confident without seeming arrogant or egotistical. Reminding herself that one of the reasons she'd taken Averill up on his offer today was to forget about her problems—including those inherent with being in love with a married man—she turned her attention, instead, to the glorious scenery that could have graced the cover of a brochure put out by the Santa Barbara tourist bureau.

Gulls whirled overhead, their strident cries carried off by the ocean wind. Every so often one of them would go hurling downward, disappearing beneath the water, reappearing moments later with a flash of silver in his beak. Long-billed pelicans and wide-winged cormorants skimmed along the surface of the water; sea lions dozed atop sun-warmed rocks.

Averill steered the boat into a sheltered cove, where they sat on the polished teak deck and shared the lunch of cold chicken, pasta salad and crunchy French bread Eleanor's cook had packed into a wicker basket. The doctor's contribution to the picnic was a bottle of Napa Valley chardonnay.

The outing proved even more relaxing than Averill had promised. Alex thoroughly enjoyed the glorious day, the brisk sail, the congenial company.

"Thank you," she said after they'd returned to the yacht basin. "I had a wonderful time."

"The pleasure was all mine." His smiling eyes swept over her, taking in her face, flushed prettily from the sun, her sunset-bright hair, which had been whipped into an enticing froth by the sea breeze, her long, tanned legs, shown off by her daffodil yellow denim shorts.

"You know," he said, as he took her hand and helped her off the gently rocking ketch onto the floating dock, "if I were twenty years younger, I'd prove to you that there's a great deal more to life than work." He shook his head in disbelief. "In my day, a lovely woman like you certainly wouldn't still be running around unclaimed."

Alex had two choices: she could be irritated by his blatantly chauvinistic statement, or she could take his words as a masculine, if slightly dated, compliment and be flattered. She chose the latter.

"I do hope you're not calling me an old maid," she said with a light laugh.

"Not at all." He looked honestly horrified that she might think such a thing.

"Good. That being the case, I should tell you that I don't think you're old at all." Feeling remarkably carefree, she linked her arm through his. "In fact, next time you're in L.A., I insist you let me reciprocate by taking you out on the town."

"I'm speaking at a conference in the city next month. Why don't I come down in the ketch? We can sail to Catalina and I'll let you buy me lunch at Las Casitas."

"It's a date. I've never been to Santa Catalina Island."

"You haven't?" He stopped in his tracks and looked down at her as if she'd just sprouted a second head. "My prescription for you, Alexandra Lyons, is regular doses of sun and salt air. And I intend to schedule in regular checkups to ensure you're following orders."

Alex laughed, as she was supposed to. "Yes, Doctor."

Chapter Twenty-Five

The lightened mood instilled by the brisk sail disintegrated when the terrifying dream returned that night. To make matters worse, the next morning Zach arrived at the house to discuss the logistics of the Chicago opening with Eleanor.

Watching Zach and Miranda was like watching a Tennessee Williams play. Miranda, who seemed in no hurry to return to her work at the London Lord's, was her typical theatrical self, ensuring her place at center stage, while Zach glowered and remained silent.

As if conjured up by some special-effects department in the sky, a storm front coincided with Zach's arrival, driving away the benevolent sunshine with wind gusts, pelting rain and fog.

When Miranda cursed viciously at yet another servant for some minor imagined transgression, Alex decided that rain or no rain, she had to escape.

She went out to the six-car garage and took the Mercedes two-seater Eleanor had generously made available to her during her stay. She drove past the Montecito Country

Club, continuing on through the center of town to the coast, passing by sandy East Beach, where the usual weekend arts-and-crafts show had been rained out.

She passed Stearns Wharf—which Averill had told her was the oldest operating wharf on the West Coast—and the yacht harbor, where she was tempted to stop and see if the doctor was working on his ketch, as he was every other weekend he wasn't sailing. She felt an overwhelming urge for some easy, uncomplicated companionship.

Worried that after his remarks about her lack of dating he might think she'd set her sights on him, Alex stopped, instead, at the breakwater and walked along the half-mile manmade marvel, attempting to work off her anxiety.

She stood at the end of the breakwater for a long time, watching the white-capped waves roll in and thinking of Zach. Sea mist dampened her face and went unnoticed.

For whatever reason—Alex knew it wasn't love—Zach appeared determined to make the best of his marriage. Which meant he was off-limits.

Averill was right about one thing: she'd been living unnaturally. It was time she started dating again, if for no other reason than to get on with her life. She'd come a long way from the naive young acolyte who'd let Debord steal her designs, then throw her away as if she were a stale croissant left over from breakfast.

She was an Emmy-winning designer, dammit! She had a fulfilling, glamorous career, and thanks to Eleanor Lord, she was a businesswoman with her first licensing agreement. The thing to do, Alex told herself firmly, was to quit mooning over a man she could not have and get on with her life. It was time, past time, that she put the man out of her mind!

Which wouldn't be all that easy to do, considering the fact that they still had to work together on the Blue Bayou project. But she'd already accomplished so much, had come so far. Her mother had always assured her that she could do anything she put her mind to. So, from now on, she would simply put her mind to burying whatever feelings she had for Zach deep inside her.

The wind picked up and the temperature dropped, causing Alex to realize she'd been standing out in the rain for a very long time. Shivering, she headed back for the car.

Not yet ready to return to the estate, she continued her drive through the fog-draped Santa Ynez Mountains. With the heater going full blast, she warmed up quickly. She tuned the radio to a rock station; the windshield wipers added a *swish-swish-swish* counterpoint to Bruce Springsteen's driving beat.

For a long time, as she maneuvered the car around the curves, she continued to give herself a stern pep talk. "Zach? Zach who? Oh, Zachary Deveraux, *that* Zach. He's only a business associate. Nothing more."

She could tell herself that all day. And all night. But more than an hour later, after she'd made a U-turn in the middle of the road and headed back down the mountainside toward the Montecito estate, Alex realized it was folly to keep lying to herself.

The frightening truth was that despite all her good intentions and stalwart resolutions, if Zach ever wanted her, she would give herself to him.

Immersed in her tumultuous thoughts, she hadn't noticed that the little sports car had begun to pick up more speed than was prudent, given the slick conditions of the road.

Alex pumped the brake lightly. When it failed to gain purchase, she tried again. Nothing.

Again, harder.

Again, nothing.

Risking putting the car into a deadly skid, she pushed the brake pedal all the way to the floor. Instead of coming to a screeching halt or even slowing down, the car picked up speed.

Trying to remain calm, Alex downshifted, which, considering the steep grade she was descending, proved ineffectual. The engine whined as misty trees sped past the windows.

Now she was scared. Leaning forward, she hung on to the wheel with both hands, trying to steer around the treacherous wet curves. Time slowed. She wondered if her life would begin flashing before her eyes.

Alex sincerely hoped not; seeing through the slanting rain was hard enough without having to watch a rerun of past mistakes.

Unfamiliar with the mountains and having paid scant attention to her surroundings earlier, she had no idea how far she still had to go before reaching level ground. As she sped past a side road leading to a winery, she hoped the wild ride would be over soon.

It was. But not in the way she'd hoped. As the car raced around a snakelike series of curves, the tires hit a particularly wet patch of roadway and began to hydroplane. The rear of the car fishtailed, sending her off the pavement, over an embankment, where the front end of the Mercedes settled with a great sucking sound into the mud.

Alex was thrown forward, but her seat belt held, keeping her safe. Safe, she determined once she could breath again. But lost. And the rain was still coming down.

Cursing in a way that even Miranda might have admired, had Zach's wife been unfortunate enough to be out in such horrid weather, Alex managed to push open the door. And then, as the skies opened up still more she began to walk.

Although the winery tasting room was closed, Alex was fortunate to find an employee taking inventory. The young man let her in, retrieved a handful of paper towels from the rest room and, while she called the house to explain about the accident and to request that one of the servants come retrieve her, poured her a very large and very tasty glass of estate-bottled *pinot noir*.

Since she hadn't eaten anything but a grapefruit and a cup of coffee at breakfast time, which was, she realized, glancing down with surprise at her water-fogged watch, more than eight hours ago, the smooth, ruby red wine went straight to her head, creating a comfortable glow. Indeed, the feeling was so pleasurable, she didn't refuse a refill.

Thirty minutes later, Zach arrived, looking every bit as foreboding and dangerous as the weather.

"I didn't ask Eleanor to send you." Alex blinked with surprise at the sight of Zach practically filling the tasting room doorway.

"I volunteered."

"Oh." While far from drunk, Alex was relaxed enough to be able to ignore his lambent fury. "Well, it was certainly nice of you to come out in the rain this way."

"You can thank me later." He pulled a bill from his wallet and tossed it onto the oak bar.

The young man pushed the money back. "It's on the house. My pleasure."

He was talking to Zach, but his gaze was on Alex.

"Zach, this is Steve," Alex said with remarkable cheer, considering the events of the past hour. "Steve, this is Zachary. My, uh, business associate."

"Nice to meet you," Steve said without so much as a glance Zach's way.

Seeing Alex through the other man's eyes, observing the familiar aching on his young face, irritated the hell out of Zach.

"Mrs. Lord appreciates you helping her houseguest," he muttered. He took hold of Alex's arm and yanked her off the bar stool. He also left the bill where it was.

"Come back some time when you're not in such a hurry," Steve called out after them. Zach knew damn well the irritatingly good-looking Steve was not talking to him.

"Thank you, I'll do that," Alex said. Her sunny smile, as Zach dragged her across the wooden floor, could have banished all the rain clouds overhead.

"Wasn't he nice?" Alex asked as they drove away from the winery in Zach's Jag.

"A real prince," Zach muttered. "You certainly didn't waste any time making another conquest."

"What?" Alex glanced toward his rigid profile. "What are you talking about?"

"First you have Averill practically tripping all over himself to take you sailing, and now your new little friend Steve—the guy reminded me of my old hunting dog, Duke, slobbering over a juicy steak bone. By the time you leave town, you'll probably have every male within a thirty-mile radius of Santa Barbara lusting after you."

Was he actually jealous? The idea was both surprising and encouraging. "That's not a very nice thing to say."

"In case you haven't noticed, sweetheart, I'm not exactly in a very nice mood. Have you noticed how fate keeps decreeing I step in and rescue you from your own stupidity? Kinda makes you wonder what I must've done in a past life to deserve such lousy karma, doesn't it?"

So much for encouraging. The warm glow instilled by the wine was shot to smithereens by his gritty tone and unkind words. Refusing to respond, Alex folded her arms and pretended avid interest in the scenery flashing by the passenger window.

Neither one of them spoke for a long time. Finally Zach said, "I arranged for a tow truck to pick up the Mercedes."

"Thank you," she answered stonily, still refusing to look at him.

"In case you're interested, it's not that banged up."

"Oh, I'm so glad," she said on a burst of honest relief. "I was afraid I'd totaled Eleanor's car."

"If you were so concerned about the damn car, you shouldn't have been driving so fast. Christ, Alex, don't you have any more sense than to speed on a wet highway in the rain?"

"Speeding? You think I was speeding?"

"If you'd been driving at a halfway prudent speed, you wouldn't have gone off the road," he said with the unwavering logic she usually admired.

She gave an unladylike snort. "Gee, you've got a helluva lot of faith in me."

"You're not exactly a model of restraint, sweetheart."

Alex knew he didn't mean the term as an endearment. "I am, too!"

Didn't he realize how much restraint it had taken her not to pull out all the stops and seduce him?

Most of the time, Alex didn't think it would be all that difficult to lure Zachary into her frustratingly lonely bed; at other times, such as now, she almost got the impression that he didn't like her at all.

And women were supposed to be the changeable ones, she thought darkly. Men might not suffer PMS, but they damn well had their own share of mood swings, nevertheless.

He brought the car to a halt at a four-way stop. "Honey, you wouldn't even know how to spell restraint."

That did it. To hear such a disparaging tone from the man she loved was the last straw in a very trying day.

"Go to hell." Unfastening her seat belt with trembling fingers, she opened the door and began walking angrily down the road.

Chapter Twenty-Six

"Goddammit, Alexandra!"

He'd been panic-stricken when her call had come. All during the nerve-racking drive to the winery, thoughts of Alex lying in the roadway, broken and bleeding, had billowed in his mind like dark and deadly smoke from a sugarcane field fire.

Wanting, needing, to get to her as quickly as possible, he'd disregarded personal safety and all state speed statutes, racing into the mountains, planning to take her into his arms, to soothe her, to love her.

But then he'd found her sitting coyly atop that bar stool, sipping wine as if she were in some damn nightclub, flirting with that blond beachboy, who in turn looked as if he'd been struck by lightning, and every one of Zach's good intentions had disintegrated.

He was, admittedly, furious. Furious at her for risking her life, furious at himself for allowing loyalty to Eleanor and responsibility toward Lord's to prevent him from simply saying the hell with the company and his marriage and taking what he wanted.

And what he wanted, dammit, was Alex.

"Dammit, Alexandra," he complained, driving slowly along the edge of the road, "would you quit acting like a spoiled brat and get back into this car?"

She didn't answer; nor did she so much as spare him a glance. She just kept walking, her hooded cardinal slicker brightening the dismal gray day.

"It's another ten miles to the house."

"I run ten miles all the time."

"Not in weather like this."

She turned. "It just so happens that I like walking in the rain. And for your information, Mr. Know-It-All Dever-aux, if you check with a mechanic after the tow truck driver pulls the car out of that ditch, you'll discover that the brakes gave out. I wasn't speeding."

"Are you saying the brakes failed?"

"Got it on the first try. I guess the famed German auto-motive engineering isn't all it's cracked up to be." She turned away and began marching down the road again.

This was ridiculous. He couldn't follow her all the way back to Eleanor's. Muttering a string of pungent curses, he pulled the car over to the side of the deserted roadway.

He moved quickly, planning to drag her, kicking and screaming if necessary, back to the car.

She didn't look back when she heard the car door slam. Nor did she pause as his long, determined strides brought him alongside her.

"Go away. And leave me alone."

"The hell I will," he snarled, his temper approaching boiling point. "You're coming with me."

But he'd no sooner grabbed her arm when Alex sur-prised them both. Swinging her fist wildly, she connected firmly with his jaw.

"I said, leave me alone!" she shouted, her words whipped away by the driving wind.

"Too late." It was the last straw. Ignoring the surprising pain in his jaw, he grabbed hold of the front of her slicker and pulled her toward him. Water streamed down his furious face.

"I'm sick of this," he shouted. "I'm fed up with this entire fucking charade."

A lesser woman would have been intimidated by the savage gleam glittering in his midnight dark eyes. Alex tilted her head—disregarding her hood as it fell backward, exposing her head to the driving rain—and met his dangerous gaze with a challenging glare of her own.

"What charade?"

"For starters, my sitting in my office, drinking in your scent, trying to keep my mind on facts and figures when all the time I'm wondering what you're wearing beneath those outrageously sexy outfits you insist on wearing, instead of proper little pinstriped dress-for-success business suits.

"I'm sick and tired of spending some of the most miserable nights of my life lying alone in bed, imagining you across town—so near, and yet so impossibly far away—and wondering what you're doing. Or worse yet, who you're doing it with.

"I'm sick of remembering that night, when I held you in my arms and wished that I possessed the power to stop time. I'm sick of going to sleep so horny my balls ache and having to take cold showers every morning to get rid of the goddamn hard-on that comes from dreaming about you.

"And mostly I'm sick of having spent all this time wishing for what might have been and kicking myself for not having made love to you when we had the chance.

"I've wanted you more than I've ever wanted any woman in my life. But because I care about you more than I've ever cared about any woman in my life, I've been killing myself trying to keep from hurting you. And what the hell have all these good and noble intentions gotten me?

"A punch in the jaw from a snotty, stubborn female who doesn't even have enough common sense to come in out of the rain!"

He was definitely on a roll. Alex, who was finally seeing the fire she'd always suspected dwelt beneath that infuriatingly remote exterior, stared up at him in awe. She knew she should find such violent emotion frightening. But knowing that Zach would never actually harm her, she was finding it thrilling.

His head swooped down and Alex cried out as his mouth captured hers in a hard, rapacious kiss.

She began kissing him back, desperately, hungrily.

The rain sluicing over their taut, straining bodies went ignored as they consumed each other with deep kisses. They were caught in the unrelenting grip of something powerful and ageless and primal. Something that could no longer be denied.

"If that wasn't an earthquake," she said breathlessly, "we're in trouble."

"It was no earthquake." His lips skimmed hotly up her face; he pulled her hard against him.

Zach wanted to take her here and now. He wanted to drag her to the side of the road and bury his throbbing shaft in her silken, welcoming warmth. Deep, then deeper still. Until he could touch her womb.

Alexandra wanted him to do exactly that. And more.

"Do you have any idea how long I've wanted you?"

"How long?" Her shaky laugh was half seduction, half promise.

"Forever." His declaration was half wonder, half certainty.

A rush of warmth flooded through her, so deep and hot she was amazed that steam wasn't rising from her skin. She rained kisses, stinging, avid kisses all over his wonderful, handsome face. She continued to kiss him as he carried her back to the car.

He set her down on the back seat, impatiently ripped open her slicker, then covered her body with his. He was hard and aroused, and the movement of her hips against his aching groin created a building pressure that made him feel on the brink of exploding.

One final last voice of conscience, lurking in the far reaches of his mind, struggled to make itself heard. He pushed himself up on his elbows. Her cheeks were flushed the deep, pink hue of the Old Blush blossoms in Eleanor's rose garden, her lips were slightly parted, her hair was a gleaming wet tangle. Her eyes shone with a dazzling gold light.

She was, as always, the most beautiful, alluring woman he'd ever seen. But as his *grand-mère* had always told him, and he'd learned the hard way with Miranda, beauty was only skin-deep. Alex's true beauty, Zach knew, was a deep-seated, inner beauty of heart and spirit that would make her still stunning on her one-hundredth birthday.

"I don't want to hurt you."

Caught up in ancient, primal needs, Alex misunderstood his concern. "You won't."

He decided to try one last time. Then he wouldn't be responsible for the consequences. "I can't give you what you want, Alexandra. What you need."

She smiled at that. A slow, fatally seductive smile that beautiful sirens had been using to lure men to their doom since the dawning of time.

"Oh, I think you're wrong about that," she murmured silkily. Lifting her hips, she rubbed her pelvis against the placket of his jeans.

When her hand moved in the direction of his painful tumescence, Zach grasped it and lifted it to his lips. "That's not what I meant." He kissed the soft, delicate flesh at the center of her palm. "You deserve a man who can promise you a future."

She didn't want to think of that. Not now. Not when every nerve ending in her body felt as if it were on fire. "You talk too much." Dragging her hands through his hair, she pulled his head down and gave him another long, heartfelt kiss.

"I don't want to think about the future," she insisted against his lips. "I only want to think about now. And how much I want you."

For months, he'd fought his feelings. Fought her. And now he wouldn't, couldn't, fight any longer.

Consequences be damned. Zach surrendered to her husky voice trembling with pent-up emotion, the seductive movement of her hips, her lips, plucking so enticingly at his. He surrendered to the inevitable.

He pulled down her jeans, saying something pungent and profane when the wet denim clung to her smooth legs. Today's panties were the bright blue color of cornflowers, tied low on her hips with narrow white satin ribbons. He cupped his palm against her silk-covered mound and elicited a soft, shuddering moan of pleasure.

"Christ." Edging his way beneath the lace-trimmed leg band, he eased a finger deep inside her. Her voluptuous flesh was as hot as hellfire, as wet as her lusciously ripe mouth. "You are so hot," he rasped. "So ready for me." He kissed her again, tasting the rain. Tasting her.

"More than ready." Leaning up on her elbows, she began tearing with urgent frenzy at his zipper. "I want you, Zach." She knew she was begging. But she didn't care. She'd have gotten down on her knees if necessary, if only to end this agonizing torment. "Now. Please." A sob of relief escaped her ravished lips when his penis burst free, as hard and smooth as polished marble, rampant with vitality.

When she stroked it wonderingly, from its base amid its nest of crisp ebony hair to its silken tip, spreading the gleaming bead of cream with an innocently seductive fingertip, reason shattered.

Zach ripped at the satin ribbons and tore away the scrap of blue silk. Their lips fused again as together they fought to pull down his own wet jeans. He plunged into her, taking her with a ravenous hunger he feared could never be quenched.

All thought evaporated. Passion burst from their hot, wet pores. When her body went rigid beneath him, he buried his mouth in her throat and moved his hips in one deep, final thrust. She cried out, clinging to him as they came together, proving to Zach that sometimes fantasies really did come true.

Chapter Twenty-Seven

Alex had known this would happen. Just today, she'd admitted the inevitability of making love with Zach, little suspecting that the opportunity would come so soon.

No, she reminded herself, *this was not making love.* This was sex. Hot, fast and thrilling. But it was not love. At least not on Zach's part.

His passion had been born from anger and jealousy, and perhaps, she conceded, from a fear she'd been injured in her accident. But none of those reasons, as understandable as they were, equaled love.

He was lying on top of her, their legs tangled, their hearts still beating in unison even as the shared rhythm gradually slowed. He lifted his head and looked down into her face, his dark eyes as grave as his expression.

"Alex—"

"No." She caught his hand as it brushed away the tangled damp hairs clinging to her cheek. "If you dare apologize—"

This time it was he who cut her off with a quick, hard kiss that would have sent her reeling had she not already been lying down.

"I wasn't going to apologize. Well, maybe I was," he allowed when she gave him a knowing look. "But not in the way you think. I'm not at all sorry this happened. But I *am* sorry that when I finally did get around to doing what I've wanted to do for months, for years, what I should have done that first night . . ."

He frowned and shook his head in obvious self-disgust. He hadn't even bothered taking off her raincoat or sweater.

"Lord, Alexandra, never in my wildest dreams did I envision making love to you in the back seat of a car like some oversexed teenager."

His tender gaze threatened to be her undoing. Afraid that her love for him was written across her face in bold, black script, Alex wiggled out from beneath him and began struggling to locate her clothes.

Her panties had landed atop the back of the front seat; they were, she decided, observing the torn ribbons, a lost cause.

"I'll buy you a new pair."

"That's not necessary." She shoved them into her slicker pocket and started working on turning her jeans right side out.

"I said I'll buy you a new pair."

"Fine. Do whatever you want." She began to struggle into the tight jeans, which wasn't all that easy, from a sitting position, with Zach watching her with those steady, unblinking eyes.

If she kept wiggling her little ass like that, he was going to end up stripping those jeans back off again, Zach mused, as he felt an all too familiar tightening in his groin.

She'd encased herself in enough ice to cover the North and South poles. Silently working his way through every curse he knew, both in English and the Acadian of his roots, Zach jerked his own pants up and wished he hadn't given up smoking during football training in his freshman year of college.

His renewed frustration gave birth to an urge for a cigarette. Or a drink. Jack Daniel's, straight up, no ice.

"Look," he said, deciding to try again, "I said I was sorry. What else can I say to try and make this right?"

"I told you, you don't have to apologize." To Alex's aghast humiliation, fat hot tears started flowing down her cheeks. "I understand, Zach."

Unable to bear the pity she thought she was reading in his expression, she turned her head away and stared out unseeing into the rain, trying to calm her whirling mind and soothe her aching heart.

"Dammit—"

"We got carried away. It happens sometimes." She took another deep, shuddering breath. "No harm, no foul. Besides—"

"I love you." He ran his hand impotently across her hunched shoulders.

"—you certainly didn't do it all by yourself. You know what they say, it takes two—"

"I love you."

"—to tango. And to tell you the truth, I wanted it every bit as much as you did."

His words, stated so calmly and matter-of-factly, finally sank in. Hope was a hummingbird—no, Alex considered, a giant golden eagle—flapping its wings inside her heart. "Are you saying—"

"What I should have told you a long time ago. I love you, Alexandra Lyons."

She flung her arms around his neck and kissed him deep and hard. "I love you too, Zachary Deveraux."

"I know."

"Was I that obvious?"

"Not really. In fact, you've been driving me crazy trying to figure out exactly how you felt. Until earlier, when you finally let down your guard."

She'd hoped that, caught up in his own explosive orgasm, he hadn't heard her cry out her heart's most closely guarded secret. But whether loving Zach was wise or prudent, or even particularly moral, given his marital status, love him she did. She'd grown weary of hiding her feelings every time they were together.

"I'm still sorry I was kind of rough. And fast," he tacked on reluctantly.

"Actually," she said with a sassy grin, "I rather liked that part." It had been incredibly exciting. But it had also been more than that. It had been, in its own remarkable way, an epiphany.

As she sat in the back seat of Zach's car, watching the rain stream down the fogged-up windshield, Alex realized that what she'd experienced with Debord had been purely sexual.

It, too, had been exciting. But somehow, she'd always remained detached, as if watching herself perform for his pleasure. Even at the moment of orgasm, there had been no real emotional connection; instead, Alex had always been aware of her reaction through Debord's eyes.

But making love to Zach had been so very, very different. It had taught her that sometimes love didn't have to be soft and gentle. It could be hard and even a little frightening. And though she knew it was wrong, the blazing lovemaking she and Zach had just shared had left her wanting more.

Zach was stroking her shoulders and making a futile but endearing attempt to finger-comb her tangled hair. "We need to talk."

She opened her mouth to argue, to assure him it wasn't necessary, then decided there'd already been enough lies and evasions between them. "Yes."

After they returned to the front seat, Zach placed a call to a worried Eleanor from the car phone, assuring her that Alex was safe and sound, but that it was going to take a while for the tow truck to arrive.

That much was the truth. What he didn't tell his employer and friend was that he had no intention of waiting around for the truck. Not when he had more important things to do.

"I don't know about you, but I'm starved," he said after he'd hung up. "I'll admit to having things backward, but I think I owe you dinner."

His smile was that warm, uncensored one she hadn't seen since his mother's wedding. "I'm not exactly dressed to go out." She plucked at her damp sweatshirt and wrinkled damp jeans.

"That wouldn't matter at one of the little hole-in-the-wall seafood places on the pier," he pointed out.

She wasn't eager to have such a long-overdue private conversation in a public setting. Nor was she quite prepared to share Zach with anyone. Not yet.

"We could get takeout," she suggested. "And talk in the car."

"Brilliant." He leaned across the space between their leather seats and kissed her, a brief, feathery meeting of lips that sent warmth shimmering through her. "Takeout it is."

Which was how they came to be parked in a deserted lot overlooking the crashing surf, sharing french fries, Big Macs, cherry turnovers and a bottle of Dom Pérignon Zach had picked up at the liquor store next to McDonald's.

"I always promised myself that the first time we made love, we'd have champagne." He popped the cork with a flair that told Alex he did it often, then poured the sparkling golden wine into two paper cups. "And music." The car radio was tuned to a local jazz-and-blues station. "Unfortunately the liquor store didn't have any candles."

She took a sip of the champagne, enjoying the way the bubbles danced on her tongue. "This is perfect," she said, meaning it.

"Are you always this easy to please?"

"I'm a cheap date," she said on a laugh. "A Big Mac and I'm all yours."

He smiled and refilled her cup. "Next time I think we can do better."

Next time. Alex's yearning heart leapt upon the words, holding them close like a talisman.

They sat there for a long, comfortable time, sipping champagne and watching the waves roll unceasingly onto the shore. The sky was a misty gray curtain; in the distance came the lonely sound of a foghorn, a counterpoint to the voice of Billie Holiday singing of love and heartbreak.

"How long?" she murmured.

"Have I loved you?"

Alex nodded.

"I don't know," he answered honestly. "It snuck up on me over time. I was attracted to you that first night, but to be perfectly honest, I think that might've been my hormones talking."

"Thank God for talkative hormones," she murmured, grateful he hadn't turned down her invitation for that drink.

"Ain't that the truth." He took a sip of champagne and looked thoughtfully out to sea. "I knew I was getting into trouble at my mother's wedding. Because, if it had been just lust, I probably would've done something about it—either that night, or after we got back to L.A., instead of letting you walk out of my life."

"You wanted to keep from hurting me."

"That was the plan. Unfortunately I think all I succeeded in doing was delaying the inevitable."

"Lucky for us, fate threw us back together again."

"I didn't mean what I said earlier." Zach ran the back of his hand down the side of her face in a slow, warming sweep. "About fate and my lousy karma."

"I know.... I think I've loved you from that first night," Alex admitted.

"Why didn't you tell me before now?"

"Did you really not know how I felt?" At times she'd thought it had been so obvious that everyone in the Lord's offices must have seen it.

Zach shrugged. For the second time in a few hours, he was feeling uncomfortably like a teenager again. *She loves me. She loves me not.* It had been years—aeons—since any woman possessed the power to make him feel so insecure.

"I thought, sometimes, you did. But whenever we'd start to get close, you'd back away."

"You were married."

"I still am," he felt obliged to say.

"I know." She sighed. "But somehow, as horrible as this sounds, back there in the mountains it just didn't matter anymore." Besides, she mused in an effort to justify her behavior, it wasn't as if Zach had a real marriage.

"No," he agreed. "It didn't."

His flat tone worried her. "I hope I didn't complicate things."

He heard the uncharacteristic insecurity in her soft voice and hurried to reassure her. "Things were already complicated before we met." Her hair had dried into a riotous halo of red-gold waves around her lovely, too-somber face. Zach tugged on the bright ends. "You are the best thing that's ever happened to me."

He kissed her again. For a long, glorious, heart-swelling time. "It's not going to be easy," he warned after they could breathe again.

She laughed at that. "It couldn't be any harder than it's been all these months, trying to keep my feelings from showing."

"That's just it." He took her hand and kissed her fingertips, one at a time, with an exquisitely sweet tenderness. "I wasn't exaggerating when I told you that things were complicated," he began slowly, reluctantly.

It wasn't easy admitting he'd made a major mistake in getting involved with an emotionally unstable woman who only wanted to parade him around on a leash in front of her society friends. But after the unintentional pain he'd caused Alex, Zach felt he owed her the truth.

"Miranda's beautiful. And sexy," Alex murmured. "Any man would be attracted to her."

"For a kid who came out of bayou Catholic schools, the kind of uninhibited sex Miranda offered was a definite turn-on," he admitted grimly. "But I guess some of those youthful catechism lessons took, after all. Because it didn't take long to realize that sex without emotional commitment isn't fun at all. It's depressing. And lonely."

"I learned the same lesson," Alex murmured, thinking back on that last, sad night with Debord. "The hard way." She was surprised and relieved to realize the memory no longer hurt. "So, why did you marry Miranda?"

"Because despite my success, I couldn't quite stop thinking of myself as the nearly indigent son of a Louisiana bayou sugarcane farmer. Miranda was beautiful, but more importantly, she was filthy rich. And she had status. And social standing."

"And that was important to you?" Alex was surprised.

He shrugged and wished again for a cigarette. "I thought it was. At the time."

Unable to believe he'd been so shallow, Zach dragged his hand through his hair. "The ugly truth was," he muttered in a voice thick with self-revulsion, "Miranda went on one of her infamous shopping sprees at a time when, as much as I hate to admit it, I'd definitely been for sale."

Alex placed a palm against his cheek and felt the muscle jerk. "You shouldn't be so hard on yourself," she said quietly. "We all have dreams. The problem is that sometimes, when we finally get to where we've always thought we wanted to be, it's an entirely different place from what we'd imagined."

Like her dream of working with Debord, she knew. "Everyone makes mistakes, Zach."

"Yeah, but some mistakes take longer to sort out."

He wasn't exaggerating. Alex listened with a sinking heart to Zach's explanation of the outstanding stock, of the raider who was threatening a takeover, of Miranda's threat to sell her own inherited stock if necessary, to keep Zach away from Alex.

"I knew she suspected we were having an affair," Alex said. "But since there wasn't anything concrete for her to be jealous about..."

"She thinks we've slept together. Which is pretty much the truth now." Once again Zach found himself wishing he'd done things right.

"There'll be other times," Alex assured him, reading the face, the mind, of this man she loved.

"A lifetime," he agreed. He kissed her again, wondering how he could have ever been so lucky to have this dazzling, intelligent, sweet person love him.

"But I'd never be able to live with myself if we achieved our happiness at Eleanor's expense," Alex murmured.

"You care about her that much?"

"I love her," Alex said simply. "I told you how, when I was little, we moved around a lot."

"I remember you mentioning that." He wondered what Alex would say if she knew he had a thick dossier listing all her addresses from shortly before her third birthday through till today. It was those first two years he'd never been able to uncover; those same missing years that had Eleanor convinced Alex was Anna.

"Whenever I made a friend at school, I'd have to leave her behind. After a while, it was safer not to make any friends."

"I can't imagine you not having friends." Especially boyfriends, Zach thought, shocked at the renewed jolt of jealousy that shot through him at the thought of her swaying in some boy's arms at the spring prom. Or even worse, making out in the back seat of some souped up Chevy after a high-school football game.

"Oh, I always got along with people, but it was easier not to let myself get really close to anyone. My brother, David, was my best friend. And then he died.

"Since then, I've only been close to Sophie. And, of course, you. And Eleanor. I know it sounds strange, but from the first, I've felt a bond with her. Almost like family."

She looked up at Zach, unaware of his reaction to her words. "Do you suppose, because I lost my mother and Eleanor lost her granddaughter, we just naturally gravitated toward one another? To fill some shared emotional need?"

"Makes sense to me," he agreed carefully, even as he wondered what he was going to do about this latest complication. For months he'd been trying to convince himself that his only barrier to a life with Alex was his marriage to Miranda.

But now he was forced to wonder how she would react when she discovered his subterfuge. Would she still love him after learning he'd hired private investigators to delve into every aspect of her life—including her affair with that sicko French designer? Would she still want to build a life with him when she realized he'd been lying to her all these months she'd been working for Lord's?

He hadn't really told her an untruth, but as Sister Mary Joseph, his fourth-grade teacher had always said, a lie of omission was just as much a sin as an out-and-out lie. Zach had the uneasy feeling that when the truth was revealed, Alex would probably agree with the rigid, ruler-wielding nun, who'd spent nine long months terrorizing the ten-year-old boys in her class.

"Well, there's only one thing to do," Alex said, oblivious to Zach's troubled thoughts.

"What's that?" Zach willingly pushed the nagging worries away. There would be, he knew, a price to pay for what he'd done. He just wasn't prepared to face it today.

He wanted, he *needed*, more time. Time to extricate himself from his marriage, time to save Lord's for Eleanor. Time to figure out whether Alex truly was Anna, and how that would affect their future together.

"As hard as it's going to be, we'll have to keep our feelings secret a bit longer," Alex decided aloud. "Until you can ensure that no one can take Lord's away from Eleanor."

"You think I can do that?"

"You're my knight in shining armor, remember?" Alex said, smiling up at him in a way that made him feel even guiltier for all these months of lies. "You can do anything."

As he drew her back into his arms, Zach hoped that she was right.

Chapter Twenty-Eight

Although he longed to take Alex to the nearest hotel where he could make love to her properly all night long, they both knew that wish would have to be postponed.

"We've the rest of our lives," she reminded him as they headed back to the estate.

And although he murmured an agreement, Zach found himself wishing, not for the first time certainly, that life wasn't so damn complicated.

Not surprisingly, their return was met with a great deal of fanfare. Eleanor, pooh-poohing Alex's concerns about the car, was vastly relieved she'd returned safe and sound. Clara, spooky as always, hinted at the possibility of some unseen forces.

"Poltergeist," she declared knowingly. "Or some restless spirit who wants Alexandra out of Santa Barbara."

Although she was no spirit, Miranda fit the description perfectly. She was furious.

"I warned you," she spat out between clenched teeth once she and Zach were alone in their upstairs bedroom. "I told you what would happen if you slept with that little slut again."

"Although I've always admired your acting skills, Miranda, someone needs to write you a third act," Zach countered. "This dialogue sounds vaguely familiar." He stripped off his sweater, went into the adjoining bathroom and shut the door.

"It's too late for a shower, you two-timing son of a bitch!" Miranda yelled at him when she heard him turn on the water. "Because I already smelled your little whore's perfume on you."

Miranda's temper, which had always been formidable, seemed to be getting worse. And, Zach considered grimly, as the room began to fill with steam, all her hostility was directed toward Alex.

Uneasy about his wife's increasing instability, Zach wanted to avoid doing or saying anything that might give Miranda an excuse to harm Alex.

Knowing he couldn't hide from his wife indefinitely, Zach exited the stall, dried himself, then wrapped a towel around his middle and returned to the bedroom to face Miranda's wrath.

"I've got a suggestion," he said as he took a pair of cotton briefs from the top drawer of the antique mahogany chest.

Miranda eyed him suspiciously. "Why do I think I'm going to hate this?"

"Actually, it's a business proposal."

"Really?" she asked with a show of disinterest. But Zach saw the familiar flash of avarice in her eyes and experienced the hope this might not be as difficult as he'd thought. "What type of business proposal?"

"This marriage has been a farce from the beginning. You're not happy. I'm not happy. So, why don't we just cut our losses? Before we end up hurting one another even more?"

She lighted a cigarette, sat down on the edge of the bed and crossed her legs. Zach remembered when even a glimpse of those smooth, white thighs could make him hard. But that was another time. And sometimes, it seemed, another world.

"The problem is, Zachary, dear, you misunderstand the situation."

"Why don't you explain it to me, then?" he suggested mildly.

"The simple truth is I'm not unhappy. On the contrary, darling, I like being married."

"How can you say that? We hardly see each other. And whenever we are together, all we do is fight."

"There's something that you don't seem to understand," she said patiently, as if speaking to a very slow kindergartner.

Once again Zach realized how superior to him she considered herself. His humble background, which had proved such a source of fascination when they'd first met, was routinely thrown back in his face as proof of his lower status.

"I'm trying to understand," he said.

"The truth, as unpalatable as it may be, is that I am no longer a young woman. And in my world, divorced women of a certain age are often pitied.

"Which is why having a husband—" she exhaled a stream of blue smoke and looked him up and down as if he were livestock she was considering purchasing "—even an absent one, gives a woman much needed cachet."

"You had two husbands before me," he pointed out. "You'll get married again."

"Perhaps." She stood up, ground out her cigarette in a crystal ashtray and walked across the room to the bureau.

"But I'll be the one to decide when and if we get a divorce."

"I could just file. God knows I've got grounds."

"So do I. Don't forget, Zachary, when it comes to adultery, what's sauce for the goose is sauce for the gander. Neither of us has remained faithful to our vows."

She extracted a folded piece of paper from beneath a pile of scented French lingerie. "You may be interested in this."

Curious in spite of his building frustration, Zach snatched the paper from her hand, his heart clenching as he read the three typed paragraphs.

"This is a memo from Nelson Montague."

"To his Hong Kong banker," Miranda agreed with a sly smile that made Zach's flesh crawl. "Revealing his plans for Lord's. After he takes over, of course."

Zach shook his head. "It's insane to think he can turn a thriving upscale chain like Lord's into Wal-Mart."

"More like Loehmans," Miranda corrected. She was smiling like a sleek cat who'd just swallowed a particularly succulent canary. The only thing missing was the yellow feathers sticking out from between those glossy vermilion lips. "Seconds, factory overruns, clothing that didn't sell because the sizes were too large or too small, or just didn't survive the fleeting time span of fashion fads."

"I know the kind of store you mean," Zach countered sharply. "And it damn well doesn't belong on Rodeo Drive."

"Oh, he intends to spin the Beverly Hills store off and sell it to Saks," she informed him, reminding Zach that in her own way, Miranda was no gorgeous blond bimbo. On the contrary, she had a very good head for business when it suited her.

"As for the others," she revealed, "buyers are already waiting in the wings."

"He intends to dismantle the entire chain?"

Which would, Zach thought, effectively put an end to the Alexandra Lyons Blue Bayou collection.

"That's the plan," she said cheerfully. "But all's well that ends well. The price per share he's offering will make the stockholders very, very rich."

"If they sell."

"Oh, enough will sell, Zachary. There's no limit to what people will do to make a quick profit." Her smile reached all the way to her eyes at the thought of all that lovely money. "Nelson taught me that."

"And did he also send you to me with this memo?" That was the part that didn't make any sense. The Australian raider was not known for tipping his hand.

"Of course not. Actually, I confess to being a bit naughty. I stole it from his briefcase while he was sleeping."

"And now you're selling the information to the highest bidder."

"In a way. This is my trump card, Zachary. We both know I hold the deciding stock. If I vote with you and Aunt Eleanor, Lord's will continue as is. If I choose to vote with Nelson..." She shrugged. "Well, I believe the memo's more than clear as to his plans."

"You realize this would kill your aunt."

"Now who's being overly dramatic? Auntie's a tough old bird. If she could survive the murders and the kidnapping and being widowed, she'd undoubtedly survive losing her beloved company."

"You're sure of that, are you?"

"Actually, I'm that sure of you, darling. As much as you'd love to set up housekeeping with your little chit of a designer, you possess the fatal flaw of loyalty.

"You won't even attempt to divorce me, because if you do, I'll play that trump card. Then we can both see exactly how much dear Auntie's heart can take."

Listening to her hateful words, watching her hard expression, Zach wondered how he could have been so blinded by lust not to have seen that Miranda was more than calculating. She was either very sick or very evil.

That idea sent another shock wave ricocheting through him. "Are you responsible for what happened to Alex today?"

"What are you talking about?" Her surprise appeared genuine.

"Did you have anything to do with that accident?"

"Are you accusing me of tampering with the brakes or something on your lover's borrowed car?"

"You want Alex gone."

"Of course I do. But gracious, Zach, I certainly don't have to stoop to murder to get rid of such an insignificant little problem. Besides," she pointed out, "if I even understood automobile mechanics, which I don't, I'd never risk breaking a nail."

She held out her hands as proof of her innocence, displaying ten long, perfectly manicured fingernails that sparkled like rubies.

"You could have gotten someone else to do your dirty work."

"But I already have, darling." She came and stood right in front of him and ran one of those ruby nails along the grimly set line of his lips. "I've got you." She pressed a kiss against his hard mouth, then laughing, left the room.

Cursing viciously, Zach crumpled the stolen memo into a ball and flung it across the room. As his Grand-mère Deveraux would have told him, he'd made his thorny bed; now it was up to him to lie in it.

Even if that meant he was destined to spend his nights alone. Thinking of a woman he didn't dare have.

Chapter Twenty-Nine

Although it was difficult, Alex and Zach managed to keep from giving Miranda any reason to sell her stock to the Australian corporate raider. Returning to the rigid self-restraint they'd both exercised for so long, they tried to pretend to be content with stolen kisses behind closed office doors.

They had hoped, in the beginning, that they might steal some private time together, but Alex grew increasingly aware of a man who seemed to be wherever she went. A man who was so unremarkable she might not have noticed him if Zach hadn't warned her that Miranda might hire a private detective.

Well, she obviously had, and although Alex was certain the poor guy must be bored stiff by her uneventful lifestyle, she also had to award this round to Miranda. Because while Miranda might not have any compromising videos or incriminating photographs to look at, she had effectively managed to stop Alex and Zach from making love again.

Alex was in her Venice bungalow, cutting out a piece of brightly flowered silk and singing along with Madonna, who was claiming to be a material girl, when the doorbell rang.

"Damn," she muttered, putting the shears aside. She was working on the dress she planned to wear for the Chicago debut and her mind was constantly filled with design changes. Her outfit had to be absolutely perfect. It had to display her talents, her individuality, her spirit. It had to speak to all those potential buyers, not to mention knocking the socks off the characteristically blasé fashion press.

Which was, Alex admitted as she looked through the peephole at the uniformed man, one helluva lot of responsibility to heap on a yard and a half of silk.

"Ms. Lyons?" he asked when she opened the door.

"Yes."

He handed her an envelope. "If you'll read this, ma'am, I think it should explain what I'm doing here."

Alex recognized Zach's bold scrawl immediately. She skimmed the brief note, which didn't tell her anything except that an emergency had come up and she was to go with the driver.

"What kind of emergency?" she asked.

"I don't know, ma'am. I'm only following orders."

Trusting Zach implicitly and worried enough that she wasn't about to waste time arguing, she grabbed up her purse and followed the driver out to the car.

They drove through the valley to the small Ontario airport, where she found the Lord's executive jet waiting for her. As she entered the cabin, she was surprised not to find Zach waiting aboard. "Isn't Mr. Deveraux joining us?" she asked the steward who welcomed her aboard.

"No, Ms. Lyons. You're our only passenger." He gave her a bright, professional smile and instructed her to fasten her seat belt. "Mr. Deveraux instructed a bottle of champagne to be opened as soon as we're airborne."

"Where are we going?"

"To Phoenix."

A little more than an hour later, Alex was being ushered into a luxurious suite at the five-star Arizona Biltmore Hotel.

"I've been going crazy waiting for you," Zach said in greeting her. His broad hands stroked her face, as his clever lips skimmed her cheek.

As always, her heart took a little leap at the sight of him. "This is a wonderful idea. But is it wise?"

"Miranda's in London."

"But that horrid little man she hired—"

"Is probably posting bail by now."

"Bail?"

"Loitering is against the law," he said. "Seems one of your neighbors got tired of seeing him parked across the street and anonymously called the cops, who weren't very pleased to learn that a guy whose P.I. license had been yanked six months ago was hanging around their jurisdiction with a concealed weapon in his possession."

"How did you know about his license?"

Zach shrugged. "You'd be amazed what you can find out with a computer these days."

"That was very clever of you," she allowed. "But there's just one little problem."

"What's that?"

"Your driver didn't give me time to pack."

His hands shaped her curves from shoulder to thigh. "Don't worry, sweetheart. For the weekend I've got in mind, you're not going to need any clothes."

She laughed and twined her arms around his neck. "Oh, goody."

The first time, when he'd taken her so ruthlessly in his car, all his hunger had come clawing out of him. Now, as he kissed her temple and breathed in her scent, Zach felt the knot in his gut beginning to loosen.

"You have to tell me what you like." He nibbled on her ear as his hands moved up and down her back. "What you want."

His caress was making her bones melt. She closed her eyes and swayed against him. "I want you to kiss me."

He complied, kissing her slowly from one corner of her lips to the other. "Like this?"

"That's an excellent start," she whispered. Her breath was like a soft summer breeze against his mouth.

"That's all it was, baby," he promised. "A start."

His tongue created a ring of fire as it circled her parted lips. A matching warmth flickered between her thighs. "Has anyone ever told you you're a very good kisser, Zachary?"

"Someone has now." He deepened the kiss, keeping it soft and gentle for a long, glorious time.

Entranced by the way he could make her float with only his mouth, Alex felt as if she'd fallen into a bed of feathers. Or clouds.

"Better than good," she declared. "You, Zachary Deveraux, are world-class."

"And you're prejudiced."

Seduced by the slow, deep kisses himself, he lifted her into his arms as tenderly as if she were a piece of Eleanor's precious crystal, rather than a flesh-and-blood woman. No man had ever treated her with such care.

"I won't break," she murmured as he placed her gently on the bed. The mattress sighed as he lay down beside her.

"I know. That's one of the things I love about you." He took off her outer clothing, treating each piece of revealed flesh to a sweet, seductive torment with hands that were heartbreakingly gentle, with a mouth that was warm and sensuous. "You can be strong and soft at the same time. Like steel wrapped in satin."

A delicious time later, he'd worked his way down to her teddy—a brief confection of silk and midnight lace.

And then his clothes were gone, as well, and he held her against him.

Even as her mind became wrapped in a gauzy pleasure, a tiny portion of her brain reminded her that this was supposed to be an activity for two people.

"I want to make love to you." She lifted her hand to his chest.

"Later." With his eyes on her, he kissed her fingertips individually. "This first time is for you, Alex. So relax. And just take."

His hands felt so good, stroking, soothing, calming, that she could not summon the strength to argue. So she closed her eyes and gave herself up to these shimmering sensations and allowed Zach to set the pace.

He tasted her and sent her floating. He savored her and made her fly. He murmured his love for her over and over again and made her melt. Though his hands remained gentle, there was a quiet, unyielding strength beneath his tender touch.

His lips took a slow, erotic journey, hot against her glowing flesh. "Promise me something," he murmured.

As his mouth dampened the ebony silk covering her breasts, Alex writhed in mindless pleasure. "Anything."

The word that shuddered from between her trembling lips was the truth. Alex was willing to do whatever Zach wanted. As the treacherous assault continued, she was willing to go wherever he took her.

"Promise me you'll never quit wearing this sexy underwear." Zach knew, without the faintest shadow of a doubt, that the sight of Alexandra clad in her skimpy French lingerie would still excite him when they were in their nineties.

"I promise," she gasped as his teeth tugged on a nipple.

When his palms pressed against the insides of her quivering legs, she willingly opened to him, knowing, even through the mists clouding her mind, that she'd never been more vulnerable. Not even that horrifying time with Debord.

And yet, as his teeth nipped at the sensitive flesh of her inner thighs, as his tongue soothed away the marks, as his heated breath warmed her feminine core through the silk her desire had already dampened, Alex had never felt safer. Because Zach loved her. And love, she discovered, was stronger than desire, more powerful than need. It was everything she'd been waiting for without having known she'd been waiting; Zach was everything she'd been yearning for, without having known she'd been yearning.

He peeled the silken barrier down her body with deft, expert hands. The same hands created trails of shimmering pleasure through the downy golden red curls at the juncture of her thighs. When his mouth settled on her throbbing, swollen clitoris, she felt a blaze of hot pleasure.

Zach slipped a finger inside her and found her warm and wet. "You are so incredibly soft." His words vibrated against the ultrasensitive flesh he was kissing as deeply, as erotically, as he'd kissed her mouth. "And sweet."

Nearly weeping, she arched against him, trusting him implicitly, loving him wholly. Her skin was so sensitized that the mere brush of a fingertip made her burn. Every nerve ending in her body had contracted into one tight, hot ball. As she struggled to fill her lungs with air, the ball imploded, leaving her limp, boneless and dazed.

She's so responsive! Zach thought. So sweet. And she's mine. All mine!

He held her trembling body tightly against his. He buried his face in her hair and thanked whatever fates had brought this woman to him.

She remained safely in his arms until the shudders racking her body ceased. She wanted to tell Zach everything she was feeling, but her mind, still numb from such exhilarating pleasure, could not think of the words.

All she could do was show him. She turned in his arms and pressed her lips against the pulse at the base of his throat.

"I love you," she whispered. She slid down his body, her mouth blazing a hot, wet trail that bisected his torso. "Love you." Her hands slid across his shoulders, down his slick sides. "Love you."

As she had done earlier, Zach willingly surrendered his power, allowing Alex to set the pace. As he had done earlier, she drew it out, reveling in the feel of his steely muscles clenching beneath her exploring hands, his quick intake of breath when she blew a soft, teasing breath across his taut stomach, his ragged groan as her lips embraced his rock-hard shaft.

Heat was thundering through him. Her sensuous tongue was stroking his throbbing cock from balls to tip in a way that threatened to blow whatever self-control he still possessed to smithereens.

"Honey," he groaned, grabbing handfuls of her thick bright hair, "if you don't stop right now, I'm going to... Oh, sweet Christ, Alex..."

He felt the pressure building at the base of his spine. Just in time, he pulled away, yanked her into his arms and held her tightly against him, drinking in deep gulps of breath as he struggled for control. When the storm was successfully, albeit temporarily, banked, Zach rolled her onto her back and braced himself over her. With hands that were far from steady, he pushed the tousled red-gold waves away from her face. "I love you."

He slid into her, heat to heat, flesh to flesh, male to female. With a sigh and a murmur, she opened to him, enfolding him with absolute generosity.

Later, as she lay in his arms, waiting for her heartbeat to return to normal, Alex, who'd sworn to herself she would not complain, murmured, "I wish we could stay like this forever."

"I know." Zach sighed, a deep breath thick with regret and lingering frustration. "Hang in there, sweetheart. I've got a plan. The only problem is it's going to take some time to pull it off."

Having no other choice, Alex trusted him. And waited.

The little girl huddled in the back of the closet, her eyes squeezed tightly shut as if that might keep the monsters that lurked in the dark at bay.

Those same monsters had killed her mommy and her daddy. The memory of all that blood remained riveted in her mind's eye, a dark crimson flag that would not go away.

She'd feared that the monsters would kill her, too, but then Rosa had swept her up and carried her out of the house. Clad only in nightgowns, feet bare, they'd made their escape.

Rosa had cried loudly as the car sped through the black night; Anna had not. The horror of what she'd witnessed had rendered her mute.

And then it was day again and they were hiding in the hotel room, awaiting the telephone call that Rosa assured Anna would fix everything.

But the call never came. Instead, the monsters found them. And then they murdered Rosa, just as they'd killed her parents.

Because they'd locked her away in this dark closet, Anna hadn't seen the monsters kill her nanny, the woman who had always seemed more like a mother to her than her own glamorous one.

But Anna had heard Rosa's desperate pleas. And even putting both hands over her ears had not kept her from hearing Rosa's broken sobs. Or her bloodcurdling scream.

And then, finally, even more terrifying, a long, empty silence descended.

The little girl lost all sense of time or place. She only knew, with every fiber of her tense young body, that the monsters—those same ones who'd lurked beneath her bed every night just waiting for Rosa to turn off the light—were still out there.

Just on the other side of the door.

Waiting to eat her, the same way the big bad wolf had gobbled up little Red Riding Hood's grandmother.

And so, unable to do anything else, she hunkered deeper into her fear and waited.

Hours later, Anna was jolted from a restless sleep by the sound of her own screams. At the same time, the closet door was flung opened, flooding the small cubicle with blinding light.

Terrified that the monsters were about to devour her whole, Anna screamed louder and began to kick at the intruder....

"Alex! It's all right. It's only a dream!" Zach shouted.

Immersed in her own horror, Alex couldn't hear him.

"It's all right," he insisted, sucking in a sharp breath as a flailing fist slammed against his ribs. "You're safe, sweetheart. No one's going to hurt you."

The struggle continued for another minute, a time that seemed longer to both Zach and Alex. Finally his soothing voice and gentling touch had their effect.

As his wide hand stroked her hair, Alex looked up at him. Fright still lingered in her expressive eyes.

"I had another nightmare."

"I know." He pressed his lips against her hair. "But it's all right. You're all right."

"Yes." Alex sighed and rested her cheek against his bare chest.

Zach listened to her breathing return to normal. Beneath his stroking hand, her flesh warmed. "Feeling better?"

"Uh-huh." She nodded. "I was dreaming of Anna," she murmured drowsily. Secure in his arms, she had already begun falling back to sleep.

Zach decided he must have misunderstood her. "Anna? You were dreaming about Anna Lord?"

"Mmm." She nestled closer against him. "I was dreaming about when she was kidnapped."

His blood chilled. "Oh?" he asked with a studied calm. "What about it?"

But Alex had fallen asleep again. Leaving Zach to watch her. And wonder.

The following morning, to Zach's secret frustration, Alex could recall nothing of her terrifying nightmare. Which kept him from learning if the dream had only been of things Clara and Eleanor had told her, or something else. Something only Anna Lord would have known.

After *croissants* and strawberries in bed, and another leisurely session of lovemaking, Alex reluctantly returned to Los Angeles.

As he watched the executive jet take off into the vast, blue Arizona sky, Zach was forced to ponder the possibility that, as amazing as it might seem, there was an outside chance, just perhaps, that Eleanor was right about Alexandra Lyons.

Chapter Thirty

On the day of the Chicago opening, there was more excitement than the time Queen Elizabeth and Nancy Reagan visited the Long Beach Lord's. Behind the scenes, as she made last-minute adjustments to the models' gowns, Alex's heart was beating so hard and so fast she was certain it would leap from her chest.

They'd flown to Chicago the previous day on the Lord's executive jet—Alex, Zach, Eleanor, the actresses and models, and, of course, Sophie. Concerned about the slight angina attack Eleanor had suffered a week prior to the trip, Averill had come along, as well. As had Miranda, who seemed determined to keep her husband away from Alex.

A by-invitation-only fashion show was planned for those valued credit-card holders and the fashion press. Afterward, the public would be allowed into the newest store on Michigan Avenue's Magnificent Mile.

The Blue Bayou boutique was on the sixth floor, set advantageously between designer gowns and fur coats. It was a romantic setting, with soft, piped-in music, tufted blue ottomans and deep-cushioned sofas designed to make a waiting husband or lover as comfortable as possible.

The set for today's fashion show resembled an old plantation; the designer—one of several set designers borrowed from the television show—had twined fragrant pink, red and white flowers around *faux* Grecian marble pillars. A pair of trees draped in Spanish moss flanked the stage.

A white satin-covered runway bisected the boutique; on either side were gilt chairs; a rose had been placed on each white brocade seat.

"It's absolutely stunning," Alex breathed softly, staring at the boutique above which, as Eleanor had promised, her name appeared in sky blue neon.

She'd seen the drawings, of course. And she'd been here the previous evening, but although she'd stayed till past midnight, the stage had still been little more than scaffolding, and the flowers had been safely stored in the florist's walk-in cooler.

"Not as stunning as the clothes," Eleanor answered. "I knew you were talented, Alexandra, but you've surpassed even my expectations."

Having discovered exactly how demanding Eleanor Lord could be, Alex took her words as high praise indeed.

Only minutes before the show was to begin, Zach appeared backstage. After some vague and incomprehensible remarks about needing her input on pricing structure, he led her into a nearby dressing room and shut the door.

"Zach," she whispered, "the show's about to begin."

"Not for another five minutes." He played with the ends of her hair. "Have I ever told you that I love your hair?"

"Yes, but—"

"Relax, sweetheart. They haven't even opened the downstairs doors yet.... I do, you know." He ran his hand down the mass of waves. "I love the color. The scent." He kissed the top of her head. "I love the feel of it draped over my chest. My thighs."

His unthreatening touch was a direct contrast to the seductive images his words were currently invoking. She put a hand on his chest, whether to draw him closer or push him away, Alex could not quite decide.

"Dammit, Zach," she complained on a soft, shaky little laugh, "you have rotten timing."

"I know." He lifted her hand from his white dress shirt and began nibbling on the sensitive flesh at the inside of her wrist. "It's my single flaw. But I promise to improve."

When he scraped his teeth against her knuckles, Alex's knees turned to water. "You're driving me crazy."

"That's the idea. Because you've been doing the same thing to me and I refuse to make the trip alone." He folded her fingers and returned her hand, enveloped in his larger one, to his chest. His smiling mouth was a breath away from hers. "I wanted some time alone with you, just the two of us, before you got even richer and more famous."

She looked up at him in surprise. Could he possibly think her financial status would make any difference to her love? "It won't change how I feel."

"I know." His soft sigh was one of pleasure, not regret or sorrow. He lifted his eyes upward, to a heaven that, until Alex, he'd never been totally sure he believed in. "Thank you."

And then he lowered his lips to hers.

The kiss was soft, but deep. The kind of kiss a woman could drown in. The kind that could make a woman float. A soft breath escaped her parted lips as Alex closed her eyes and followed Zach into the mists.

"I love you," he murmured, unwilling to relinquish her lips when the warm, stolen kiss ended.

"I know." She smiled up at him, her heart glowing in her eyes. "And that makes everything worthwhile."

"I'm glad to hear you say that." Reluctantly he released her, smoothing out imaginary wrinkles the embrace might have caused in her bright silk dress. "But I think this is where you're supposed to tell me that you love me, too."

"I love you." She kissed his mouth. "Love you." His chin. "Love you." His throat, above the perfect Windsor knot of his tie. "Love you."

His body was growing hard. Not wanting to face all those waiting women in an aroused state, he laughed and put her a little away from him. "That's all I wanted to hear." Still grinning, he gave her a proprietary once-over. "You look gorgeous."

"Thank you." She gave a quick curtsy. "I thought about wearing something softer hued, to match the set, but red always gives me confidence."

The silk dress, with its deeply scooped neckline and short skirt was emblazoned with huge poppies. The way the material hugged Alex's curves was enough to make any male with blood still flowing through his veins want to pick those bright flowers.

"It suits you." He gave her another proprietary look and forced himself not to think of what vibrant confections she was wearing beneath the flowered silk. "But something's missing."

"Missing?"

She spun around, studying herself in the three-way mirror. At Eleanor's suggestion, the lighting in the dressing room was a warm and complimentary soft pink, vastly different from the usual color-draining fluorescent. It was lighting designed to make a woman look her best.

"I'm no expert on female fashion, but I think it needs this." He pulled a gray velvet box from his suit-coat pocket.

"Oh, Zach!" Alex gasped as she looked down at the slender chain of hammered gold accented with a diamond heart. "It's spectacular."

"Not as spectacular as you. But they haven't invented a gem that even comes close, so I suppose it'll have to do."

She grinned her pleasure at both his flattering words and his extravagant gift. "Flatterer." Turning around, she lifted her hair, baring her neck. "Would you put it on?"

As he fastened the chain, Zach found himself yearning for the time when such intimacies wouldn't have to take place behind closed doors.

Soon, he told himself as they left the dressing room. If everything worked out according to plan, in a few short weeks he would be a free man.

It had been Eleanor's idea that Alex describe her own designs, insisting it would increase the name recognition of the line. Afraid she'd suffer from stage fright, Alex had reluctantly agreed.

Giving in to Alex's belief that live music would be preferable to taped, but wanting to keep costs from soaring into the stratosphere, Zach had compromised with a jazz quartet. The musicians, who hailed from New Orleans, fit both his and Alex's criteria: they were talented and came cheap. And the music, Eleanor had pointed out with her usual marketing flair, was perfect for the Blue Bayou theme.

The fashion show began with daytime wear: graceful, fluid dresses created from whisper-soft silks printed with impressionistic images of flowers and leaves, seductively draped to enhance any woman's figure. Along with the romantic dresses were narrow little suits reminiscent of the fifties, worn with sequined bustiers or crayon-bright silk camisoles.

"Of course, every woman needs a special dress for an afternoon at the theater," Alex read from her script. She lowered her voice. "Or for that forbidden midday assignation."

There was a ripple of excited recognition as Mary Beth, whom every woman in the room loved to hate as the amoral mistress Tiffany, walked out from behind one of the Grecian pillars.

When she unfolded from her cocoonlike fuchsia stole, displaying the snug minidress embroidered with silk flowers, the audience gasped their surprised pleasure, then applauded.

"When temptation is the name of the game, dare to outdazzle the bright lights of Monte Carlo," Alex read, "in a short, sassy, sparkling evening gown...."

"Wear this and everything stops but the music," she described the strapless floor-length tube of clinging red silk.

"And for your gypsy soul..." A trio of models twirled down the runway, resembling flamenco dancers in their calf-length black, red or gold mousseline dresses cascading with ruffles.

The spontaneous burst of applause for the same design Debord had so harshly rejected made Alex's heart soar. Her nervousness vanished; the remainder of the show passed in a glorious blur.

After she'd taken countless bows, the doors to the newest Lord's store in the diamond-bright chain were flung open to the public with a flourish by white-gloved young men wearing red jackets.

Hordes of women clogged the escalators to the sixth floor. The resulting stampede attested to a pent-up demand created by what had been essentially a weekly, hourlong television commercial for Alexandra Lyons clothes. When the number of shoppers quickly swelled to 20,000, the store's security people—whose idea of an incident might be two women fighting over a cashmere sweater—got nervous and ordered the doors temporarily closed until order could be restored.

Once again Eleanor's instincts proved flawless as shoppers proved thrilled to be able to buy the same mint green, satin peignoir set the beleaguered wife had been wearing when arrested for murder on the season-ending cliff-hanger. Another popular outfit turned out to be the royal purple silk suit Tiffany had worn on that same episode when she went to the morgue to identify the body of her much older third husband.

As the cash registers rang up the sales, shoppers revealed both their good and bad sides. According to Zach's up-to-the-minute computer tallies, the saintly wife's classic, yet sexy business suits were the best sellers in the daytime wear, the ex-wife captured the cocktail dress crown, while the mistress won the battle of the underwear, hands down.

Even Zach, who had never understood Miranda's obsession with couture clothes, had to admit that the sight of seven hundred dresses and five hundred peignoirs streaming from the store like the soap's leading character's black gold, was quite a sight. If first-day receipts were any indication, the Alexandra Lyons collection was going to be a smashing success.

By the time the harried security guards shut the doors at the end of the day, Lord's had sold most of the Blue Bayou stock and was into back order. Indeed, any woman who wanted to get married in Tiffany's pearl-and-rhinestone-studded wedding gown would have to postpone her ceremony for several weeks to allow the Brooklyn factory to catch up to demand.

The following morning brought even more good news. During a breakfast meeting prior to the return flight to California, Zach announced that on Wall Street, the opening of Lord's shares had been delayed forty-five minutes after the bell because of the crush of would-be investors clamoring for the stock.

When trading finally did begin, Lord's shares went up considerably. As the company jet crossed over Kansas, the stock had continued to climb and showed no sign of slowing.

It was official. Both the fashion press and the financial media had declared the Alexandra Lyons Blue Bayou collection an unqualified success.

The news came as a vast relief to Alex, who'd harbored a secret fear that perhaps Debord may have been right about her designs not being marketable.

Life would be perfect, she considered as the pilot pointed out the Grand Canyon below, if only for one thing.

If only she could share her happiness with Zach.

Alex was sitting in the richly appointed cabin, lost in thought, idly watching the clouds, when Miranda suddenly appeared in front of her.

"Congratulations. How does it feel to be fashion guru to the middle class?"

Zach's wife's words were not meant, Alex realized, as a compliment. "I'm pleased people like my work."

"Isn't that nice." Miranda lifted the crystal old-fashioned glass to her lips. From the way she was swaying ever so slightly on her Charles Jourdan high heels, Alex suspected it was not mineral water Miranda was drinking. "It's not going to work, you know."

"What isn't going to work?"

"This little act you have going." She waved her arm, splashing vodka onto Alex's white jeans.

Alex pulled a tissue from her purse and began dabbing at the moisture. "Act?"

"You're nothing but a scheming little opportunist," Miranda spat, pointing a scarlet fingernail into Alex's face. "Or are you going to deny you slept with Debord to get that job in Paris?"

Alex's first thought was surprise that Miranda knew about her affair with the designer. Her second thought was that Zach's wife had garnered the attention of everyone on board.

"You've got your facts wrong, Miranda," Alex managed to reply calmly.

"That's what you say." She leaned forward, her red lips twisted into an ugly sneer. "You're not only a conniving slut—you're a liar."

Zach, who'd been in the cockpit with the pilot, returned just in time to hear his wife's poisonous accusation. "You've had too much to drink, Miranda." He took hold of her arm and tried to take the glass from her hand, but she pulled away.

"That's where you're wrong, darling. Because I haven't had nearly enough to get the taste of your little trollop out of my mouth." Throwing back her blond head, she finished off the rest of the drink. "I know you're sleeping with my husband," she hissed at Alex. "I also know why. Because you're using him to infiltrate yourself into my aunt's life."

Miranda glanced around, her daggerlike eyes sweeping the room to settle momentarily on Eleanor before returning to Alex.

"Just because Aunt Eleanor believes you're her long-lost granddaughter, don't think for a minute that anyone else is that gullible."

Alex knew she shouldn't respond to such outrageous, drunken accusations, but she couldn't let that one pass. "That's ridiculous."

"I agree it's ridiculous to think you're Auntie's dear departed little Anna," Miranda agreed. "But it's not the first time she's been made a fool of by a scheming little swindler. Just ask your lover."

Her sleek blond hair flew out like a shimmering fan as she tossed her head in Zach's direction. "One of my husband's corporate duties is investigating all the fraudulent Annas.

"And you should see," Miranda said wickedly, lowering her voice to a conspiratorial tone, "the fat, juicy file he's compiled on you."

No! It couldn't be true. It was merely a delusion born in the murky reaches of Miranda's vengeful, alcohol-sodden mind.

Miranda had never liked her. And she had threatened to make trouble. This was just Zach's wife's latest volley in their ongoing war.

After all, Alex assured herself, Zach loved her. He wouldn't lie. He wouldn't pretend. He wouldn't make a fool out of her. He couldn't. *He loves me!*

Alex looked up at Zach, willing him to tell her that his wife's hateful words were a lie.

Her blood chilled as she read the answer in the stony set of his jaw, the unrelenting bleakness in his dark eyes. For a long, suspended moment, nothing seemed to function— her mind, her heart, her lungs.

Then she felt her heart splinter into a million pieces as Alex realized that, for once, Miranda was telling the truth.

Chapter Thirty-One

The cabin had gone deathly still. The strained silence was palpable; Alex could practically feel it ricocheting around her, like machine-gun bullets against the walls of a dark, cold cave.

Not now, dammit! Zach thought, more furious at Miranda than he'd ever been. But he should have expected such treachery from his wife. Up till this horrible moment, it had been Alex's day of triumph. Miranda had never been willing to cede center stage.

"It's not the way it sounds," he said finally.

Dear God, how she wished that were true! But his expression proclaimed his guilt every bit as loudly as if he'd shouted it on a bullhorn.

He started toward her, but was brought up short when her hands whipped out. "Just tell me one thing," she said through lips that had turned to stone. Could that really be her voice? It sounded so thin. So cold. "Did you investigate me?"

He dragged his hands through his hair in a frustrated gesture she'd come to recognize. "Yes. But—"

Trapped in the icy pain of shock, Alex pressed a hand to her stomach as if to ward off a killing blow. "Because you thought I was some kind of swindler?"

She couldn't believe it. She'd loved him. He'd told her he loved her. How could he think her capable of stealing money from an old woman?

"No, he didn't," Eleanor answered for Zach.

Alex spun around in her seat, prepared to turn on the elderly woman. The pained expression on the lined face took a bit of the furious wind out of Alex's sails.

Eleanor rose unsteadily from her place at the front of the cabin. Her left hand, laden with diamonds, clutched the back of the seat. "Zachary never thought you were a swindler, Alexandra, dear. You must believe that.

"And whatever he did, he did out of loyalty to me. Because I truly believed you were my missing Anna."

"Why didn't you say anything?" Alex's composure was cracking. It was imperative she keep her anger cold. Controlled. She had to think clearly. *Think, not feel.*

"I knew you were my granddaughter when I saw you on television," Eleanor alleged. "But Zachary counseled restraint—"

"Oh, Zachary's always been a virtual pillar of restraint," Alex broke in, shooting him a sharp, bitter look.

She'd trusted him, dammit! She'd believed in him. She'd opened her heart, her body, to this man. How many times was she going to have to stick her hand into the damn flame before she learned not to do it anymore?

"You have to understand, dear. Miranda is correct about my having made a fool out of myself once before," Eleanor revealed reluctantly. After all these years, it was obvious the mistake still stung her not inconsiderable pride. "Because I ignored Zachary's misgivings. This time I chose to heed his warning."

"Makes sense to me," Alex agreed bitterly. "Why make a fool of yourself when you can all make a fool out of me, instead?" Her words hit their mark. The color drained from the elderly woman's face.

"I'm sorry," Alex mumbled when Eleanor took a deep, shuddering breath. "But you should have told me."

Averill, his somber expression revealing both professional and personal concern, took hold of the elderly woman's arm. "Eleanor," he coaxed gently, "please, sit down."

Looking frail and old, Eleanor sank onto a seat across the aisle from Alex. Averill's fingers were on her wrist, taking her pulse even as he gave Alex a warning look.

The plane began its descent into LAX.

"You're right, of course," Eleanor agreed after she'd regained her composure. "We should have given more thought to how you would feel when we broke the news to you about your true identity."

There were so many questions Alex wanted to ask. So many accusations she wanted to fling at Zach. But Eleanor's pallor was frightening. "There's something important you're overlooking," Alex said, gentling her tone and her expression.

"What's that, dear?"

"I understand your need to find your missing granddaughter. But I'm not her. I'm not Anna."

"Of course you are," Eleanor returned patiently.

"Eleanor—"

"There is one way to find out," Averill suggested.

"What's that?" Zach asked, ignoring the icy looks directed his way by both his wife and the woman he loved.

"A DNA test."

"I've read about that," Eleanor said. The idea seemed to perk her up a bit. "Isn't it also known as genetic fingerprinting?"

"That's right. It's a controversial procedure in the courtroom, but there have been documented cases of DNA matching being used to determine paternity. It's also very expensive."

Renewed color returned to Eleanor's ashen cheeks. "Whatever it costs, the money will be well spent." She reached out across the aisle, took both Alex's hands in hers and said, in a pleading tone that wavered with age and emotion, "Please, Alexandra, say you'll take the test."

This was impossible! She knew who she was. She was Alexandra Lyons. She'd been Alexandra Lyons all her life. Such a test would be a waste of time, money and emotional energy.

But if it freed Eleanor of this obsession... "What would I have to do?" she asked Averill.

"Not that much. We can get sufficient DNA from a simple blood sample."

"I hate to even bring this up," Alex said with a worried, sideways glance at Eleanor, "but how would you obtain DNA samples from Robert and Melanie?"

"Those should be available from the police. The files were never closed."

Alex found the idea of digging through moldy police files for old blood samples from murder victims almost too morbid to contemplate.

"I'll have to think about it," Alex said as the jet's landing wheels touched down.

"Of course, dear," Eleanor replied generously.

Having come to know the woman well, Alex realized such patience did not come easily to her.

Refusing the offer of the Lord's limousine, Alex headed in the direction of the taxi stand. Zach followed directly on her heels.

"Go away!" she shouted. The icy shock had worn off. Her eyes glittered with tears of anger. Tears of betrayal.

He put a hand on her shoulder. "You have to let me explain."

"There's nothing to explain." She shook off his touch. "Unfortunately I understand all too well. Eleanor believed I was a missing heiress, and since you're always so concerned about saving Lord's precious money, you investigated me to prove that I was just another in a long line of fraudulent claimants."

"I never thought you were a swindler, goddamn it." He tried to find a way around the hurt. The lies. "I just didn't think you were Anna."

"But Eleanor did."

Fighting desperation, he shoved his hands into his pockets to keep from touching her again. To keep from dragging her against him and kissing her senseless until she could see, until she could feel, how much he loved her. "Yes."

"And everyone knows you'd do anything for Eleanor Lord. Even prostitute yourself."

Frustration soared, mingling with his own flare of anger. "What the hell are you talking about?"

"You slept with me."

"Because I love you, dammit. What happened between us had nothing to do with Eleanor's belief you were Anna."

"It had everything to do with it. But believe it or not, I can't help admiring your loyalty, Zachary, even while I despise your methods."

She stopped long enough to look up at him, her misty eyes dark with pain. "It was all a lie, wasn't it? New Orleans, your mother's wedding. Everything."

His betrayal cut so fatally deep, Alex could no longer even believe that Zach had loved her. She felt tired. And used.

She was looking at him as if he were something that had just crawled out from beneath a rock. Her anger he could handle. Lord knows he'd had enough experience with Miranda. But Zach had no way of knowing how to cope with Alex's despair.

"I never lied to you, Alex."

"You didn't tell me the truth. And in my book, Zachary Deveraux, that's the same thing."

As she walked away, head held high, spine as straight as a rod of steel, it crossed Zach's mind that Alexandra Lyons and that unbending arbiter of veracity, Sister Mary Joseph, had a lot in common.

The following morning, after a restless night, Alex reluctantly agreed to Averill's DNA test.

She met him in a laboratory at the UCLA medical school, where a white-smocked technician pricked the end of her right index finger, drawing a bright red bead of blood.

And then the waiting began.

Chapter Thirty-Two

Not only was DNA testing expensive, it was, Alex learned, time-consuming. Days passed. Fifteen long days and even longer nights, which Alex spent reliving every event of her life.

She was barely able to sleep. Which was, in its own way, a blessing, because whenever she did drift off, the nightmares would return, more terrifying, more ominous than ever.

This time she could see the house, which had been draped in mist in her earlier dreams, clearly. It was Casa Contenta.

And when the monk raised the glittering knife to strike her, his brown cowl fell back, and in the slanting light of a full moon, Alex found herself staring directly into Zach's traitorous face.

She couldn't eat. Time, which was reputed to heal all wounds, did nothing to ease either her anger or her grief. She'd never been a woman of ambivalent feelings. During her life she'd felt love and hate.

Not until Zach's betrayal had she realized it was possible to feel both at the same time.

Just as she'd done when she'd set out to learn about Eleanor's will, Miranda dressed for her late-afternoon visit to Averill with extreme care.

She was wearing a new Valentino cream suit with gold piping that showed off the golden tan recently acquired in a Beverly Hills salon. Although a dread of wrinkles had already made her eschew the sun, Miranda knew that Averill preferred women who appeared to glow with good health.

"As if skin cancer could ever be healthy," she muttered as she pulled her Rolls into the office parking lot.

Peeking between the lapels of her fitted suit jacket was the lace top of her camisole. Her ivory-hued, lace-topped stockings ended at midthigh. She'd spent two hours this morning having her blond hair whipped into a frothy, windblown cloud. Diorissimo had been smoothed and spritzed over every inch of her supple, well-toned body.

She judiciously checked her reflection in the mirror, applied a bit more peach lip gloss and smiled her satisfaction.

Averill's office nurse had no sooner announced her than the door to the doctor's sanctum sanctorum opened.

"Miranda," he said with his trademark smile, "what a pleasant surprise."

"I was in the neighborhood—" she slipped her creamed and manicured hands into both his outstretched ones "—and thought I'd drop in."

"I'm glad you did." He hugged her briefly. "You smell like springtime."

Her smile was as dazzling as the diamonds surrounding the pearls gleaming at her earlobes. "Aren't you sweet."

She allowed her body to stay against his for a heartbeat too long. "I do hope I'm not interrupting anything important."

"Not at all. As a matter of fact, your timing's perfect. My last patient of the day just left." He glanced at his nurse. "In fact, Terri, if you'd like you can take off early."

The nurse did not hesitate. She grabbed her bag and was out the door, leaving Averill and Miranda alone in the office.

Just as Miranda had planned.

"Would you like a drink?" Averill offered as he ushered her into his inner office. "I've a variety of hard liquor here in the office, but if you'd rather have a glass of wine, we can go down the street to the Biltmore."

"Perhaps later." She sat down on his sofa and crossed her legs in a way that allowed an enticing glimpse of the lacy top of her stocking. And the smooth thigh above it.

She watched the good doctor watching her and felt a glow of female satisfaction. Men were such fools for sex, she thought. Which wasn't so bad, really. Not when it made them so easy to manipulate.

"Actually, I came here to talk with you, Averill. About Alexandra's DNA test."

"Oh?"

He folded his hands atop his desk. His expression turned professionally inscrutable. "What about it?"

"I'm sure you can understand that I'm not exactly a disinterested party."

He nodded. And waited for her to continue.

"After all, I do care a great deal for Aunt Eleanor. And I'm so worried that finding out Alex is not Anna—which we all know is the way that test is going to turn out—will come as quite a blow."

"She's pretty convinced the test will back up her beliefs," Averill said.

"I know." Her soft intake of breath made her breasts swell enticingly. "Well, I thought that if perhaps I could have advance warning, I could make certain I'm at the house. To prepare Auntie."

Averill leaned back in the chair. His intelligent blue eyes studied her for a long moment. "Are you suggesting I give you the results of the test before I tell anyone else?"

She met his gaze with a level one of her own. "That's exactly what I'm suggesting." She recrossed her legs with a swish of silk. "I promise you, Averill, I will be very grateful."

He pressed his fingers together and smiled at her over the tent of his hands. "You know, Miranda, I've always admired you."

"As I've admired you," she said silkily.

He nodded. "I've always admired your beauty and your drive. And your unrelenting avarice."

She stiffened. "Excuse me?"

"You've got balls, lady," Averill allowed. "And although I have no doubt that what you're offering would be world class, I'm afraid I'm going to have to pass."

"Pass?" Her voice rose. Her eyes glittered dangerously. "Are you saying you refuse to cooperate with me?"

"Actually, I'm saying that I can't betray my medical principles, Miranda. Not even for the fuck of a lifetime."

"You're going to be very sorry, Averill."

He looked up at her heaving breasts, flushed cheeks, her glossy, parted peach lips, and sighed heavily.

"Believe me, sweetheart," he said, his voice thick with regret, "I already am.

"But—" he held up his hand to forestall her intended renewed effort "—I'm still not going to give you first crack at Alexandra's test results."

Unaccustomed to rejection, Miranda slapped him. Hard. Then she stormed out of his office, slamming first the inner door, then the outer door behind her.

As he heard the framed diplomas on the waiting-room wall fall to the floor, Averill shook his head and wondered idly if Hippocrates had ever faced a similar ethical dilemma.

"You know," Sophie said, studying Alex's shadowed eyes and pale cheeks, "you look as if you're getting ready to audition for a remake of *Night of the Living Dead.*"

"Thanks for the compliment," Alex muttered. They were sitting in Alex's kitchen, the box of doughnuts Sophie had brought with her between them.

"I'm worried about you."

"I'm fine."

"Like hell." Sophie licked the glaze from her fingers. "Call the man, Alex."

Alex opened her mouth to insist there'd be snowball fights in hell first when her telephone rang.

"The machine'll get it."

Immediately upon their return to Los Angeles, Zach had called several times a day, first begging, then, as his frustration obviously built, demanding to talk with her.

But she'd steadfastly refused to pick up the phone, leaving him no choice but to leave a series of messages on her recorder.

Two days ago the calls had stopped. Alex had taken the sudden silence as a sign that Zach had given up.

"Alex?" The masculine voice was smooth and cultured and unthreatening. "It's Averill. I just wanted you to know that I've got the test results back—"

Alex dived for the phone. "Averill, hi. It's me."

"Well, hello, Alex. How are you?"

"Fine, thanks," she lied. "And you?"

"Never been better. The reason I called—"

"I know. The test."

"Yes." He cleared his throat. "What are your plans for this afternoon?"

"Actually I don't have any." Other than avoiding Zach.

"Good, good," he said absently. There was a moment's silence, then Alex heard him talking with someone apparently in the room with him. "Sorry, Alexandra," he said when he came back onto the line, "but my nurse needed me to sign some prescription forms."

"That's okay." Alex took a deep breath. "Well? Was I right? Did your test prove Eleanor wrong?"

He cleared his throat again, revealing atypical discomfort. "Actually, Alex, if you don't mind, I'd prefer to discuss this with both you and Eleanor at the same time."

"You want me to come up to Santa Barbara? Today?"

"I thought that might be best. The strain of waiting has been hard on Eleanor. I'd rather she not make the trip to L.A."

"I'll leave within the hour, Averill."

"Thank you, dear. I'll tell Eleanor you're coming. The news will please her, I know."

"Well?" Sophie demanded after Alex had hung up.

"He wants to break the news to both of us at the same time." Alex sighed. "Poor Eleanor. You know, I really want to be angry at her, but I keep thinking how desperate she must have been all these years."

"You never know," Sophie suggested. "Eleanor Lord may get her wish today. And you may become one of the youngest millionaires in the country."

"Right. And pigs will begin flying all over Los Angeles."

London

Zach had known that the hunch he'd come here to play was a long shot. But he'd played it to win, and it had paid off.

He'd spent the past six hours locked in deliberation with the governor of the Bank of England, the chairman of

Lloyd's and the publisher of the *Times,* enough royalty to fill several pages of *Burke's Peerage* and several members of Margaret Thatcher's egalitarian meritocracy.

And now, business concluded, he had one last matter to take care of before he could return home to Los Angeles. And Alex.

He knew it wasn't going to be easy breaching her seemingly concrete parapets. But breach them he would. Zach had not achieved such a high level of success by taking no for an answer.

Typically, for London, it was raining. The sky was a gloomy pewter, the streets were gray, the stone buildings were draped in a slate mist. But the dismal weather could not dampen Zach's enthusiasm. All during today's meeting, it had taken every bit of self-control he possessed to keep from thinking about how, in a few short hours, he would be making love to Alex.

Miranda's town house was located in Belgrave Square. Formerly Elysian Fields, where sheep had once placidly grazed, Belgravia, as it had come to be known, was an oasis between the feverish shopping streets of Knightsbridge and traffic-congested Picadilly.

"You can wait," Zach instructed the driver as the taxi pulled up in front of the Regency London building. "I won't be long."

"Whatever suits you," the driver said with a shrug as he turned off the engine and plucked a racing form from the floor of the front seat.

Zach let himself in with his key. The town house was dark. Hushed. The only sound was the steady *tick-tick* of the mantel clock.

The bedroom was dark, as well, but the adjacent bathroom was illuminated with the flickering glow of candles.

"Miranda?"

Zach stopped in the open doorway, struck momentarily mute by the sight of his wife and Marie Hélène Debord lying together in the old-fashioned, claw-footed bathtub. The Frenchwoman's hand was on Miranda's naked breast, Miranda's firm thigh was twined around her companion's hip.

"Zach!" Miranda stared up at him. Marie Hélène, Zach noted through his shock, merely curled her lips in her cool, trademark superior smile.

He'd always known his wife had taken lovers. That being the case, he supposed the sex of those bed partners really didn't make a helluva lot of difference.

"Get dressed." He yanked a thick towel down from the heated rack and tossed it at her. "There's something we need to discuss."

Feeling amazingly calm under the circumstances, Zach went back into the living room, poured two fingers of single malt Scotch into a glass, reconsidered, and added a healthy splash more.

He'd no sooner polished it off when Miranda appeared, clad in an emerald silk robe, looking flushed and guilty.

"If you're going to drop in like this, Zachary, it would be nice if you had the decency to telephone first."

"So I don't interrupt when you're entertaining your lovers?"

"Well, it was an unpleasant surprise." She rubbed the nape of her neck. "I suppose you're going to lecture me again."

"Personally, I don't care what you do, or who you do it with, Miranda. I haven't for a very long time. Which is why it's time we put an end to this farce of a marriage that should have been declared dead at the altar."

"You can't divorce me." Her expression turned hard, making her face ugly. "Don't forget, if you even try to leave me for Alexandra Lyons, or anyone else for that matter, I'll sell my stock so fast your uncivilized, barbaric backwoods Cajun head will spin."

"Threats aren't going to work today. It's over."

"I'll call Nelson Montague."

"Go right ahead."

She paused, her hand on the telephone receiver. "You realize this will give him control of Lord's."

"There is no way that pirate will ever gain control of Lord's. I've seen to that."

"What the bloody hell are you talking about?" Her eyes remained as hard as emeralds, but her peaches-and-cream English complexion turned as white as the papers he had brought for her to sign.

"Eleanor and I have just purchased all the outstanding stock belonging to the British consortium. Which leaves you and your Aussie pirate out in the cold."

"That's a lie! They promised that stock to Nelson. I saw the preliminary agreement!"

"That was before they knew about his true plans for the company. I have you to thank for that, Miranda. If you hadn't stolen that memo, I wouldn't have had such an effective weapon.

"As it turns out, the London group is big on tradition." It was what he'd been counting on. "And though they'd decided to finally sell their stock and take a hefty profit, none of them wanted to be responsible for turning an upscale, fifty-year-old department store chain into the five-and-dime."

"Damn you!" Furious, she slapped him, the sound of her palm hitting his cheek like a gunshot.

"If you want to blame someone," Zach said calmly, ignoring her outburst, "I'd suggest you blame your father. If he hadn't sold his stock to pay his gambling debts, it would have remained under family control."

He pulled an envelope from the inside breast pocket of his suit jacket. "Here's a check for your outstanding shares, made out for twenty percent above today's market closing price."

"What makes you think I would sell my stock to you?"

"In the first place, I'm offering you an extremely generous profit. Then there's always the fact that your social cachet might plummet if all your society pals find out about your little playmate." He tilted his head toward the bathroom door.

When he'd come here today, he'd hoped to use Miranda's deep-seated greed to convince her to sign; he hadn't expected her to give him a more powerful weapon.

"That's bloody, fucking blackmail."

"You'd be the one to know," he drawled sapiently. "Having used the tactic yourself so many times."

"I'll kill myself if you leave me." It was a last-ditch effort that had succeeded before. This time it failed.

"That threat may have worked once," Zach allowed. "But don't forget, baby, we hadn't been married long. I hadn't seen through your slickly applied veneer yet.

"Besides, you'd never do it," Zach said. "You're too narcissistic to ever hurt yourself." He pulled another check from his pocket. "And to sweeten the pot, Eleanor's willing to give you your inheritance up front."

"I can't believe you actually went to Eleanor with this."

"Lord's is her company," he reminded Miranda. "She was entitled to the opportunity to save it. Face it, sweetheart," he said as she snatched both checks from his fingers, studying them with avid green eyes, "this deal is as good as it's going to get.

"In fact, the offer for your shares automatically drops ten percent per minute." He glanced down at his gold watch. "Beginning now."

He placed the deed of transfer on the nineteenth-century partner's desk he remembered her unearthing at an antique store on Bleeker Street during his first visit to the city and held out his pen.

"You bastard." She took the gold pen from his outstretched hand and signed her name in a furious scrawl far removed from her usual stylish script.

"My lawyer will be contacting yours in the morning to work out the details for the divorce."

At her mumbled obscenity, his eyes hardened to black stones. "I wouldn't advise your stalling on this one, Miranda. Unless you want to see exactly how uncivilized we barbaric backwoods Cajuns can be."

"Bastard," she repeated through clenched teeth.

"Goodbye, Miranda." Zach folded the transfer agreement and returned it to his pocket. "It's been interesting."

Feeling remarkably lighthearted and blessedly free— free!—he walked away, not pausing when the porcelain Ming vase shattered against the doorjamb only inches from his head.

As he returned to the waiting taxi, Zach was whistling.

Chapter Thirty-Three

Though Alex knew Eleanor was about to be proved wrong, she could not rein in her anxiety as she drove up the coast to Casa Contenta. By the time she entered the mansion, her nerves were screaming.

"My dear," Eleanor said, "thank you so very much for coming." She took both Alex's unnaturally icy hands in hers. "I had tea and cakes prepared. Will you join me?"

"Of course." They were both skirting around the real reason for her being there. Which was, of course, like ignoring a dead elephant in your living room.

Averill was waiting for the women in the solarium. After greeting the doctor politely, Alex glanced down at the white, wrought-iron table, relieved to find it set for only three.

Eleanor did not miss Alex's surreptitious study of the table settings. "Zachary is in London. He's returning to L.A. this morning."

"If you don't mind, Eleanor," Alex said, her voice as tight as the fist that gripped her heart, "I'd rather not discuss Zach." There. She'd done it. Said his name without choking. Alex figured that was progress of sorts.

"Whatever you wish, dear." There would be time, Eleanor assured herself, for the young people to iron out their difficulties.

Alex was forced to wait while Eleanor poured the tea neither of them really wanted.

"I suspect you ladies have been on pins and needles, these past weeks," Averill said as he accepted a raisin-studded scone from the plate Eleanor passed him. "So, shall we get to it?"

At that moment, Alex could have kissed him. He met her eyes and smiled his understanding of her impatience.

He reached into the alligator briefcase on the chair beside him and pulled out a thick sheaf of papers. On the top page was a colorful graph resembling the bar code scanned for supermarket prices.

"As I said, it's a complicated test," he began. "You'll recall that human beings have forty-six pairs of chromosomes, each chromosome consisting of a long string of genes that are, in turn, composed of strands of deoxyribonucleic acid, which is a chemical that carries the, uh, computer programming codes, I suppose you could call them—"

"Averill." Eleanor lifted her hand. "Alexandra and I have both taken high-school biology. We know what chromosomes are and we also understand, as well as any layperson needs to, what genes do. So, do you think you could just skip the lecture and cut to the chase?"

"Of course," he said. "I'm sorry if I bored you."

"We're just a little anxious," Alex said quickly.

"You don't have to apologize, Alexandra," Eleanor countered. "Averill is quite accustomed to my bad manners. Aren't you?"

"I wouldn't touch that line with a ten-foot pole," he responded mildly. "Okay. The bottom line is that there's no match."

His words landed in the center of the table like a bomb. Alex would have not been surprised to see the flower-rimmed Royal Doulton tea plates and delicate cups shatter.

"Are you saying Alexandra is not my granddaughter?"

"Yes." Averill exchanged a glance with Alex and she knew they were thinking the same thing. Neither of them would have willingly harmed Eleanor Lord. Yet that was what they'd done. "I'm sorry, Eleanor."

"How conclusive is that test?" Eleanor demanded.

"Very conclusive. Alex is a charming, intelligent young woman. And it's more than a little apparent that you and she have a great deal in common. But she is not Anna."

"Well." Eleanor exhaled a deep breath and turned her gaze out over the estate. Outside the windows, the groundskeepers were raking the red clay tennis courts. She was silent for so long that Alex thought the older woman had forgotten their presence until she turned from the window and faced her.

"Fate is a powerful force, Alexandra. It was fate that brought us together—in so many ways that are every bit as twisted and interconnected as those genes Averill says proves we're not related by blood.

"But it doesn't matter," Eleanor insisted, reaching out to cover Alex's hand with her own blue-veined one. "You could not be any closer to me if you were my own flesh and blood, Alexandra. And that's all that matters."

"Yes." Alex nodded. "That's all that matters." She'd never meant anything more in her life.

For a quarter of a century Eleanor had been obsessed with finding her missing granddaughter. Now, as she embraced Alexandra, she finally gave up the quest.

There were tears. And laughter. Then more tears. Then emotional healing.

"It wasn't Zachary's fault, you know," Eleanor said after they had moved from tea to champagne.

Alex took a long sip of the sparkling wine and tried not to think about the day she and Zach had drunk Dom Pérignon from paper cups. "He lied to me."

"Only to protect me. The man was horribly torn, Alexandra."

"I understand that." Alex leaned forward and refilled her glass. "But if he loved me, really loved me..." Her voice drifted off as she ran a fingernail along the rim of the flute.

"May I ask a question?" Eleanor said.

"Of course."

"Do you love Zach?"

Alex didn't want to. She had tried with every fiber of her being to exorcise him from her mind. Her heart. But she might as well have tried to stop the sun from rising in the east or those waves outside the windows from ebbing and flowing.

"So much it hurts."

"Well, then," Eleanor said with her usual brusque, decisive manner, "that's all that matters, isn't it?"

"I don't know," Alex murmured.

"I've always believed that when your head and your heart seem at odds, it's best to go with your heart," Eleanor advised gently.

Eleanor wondered if they'd like to get married here, at Casa Contenta, then remembering that this was the scene of Zach's first disastrous wedding, reconsidered. The country club was always nice. Or perhaps the winter home she kept on Kauai.

Kauai, Eleanor decided. Outside, on the lanai overlooking the peaceful blue lagoon, with the scent of Plumeria and bougainvillea drifting on the trade winds. Alexandra would make such a lovely bride. She deserved a wedding fit for a fairy-tale princess, and Eleanor intended to see that the day lived up to her darling Alex's most romantic fantasy.

"Eleanor," Averill murmured, interrupting into her pleasant thoughts. "As much as I hate to break up this party, it's past time for your nap."

"Oh, pooh," she complained. "I do wish you'd stop treating me like an old woman."

"You are an old woman," Averill countered, smiling. "The goal is to keep you healthy so you can get even older."

"But I want to talk with Alexandra some more."

"She'll be here when you wake up. Won't you, Alex?" Before she could answer he suggested, "In fact, why don't you spend the night?"

Alex had intended to return to Los Angeles as soon as she'd learned the results of the DNA test. Truthfully, she didn't want to spend another night upstairs, where she'd suffered those frightening nightmares. But one look at the hope etched blatantly into the deep lines of Eleanor's face and she felt her resolve crumbling.

"I'd love to spend the night."

"Thank you, dear." Eleanor rose from the table and kissed Alex's cheek. "You've made me a very happy woman." That said, she allowed the doctor to escort her upstairs.

Alex took the opportunity to call Sophie and let her know about the negative results. She was still in the solarium, sipping champagne and looking out at the ocean when Averill returned.

"That was very nice of you," he said.

"What?"

"Agreeing to spend the night. I'm sorry, Alex. I was so concerned about Eleanor, I forgot about the nightmares."

"That's all right. They're only dreams."

"Of course."

"And dreams can only hurt if Freddy Krueger's starring in them."

"Freddy Krueger?"

Alex laughed, feeling foolish. "He's a character in a movie. He has horrible long fingernails and slaughters high-school students who dream about him. *Nightmare on Elm Street.*"

"I must have missed that one."

The idea of this debonair man sitting in a theater with a bunch of screaming teenagers watching the satanic sand-man slashing away at defenseless dreamers made Alex laugh again.

"I have got an idea," he said suddenly. "How would you like to go for a sail?"

"Today?" Alex glanced out at the line of clouds building on the horizon.

"That rain is hours away," Averill assured her as if reading her mind. "We'll only stay out a short time. Just long enough to help you relax so you can sleep without worrying about nocturnal visitors. It's better than pills."

Remembering how her day on the water had calmed her nerves the last time she'd been bothered by the night-mares, Alex made her decision. "I like your prescription, Doctor."

Although Alex trusted Averill's sailing skills implicitly, as the sky grew darker and the water became choppier, she began to feel uneasy.

"Eleanor's probably awake by now," she said. "Perhaps we should go back in. Before she begins to worry."

He turned from trimming the sail. "Eleanor knows you're with me, Alex. She won't worry."

The wind picked up, blowing her hair into a frothy tangle. "Still, with her heart condition and all . . ."

"Don't tell me you're afraid."

"Of course not," Alex said quickly. A little too quickly. Averill gave her a sharp, knowing look. "All right," she admitted reluctantly. "I am a little nervous."

"Don't you trust me?"

"Of course, but—"

"Alex, Alex." He laughed off her concern. "I've sailed in worse squalls than this. Don't worry, I know what I'm doing."

She tried to relax. She watched him move around the wet and slanting teak deck, as graceful as a cat walking along the top of a fence. He knew what he was doing, she reminded herself, observing his deft skills. He'd never risk his own life.

She told herself that over and over again, but as the sky grew even darker and thunder boomed ominously beyond the thick fog bank blowing in from the horizon, she began to find it more and more difficult to relax.

A frisson of fear skimmed along her nerve endings when she noticed that, instead of turning the ketch back toward the shore, he was actually taking it farther out to sea.

"Please, Averill," she said. "I want to go back now."

"I'm sorry, Alexandra. But I'm afraid that's impossible."

"What do you mean?"

"I mean it's all your fault," he explained. His voice was calm.

A wave hit the side of the ketch, splashing her. She dragged her hand down her face, wiping away the salt water. "What's my fault? Surely not the weather."

"I hoped I wouldn't have to do this." He shook his head with what appeared to be honest regret. "But then you began having those damn nightmares. Over and over again."

"I don't understand. What do my nightmares have to do with anything? We'd agreed they were only dreams." Alex wasn't afraid. Not yet. But she was confused.

"That's what we'd agreed. But you have to understand. I can't take the risk."

"Risk?"

He shook his head. "Everything went wrong that night," he said as if he hadn't heard her. "Melanie wasn't supposed to die, dammit! Only Robert."

Somehow, some way, she'd deal with this, Alex told herself. "I don't understand."

"Robert met Melanie in L.A., when she was under contract to Paramount. But her career was going nowhere and she was tired of struggling to make ends meet, so he seemed like the answer to her prayers.

"But after he brought her to Santa Barbara, it didn't take long for her to get bored. The town," he said unnecessarily, "is not known for its nightlife. And Robbie was trying to lock her away like one of Eleanor's damn hothouse flowers. But Melanie Patterson was a vibrant, exciting woman. So she turned to me for the stimulation she needed so badly in her life."

"You had an affair with Melanie Lord?"

"Not an affair," he retorted. "I loved her. I'd have done anything for her."

"Even kill your best friend?"

Averill didn't directly respond to her question. "I grew up in Robert Lord's shadow," he said, his eyes focused on some unseen horizon. "My father was Eleanor and James's gardener. When we went away to college, Robbie got a Chrysler convertible. I got a job washing dishes in a sorority kitchen.

"After graduation, Robbie got another new car, a Porsche this time, and went to Harvard law school. I managed to swing some financial aid for medical school, but it took me fifteen years to pay off my student loans. Fifteen damn years.''

"That must have been hard."

He gave her a long, unfathomable look. "Yes."

"But then you began to make a great deal of money," Alex said. "You were able to buy your Ferrari and this gorgeous ketch—"

"That's not the goddamn point!" he roared as the ketch reeled on the increasing waves.

Alex swallowed. "I'm sorry. I didn't mean to belittle your struggles."

"Everything always came so easily to Robbie. But then, I had something of his. I had his wife."

"Whom you loved," she said, trying to remain calm. The thing to do, she decided, was to keep him talking. Until she figured out a way out of this.

"Love doesn't begin to cover what I felt. Obsession comes close, but it's still not a strong enough word. Which is why, when she began insisting that the only way we could ever be together would be if Robert were dead, I believed her."

Alex didn't know which she found more horrible: the story itself, or the fact that she was beginning to believe it. "Why didn't she just get a divorce?"

"I suggested that. But Melanie pointed out that if we stayed in town, the scandal would damage my reputation. She said we'd have to move away and I'd be forced to start another practice somewhere else.

"She convinced me it was ridiculous that I should have to struggle all over again when I could marry Robert Lord's widow and have the entire Lord fortune at my fingertips."

"I can't imagine you agreeing to that," Alex said truthfully.

"I can't, either. But at the time, Melanie's sexuality, along with the lure of more money than I'd ever dreamed of, proved terribly seductive. The plan was to kill Robbie on a night when everyone would be out at a party at the club.

"I'd given Melanie something to put in Robbie's drink to make him nauseated. When he was unable to go to the party, Eleanor and Melanie left without him. It was a very clever plan."

Averill's normally kind eyes lighted with pride, and he looked at Alex as if expecting praise.

She wasn't about to risk disappointing him. "Very clever."

"It should have gone off like clockwork. I'd shoot Robbie, then mess up the room, making it look as if he'd interrupted a burglary in progress. The only problem was that Robbie had overheard us plotting his murder. That's when he came up with his own plan. A plan to kill the man who'd stolen his wife."

Alex lifted a hand and rubbed her temple. *"Robert Lord* was going to kill *you?"* If it weren't for the bracing salt spray constantly splashing onto her face, she'd have thought this was just another nightmare.

"Robbie was an extremely jealous man. And he'd begun to drink heavily the past six months. Neither Melanie nor I realized that his drinking had been triggered by his finding out about our affair."

Averill shook his wet head. "It was a ridiculous scenario. There we were, lifelong childhood friends, facing one another across the library like two cowboys at the OK Corral.

"The idea of either of us actually committing murder was so ludicrous we both put our guns away. And," Averill said with regret as he raked his hand through his wet hair, "it would have all ended right there if Melanie hadn't returned unexpectedly. She was afraid I'd lose my nerve."

He laughed at that, but the sound held no humor. "As it turned out, she was right. She began taunting Robbie, telling him what a failure he was as a man. She told him that he'd never satisfied her sexually, that she'd only married him for his money. Unfortunately Robbie was drunk and Melanie, who always knew how to find someone's sore spot, definitely hit the bull's-eye that night.

"When he picked up his revolver from the desk and aimed it at her, I tried to take it away. We wrestled and somehow it went off. The bullet struck Melanie in the throat."

As he described the incident, flashes of Alex's nightmares flickered on the screen of her mind. Her flesh turned an icy cold that had nothing to do with the soaked red sweatshirt and jeans clinging to her skin.

She closed her eyes. A vision, imprinted deep on her subconscious, flashed behind her closed lids. The sound of gunshots reverberated through her head. She began to shake violently.

Then suddenly, shockingly, it all flooded back, distant, horrifying memories locked in a child's subconscious.

"Oh, my God! It was you!" Her eyes flew open and she stared at Averill in horror. "You killed my father."

My father. Those impossible words echoed in her mind like the deep, warning toll of a bell. Her hands tightened around the water-slick brass railing, and she held on for dear life, as if to keep from sliding off the face of the earth. Her life, the entire world as she'd always known it, was spinning dizzyingly around her, tilting dangerously out of control.

"I didn't kill him. After Melanie was shot, the damn gun fell to the floor and fired again. The bullet entered Robbie's chest and struck his heart. He died instantly.

"I was kneeling over Melanie's body when I looked up and saw you standing in the doorway of the library, watching me with an expression of absolute shock. And horror. The same way you're looking at me now.

"You were supposed to be in bed, dammit! Rosa had been well paid to give you a sleeping pill, take one herself and stay in her room. That way, the next morning, she could truthfully tell the police that she'd heard nothing."

Alex wrapped her arms around herself to ward off the chill that had seeped deep into her bones. She wasn't Alexandra Lyons at all. She was Anna Lord. Her entire life had been a lie.

"But what about my mother?" she asked numbly. "I know she loved me. How could she have lied to me all those years?"

"It was precisely Irene's love that put you in this untenable situation in the first place. I met Ruth Black—the woman you knew as your mother—when I was going to medical school in North Carolina.

"I was doing illegal abortions to supplement my income. Ruth, who was unable to earn a living at her dressmaking business, was working as a clerk at the North Carolina state adoption agency. There she saw couples who, for various reasons, couldn't meet the state's rigid adoption requirements. We both realized that we had something to offer one another."

"You had access to pregnant women," Alex said slowly. "My mother knew people willing to pay handsomely for a child."

No. Not her mother. Her mother had been Melanie Lord. A murdered, adulterous actress. And the woman she'd thought all her life to be her mother had been engaged in black-market baby selling. Alex felt sick.

"It seemed a match made in heaven," Averill agreed.

Or hell, Alex thought, devastated. So many lies. Years and years of them. A lifetime.

"When I graduated from Duke and returned to Santa Barbara, I brought another doctor into the scheme so Ruth's income wouldn't drop off."

"How generous of you." Despite her fear and shock, Alex could not keep the sarcasm from her voice.

"She thought so. Only one person knew what happened the night Robbie and Melanie were killed."

"Me."

"Yes. Since Rosa knew of the plot, she'd have to be eliminated, which was, of course, unfortunate, but at the time I couldn't think of any other choice. But you..." He shook his head and his gaze softened. "You were an innocent child. I couldn't have a child killed."

The man was, Alex thought, one helluva humanitarian. She glanced grimly out at the rough sea and ever darkening sky, then back at her captor.

"I called Ruth," he went on, "and without telling her the circumstances, asked if she could place a two-year-old girl. She said she could. That little piece of business out of the way, I warned Rosa she was an accessory to murder and instructed her to take you to Tijuana and wait for Ruth's arrival.

"Finding someone to stage Rosa's suicide was easy. The bars were filled with men willing to do anything for a few hundred pesos.

"Unfortunately Ruth fell instantly in love with you. She called me from Mexico and told me she was keeping you for her own. Then she disappeared. I decided she must have seen the national news coverage of the double murder and kidnapping and changed both your names. After a few years, I felt safe enough to stop looking for you."

"But what about David? What about my brother?"

He shrugged. "I'd heard through the grapevine that Ruth had a son of her own. Obviously, after she brought you back from Mexico, she got new birth certificates for both of you." He rubbed his jaw. "That was clever, actually, I never would have thought to look for twins."

Suddenly a scene flashed in Alex's mind, like one of those black-and-white horror movies shown on cable television at four in the morning.

After hours in the dark, the closet door had finally opened, flooding the small cubicle with blinding light. Terrified that the monsters were about to devour her whole, the little girl screamed and kicked out at the intruder.

"It's going to be all right!" a female voice shouted.

The woman struggled to avoid the child's kicks at the same time her hands attempted to capture the flailing fists. Finally Anna's arms were locked against her sides and she was lying across the woman's lap.

Her pupils were enormous in her frightened amber eyes; her complexion was as white as her lace-trimmed nightgown, and an enormous handprint, a souvenir of the monster's brawny paw, cast a dark shadow across her pale cheek. Her exertion had her breathing heavily; her thin chest rose and fell beneath the cotton gown.

"Shh, baby," the woman crooned in a very unmonsterlike voice. "It's all right." The woman had blond hair, like Anna's mother. And while not as beautiful, she had a kind face and gentle eyes.

Even as she longed to believe this stranger, Anna remembered how convincing the wolf had been when he'd greeted Little Red Riding Hood wearing her granny's ruffled white cap.

Anna squirmed, trying to get away, but the woman's hold tightened. "As soon as you're calm, I'll let you go," she promised with a warm smile that reminded Anna painfully of Rosa. "I can't let you run away, baby. There are too many dangers out there. Too many bad things that could happen to a little girl.''

As if anything could be worse than what she'd already been through! Anna knew, with a child's absolute clarity, that she could no longer trust anyone. That being the case, she glared up at the woman, trying to resist the comforting hand that was now brushing her dirty, tousled hair away from her face.

"I'll bet it was scary in that closet," the woman murmured, her gentle touch meant to soothe. "I remember, when I was a little girl just like you, I was afraid there were monsters hiding in my closet, waiting to pounce on me as soon as my mother turned off the light."

Anna refused to answer. But she couldn't keep the truth of her own fears from flooding into her eyes.

The woman nodded knowingly. "You don't have to be afraid anymore, sweetheart. I promise I'll keep all those mean, nasty monsters away from you. They'll never hurt you again."

Anna flinched when the stroking fingers brushed the tender bruise on her cheek.

"I used to have bad dreams sometimes, too," the woman revealed on a soothing, almost hypnotic tone that gradually had Anna relaxing muscle by wire-taut muscle. "Do you ever have bad dreams?"

Not yet ready to trust implicitly, Anna's only response was a slight, almost imperceptible nod of her head.

"It's no wonder. After what those monsters have put you through." There was an edge to her voice, a cold, barely restrained fury that Anna realized was not directed toward her.

"But that's all over now," the woman said. "And you know what? I have an idea that will keep the monsters away. And help you to forget all your bad dreams." She paused. "Would you like to hear it?"

This time Anna's nod was a bit more assertive.

"I thought you might." The woman's smile melted some of the icy fear lingering in Anna. "The problem, the way I see it, is that Anna Lord is the little girl afraid of monsters. It's Anna whose Mommy and Daddy have gone to heaven to live with the angels. And it's Anna who has the nightmares. Isn't that right?"

Anna nodded.

"Poor Anna. She's had a very bad time. So the thing to do," the woman said with authority, "is change your name."

"My name?" Anna asked in a small, frail voice.

"Exactly." The woman rewarded her with a smile. "From now on, your name is Alexandra Lyons. And you are a bright, happy little girl who doesn't have any nightmares."

It was like pretend, Anna thought. She played that all the time. A princess was her favorite, like in the fairy tales her nanna Eleanor read to her every night before bed.

"Who are you?" she finally asked, her voice a little stronger this time.

"Who am I? Why, I'm Irene Lyons," Ruth Black lied adroitly. The die was cast; regardless of the danger, there would be no turning back. "Alexandra's new mommy."

Anna considered that for a long, thoughtful moment. Then wanting—needing—to put the horror of the past five days behind her, she wrapped her arms around the woman's neck and allowed herself to trust....

Finally it was all so clear. Finally Alex understood why they'd moved so often during her younger years. Obviously she'd been afraid Averill would kill them both to keep his secret safe.

Still not wanting to believe this nightmare, Alex grasped onto one last all important detail. "But the DNA test proved I'm not Eleanor's granddaughter."

"There was no test. I faked the test and the results to convince Eleanor that there was no way you could be Anna. But I knew you were."

She really was Anna Lord! The idea was too enormous to take in all at one time. The sky opened up, the rain pelting down like bullets. Like the bullets that had killed her mother and father.

"So, that's the whole tawdry story," Averill went on. "And it would have ended there, if Eleanor hadn't been watching that damn Emmy broadcast. I was afraid that when you saw the house, you'd remember. But you didn't. So I waited, hoping Eleanor was mistaken again. That you weren't Anna.

"But it became increasingly apparent that you were, and when you started having those nightmares, I knew you were on the brink of remembering. So, as much as I loathe the idea of killing, surely you can understand why I can't let you live."

Panic bubbled up in Alex's throat. "Averill, please," she protested, "don't do this. I won't tell anyone what you've told me today. It'll be our secret."

She never had been any good at lying. She knew, as his eyes swept over her face, looking hard and deep, that he wasn't fooled.

"I'm honestly sorry, Alex. But surely you can understand I don't have any other choice."

As he approached her, deadly determination glittering in his steel blue eyes, there was a deafening crack of lightning directly overhead.

Chapter Thirty-Four

Zach was growing more frustrated by the minute. He'd arrived at Alex's place, laden down with roses and champagne and a ring he had every intention of convincing her to accept, if he had to camp out on her damn doorstep until she finally gave in.

When she wasn't there, he tried the studio, only to learn from Sophie that Alex was spending the night in Santa Barbara. Zach took that news as a sign that perhaps her anger was abating. When Sophie went on to reveal the negative DNA results, Zach was surprised. He'd come to believe that Eleanor had been right this time.

"She still claims to be mad as hell at you," Sophie told him matter-of-factly. "But if you want my opinion, I think it's just injured pride talking."

"I'm going to make it up to her."

"You'd better." Sophie waved her letter opener at him. "Or I'll cut out your heart and feed it to the critics."

With that threat ringing in his ears, Zach drove to Santa Barbara. He found Eleanor in a state. He'd never seen her like this before. Her eyes were wide and frightened. Her hair was a witch's tangle around her ashen face.

"Thank God you're here!" she cried.

"What's wrong? Your heart?"

"No." She shook her head violently, causing hairpins to scatter onto the tile floor. "It's not my heart. It's Alexandra!

"She and Averill went sailing. When I came downstairs after my nap, they still weren't back. Naturally I was worried, so I called the yacht harbor. Averill's ketch hasn't returned to its slip!"

Zach took one look at the storm pelting the windows and called the Coast Guard.

"She's not Anna, Zachary," Eleanor told him as he hung up the phone and headed toward the front door.

"I know. Sophie told me." He retrieved a squall jacket he kept in the front closet. "But that doesn't matter, does it?"

"No," Eleanor agreed. "I love her, Zach. So much." Tears filled her eyes and slid down her cheeks.

"So do I." He brushed the moisture away with a tender fingertip. "And don't worry." He gave Eleanor a quick kiss on her wet, weathered cheek. "She's going to be all right."

She placed a trembling, beringed hand against the side of his face. "Promise me you'll find her, Zach." Her voice quivered with age and emotion. "Please."

"I promise." With that he was gone. To find Alex. And bring her back home where she belonged.

Although her heart was racing, some detached part of Alex remained calm. She tensed every muscle in her body to keep from trembling. There was a way out of this, she assured herself. She just had to stall long enough to think of it.

"There's something I don't understand."

Averill stopped in his tracks. "What's that?"

"Were you the person who came into my room to frighten me that first night at Casa Contenta?" Although she'd certainly suffered enough bad dreams after that terrifying incident, Alex had never truly believed it had been a nightmare.

"No." He shook his head. "I always figured that was either Miranda or Clara."

Clara, Alex decided. Miranda was too straightforward. Not that she wasn't above threats; she just enjoyed making them directly. Clara, on the other hand, had a motive of sorts. If she could convince everyone of ghostly goings-on at the estate, her position as resident psychic would be strengthened. A scent teased at Alex's memory. The aroma of orrisroot that usually surrounded Clara like a noxious cloud. It had been in her room that night. She'd just been too upset to identify it.

Then later, when she was alone with Zach, her mind had been too clouded with desire to think straight.

"But you did do something to my brakes," she guessed.

"I didn't have any choice. Surely you understand I couldn't allow to you remember what happened that night."

"But I do remember. And what I didn't know, you've told me."

He shrugged. "It doesn't matter anymore."

"Because you're going to kill me."

His lips pulled into a grim line, but he neither confirmed nor denied her accusation. "It's all your fault, Anna. You never should have come back."

The wind was wailing like one of Clara Kowalski's lost spirits. Her wet hair was sticking to her face. Alex shoved it out of her eyes. "You'll never get away with this, Averill."

"Of course I will," he said with that same calm self-confidence she suspected eased innumerable worries in the examining room. "It's too bad, really." He resumed moving toward her, murder on his mind and in his eyes. "Eleanor has already suffered so many misfortunes. It's a pity she has to survive the tragedy of you falling overboard in the storm.

"Of course, I'll tell people how desperately I tried to save you. But the ketch almost capsized, and the deck was so slippery I couldn't get to you in time."

He was inches away. "So you went sliding off into the sea. To your death."

When he began ripping at the fasteners of her orange life jacket, Alex realized her entire life had narrowed down to this one fatal moment.

With a fierce strength she'd not known she possessed, she fought back. Her fingernails tore into the flesh of his tanned face, her fists pounded his chest. But he was so strong! And every bit as determined to kill her as she was determined to remain alive.

Providentially, another drenching wave washed over the railing, causing him to slip just enough that she could break free of his iron grip.

Knowing she had no other choice, Alex closed her eyes and dived headfirst into the whitecapped maelstrom.

And then she began to swim. For her life.

Zach leaned forward in the copilot's seat, scanning the horizon with a pair of binoculars as the Coast Guard helicopter flew low over the storm-tossed waves.

"The guy's an experienced sailor," Zach complained. "What the hell made him go out in weather like this?"

"Beats me," the pilot said. "Every time we get a storm, we have to launch a search for a few hotshots who think they're invincible."

Zach had seen television news footage of idiotic daredevils being pulled from the surf during a heroic rescue. But Averill Brandford was neither an idiot nor a daredevil.

So what had possessed him to take Alex sailing before a storm that had been forecast for the past forty-eight hours?

"We have to find them, dammit!"

"Hey, there's no point in borrowing trouble. The doctor's boat is not exactly a dinghy. If the guy's as experienced as you say, the chances of them capsizing are slim. Don't worry, pal. They've probably just blown off course."

Zach hoped that was true. But some inner voice was telling him that Alex was in very real danger. And that time was running out.

"Just keep looking," he growled.

"That's what we're doing," the pilot answered with an easy calm that suggested such rescue missions were routine.

The sun, managing only the merest sliver of light through the angry clouds, had almost set into the water. Zach commented uneasily that it would soon be dark.

"That's not as bad as it sounds," the pilot said. "We'll be able to spot the running lights of the ketch. And on top of that, this baby's fitted for night-vision viewing."

His words did nothing to ease Zach's panic.

"What's that?" he asked suddenly, pointing down at something in the water. Something a great deal smaller than Averill Brandford's sleek white ketch.

"Just a buoy."

"No. That orange speck."

"Probably a piece of driftwood," the pilot guessed. "But we may as well take a look."

He dived lower. "Damned if it isn't a person! Get the ring out," he called out to the third man in the chopper.

Zach was both relieved and terrified at the sight of Alex, clinging to the rocking buoy.

While the man tossed the rescue ring out the open door, Zach shouted out to Alex over the helicopter loudspeaker. His voice cracked with emotion. Taking a deep breath, he cleared his throat and tried again.

Although she'd always considered herself a strong swimmer and she was in a life jacket, Alex had never battled such turbulent waves. She'd shouted instructions to herself in her mind: *Right arm. Left arm. Right. Left. Kick. Kick. Kick, dammit!*

Just when she'd thought she could swim no farther, one particularly violent wave had thrown her against the buoy.

She didn't know how long she'd been clinging to the buoy. But it seemed like forever. Her body, which earlier had been cold, was beginning to turn numb. So numb...

A sound rose over the roar of the surf. It was growing closer. She looked up just as the Coast Guard helicopter flew into view.

She heard a voice, but could not make out the words. When a ring attached to a rope came flying out of the open doorway, she assumed she was supposed to take hold of it. But it landed too far away. And she wasn't about to let go of the violently rocking buoy and swim for it.

The man in the doorway pulled the rescue ring back up and tried again. And then a third time. But each attempt fell short. And when the copter tried to fly lower, the wind from the rotor stirred up the water so badly, she almost disappeared beneath the waves. Alex began to despair.

And then, wondrously, the rope appeared again. But this time a man was riding it down. As he neared, Alex feared that she was hallucinating.

Perhaps, she thought wildly, this was what happened when you died. Perhaps those stories about shining lights and tunnels were wrong. Perhaps your last conscious thought was of the one you loved. Or perhaps the man descending from the sky was an angel who coincidentally resembled the man she loved.

"Alex, it's going to be all right, goddammit!" he shouted. "You're going to be all right."

Although she was definitely no expert on near-death experiences, Alex did not believe any angel worth his wings would use such language.

"Zach?" She stared up at him, strapped into a safety harness, hanging from a steel cable just over her head.

"It's me, sweetheart," he assured her. "And we're getting you out of here." She forgot that only days ago she'd been furious at him for deceiving her. Wanting to cover his wonderful face with kisses, she forced herself to follow instructions, latching the safety belt that would hold her to him and the cable.

Then, finally, wonderfully, she twined her arms around the strong column of his neck and together they were raised higher, then higher still, up to the hovering helicopter, where the copilot helped them into the cockpit.

"We have to stop meeting like this," Zach said as he wrapped her in a heavy blanket.

Her teeth were chattering and she was shaking violently with cold and lingering terror. "Y-y-you won't believe what happened!"

"You can tell me all about it later." Zach put his arm around her and drew her close.

She wanted to tell him everything, in vivid, horrible detail. But her exhaustion was too great. Tears born of relief and sorrow flooded her eyes and streamed down her cheeks.

She put her head on his shoulder, his strong, wonderful shoulder, and closed her eyes. "Zach?"

He kissed the top of her head. "Yeah, honey?"

"Eleanor was right."

"About what?" he answered absently. His thoughts were still on that breath-stealing moment when he'd spotted her hanging on to the buoy in those storm-tossed waters.

"About me." Now that she was safe, fatigue claimed her. Her eyes drifted shut. "I'm Anna."

Epilogue

Santa Barbara
Five years later

The sun shone the day Alexandra Deveraux buried her grandmother.

Beside her, his strong arm around her waist, Zach held four-year-old Ellie's hand, while Alex held the baby, Gabriel—named for Zach's father—in her arms.

"I'm so glad Eleanor lived to see her great-grandchildren," Alex murmured. "I'm grateful we all had the chance to become a real family."

"She never stopped loving you, Alex." Zach bent and brushed a tender, husbandly kiss against her temple. "All those years, she never gave up hope."

"I know it sounds crazy, but I feel as if she's still with us. Even now."

"It's not at all crazy. I can feel her, too." Although Zach had grown up surrounded by a large, loving family, he could not have loved Eleanor more if she'd been his own grandmother. "And her spirit lives on in the kids."

"Do you know what Grand-mère Eve says?" Ellie looked a long, long way up toward her father, her keen young eyes brilliant with golden facets that radiated outward, like the rays of the Santa Barbara sun.

"What does she say?" Zach asked.

"She says that Grand-mère Eleanor is an angel now. And she's watching over me. Like my very own guardian angel." Her voice went up a little on the end, as if seeking reassurance that the comforting words were true.

There were days, and this was one of them, that Zach would drink in the sight of his beautiful daughter and son, and marvel that any man could be so lucky.

Zach would have happily married Alex and never asked God for another thing so long as he lived. These two remarkable children, this vivid, breathing legacy of their love, represented more blessings than he would have ever dared ask for.

"My mother is a very smart lady," Zach assured the little girl. He tousled her marmalade-hued hair that was so like her mother's. "And I think your *grand-mère* Eleanor will make a terrific angel. Don't you agree, darling?" he asked Alex.

"The best." Alex returned his fond smile with a slightly teary one of her own.

She ran her fingers over the marble stone that marked Eleanor's final resting spot, high on the lush wildflower-studded hillside beside her beloved husband, James. Nearby, on the other side of the Lord family plot, Robert and Melanie—the parents Alex still could not remember— were buried.

The horrifying events of that fateful day when she'd learned her true identity and Averill had tried to kill her were blessedly fading from her mind, misty memories she chose not to dwell upon.

When the Coast Guard located the ketch the following morning, Averill had not been on board. Since he was an excellent sailor, Eleanor, Zach and Alex had presumed the doctor had chosen to take his own life, rather than suffer the scandal. Not to mention spending the rest of his life in prison.

"I'll bet Grand-mère Eleanor's up in heaven right now," Ellie said. "Telling all the other angels what to do."

Zach and Alex laughed at the all too accurate notion.

As they returned to the estate, not to mourn Eleanor Lord's death but to celebrate her remarkable life, Alex thought that although she would always consider Irene Lyons—or Ruth Black—and her brother, David, her true family, during these past years with Eleanor, she had also come to feel, in many ways, like a Lord.

But best of all she was Alexandra Deveraux now. She and Zachary had planted the roots of their own dynasty deep into the rich, sun-warmed soil of Southern California.

Mira Books

Proudly presents
the newest novel from

JOANN ROSS

Confessions

For a sneak preview
of this thrilling romance,
please read on....

Look for *Confessions*
in early 1996

Chapter One

Laura Swann Fletcher had never realized how long five minutes could be. Especially when you were holding your breath.

She scowled at the vial atop the cultured marble countertop, as if intimidation could speed up whatever mysterious chemical reactions were taking place inside it.

Heat lightning flashed outside the bathroom window, hinting of the storm to come. A distant taste of rain rode on the sultry air. Normally, summer storms in Arizona's high country never bothered Laura.

But tonight was different. Tonight she felt as if the electricity had gotten into her blood, making her edgy.

"Hurry up," she begged. As if she didn't have enough to deal with. "Please, hurry up."

She took a deep breath that should have calmed, but didn't. "It's only stress," she insisted, as if saying the words could make them true.

Perhaps she should have taken Fredericka Palmer up on that offer of Valium. Only last week her longtime best friend had professed concern about her. *If only Freddi knew the whole story*.

"Dammit, get hold of yourself." Laura hardly recognized the high, nervous voice. She pressed her palms against her rib cage and, taking several more deep breaths, willed herself to relax.

But her mind continued to churn restlessly, tossing up the myriad problems that had been plaguing her. Problems without end. Dilemmas without solutions.

Nerves humming, Laura decided to see if one all-important call she'd been waiting for had come while she'd been out buying the home pregnancy kit.

The answering machine was downstairs, in the den. The red light was blinking, signaling four calls. She pushed the Rewind button. Then, Play.

Unbearably restless, she prowled the plank floor.

Beep. "Laura. It's your father." His recorded voice was gruff as always, but she thought perhaps it was only her imagination. His next words confirmed that it wasn't. "I heard a story today that damn well better not be true. If you're there, pick up."

There was a slight pause as he waited for her to do as instructed. As she always had. "Hell." Another frustrated pause. "When I get back from Santa Fe, you and I are going to have a talk. Because you've got a lot of explaining to do, girl."

So, he'd found out. Even as Laura reminded herself that she'd been going to tell him herself, painful memories, buried but never forgotten, snaked through her.

She looked down at her watch.

Two more minutes.

She continued to pace.

Beep. "Laura, it's Alan. Thunderstorms kept us on the ground at National, now we're stuck on the runway at O'Hare. We're going to be late getting into Phoenix, then with the ninety-minute drive to Whiskey River, it'll probably be past midnight before I get home. Don't bother waiting up."

It was not the first time her husband had been delayed while on a trip with Heather Martin, his ambitious and sexy chief of staff. Laura doubted it would be the last. The difference was, this time she honestly didn't care.

Alan Fletcher was a rising political star, the brightest, most promising light in the Republican political firmament. Having won reelection to the U.S. Senate by a landslide, he was being touted as the party's best hope to regain the White House.

Laura had never enjoyed living in Washington. She hated the artifice, the parties that were nothing but power plays, the emphasis on political prestige rather than character. The role of wife had been difficult enough. The idea of becoming First Lady gave her hives.

Beep. "Hi, Laura. It's Mariah. Kill the fatted calf, the prodigal daughter is coming home! Do I have a lot to tell you! Guess it'll have to wait until I show up on your doorstep, which should be around midnight, which I know is an ungodly hour, but I'm dying to share my news with my big sister. Love ya."

Damn. Laura dragged a trembling hand through her auburn hair. Trust Mariah to choose this weekend to return to Whiskey River. Nothing like throwing a lighted match into an already volatile situation.

Then again, Laura considered, if anyone could appreciate what she was about to do, it would be the woman who, like their glamorous mother, had been banished from the Swann family.

She looked at her watch again.

Only one more minute.

Beep. "Hi." The deep, intimate voice sent a familiar heat surging through Laura.

"I just wanted to make sure you're okay. Hell, the truth is, I'm worried about you, babe. I still wish you hadn't insisted on doing this alone.

"Christ, Laurie—" she could picture him dragging his hands through his thick black hair "—I don't remember you being so stubborn twenty years ago. If you had... Oh, hell. Forget I said that. One day at a time, right?"

"One day at a time," Laura whispered.

It was the same thing she'd been saying for months. The problem was, she knew Clint Garvey would not wait any longer. The last few times they'd managed to be together, they'd wasted valuable time—time they could have spent making love—arguing.

Finally, last weekend, Clint had issued an ultimatum. She knew, with every fiber of her being, that if she didn't keep her promise to leave her husband, she would lose the only man she'd ever loved.

She sighed as she looked down at her watch again.

Finally!

The indicator's damning red Plus sign confirmed what she'd suspected all along. It hadn't been stress that had caused her to feel so tired lately. And it hadn't been flu that had brought about the occasional bouts of morning queasiness.

She was pregnant.

With her lover's child.

Timing, Laura considered weakly, was indeed everything.

With her back against the wall, both literally and figuratively, she slid down to the tile floor, wrapped her arms around her bent legs and rested her forehead on her knees.

What on earth was she going to do? A fleeting dread shot through Laura. Her first thought was that Clint would think she'd been lying when she'd assured him that she could not get pregnant. But how could she have known otherwise? After having spent years trying to conceive?

When pollsters had informed her husband that a pregnant wife was worth from eight to fifteen points in the opinion polls, Alan had begun dragging her to infertility clinics all over the country. None of the increasingly esoteric, uncomfortable and horribly embarrassing treatments had worked.

Finally, last year, after her thirty-sixth birthday, Laura had given up the quest for a child. Alan, needless to say, had not been pleased. It was, after all, a great deal easier to campaign on a family-values platform with a smiling wife and darling children by your side.

Alan. Laura groaned. Her husband was going to be absolutely furious. What if he attempted to pay her back for her infidelity by refusing to grant her a divorce? Worse yet, what if he decided to claim this child for his own?

"I won't let that happen!"

Laura reminded herself that her husband's most consistent personality trait was that everything Alan Fletcher said, everything he did, including marrying her, was geared solely to enhancing his career. If he attempted such a ploy, she'd hold her own press conference and tell the entire world the truth.

Ronald Reagan had proven that a divorced man could get elected president. But would voters choose a candidate involved in a messy paternity battle? Laura didn't think so.

It's going to be all right," she assured herself. And her baby. "Granted, this complicates things. But Alan will see that a quick, quiet divorce is in his own best interests."

Latching on to that optimistic thought, she pressed her hands against her still-flat stomach in an unconscious gesture of maternal protection.

Her churning mind gradually calmed as she began to view her unborn child—hers and Clint's child—as a reward for all the pain they'd suffered.

There would still be problems. Problems with her autocratic father, with Alan, with the press. And there was no way this baby could ease her current troubles regarding the ranch.

But as she ran a bath in the ancient, lion-footed copper tub, for the first time in a very long while, Laura felt capable of sorting everything out. A heady, forgotten confidence flowed warmly through her veins. Dual feelings of joy and wonder bubbled up from some hidden wellspring deep inside her.

Sometimes miracles really did happen.

Laura was soaking in the perfumed water when the storm that had been threatening earlier arrived. The sharp staccato of rain sounded on the roof. Thunder rumbled. A bolt of lightning forked just outside the window.

Suddenly, a sound like a Klaxon blare echoed through the house.

An irritating flaw in the security system was that the sensors on the windows couldn't tell the difference between a storm rattling the glass or an intruder breaking in.

She rose from the water, wrapped a towel around herself and ran back downstairs, leaving a trail of wet footprints. After deactivating the blaring alarm, she placed a call to the sheriff's office—which was automatically alerted each time the alarm went off—assuring the dispatcher it was a false alarm.

"Stupid thing," she muttered, clutching the towel to her breasts as she glared at the computer control panel. Alan had been promising to change the system for months. After tonight, Laura vowed, she was just going to tear the damn thing out.

At the age of thirty-seven, Laura was determined to re-claim control of her life. Along with the house and the twenty thousand acres of prime Arizona ranch land her grandmother Ida Prescott had bequeathed her.

After years of unhappiness, she'd returned home to Whiskey River. Where she belonged. And where she had every intention of spending the rest of her life with the man who, for eight blissful hours, in what seemed another life-time, had been her husband.

Laura returned back upstairs, traded her towel for a long sea foam silk nightgown, then climbed into the cedar log bed.

Knowing she'd never be able to fall asleep, she sat bolt upright and twisted her hands together atop the Sunshine and Shadows quilt she and Clint had unearthed in a quaint Shenandoah Valley antique shop during a clandestine, love-filled weekend. The same weekend their child had been conceived.

The storm stalled overhead, wrapping the house in its grip. Rain pounded against the windows. Thunder boomed like cannon fire; psychedelic flashes of lightning streaked across the sky. Wind wailed outside the bedroom window like a savage spirit.

It was going to be, Laura thought, a very long night.

Although she'd not considered it possible, Laura even-tually fell asleep. She dreamed of Christmas, could actu-ally smell the pungent scent of the pine tree taking up most of the living room. Beneath the tree were gaily wrapped presents. Enough toys to fill F.A.O. Schwarz spilled over the floor.

A fire blazed in the fireplace; fat white flakes drifted down like snowy feathers outside the window, creating a scene straight out of Currier and Ives.

Laura saw herself sitting on the couch in front of the fireplace, Clint sitting beside her. A little boy with her husband's jet hair and solemn dark eyes sat on her lap, listening intently as his father read aloud from Dylan Thomas's *A Child's Christmas in Wales*.

It was an idyllic scene, born of Laura's most private yearnings. One she was loathe to leave. Which was why, when the sound of the bedroom door opening filtered into her consciousness, she fought waking up.

The bedroom lamp, operated by a wall switch beside the door flashed on. Still struggling to hold on to her dream, which was rapidly disappearing like morning mist over the tops of the tall ponderosa pines outside the ranch house, she mumbled an inarticulate complaint.

The dream faded from view. Laura reluctantly roused, blinking against the blinding light.

Her sleepy mind recognized the familiar face. As her lips curved in a groggy, puzzled smile, a sound like an early Fourth of July firecracker shattered the nighttime stillness.

Startled, and unaware she'd been shot, Laura pressed her hand against the searing heat at her breast. Crimson blood flowed over her naked flesh, staining her fingertips.

Still uncomprehending, she stared up at her attacker, tried to ask *Why?* but discovered she'd gone mute. A mist covered her eyes.

Silvery rain snakes streaked down the bedroom window. Her wounded heart continued to beat.

Pumping out precious blood.

Laura's last conscious thought was regret that she hadn't told Clint about their baby.

And then, as a second sharp retort filtered through the fog clouding her mind, Laura Swann Fletcher surrendered to the darkness.

Over 12 million books in print!

Love or deception? Find out this February in

Starlight

Rand Prescott is a man who stubbornly refuses to open his heart. Karen McAlister is a woman who has to prove that her vows were said in love and not deception. Now she must try everything to convince Rand that they were meant to be together—forever.

When wedding vows aren't enough...

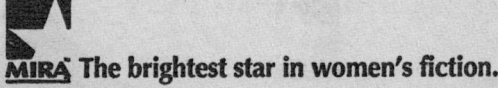

If you love the intriguing tales of

JoANN ROSS

Act now to order another thrilling escapade
by one of MIRA's exceptional authors:

| #66022 | DUSK FIRE | $4.99 U.S. ☐ |
| | | $5.50 CAN. ☐ |

(limited quantities available)

TOTAL AMOUNT	$	
POSTAGE & HANDLING	$	
($1.00 for one book, 50¢ for each additional)		
APPLICABLE TAXES*	$ _____	
TOTAL PAYABLE	$ _____	
(check or money order—please do not send cash)		

To order, complete this form and send it, along with a check or money order for the total above, payable to MIRA Books, to: **In the U.S.:** 3010 Walden Avenue, P.O. Box 9077, Buffalo, NY 14269-9077; **In Canada:** P.O. Box 636, Fort Erie, Ontario, L2A 5X3.

Name: _____

Address: _____ City: _____

State/Prov.: _____ Zip/Postal Code: _____

*New York residents remit applicable sales taxes.
Canadian residents remit applicable GST and provincial taxes.　MJRBL1

MIRA